DEATHSPORT – O
THIRD REICH

Alex's left struck hard
felt the flesh yield, sepa
gasped in shock. Alex
solar plexus, and Erich
spittle as he jacknifed i
low now, and Alex's left hook caught him
sharply in the eye. He sagged backwards against
the stone wall of the bridge. Alex struck with a
right cross which crashed into Erich's nose.
Erich raised his arms and held his elbows close
to his sides to defend himself, but Alex ripped
through with punch after punch into the
stomach. Blood spurted from Erich's mouth and
nose, and Alex felt himself growing stronger,
more dangerous. Erich's head rested on his
shoulder; Alex stepped back and fired a blow at
his nose. The big man's knees gyrated crazily
under the relentless barrage. When he let Erich
fall, the body sank to the ground and lay
motionless ...

Arena is the stunning new supersaga by
Norman Bogner, bestselling author of *Seventh
Avenue*, of a family's search for the Promised
Land and their struggle to build an
indestructible empire.

Arena

NORMAN BOGNER

SPHERE

SPHERE BOOKS LIMITED
30/32 Gray's Inn Road, London WC1X 8JL

First published by Sphere Books Ltd 1979
Copyright © Norman Bogner Enterprises, Inc. 1979

Reprinted 1980

TRADE
MARK

SPHERE

Set in Linotype Plantin

Printed in Canada

For Lori
and my Parents
with love

It is not the critic who counts, not the man who points out how the strong man stumbled or where the doer of deeds could have done them better. The credit belongs to the man who is actually in the arena; whose face is marred by dust and sweat and blood; who strives valiantly; who errs and comes short again and again; who knows the great enthusiasms, the great devotions, and spends himself in a worthy cause; who, at the best, knows the triumph of high achievement; and who, at the worst, if he fails, at least fails while daring greatly, so that his place shall never be with those cold and timid souls who know neither victory nor defeat.

THEODORE ROOSEVELT

BOOK ONE

One

An itinerant sausage peddler flicked the rivulets of sweats which pooled under his eyelids, then raked the hot coals below the grate where his bratwursts and hocks of Black Forest ham were frying. In all the years he had his stall outside Alex Stein's gym, he had never seen such a mob lined up, and his business had never been better. The customers did not even wait for him to make change. They simply battered their sausages with the spicy Düsseldorf mustard and bolted back to the entrance where they waited on the steps, craning their necks forward to get a view of the celebrities who had mysteriously appeared from large chauffeur-driven Mercedes staff cars. Pompous uniformed chauffeurs lined the Franz-Joseph-Strasse of Schwabing, Munich's bohemian district.

The sausage peddler had never been inside the gym although he saw Alex Stein each day and tipped his cap courteously. He had once asked Alex what the attraction was, since all that could be seen was boxers training. Alex's explanation puzzled him. 'Grown-ups hang around athletes because it's a form of salvation.'

But today, the beginning of June 1938, the doors of the gym were closed to the public, and a cadre of black-uniformed SS men stood at the doorway demanding the papers and credentials of everyone who wanted to enter. The armed *Waffen* guard had their orders.

Inside, sitting below the ring apron, were three of the men who controlled the destiny of Germany: Dr. Josef Goebbels, minister of propaganda; Reichsführer Heinrich Himmler, head of the Gestapo; and, spread over two seats, Hitler's newest field marshal and head of the Luftwaffe, Hermann Göring, his medals stretching across his chest like a tray of assorted canapés.

In the ring, circling, moving sluggishly, were two boxers, virtually indistinguishable in their leather headgear. Max Schmeling tucked his chin low into the hollow of his left shoulder. In a clinch, he caught an uppercut and shoved his sparring partner off.

His trainer shouted, 'Move, Max! Feint.'

Max rolled his head out of range and tattooed his sparring partner with a series of feeble jabs.

Alex Stein stood some distance from the ring, holding the heavy bag. By his side was Arthur Buelow, Schmeling's manager, waiting for Alex's reaction.

'He was never fast, but now he can't even move laterally. Shit, he's got to cover up better than that.' Alex lost patience and shouted, 'Dammit, use the ropes, Max.'

'He's thirty-three,' Buelow replied.

'Tell Joe Louis, not me.'

'He beat him once,' Buelow protested.

'Louis trained on a golf course for that one.... He's in shape this time. When Max first fought him, Louis was just another contender. He's the champion now. That makes a difference, wouldn't you say?'

Buelow contemplated the three officials observing Schmeling's graceless weaving. They applauded his clumsy left hook and the occasional right cross he landed high on his sparring partner's head.

Schmeling had fought in beer halls and clubs throughout Germany in the twenties. He'd been a poised boxer with a sudden, flashing punch. The figure in the ring, Alex knew, was a wraith, spongy-muscled, lethargic, doomed as a fighter. His timing was off, his reflexes leaden, calcified by time and fame. Even during his triumphant period as a heavyweight, when he'd held the championship for two brief years, he had carried the stigma of paper champion. He had been *given* the title when the referee disqualified Jack Sharkey for a questionable foul in the fourth round. Schmeling had won by default and the victory had left a rotten taste in sports circles. In the rematch with Sharkey, he had been outpointed over fifteen rounds.

But he had defeated the black man legitimately once. And principles of racial purity dictated that no man from an inferior race could possibly triumph over an Aryan.

In the mirror used for shadowboxing, Alex caught a glimpse of himself. Thick, coarse hair curled over his ears. His nose had once been hawklike but it had been broken at the bridge four, or was it six, times. His eyes were hazel-colored, large, resolute, and he walked with serene authority, giving off an aura peculiar to enormously muscled short men whose chests are overdeveloped. Even relaxed there was a violent, coiled aggression in his manner. He was thirty-four years old and like one of those bronze miniatures of Cellini, a swirl of S curves leaning forward on a pedestal, there were intimations that he would last forever – that he was forged.

His was a family history of encountering disaster. Their road from the past led from czarist St. Petersburg, where the Cheka had tormented his grandfather who had taught fencing and boxing to hussars, to the murky settlements of gypsies and outcasts along the Vistula.

For a period the Steins had settled in Cracow, but after five years of roving, Alex's father, who supported them by giving exhibitions in mining towns, on large farms, in tavern gardens, finally fell victim to powers beyond him in Gora in the province of Wroclaw.

Alex was nine at the time, traveling with his father as his second. The two had covered the dismal hinterlands of Poland, driving a cart drawn by mud-caked, stinking oxen. Then Abe Stein had fought the local blacksmith for nearly two hours. The blacksmith had collapsed, his eyes swollen, his mashed nose purple, his flesh bleeding, his knuckles broken. The hog butchers who put up the purse had been drinking coarse, rough, one-hundred-and-fifty proof slivovitz while the men fought. Now they encircled Abe, wielding their flashing cleavers. Powerless, Alex had watched them hack his father to pieces, methodically, surgically. They began with his fingers, his arms, legs, his testicles and penis, until merely a writhing, bloody trunk remained. The boy cowered in the back of the wagon, whining, yelping vainly as they fed the hogs the severed remains of his father. It was unconscionable for a Jew to fight as well with his fists as Abe Stein had; it upset the balance of nature.

'Alex, we came to you because you're the best strategist we have in boxing,' Buelow asserted.

I'm also a Jew and I don't want any part of this, he thought.

'Alex, your people are having lots of problems which they themselves created,' Buelow noted insidiously. 'You've been allowed to keep your gym because of Himmler. Boxing is important to the party, so you've been given a dispensation.'

Alex couldn't argue the point. The Nazis had graciously decided to overlook the fact that he was a Jew because it suited them.

'Schmeling's not a bad fighter but he's too slow. Look at the way he sets up before hooking. Louis'll counterpunch before Max throws a punch.'

'Will you help us?'

'You rented my gym for the day, but you didn't buy *me*.'

'Well, if you're smart you'll study Louis's fight films. I've set up a screen and projector in your office.' Buelow paused and stared superciliously at him. 'Alex, if you don't co-operate, the Gestapo has orders to close down your gym and take your family into custody. Nine Prinz Albrechstrasse ... think about that.'

Buelow moved off, a white-faced snake of a man, and took a seat beside Göring. Alex studied these uniformed criminals who had invaded his gym.

Even he had to admit that the Nazis had accomplished a brilliant feat of political engineering. In six brief years they had taken control of the army, the Reichstag, passed new oppressive legislation and put men in uniforms. The tramps, the criminals, the unemployed malcontents, the vagabonds of German society, boorish untutored emotional masses marched to the tune of the Horst Wessel lieder.

Munich, his city, had been transformed into an armed camp. Soldiers were everywhere. In his local tavern he had to wait on line behind a sea of black and gray uniforms for a drink. Some benches in the parks were painted yellow, and Jews could sit only on these; a new humiliating law had been passed forcing every male Jew to have his identity card stamped with the name Israel and every female with Sarah. In defiance, he had not taken his card into the local police station.

Alex walked into his small office beyond the ring. A blond SS officer in a well-cut gray uniform was waiting for him. He was sitting on Alex's scarred wooden desk, his gleaming black boots resting on a rickety wooden folding chair. He had washed-out gray eyes, a fine aquiline nose, and a humorous world-weary smile.

'I am Major Von Fritsch.'

He was in his early thirties and he was one of those posturing men who have passed from adolescent pomposity through mannered arrogance and whose experience terminates at thirty when everything has been learned, nothing under-

14

stood, and all that remains is a corseted facade of dandyism.

'I have been assigned by Himmler to see you work with Schmeling. Since we're going to be inseparable, I took the trouble of studying your record, and it puzzles me. You were a boxer, you train fighters, and you still own a gymnasium. Isn't that an odd profession for a Jew? I always thought you people picked businesses involving easily movable goods ... or acquired valuable pieces of paper which you could stuff into a briefcase. The Börse, trading, diamonds, lending money.'

'You forgot something, Major. We can't wait to rape blue-eyed country virgins and we all carry venereal disease.'

Fritsch's laughter had a brittle sound. He lowered the warped green shade covering the glass door and drew the curtains. A white projection screen hung ready. Fritsch focused a Eumig projector. 'One last caution, no matter what you've been accustomed to before in your dealings with people, let me assure you that our association is predicated on your absolute obedience to me. Just remember I have the power to hurt you and the pain will be like nothing you've ever conceived. There, I've declared my hand, Herr Stein.' He paused for a moment in the darkened room. 'The first film is Louis versus Braddock, and let's hope that you make some remarkable discovery to help Schmeling.'

The projector flashed a picture of the crowd in Yankee Stadium. Alex leaned back in his chair, his chin digging into the heavy calloused palm of his left hand. Braddock, the Cinderella Man, was past his prime and had not fought for almost two years. He sprang out in a low crouch. Alex noticed that Louis was still inclined to drop his left when he threw a right cross. It was a question of poor balance which he had not yet overcome. Weaving out of the crouch after Louis had missed with a left hook, Braddock crossed with a right and dropped Louis for a count of two. But Louis was apparently unhurt and he used his left jab effectively. In the second round, Louis began throwing combination punches that penetrated Braddock's frail defense. Round after round, Louis stalked him, an avenging angel, hitting him at will.

'What's keeping Braddock up?' Fritsch asked.

'His balls,' Alex replied. 'A champion doesn't ... Oh, what the hell.'

Braddock's face was cut and there were swollen, warped mouses over both eyes where Louis's relentless jab repeatedly struck. By the eighth round, Braddock's reflexes were gone. Louis hooked him to the temple, dug another vicious left into the solar plexus, lashed him with a right cross to the side of the jaw. Braddock collapsed and lay face-down, motionless, glued to the canvas.

'The speed of the punches ... it's unbelievable,' Fritsch said with stunned admiration.

'That's what Schmeling's up against.'

The next film they studied was an earlier fight: Louis against Bob Pastor. Pastor was plainly terrified. He bolted around the ring round after round, an unwilling participant in a dispute, rarely throwing a punch, just keeping away from Louis and never allowing Louis to corner him. In a newspaper account Alex had read at the time, the fight was described as a ten-round bicycle race. Louis won an easy decision.

The final fight that Fritsch ran was of Louis against a gallant British fighter by the name of Tommy Farr. Farr's tactics were decidedly different from Pastor's. He tenaciously carried the fight to Louis, remained close to him, not giving him room to punch, and he hit Louis often as they slugged toe to toe.

In the fourth round, when Louis shot a sharp right to Farr's nose, Alex noticed something about Louis's style that he had not detected before. Alex moved his chair closer to the screen and studied Louis's face for the next eleven rounds. He grew increasingly excited as his suspicion was confirmed, but he kept his expression one of indifference. He was aware of Fritsch's eyes on him.

Fritsch could restrain himself no longer. 'What is it?' he demanded.

'I'm not sure,' Alex said, switching on the lights. 'It must've been my imagination.'

Fritsch's anger betrayed that he was under pressure. 'You're going to have to tell me what you saw. I need concrete information.' When Alex regarded him blankly he blurted out in a shrill voice ... 'Give me something – lie if you have to ...' Fritsch's hand glided to a Luger strapped on his hip belt in a shiny black holster.

'Before you can get that gun out, I'll deck you. Then

Himmler will send you to the Ruhr, supervising coal shipments. Now do yourself a favor and tell him I'm thinking.'

Fritsch lowered his hand and fretfully observed. 'You're not like the rest of them.'

'The rest of who?'

'*Juden.*' A respectful smile crossed his lips. 'They do what they're told – they *cooperate*. You should learn from them.' He clicked his heels. 'Himmler is waiting.'

Alex followed Fritsch through the string of loam-faced, flabby pugs selected by Himmler to spar with Schmeling.

'What's your opinion?' Alex was asked in a calm, almost deferential voice by Himmler who peered myopically at him, a gleaming pince-nez magnifying the size of his innocuous gray-blue eyes. He was neatly dressed in his gray Reichsführer SS uniform, slender, a bit shorter than Alex. He might have been a train conductor or a tobacconist. Alex examined the soft, fragile hands, then saw that Himmler had a fey smile on his face. There was a certain adolescent effeminacy about him. The smile broadened, revealing a fine set of unstained teeth and a receding chin. 'Come now,' the voice coaxed, 'you're the expert.'

'I need time to develop the right defense for Schmeling.'

'Defense? Surely you can think of a more positive approach.' There was a curious obsequiousness in Himmler's manner which troubled Alex. He possessed the terrible power of a civil clerk.

'Let me put it to you simply ... if a fighter defends himself well and his opponent tires in the late rounds, he can take advantage of his weakness.'

Himmler betrayed no emotion. His smile seemed carved on his thin, bloodless lips.

'My aide formed the impression that you weren't going to be cooperative. I hope he misjudged your attitude, Herr Stein.'

'I can't work miracles ... the fight's in three weeks.'

Himmler drew him close and Alex smelled the sweet violet cashews he chewed.

'Let me put some facts ... *simply* to you,' he began in a pedantic schoolmaster's voice, 'based on my research. In archaeological excavations made by specially trained SS men, we have determined that the skulls of negroes are no different from the giant African apes. They have a smaller

17

brain than the Aryan. When these beasts were transported to America, their bodies were covered with hair and they had no language. The slave-masters trained them to speak their tongues, so that they could communicate and do their work more efficiently.

'Louis is descended from these animals – he is a mere generation away from his ancestors who emerged from the slime pits of primeval Africa.' He paused and asked in a conspiratorial hush: 'You're aware of these facts, aren't you?' Before waiting for a response from Alex, he resumed: 'It's clear to all of us that Schmeling will be fighting a man with the mind and brain of a three-year-old child. It can't be much of a contest.'

Alex shook his head in disbelief and Himmler took this for assent.

'The prestige of the Third Reich is at stake, Herr Stein. The Führer has already decreed Schmeling's victory.... I myself have contributed to Schmeling's training program by suggesting to Buelow that he place Max on the same dietary regime I recommend to all SS men – raw leeks and bottled mineral water for breakfast....'

Himmler left him to join the group beside Schmeling. Alex reeled dizzily against the wall, then strode through the door of the gym to the street where a cordon of SS enclosed him, demanding to see his credentials.

'Schlemiels. I own this gym,' he shouted at them.

He stopped at the sausage vendor and bought a fragrantly charred *Weisswürste* on a hot crisp roll, then sat down on the curb under a blooming linden tree. At his feet were heart-shaped leaves and clusters of cream-colored flowers which had been trammeled by the spectators waiting for a glimpse of Schmeling. A whisper of a breeze curling from the Isar River lofted memories of the summers he had spent as a teenager camping in Deggendorf, at the foot of the Bavarian forest where the Isar sprang to life. He met his wife Miriam there at a farm where she had been hired to pick hops for the *Bockbier* season. He imagined he heard the great, silver-flecked drays clip-clopping down the rutted country lanes as they pulled the massive wagons sent by the breweries of Dortmund, Munich, and Würzburg.

I loved her as a child, he thought to himself, half closing

his eyes, then squinted through the spangles of sunlight at Georg, the young manager of his gym who was running toward him.

'Mrs. Stein is on the phone – she's crying. I can't make any sense –'

'What's wrong?' Alex asked in alarm.

'I don't know.'

He rushed into his office and picked up the receiver. The desolate wail of his wife was so harrowing that the receiver shook in his hand. She was barely coherent.

'Miriam! Miriam! It's me!'

'I went to the school. . . .'

She broke off and her sobs were punctuated by breathlessness. She sounded as though she were being strangled.

'The school,' he repeated as though reminding an amnesiac of a lost train of thought.

'I was going to take them to the Marienplatz for shoes . . .'

Again there was the awful wrenching monody of her cries.

'Jonathan and David?' he asked. 'What happened?' He heard his own voice echo like an animal's death gurgle.

'They took the boys . . .'

'Who?'

'The Gestapo,' she said forlornly. 'When I fought with them, they threw me down in the street in front of the children . . . a man kicked me . . . Alex, he kept kicking me –'

'Miriam, where did they take the boys?'

'I don't know.'

'Listen to me, *Liebchen*. Leave the house. Take the tram to Sam's pension.' There was a silence at the other end and he waited for her to respond. 'Miriam?'

'Yes.'

'Don't take a taxi.'

'Does it matter now?' The sorrow in her voice seemed like a note played on flute, then lost in the percussion of her grief.

The phone went dead. When he tried to call his home again, the operator told him that the line was out of order.

Two

At the corner of the immense Burgerbraukeller which straddled an entire city block like some primitive colossus designed as a tribute to beer – the workingman's aphrodisiac – a small, yellow-bricked, three-storied building stood incongruously, a mere tangent, touching the thigh of a giant. The sign displayed outside was neatly printed and attached to a metal rail:

Weissbeck Pension

The garden was filled with a variety of Dutch tulips, climbing roses that gerrymandered over pinewood trellises, an arbor of fruit trees among which stone benches were placed for guests of the pension. A shallow pond filled with goldfish abutted the garden wall.

Sam Weissbeck bitterly attended to his daily task of cleaning the pond. Each night when the Braukeller closed, violent drunks trampled the garden, vomited on his flowers, urinated on the benches and defecated in the goldfish pond. Occasionally they would break windows on the ground floor. But Saturday nights were the worst. Prostitutes would come in droves from their haunts on the Nymphenburgerstrasse, shouting, bartering with the men staggering out of the beer hall. Raucous, caterwauling shrieks fissured the night, disturbing the few boarders who still remained at the pension. Sam's eight-year-old daughter, Lenore, would creep into his room when the whores and their sweating pickups climbed into the garden, sprawled on the grass, and lowed like farm animals. The steps, the benches, even the small chapel behind the house where his beloved Judith lay buried would be caked with semen and the lawn littered with blobs of used condoms, bloated like jellyfish beached by a poison tide.

Sam no longer called the police.

He was a Jew.

His complaints carried no weight. In fact the merest cheep of dissatisfaction that he registered brought with it alarming consequences. The police had threatened to jail him for running a brothel, selling spirits without a license, keeping an unclean kitchen, dealing in stolen goods. It wasn't merely that he was a Jew, but that he stood in the way of the beer hall's plans for expansion. In 1935, after the passage of the Nuremberg Laws which deprived Jews of their right to own property. Sam had prudently arranged with the help of a friendly notary and the family *Advokat* to sell the pension to his wife and her father: both Judith and her father were Lutherans. Sam's new position on official forms was 'domestic porter.' Notwithstanding this stratagem, flotillas of lawyers, judges, and their clerks employed by the brewery tried to force him out so that the Burgerbraukeller could, as one of its directors put it, 'turn the corner and find its place in the sun.' The courts upheld the rights of the new owners, thus beginning an accelerating reign of terror.

Hundreds of workmen had been brought in to enlarge the beer hall. A gigantic concrete wall replaced the old timber one. The wall surged higher and higher like a parasite consuming its host. Pnuematic drills tore up the pavement; additional sewage lines were connected. The work was unending, unremitting and Sam's regular boarders left.

Of the fifteen rooms in the pension only four were now rented and these by loud, provincial commercial travelers, greasy peddlers, monsters of frugality. They ravaged his table, licking spoons, sopping up gravy with their filthy fingernails when he pleaded that there was no more bread with the evening meal.

But Sam was a stubborn man. The property was sacrosanct. He was convinced that only in bricks, mortar, a plot of ground could a man establish any permanency. The pension had efficacy, underwrote a claim to the future, and he would rather die than give it up. The property took on a living presence, growing before his eyes each day like his daughter Lenore. No one, not the beer hall's lawyers, nor the Nazis, could drive him out. If he lost the pension, he forfeited his soul. As an orphan he had been shifted from one foundling home to another; he had nurtured all of his life the fantasy of owning, possessing a piece of ground that would always belong to him.

In order to purchase the pension he had squeezed every penny, working for years as a toilet swab, kitchen porter, busboy, salad man, waiter, bellman. By the time he asked for Judith's hand he could proudly tell his father-in-law-to-be that he was the *owner* of a small pension which would one day be a great hotel rivaling the majestic Vier Jahreszeiten. His passion for Judith and the recklessness of his ambition persuaded her father that Jew or not, Sam was a good man who would care for his daughter. In the year of their marriage, 1929, the stock market had crashed on Wall Street and the founder of the Nazi party was domiciled on the other side of the river in two small upstairs rooms, living off the royalties of a book he had written in prison and cash fees for lectures.

Sam and Judith had their wedding reception in a small nightclub in Schwabing called the Nachteule where Sam had once worked as a waiter. His best man was his boyhood friend Alex Stein. Victor Conte, the owner-impresario of the club, charged them only his cost for the food and liquor. As a present to the couple, Victor provided the room, musicians, waiters and a heart-shaped floral wreath.

No one present at the Nachteule wedding festivities was aware of the fact that the moody author-lecturer had just forsaken his bohemian habits, had used the war chest of the Nazi party to take possession of his first Mercedes on the evening of the wedding reception. A uniformed chauffeur came with the open touring car.

Thus when Judith and Sam returned to the Pension Weissbeck to spend their wedding night as their own first guests, Judith had noted with that eye for good society that marked her as the observant wife of a burgher: 'Look, Sam, even though the beer hall's beside us, we're getting a good class of people.'

Parked in front of the pension was *the* Mercedes. Emil Maurice, the chauffeur, leaned against the spare tire casing and tipped his cap courteously, wishing the newlyweds a *guten nacht*. Beside him was a blond girl with pellucid blue eyes and the sensitive expressive features of a Rubens nymph. She smiled amicably at them, and as Sam opened the front door he heard the girl's high heels clatter on the steps behind them.

'Are you still open?' the girl asked.

'Well, it's –' Sam began, then thought better, embracing this harbinger of future trade. 'What would you like?'

... said, walking through to
... om the cold room. She broug...
... nded Sam the corkscrew, and
... unwrapped the special sur-
... they left the reception.
... the white, kid-glove
... letters. PENSION

lea...

WEISSBECK – ... om

'Only Alex would be so ... ... exclaimed.

Sam took out his fountain pen and wro... on the first page.

Mr. and Mrs. Samuel Weissbeck, August 23rd, 1929

'We were just married,' Sam told the girl, offering her a glass of chilled hock.

'Congratulations ... Look, I won't stay long. I'm waiting for my uncle who's at a meeting at the beer hall,' she said with disdain. 'He doesn't like me to drink.'

'Well, you'll tell him it was a celebration. You're our first guest,' Sam said exuberantly. He offered her his pen. 'Will you do us the honor of signing our book?'

'A pleasure.' As she took the pen her hand froze. The voice of man, honed by outrage, came from outside.

'Geli, Geli, where the devil are you?'

The girl's eyes fluttered nervously and she quickly scrawled her name, then extended her hand first to Judith then to Sam.

'My name is Geli Raubal. I wish you both happiness.'

The door burst open and a well-dressed man in a dark suit and trench coat glared at them with the furious expression of a betrayed lover.

'Why didn't you wait in the car?' he demanded.

'I was bored ... don't embarrass me. These people were kind enough to offer me some tea.'

His face altered and there was a desire to yield some softer passion, an alien emotion of relief, gratitude. He removed his soft black felt hat.

'Thank you for looking after my Geli,' he said.

'Come sign their book. They've just been married. We're their first guests. They've been so hospitable to me ...'

He took the pen from her, affixed his signature, and added,

'May your house prosp
allowed the girl to ho
smitten by an overwh
the two walked to th
put his arms around
'I can't make ou
Imagine prop
married man in
Judith in his ar

over
child. As
he man stop,
said as Sam locked up.
r uncle. He's just another
younger girl,' he replied, taking

It was two ye... since Judith had died, and the memory
of her warm bo... her ebullience, enabled Sam to resume
his housekeepi... chores. He picked up the sack which
jangled with ... beer bottles, broken glass and the refuse left by
the m... ...en the previous night. He paused at Judith's grave,
placed a bunch of freshly cut violets beside the stone and
spoke to her as he did each day before going to the kitchen
to prepare the evening meal for the day's boarders. To cut
costs he had discharged the cook the previous week.

'I love you, my darling. And I won't give up.' He stretched
out his arms as though embracing the house and garden.
'This is ours and someday you'll know I was right. We'll have
the big hotel I promised you. Lenore is helping me.' He
passed through the garden door to the alley where the dust-
bins were kept and slung the gunnysack onto the top of the
heap. As he was about to go back into the house, he saw a
woman lying just beyond the bins. A tremor rippled through
his bones as though jarred by electricity. He stooped to the
ground. There were red bruises on the woman's cheeks, and
blood seeped through the bodice of her fine lace blouse.

'Miriam . . . Miriam . . . God –'
He lifted her in his arms and staggered with her to a downstairs bedroom. She was deadweight and hardly breathing.
Hesitantly, he opened her blouse to listen to her heart. The
cavity between her breasts had a nasty gash. He went to the
sink, ran the cold water, and with a clean towel staunched
the flow of blood and cleaned her wound. But he was at a
loss as to what next to do. She lay on the bed, sibilantly
groaning. He remembered that there was some household
ammonia under the sink and he left the door ajar and rushed
into the kitchen.

One of his boarders, Karl Bauer, a stocky, bearded traveler

in p

home

dark b

furtive man

who made monthly visits from h

lurking outside the larder. He had

'What's going

as he was caught re... ...ant eyes, pomaded hair, and the

'The pork cutlets at din... said, taking the offensive

the potato soup was salty ag... slab of Muenster cheese.

ject I can't bring myself to disc... as a whore's ass and

for another room, Weissbeck, unless... spaetzle is a sub-

provement.' He wagged a thick finger at... king of looking

your table at the evening meal. Make no mis... be judging

good nature. It has limits ... The Alpenhof has go... my

menu each weekend. ... Do you take me for a fool – I'm the

man who supplied the urinals and commodes to the Neu-

schwanstein Castle!' When Sam turned his back, Bauer

placed the cheese in the tattered pocket of his patched ro...

Sam located the ammonia but Bauer blocked his path. 'Not so fast, I'm not through with you yet. When I passed number eight, he had his door opened and was masturbating. He was watching the nymphs outside on your lawn with their clients. There are cures for such things, spas ... Baden, the waters, the ice-cold sitz baths which shrink the prostate. I'm a respectable traveler. I won't tolerate foreplay outside my window – baying. Mark me, carnal acts destroy the digestive system.'

'Herr Bauer, let me pass.'

'I'll file reports on these incidents.'

'Go ahead,' Sam said angrily. 'But let me tell you the next time I catch you stealing cheese I'll give *you* notice.'

'Threats now,' Bauer muttered, then retreated to the back garden.

Sam poured some ammonia on a ball of cotton and held it under Miriam's nose. She jerked her head away and he held her in the crook of his arm. Her eyes rolled and she hiccuped violently.

'I think I want to be sick,' she said.

'I'll bring a basin.'

'No, let me go to the toilet.'

He helped her out into the passageway and debated ringing a doctor, then he asked, 'Shall I get Alex?'

'No, he's on his way.'

When she came out, her ....ol and took them.'
then she fell sobbing into... small, chiseled nose, the
'The Gestapo came t... disfigured by the calamity
The delicacy of his ...ly bent toward her like a weed
softness of his gray...
of her statement. ...
held fast by win...

'Why?' he ...on't understand ...' As an afterthought
'I don't k don't even look Jewish. If you had to pick
she said, a group you'd never think —'
them o... there have been some mistake?' he asked, ever the
'C... optimist.

Miriam shook her head disconsolately.

'I wish ... but they're efficient. No question about that.
They had their names and their school photographs.'

Sam was stricken by Miriam's collapse. She was usually
a forceful woman, well organized, intelligent, who had adjusted to living on borrowed time. Now her dark hair, worn
like woven strands in a tight bun, hung limply over her
shoulders. And her full lips, with a tendency to smile even
when she was upset, were shivering. She was a lost, an-
guished mother. But what could he say to reassure her that
would not emphasize his own impotence? They were victims, outcasts, beyond the perimeters of law and human
justice. The dynamism of the Nazi power had overwhelmed
them and only God would hear their appeals.

They sat down in the parlor which had originally been his
and Judith's sitting room. After her death, Sam had given
it over to the boarders, so that now it was an unholy ragout
of armchairs bought in fire sales, sofas acquired from bankrupt offices, tables and lamps damaged in shipment to stores.
The maroon frayed carpet with its patterned birds alighting
in trees, a feeble counterfeit of an Aubusson, had once graced
the office of a provincial stationmaster. On the walls hung
gloomy nineteenth-century oils from the *Sturm und Drang*
school of painting, figures taking shelter under gnarled oaks
as cataclysmic tempests cleaved open the dark gray skies, en-
gulfing the fugitives in a world of malevolent forces. Sam
had taken a perverse pride in putting together this farrago
for the Bauers of the world. Here was drama, the room
seemed to shriek. But Miriam's presence in these surround-

ings troubled him, for it measured the decline of his hopes and ambitions. She had visited Judith here often. Now she looked around, and it was clear that she was disoriented.

'One of the Gestapo men said that a Major Von Fritsch would have information about the boys.'

Dachau was only eight miles away from the center of town. On the way there, David ate a Nestlé chocolate bar the driver had given him when they left the school. He was quite impressed by the motorcycle escort in front of the staff car carrying him and his brother along the country road. He took his notebook from his briefcase. In it he kept the numbers of locomotives and car licenses. He slept with it under his pillow. He selected a red crayon from his case and wrote down the licenses of the motorcycles, then asked the driver what his number was.

He had his mother's bright, open face and a devil-may-care attitude that endeared him to the boys his age. He attracted the girls in the school with glib stories of how his father was the lightweight champion of Europe and piloted airplanes. His mother he depicted as a musical-comedy actress, and he himself an heir to a diamond fortune.

Right now he was concentrating on not showing that he was terrified.

'We must be important for them to go to this much trouble,' he informed his brother Jonathan. David was eleven, two years older than Jonathan but not as physically strong.

'They had no reason to take us and hurt Mama,' Jonathan declared.

'She shouldn't have fought,' the driver said. 'She'll be all right.'

'Are we guests or prisoners?' David asked lightly.

'I just drive you ...'

'Do they serve kosher food at the camp?' he asked.

'You're an impossible boy,' the driver replied with a short laugh.

'David, stop it.'

'They don't hurt children,' he added confidently to cheer up his brother, but Jonathan saw him shiver as he turned his head away.

Jonathan sat looking out at the farms and the countryside,

27

mentally noting landmarks so that he could find his way back to Munich after they'd escaped. As the car passed through Dachau, he observed a sawmill, a castle on the hill, and a smallish brewery. Among the market stalls, painters and artisans hawked their wares ... just another sleepy village. Beyond the town there was a rank odor of swamps. Fog crept up from deep, slimy trenches and the sky was filled with a yellowish, nauseating miasma.

The cortege stopped in front of a shapeless concrete privy. Beyond it he saw a series of manned wooden watchtowers with aerials on their roofs.

The driver rolled down his window and said to the armed guard, 'David and Jonathan Stein to be held in detention.'

A wooden barrier lifted and the car entered a compound enclosed by ten-foot-high barbed wire. In the background were long wooden huts with tin roofs. The car stopped and the driver said, 'Out ... Now be good boys and nothing will happen to you.'

A man of middle size, with a crest of medals on his uniform, approached them. He was accompanied by two soldiers.

'I am SS Standartenführer Eicke,' he said, punctiliously clicking his heels. 'Commandant of Dachau. You are both being held in protective detention.'

'Why?' Jonathan asked. 'What did we do?'

'There are no questions here. Only one thing has any meaning – orders!'

David found the numbers of other vehicles to copy as they were escorted by the two soldiers to a hut. Jonathan peered around him at the adults in their gray-striped prison uniforms. The letter *J* was patched on their worn shirts. They had sallow complexions, stained teeth, and many of them were barefoot. They stared through him as though they were blind. Beside the hut a man tied to a wooden post was being lashed with a bullwhip.

'You can stay here,' one of the soldiers said.

'We have to get out of here,' Jonathan whispered.

'You're crazy. Don't you see the barbed wire? We'll cut our hands.'

'They're going to kill us.'

'Oh, God, don't say that,' David said, breaking down.

Jonathan pushed the cowl of black hair out of his eyes and

searched for an opening in the fence. He walked toward the barbed wire and surreptitiously looked around for anyone spying on him. As his fingers touched the wire, David pleaded with him to follow orders. He wrestled Jonathan away from the fence. Their commotion drew attention from the watchtower and a voice over a megaphone bellowed, 'Get away from the fence.'

Jonathan looked up at the guard who had a rifle pointed at him. He stepped away from the fence and brandished his fist in a gesture of unutterable rage. Then he spat at the foot of the watchtower and shouted, '*Feigling* ... coward ... I'm not afraid.'

*   *   *

The tram ride from Schwabing seemed interminable to Alex. It had taken almost half an hour to reach the Rathus where an army of tourists and their guides were blocking the tracks as they stood photographing the mechanical figures and the Mary Column. A black Citroën with four men in long black leather coats and cropped hair kept pace with the tram. Only Gestapo agents would be dressed like this in June. Alex knew he had a better chance to lose them if he were in a crowd.

The tram conductor rang the bell to get the people off the tracks. The Citroën pulled alongside the tram, and Alex crouched in the rear of his car. When the driver opened the door to let off passengers, Alex lurched out and rushed across the Rathaus square. He saw two men jump from the back seat of the Citroën and fight their way through the crowd. But he was safely hidden in a large group admiring the Münchener Kindl, the symbol of the city. The Gestapo agents strode past him. When they entered the Rathaus, Alex leaped on an unattended bicycle and rode down the Brienner-strasse.

As he pedaled hard by the bank of the Isar, he struggled with his dilemma. He was a man accustomed to free choice, but in this deranged system of Nazi government, controlled by Hitler's whim, his opposition was meaningless. They had beaten his wife and taken his sons ... and in a lawless society whoever had the power could enforce his will.

He skirted a group of Hitler Youth running wind sprints. Here were the legions of the future, dragons in Arcadia. Hitler had struck deep, rich earth, formulating a manic religion which appealed to children. He was the fourteenth apostle, displacing God, corrupting the land, filling the mouths of the people with trenchant slogans instead of prayers.

Lenore was tall for her age. Her lo[ng] had a woman's shapely contours and contributed to tha[t] of statuesque litheness which attracted the attention of ...en. Her cheekbones were high, a miracle of nature's hapha[za]rd sculpture, and her turned-up nose counterfeited a degre[e] of hauteur that antagonized the mothers of her classmates. S[he] had inherited her mother's natural reserve, and among Germans this ladylike composure passed for arrogance. Her face was oval and in her light gray eyes there was a sense of worldliness, a lack of surprise, a patient tolerance of adults and their lack of perspective.

Sam had repeatedly warned her not to walk past the beer hall. During the day it presented dangers (so he told her) that a girl of her age could not comprehend. Gangs of construction workers recruited from Stadelheim prison loitered in the trenches outside. They were troublemakers, invariably drunk on the job. They worked cheap, and once they had been paid their wages they floated like untraceable jetsam into the nether world of cheap taprooms, freight yards, or joined the roving bands of tramps and outcasts. They were the colonies of human caries in Germany's body. Some became members of the SA, the army of thugs which had been formed by Ernst Röhm.

But the allure of Rumplemeir's Konditorei, an Austrian pastry shop with its bombes, glazed apricots, its torten, and chocolates shaped like swans, was irresistible to Lenore. After school she would stand outside the window waiting for the unsold cakes of the previous day to be marked down. The Konditorei was located in the small parade of shops alongside the beer hall. It struck Lenore as silly and time-consuming to walk on the other side of the street, then cross at a busy corner. It always took ages for her to get home.

After all she was not a little girl. At the pension she helped change beds, she boiled cabbage, cleaned vegetables. The boarders always complimented her on the fluffiness of her

omelets. No, she wasn't jus... yed her father in most
responsibilities. Although... of her mother his obsessive
matters, this prohibition... a greater strain on her situation
too solicitous. Since... dy shunned by many of the other
concern for her safe... even walk with them. Wasn't it bad
at school. She w... girls whispered about her? Often they
students. She c... guttural, hectoring chorus which lodged
enough that t... ss and reverberated through her dreams
barked, 'Jud... nt.
in her consciou...
like a witch's ...

There w... evenings when Sam would sit in the kitchen
after the... washed the dishes. His newspaper would be
pressed against his nose and he would be unaware of the tears
gathering in his eyes and trickling down his cheeks. She, too,
thought about her mother – the sweet fragrance of the lily of
the valley cologne she wore, the way she brushed and braided
into plaits Lenore's blond hair – and at times Lenore wanted
to scream out, protest to a vindictive God who had permitted
this injustice.

The familiar face of one of the boarders, smeared with
whipped cream, appeared behind Rumplemeir's window.
Bauer wagged his finger at her. She overcame her revulsion
of him – fearing that she would be accused of slighting him –
and went inside. He motioned her to be seated at his table.
He closed his catalog illustrated with odd-shaped pipes, commodes, and bidets.

'Come, I'll buy you a cake.' He thrashed the air for the
attention of a waitress wheeling a cart like a dray. 'Here,
stop!' he cawed. She ordered a hot chocolate and selected
an apple nut torte from the trolley. 'Eat, *Lieblich Mädchen*,
but first' – he shoved his sweaty, porcine face to her mouth
– 'give Uncle Bauer a kiss.' Some lavatory astringent clung
to his loud, black-and-white houndstooth suit, and his hair
reeked of a dulcet floral pomade. She hesitated. He took the
opportunity to fondle her plaits. He undid the rubber bands
and her hair flowed in a thick, wavy mane.

'You mustn't do that,' she said uneasily.

'Be free like the wind. . . . You look fifteen, young lady,' he
said flatteringly. 'Who could resist you, Lenore?' She dutifully pressed her lips against his cheek. 'See, what did I tell
you? It didn't hurt a bit and look how happy you've made

me. The t[...]
forced a l[...]
book to the n[...]
provide even tha lips and you can have the wor[...]
to the showroom w ate slice on her, then opene[...]
day you might even ow bidets. 'Dresden, yes, I'm abl[...]
two conspirators sharing noon after school, I'll take y[...]
sweets. 'Der Führer has one on display. Imagine, on[...]
repeatedly stabbed his chest har self.' He drew her close,
myself took the order ... and I've in nce richer than their
of my triumph. The Direktor is going or his niece, Geli.' He
head 'BY APPOINTMENT TO ADOLF HITLER, DER his index finger. 'I
Dr. Goebbels approves. I might even give mysel to the home office
Doktor! Now what do you think of Karl Bauer?' RER' ... if our letter-

'I have to leave now.'

'What's the hurry? This is a day for celebration. I'll buy you perfume at one of the shops on the Marienplatz. They have lovely scents *pour le bain*. The bubbles rise up and embrace your body. Your skin will feel like Japanese silk – a geisha's ...'

'I'm late, Herr Bauer.'

'Then I'll accompany you home.'

He settled the bill, pinched the cashier's cheek, and played the gallant by bowing to Lenore, clicking his heels, and holding open the door. He seemed quite mad to her, but he had lost that forbidding presence that she sensed when she caught him lurking on the staircase or spying outside of the toilet.

She was light-headed in the fragrant summer air with its promise of long holidays, perhaps a trip along the Rhine with her father and the Stein family. She and Jonathan had discussed it all through the winter, spreading maps on the floor of his room. He would teach her to fish for pike and they would camp out and he would buy a red canoe and name it after her. He would do the lettering himself, draw a white heart, and inscribe 'Lenore' on the side of it. Jonathan inspired her with his wonderful ideas, and she knew that one day they would dare to admit their love and they would marry and she would have his child and it would be named for her mother. Her moments with Jonathan were the magical treasures she stored in her soul.

'... It's the blatant sexuality that I find objectionable,'

Bauer said, pausing by a le... ...m a sensitive man
... and I think that your fa... ...ve fallen out because
he doesn't recognize the ...rer and I share. The similari-
I'm a pure romantic ...nality are endless — the parallels
another correspondent ...t in the Great War, was gassed at
ties in our nature a... ...I know we may have met then. Com-
astonish me. I, to... ...ame trench. But Sam doesn't see these
Passchendaele. ...esn't understand my protests, my sense of
rades sharing... ...gallantry. You've heard the women at night,
affinities. ...surely Lenore?'
honor —

She nodded ruefully. The subject was distasteful, threatening. She forced the thoughts out of her mind. She knew what
they were doing in the garden and she tried to shut out the
flashing coupled bodies which she occasionally saw when she
had to use the bathroom in the middle of the night.

'There's nothing Papa can do. He's called the police, but
they won't help him.' She looked at him and her eyes filled
with the entreaty of the powerless. 'Don't leave us, Herr
Bauer. I know that Papa has deep respect for you.'

'Well, then, Lenore, I'll consider staying for your sake.
But we must have our secrets. It is the foundation of friendship. Mutual trust, the warm affection, the loyalties which
form a bond. I'm your ardent admirer, so allow me to be
your loving uncle. But we must not reveal our relationship
to anyone — especially your father.'

'Why not?'

'He wouldn't understand . . . and he'd draw the wrong con-
clusions. Interpretation is everything. Judge a man by his
actions . . .'

He took her hand and she was carried along by his momentum, into the *Leder* shop. The aromas of the tanned
hides were luxurious and tantalizing. Bauer started feeling
the leather for softness, texture. An assistant showed them a
range of skins.

'They must be very expensive,' Lenore said.

'Italian antelope — the very thing —' Bauer said like a cou-
turier. 'It has essence. A vest for my niece,' he commanded.
Various sizes and styles were brought out and laid on a
highly varnished wooden counter. 'Black will set off your
hair. Yes, it will bring out the hunt, the woods. You'll be my

little Diana o

She was us... helped her on w..., made of bone. She g... fitting room and an ass... thrilled by the touch of ... ather vest. The buttons w... completely grown up. A w...ed in the three-way mirro... her new vest when they met ...ught she looked beautif... Jonathan would admire... Englischer Garten. ...ic on Sunday in the

'An enchantress,' Bauer said, rub... the bodice. 'Now give Uncle a proper kis...is fingers across respond, his mouth was thrust against hers a...ore she could breath. ...he held her

He stroked her neck and breathed heavily in her ear.

'You mustn't, Herr Bauer,' she implored him.

'Do you mean you're not grateful!' Scolding. 'Well, I'll simply pack my bags and that'll make an end of it.' His face was flushed, and she trembled. 'There'll be an investigation – make no mistake about it. The first magistrate in the land, Der Führer himself, will learn about the goings-on at Pension Weissbeck. The SS will be brought in to purge the place and believe me I'll be present at interrogations ...' he inveighed, totally out of control, fulminating.

'I love the vest,' she cried, 'Please ... please ... please, *Uncle* Bauer, don't hurt us.'

He regained a semblance of his equanimity when he paid the clerk. In the street, he cautioned her to remain silent about their meeting and the gift.

'Won't I be able to show it to Papa?'

'Never, never, do you hear?' Adamant. 'I'll keep it for you in my room, Lenore, and when I invite you in, you'll model it for me. I'll be Apollo and you'll be my sister – Diana.' He chortled. 'When I least expect it, my Goethe side emerges.'

He paused with her by the Braukeller to watch the progress of the building. The men were digging trenches below her, and as she stood peering at their slick, bronzed, sweating backs, she noticed a man scrutinize Bauer, then her. The man's deep-set, black-brown eyes seemed to bore through her and she moved behind Bauer to block him out. *'Mädchen, kommt due hier. Ich will deine votze lecken,'* one of the men called out in a singsong voice. The disgusting suggestion set off a charge of obscene jeering among the other laborers. She tugged at Bauer's sleeve, but he was lost in thought, then he

smiled and approached the ...ed his hand to the man,
'Geisler' – Bauer warm...nkered belly was strippled
a colossus of beer, where ...haven't been the same since
with perspiration – 'the...
you left.'

'Geisler replied. His eyes probed

'I don't miss ...d you become a father?'
Lenore. 'Since ...er of the pension owner.' He enjoined

'She's the ...ce herself, and in an effort to conceal her
Lenore to i...he smiled companionably at the brute. 'Why
nervousne...
did you ...ve?'

'I had some trouble with a woman worker. You know the
old story ... an accusation and the man's without a defense,'
Geisler said breathing heavily. 'I did a few months at Stadelheim and I decided to try my luck in Munich. It's gayer – not
so many restraints. And I don't have to travel very far for
Oktoberfest.'

'It's a man's city,' Bauer agreed. 'Sophisticated tastes have
a home here. Certain activities are *comme il faut* for people
like ourselves. May wine festivals, strawberries, the gardens,
idyllic boat rides on the Isar *avec une petite belle amie*, don't
bring the trouble that can inhibit a man in the provinces. I
hope this work is temporary, my dear Geisler.'

'I've applied for a sales position in the Braukeller.'

'Sales, yes, there's the future. Commissions ... a man
spreads his wings like an eagle.'

'I'm a perfect advertisement.'

The two bawled with laughter and arranged to meet for a
drink. 'You'll like Herr Geisler,' Bauer said to Lenore as they
walked away. 'He's a most amusing person.' Before leaving
her at the corner to walk home by herself he said, 'Keep our
secret, *Liebchen*.'

When Lenore let herself in, she heard muffled voices, but
she distinctly made out the sound of a woman crying coming
from a downstairs bedroom. Shaken, she called out for her
father, and when there was no response she crept nervously
along the dark corridor. Her head was throbbing and she
felt feverish. She listened for a moment, and when she
recognized Alex's voice she rapped lightly on the door. Her
father stuck out his head but blocked her view.

'What's wrong, Papa –?'

...and peel potatoes for the soup,' Sam
...to this kind of treatment and she
...he here today?' she insisted.
...saw Miriam sitting on the
...a large spool of gauze.
...upport. ...d kissed her,
...in an acci-

bea...........enest with.....
Leno........ out for the towel rail for s......
  'Aunt Miriam ...' She rushed to the bed a....
then held her head in her small hands. 'Were you
dent?'
  'Don't ask questions,' Sam adjured her.
  'Aunt Miriam, don't cry, please. Everything'll be fine
  Miriam's sobbing seemed almost cauterized by the gir...
She motioned the child to sit beside her on the bed. Lenore
massaged the muscles on Miriam's neck.
  'Oh, how I've always wanted a daughter like you,' Miriam
said, kissing Lenore's hands. '*Sheine madela.*' She lapsed
into silence and her contorted face frightened Lenore.
  'Don't please ... I'll make you some strong tea with
lemon.'
  'Nothing,' Miriam replied.
  Alex took Lenore by the shoulder and forced her off the
bed.
  'I've given her some codeine ... let her sleep,' he said.
  'I hope I never wake up,' Miriam moaned. 'You can say
Kaddish for the three of us.'
  They left her in the room and huddled in the kitchen.
Lenore filled the kettle with water and set it on the range
to boil. Her confusion increased as she studied the drawn
faces of her father and Alex. Lenore's imagination spiraled
with phantoms, admonitions she heard in synagogue about
dybbuks – evil spirits who took possession of people, entering their souls and driving them mad. It struck her as
incredible that with Miriam in such agony the subject under
discussion was boxing. She peeled potatoes in a corner by
the sink as she listened.
  'You have to work with Schmeling. It's the only way,' Sam
declared.
  'But how can I guarantee that Schmeling's going to beat

Louis? That's what Fri
Schmeling, but it's usel
'Try, Alex, there's no
'Try? Don't be so da
my back as long as I'm al
'Then bargain for the
returned, you won't help
taken the boys if they w
'Jonathan? Who to
'The SS,' Ale
'I had to act
Lenore
breath
head
an

...apo will be on
...an Fritsch unless they're
...meling. They wouldn't have
...en't worried themselves.'
...ok him?' Lenore asked, quavering.
...x replied. He was filled with self-reproach.
...like a hero and insult them.'
...e felt her muscles tense until she could hardly
...e. Her Jonathan ... There was a shattering inside her
...as thoughts crashed, splintering. She heard a wail of
...guish fill the room as the men jumped up from the kitchen
table and shook her.

'She's hysterical,' Sam said. A hand lashed across her cheek and she saw a jagged white flash.

The shock of the blow brought her to her senses and she sat down at the table.

The pain kneading her temples gathered momentum until she thought her head would explode. She had heard stories at school about how the SS took people to concentration camps and then cut their bodies into small pieces while they were still alive. She imagined Jonathan writhing on the ground, beheaded.

'We'll get him back – David, too,' Alex was saying. 'I promise. Now stop crying, Lenore. We've got to think this through.'

She found herself drifting to another plane, transcendent. Only she could rescue Jonathan.

'I had a cake at Rumplemeir's,' she began, 'and I know if I speak to Uncle he'll go directly to Hitler and the SS won't harm the boys. I won't let anything happen.'

'She's raving,' Alex said.

'Lenore, darling, calm down. We'll deal with it,' Sam reassured her.

'We'll also stop the men and women from coming into the garden at night. I'll wear my leather vest for him – you'll see ...'

Sam carried Lenore to her bedroom.

The summer breeze rustled the leaves of the horse chest-

She clung to fragmented ves-

...nd you won't harm me

...she allowed herself to

...warm, textured darkn...

*　　*　　*

The telephone shook in Alex's hands but Fritsch could not see him.

'Your people must be crazy. Why would they kidnap my sons and beat my wife?' Alex demanded, taking an aggressive position.

There was a silence on the other end followed by a polite request for Alex to hold on while Fritsch made a few inquiries. The fruit trees in the pension garden formed silhouettes as evening crept forward. Men coming home from work with their evening paper descended from the tram stop. The life of ordinary Germany was normal, prosaic, Alex thought, as he waited for Fritsch to come back to the phone.

'I don't understand how my orders were misunderstood.'

'Neither do I, Major ... It isn't that simple to develop tactics after seeing a few old films. I thought someone who knew boxing as well as you would be the first to appreciate that.'

'The boys are at Dachau. They're perfectly all right,' Fritsch replied languidly. 'They're detained by mistake. I'd asked the Gestapo to guard your family, not imprison them. Why don't we meet and discuss the situation? The bar at the Regina Palast?'

'I'd rather meet at a club not far from the gymnasium. The Nachteule. It's on the Franz-Josef-Strasse.'

'Nine o'clock, Herr Stein.'

The time dragged for Alex. He had a dinner of sauerbraten blaukraut, and a dunkel beer with Sam and the other boarders. The emotion of fear was totally alien to his character, and a turbulent conflict raged within him which he could

not control. Every
Sam's commiserati...
to get his sons back,
A man has some ...
'I advise you to
There was in his na...
diplomacy. Alex deplo...
the phone was openly ...
but don't provoke him
'We're differen...
a gentle man
mean th...

only
would take.

...ully,' Sam asserted. ...which he passed off as ...de of Sam. 'Your attitude on ...e to Fritsch. Think what you like,

...t people, you and I,' Alex declared. 'You're ...I've survived by standing up for myself. I don't ...t unkindly. But, Sam, I've spent my life watching ...giving beatings and others taking them. You're in a service business. You make your living by bending, softly tapping on your boarders' doors to wake them, carrying their bags, preparing meals.

'I couldn't do it, and you couldn't watch a man having his teeth knocked out, then clean his mouthpiece and massage his neck while he spits broken teeth into a pail. A fighter's mouth looks like the inside of an erupting volcano – his cheeks turn purple, mouses swell from his eyes, when he pisses he passes blood for a week from the kidney punches. That's my world. It's ugly to a man of your sensibility. It's my kitchen . . .'

Sam shook his head, and in the cast of his eyes Alex discerned a lack of comprehension and disapproval.

'All I want is for you to have David and Jonathan back.'

Alex took Sam's hands and pulled him down to the bench at the table. He coiled his arms around his neck and hugged him. He loved Sam, and this estrangement at such a critical moment had to be resolved.

'The Nazis understand one thing – violence. In the twenties when we were children, didn't we stand by while the SA beat people on the streets, disrupted political rallies, broke into shops? Hitler realized that the Storm Troopers would make people listen to his message. Major Fritsch must have a family, a mother, a father, perhaps a wife and children – a girl he's fond of. He's human! He bleeds if he cuts himself shaving – the master race that Speer glorifies at the Nuremberg rallies – yes, my friend, their blood is no different from ours.'

'Alex, control yourself. They'll kill you without a thought.'

40

to him.

'You can't simply think

'Why not? I'm the injured
one has to accept responsibility   . If Fritsch
had struck me, beaten me, then w   have fought like
men. But he's insidious, a thinker, a plotter, an officer who
appreciates forms of strategy. You can always bring a man to
heel by attacking the people he loves, or whatever in the
name of God is precious to him.... There you have the
tactics and the power of the Nazis. In boxing you either fight
offensively or you have to defend. We've done nothing! We
allow them to kick us like dogs and we don't even cover up.'
He slapped the table with both hands and the dishes leaped
into the air. 'More! More! like this table. We beg for it:
Come hit me ... I love it. Keep doing it ... but do we at
least have the nobility, the honour of a boxer who takes a
beating and refuses to go down because some inner voice,
some fineness of spirit, raises him above beasts and makes
him last the fight? The spectators stand on their feet applauding before the final bell. They've seen a man struggle. His
courage reaches out and encompasses them, makes them feel
proud to be men. Hitler talks about the triumph of the will.
He can't appreciate the triumph of the human spirit.'

Alex left the dining room and went into the bathroom. He
ran the tap and splashed his face with cold water, luxuriating
in the chill investing his body. He swabbed himself down
with a towel, then poked his head into the bedroom. Miriam
was in a deep sleep and he closed the door soundlessly. Sam
gave him a clean blue shirt and his best tweed sports jacket.
When Alex looked at himself in the mirror he began to
laugh.

'It's a young overcoat, not a jacket. Let me have a sweater
or a Windbreaker. After all I'm not courting a woman but
going into battle.'

'I called Victor and he'll meet you at the club.'

'What time is it?'

'Seven. You've got two hours.'

'Victor will understand what I'm talking about,' he said.

The heavy scent of summer rain, dying roses, and the
beer sweat of passing workmen depressed him. He wondered

41

nished with Glockengasse No. 4711, a Rhine cologne. His sleek image was enhanced by a new cornflower blue serge suit for the occasion. He looked like an unemployed maître d'hotel from the provinces . . . a Sicilian, Cavini thought. The restaurant was too public for murder. The men's room might serve his purpose. Yes, he had to dispose of this swindler.

'Come with me to the men's room,' Cavini suggested.

'I'll pay interest,' Victor replied.

'Twenty percent.'

'Usury,' Tina chided her father.

'What then?' he asked, befuddled.

'Ten percent over five years.'

'I'd sooner bury my money in the ground.'

'Papa, it's for me,' Tina beseeched him.

'Go to the men's room, Signor Cavini, and reflect on the proposal.'

'We'll discuss it together there,' the Puntura insisted.

'Discuss business affairs of such importance, while toilets are flushed? How can we cover the topics?'

'What topics? What are you talking about?' Cavini asked, becoming flustered as he undid a strap on his suitcase.

'What do you intend to do in the men's room, wash your linen?'

'That's a possibility.'

Tina pulled the suitcase away from him and touched her father's hand affectionately.

'I'll do your linen, Papa.'

'There, it's settled,' Victor said. He raised his glass, then stood up at the table, and as Cavini and his daughter tugged at the suitcase which was now in the aisle, Victor broke into song. The restaurant diners as well as Cavini were stunned, but soon faces relaxed and hands were swaying in a conductor's ump-pah gesture, necks ululating, and hums were heard as Victor's mellifluous baritone rang out with a medley of short arias from *Cavalleria Rusticana*.

'He's demented. I'm being humiliated,' Cavini complained to his daughter who had pulled the suitcase to her side of the table.

'No, Papa. Victor often does this for business. He'll leave his card at the tables and when we have a club people will flock to it. Say ten percent, *padro mio* . . .'

The diners applauded enthusiastically and Victor took four

bows. When he returned to the table he removed from his briefcase a sheaf of papers written in German and presented them to Cavini along with a fountain pen.

'Contracts, all notarized,' Victor said, slapping Cavini's back with good fellowship.

'But I don't read German. I don't know what I'm signing.'

'Trust is the basis of family unity,' Victor averred, pressing the pen on him. 'What is your middle name, Padre Cavini?'

'Giorgio,' he replied. His hand quivered over the papers and the morass of Xs requiring his signature.

'Your name has what we in opera call syllabication. Gi-or-gio. See how the tongue grips it, toys with it, embraces it. It's a name with a posture, a bearing, and yet it has a resonance which commands respect, obedience. It's a flower. Our child, male or female, shall bear the name Giorgio.'

Victor kissed Cavini's cheeks, trilled Rossini, while Tina kissed Cavini's hands as he wrote his name endlessly on the documents.

'One thing, Vittorio, you'll pay the debt and if anyone comes from Naples and needs your help, you'll give it without asking questions.'

'You have my hand and my honor on it, Padre.'

The debt had been paid long ago, and the promise forgotten. As Victor kissed his daughters Georgie and Linda good night before leaving for the club, he had an uncomfortable sensation in the pit of his stomach. He communicated his disquiet to Tina who walked him to his Citroën sedan.

'What's wrong?' she asked. 'Problems at the club?'

'No, business is marvelous ... every night is New Year's Eve for the officers in town.'

'You'll try to help Alex, won't you?'

'Of course I will. I'm sure that this is all a misunderstanding and if he'd been a little more tactful the Nazis wouldn't have bothered him.'

They both stood by the car. The poplars and lilac bushes were threshed by the wind, and for a moment the secure life they had built seemed threatened by something unspoken. She held up her face and he lightly grazed her lips, dispassionately, preoccupied.

'Vittorio, tell me.'

'There was a message for me at the club ... a man from

46

Naples wants to see me. He mentioned your father's name.'

She had the ability to conceal her emotions, but a flush suffused her ivory skin and he felt her chest heave involuntarily against his.

'Mafia,' she said.

'That's what I assume. With all the SS men coming to the club, well, it's a problem. They work with the Italian Secret Police. Mussolini's created a very efficient service with the SIM. They come snooping around from time to time.'

'My father is asking for a favor,' she said severely.

'Tina, we don't owe him a damned thing. He's got his money.'

'Vittorio, pay my father ... it has to be done.'

There were serious problems at the Nachteule which Victor never brought up with his wife. He had achieved respectability, had given Tina the sheltered life of a country wife. She spent her time raising their two daughters in a gabled house on the outskirts of Munich. Her life revolved around the church that could be seen from their walled garden. Its steeples seemed mystically suspended in the sky, designed by God to protect the Contes. Christ's columns, Tina called them. Driving past the church, he looked down the side of the hill to his house which was swathed in blue-black tones of early night. During the day, the soft, tranquil greens of the landscape gave him the feeling of being in the country, remote, secure. Yet he was barely twenty minutes from the center of Munich's bustling life.

He had constructed a shield of charm which enabled him to endure the late nights – of asking people to wait at the bar because their table wasn't quite ready, of mollifying elderly men nervous about the young women they planned to seduce. He knew he was meant for better things – memorable, sweeping events – and not just cashiers who couldn't add or bookkeepers who had the audacity to try to fiddle him. When he thought about it, he grew melancholy for having settled for less than his actual worth. He yearned for recognition, coveted fame like a schoolboy, and collected newspaper scraps that mentioned him or his establishment, even when the names were misspelled.

The Nachteule had flourished. He had brought a new concept of entertainment to the city, cannily importing young chorus singers from the leading opera companies after their seasons had ended. No other nightclub in Munich could provide Italian opera, a romantic atmosphere, along with the good, sharp, spicy cuisine of southern Italy. His was a club that lovers frequented as well as those who appreciated good music. The Nachteule in many respects was without competition, an original which Victor had created with Cavini's money.

Victor recognized that his period in Munich was drawing to a close. Recent experiences made that clear. The shift of power to the Nazis had markedly affected the club. His clientele had become the uniformed men of the officers corps and the SS. Victor did not object to taking their money, but he found their rowdiness increasingly disturbing to the civilian regulars.

Almost overnight the Nachteule had degenerated into one of those Left Bank Parisian rendezvous where just about everything short of seduction occurs. Girls loitered around the piano bar, packing it six deep as shifts of officers came in. Highly placed SS officials openly bribed waiters for introductions to the pretty Italian singers who were working at the club. Victor saw that he was losing control of the situation, but he was unable to resist the force of arms.

The situation had reached new dangerous heights the previous week when Reinhard Heydrich had been on a tour of the city. He had come to the club with a party of other SS officers, and after spending several hours listening to the music and drinking heavily, his eye had fallen on Victor's lead soprano. As chief of the SD, the security police within the SS, his power was unlimited. His reputation as a sadist was well known. But when he called Victor to his table, his face was relaxed and good natured.

'I hope you enjoyed the singing.'

'I've always been interested in music, Signore Conte,' he said. 'It was first class. The soprano especially.'

'Silvia.'

'Yes, what can you tell me about her' – he beckoned Victor to a seat between himself and his deputy Walter Schellenberg – 'origins?' Victor had no reason to assume that Heydrich had any motive but curiosity.

'She's from La Scala – one of the lead singers in the chorus. This coming season, she'll be singing principals.' Victor noticed that the bottle of Remy Martin in front of

Heydrich was almost empty and he signaled a waiter to bring another. 'May I offer this with the compliments of the Nachteule?' Victor poured the officers a drink. The men raised their glasses and chimed, '*Prosit.*'

'What do you know about her parents, or her background?' Heydrich asked.

'Nothing. I heard her perform in *Norma* last year and invited her to join us here.'

Heydrich moodily swirled his brandy in the snifter. His eyes were a mesmeric blue and his blond, short, neatly parted hair and athletic carriage epitomized the Nordic qualities that were so close to Himmler's heart. And yet Victor had heard rumours about Heydrich ... scandalous gossip that he had some Jewish blood. It hardly seemed possible. When some of his party left the table to go to the bar in search of girls, Heydrich slipped into an expansive role.

'Very few people are aware of the fact that my father was a uniquely talented musician and teacher and I was profoundly influenced by him while I was growing up.

'My father founded the first Halle Conservatory of Music and for years some of our most gifted musicians studied with him —' Heydrich broke off and on his face there was a painful conflict. 'But then one day everything changed for my family ... when Riemann's *Musiklexikon* was published.' The timbre of his voice became singsong. 'Under my father's entry, "Bruno Heydrich," Riemann had the audacity to add, "real name Suss!"'

The veins in his temples protruded as he fought to control his anger.

'The effect on all of us was devastating. .... I mean, I ask you, a man who appreciates fine music and the civilities of life, why would my father be accused? Suss! The sound of the name even now reminds me of the hiss that comes from sewers ... the effluvium. It isn't a name but a chemical reaction. A form of poison gas.'

Victor nodded, caught the eye of a waiter who would come to the table and call him away. It was a device that he frequently used when a tiresome customer was bending his ear. When the waiter approached, Heydrich picked up his black leather crop and angrily thrust it into the waiter's stomach.

'No interruptions, is that clear?'

'Herr Heydrich, please, let me assure you that the man

meant no harm.'

'I want you to understand,' Heydrich demanded. His face again became taut and bellicose. 'It's important ... you see there was a girl from an Italian family ... a devout Catholic. She and I were friends and she studied at the Halle. She had an exquisite mezzo, clear toned, pure. We went to concerts together ... to the films. We both admired Fritzi Massary and saw her perform in her legendary *Madame Pompadour*.' Victor could hardly make sense of these moody ravings but he could gauge the dangers they represented.

'Puppy love,' Victor diagnosed. 'It happens to all of us. As a Neapolitan ... well ... I myself know the feelings, the wrench one feels as a lad when one loses,' he trilled, uniting the two of them. 'Fellow sufferers,' he continued '*Innamorato*. Why, my dear Heydrich, it's an affliction that only the the healthy youth experiences. It's an affirmation of one's masculinity.' He raised his glass. 'Let us drink to lost loves and the ladies' misfortune.' He pointed to himself. 'Look at us, enjoying our everyday existence, able to cope with adversity, and our ladies no doubt are middle-aged, brown at the edges, fruit past its time, overripe, fit only for compotes. Rejoice in your vigor, your high position, your success.'

Heydrich tortured a smile on his lips, but the hooded eyes spoke of winter storms, derangement, passionately summarizing lost hope in a cadenza of vindictiveness.

'Unfortunately, the memory of her never leaves me,' Heydrich admitted. 'I've spent years attempting to trace her ... the complex machinery of the SD has been at my disposal.' He closed his fingers and his powerful hands grasped at the air. His fist was raised. 'Nothing ... a man's deepest yearnings unlike the callow boy's are for different expressions of power.'

'Like what?'

'Retribution.'

'I don't quite follow ... '

'Silvia, your soprano, reawakened all the old buried mysteries which I myself can't fathom. At times I thought when I heard her voice and studied her features that my soul was trying to escape.'

Victor knew that he was isolated with a psychopath.

'If you care to stay for the midnight show, you'll hear her again.'

'You'll introduce me,' Heydrich ordered with a note of finality.

'She's in the dressing room . . .'

Heydrich rose from the table and stumbled forward. One of his aides came toward him and asked if he wanted his car, but Heydrich brushed him aside. He strode through the crowd with Victor. A path opened, people nervously bunched together, squashing themselves against the bar so he could pass untouched.

When they were backstage, the chattering of the artists who were on their break subsided. All that could be heard was the contact Heydrich's leather boots made with the wooden floorboards.

'The girls are changing,' Victor said awkwardly. Droplets of perspiration ran from his armpits to his hips.

'Bring her out!' Heydrich raised his arm and supported himself against the wall. 'Immediately.'

Victor hesitated, flustered. He opened his palms in a futile gesture to the singers who froze in a still-life cluster. Victor knocked on the dressing room door, whispered to the elderly costume lady.

In a moment Silvia came out. She was dark-haired, with a girlish plumpness. She held her robe closed, but the deep cleavage of her breasts throbbed apprehensively. She studied the silent, repressed expressions of the company.

Clumsily, Victor introducd them. Heydrich appeared dazed, lost in bizarre contemplation, then suddenly snapped, 'Where's your office?'

'This way . . .'

'– Well, take us there and send in a bottle of champagne.' He grasped Silvia's hand like a reproving guardian.

Heydrich spent more than an hour locked in Victor's office and when he finally came out, Silvia was splayed across his desk, unconscious. Blood seeped from her vagina and her body was pocked with cigarette burns. Victor called for an ambulance, and as he carried the girl to a sofa, he vowed that one day he would see that Heydrich paid for this act of insanity. But even before his fantasies of cornering Heydrich alone and unguarded took shape, he was stopped by Schellenberg.

'Gruppenführer Heydrich has ordered you to make arrangements for rooms so that if any SS man wants to have a

51

girl he can be sure of hygenic accommodations. Your office won't do, Herr Conte.'

No, he could not tell Tina about his problems.

Victor put his key into the back-door lock of the club. There were some metal shavings in the crevices. He slid against the wall, closed the door silently, and listened intently. His first thought was that Heydrich had returned, but he dismissed the idea. The SD invariably made a great public display of an arrest. If they were after him, they would have come to the club when it was crowded and created a drama.

Victor did not turn the light on. He could find his way through the rooms and passageways in the dark. He knew every floorboard creak. He tiptoed backstage into the gloom of the canvas sets.

He kept a 7.65 mm Mauser automatic in the clothes closet of his office. He glided past the dressing rooms and stood indecisively at the threshold. He inched forward cautiously, then reached for the doorknob of his office. He had to get to his gun.

Something wrapped around his neck, cut into his windpipe. It tightened. His heart thumped wildly, and he struggled to pull it off, but he could not reach the powerful hands behind his head. He blacked out for a moment. His knees drooped forward and his body went limp.

A flame from a lighter flickered beside his bulging eyes and a voice cried out: 'God, Vittorio. I thought it was the Gestapo.' The wire was released and Victor staggered against the wall. Motes of light flashed before his eyes and he held his hand to his mouth, trying to retch. The pulsating in his body and head was agonizing. He rubbed his neck, the pain gradually subsiding, but he had difficulty focusing on the blurred figure furiously massaging his face. His cheeks were slapped.

'I'll get some ice from the bar,' the man said, helping him into his office. A desk lamp was turned on, and Victor lunged onto his leather sofa, terrified and exhausted. A man's face slowly formed. He had lazy blue eyes, slick hair, a delicate nose, and a sallow complexion. He was broad-shouldered and his muscular arms bulged in the striped blue suit he wore. The face was familiar but he couldn't quite place it. He re-

minded Victor of a bouncer he had hired when he firs
over the club.

'You'll be all right in a minute, Vittorio. Brandy and
There, your color's coming back, like you've spent the day
at the beach in Masaniello, ehhh?' He snapped his fingers,
pressed the tip of his tongue against the front of his teeth,
gathered the spittle, and emitted a 'thith-thith.' The habit
was one that Victor recalled from his youth: known as a
Neapolitan mouth rinse, it was reserved for a girl passing on
the street to indicate that she looked good enough to eat.

The man returned with a bottle of fifty-year-old Napoleon
brandy and a chunk of jagged ice which he held in a towel
with an ice pick. He handed the bottle to Victor.

'Drink, Vittorio ... it's the best French stuff you've got.
For pussy and brandy, you got to go a long way to beat those
French.' He paced the room with an arm behind his back.
Victor took a pull from the bottle.

'I'm sorry ... so give me a "hello" already. It's me, Paolo
... Paolo Salica. I give you your first pessary when I was a
delivery boy in Santini's Farmacia ... and that dummy Marta
you wanted to bash swallowed it.'

'Il ladro,' Victor said.

'There you go, Pauli the thief. You ought to kiss my hands,
cause Tina's father offered me ten thousand lire to bring
your testicolos back to him so he could cook them in a risotto.
Me, I tell him, let the lovers live ... no one else's gonna
marry Tina after Vittorio broke the label ... nuns won't take
her, right? Leave them be, ehhh?'

Salica laughed in short, staccato bursts, toyed with the
piano wire, then slipped it into his jacket pocket. Victor remembered him. They had seen each other around Naples
cafés and nodded over newspapers. Salica was then involved
in petty deals. He always had an inventory of gaudy, cheap
stolen jewelry which he kept in a bandage taped to his calf.
He delivered messages to Mafiosi and carried purloined merchandise to fences. After a time Victor lost sight of him, and
when his name was brought up in the neighborhood, he'd
heard that Salica had developed into an ingenious wireman
and lock expert. He was acquiring a reputation. Pretty slum
girls pursued him because he invariably bought them clothes
and used them as accomplices.

'Say you're glad to see me,' Salica said.

53

'You're trouble, Pauli, and I've got enough already.'

'I'm not trouble. Come on, Vittorio, we went out when we were kids. Remember when I shit on Il Duce's picture right in the middle of the Vómero and the *carabinieri* chased me over half the roofs of Naples before giving up?'

'Mafia,' Victor said with contempt.

Salica shook his head for almost half a minute like a dummy.

'Listen, Victor, when the old man lent you the money for your club, you didn't ask questions. Thought you fleeced the Puntura, right? Well, let me straighten you out. We're the last of the revolutionaries. We never allowed ourselves to be stepped on by Mussolini. Nobody shaved our heads or poured castor oil down our throats. All right ...? You think Himmler's bad? We've got Prefect Mori ... he uses the Mafia as an excuse to kill and torture innocent people. If you're not Fascista, you're an enemy. I'm an enemy.'

'What are they after you for?'

'A banking problem.'

'Forgery?'

'I'm not Dante. I robbed the Banca di Commerciale in Naples. We lost three people ... my partner and I got away.'

Victor could not contain his astonishment. The Commercial Bank of Naples was impregnable. 'What possessed you to think you could rob the Commerciale?' he asked

'I did ... let's see –'

'The Mercantile in Viareggio,' a woman's voice answered outside the open door. She stepped inside the office. In her hand was a .22 Baretta and at a nod from Salica she put it inside her purse. She was slender, gamine, with flowing brunette hair. Her expression was watchful. 'You wanted a seaside holiday.'

'My associate, Mademoiselle Claire Vallon, known as Chou. This is my boyhood friend, Vittorio Conte.'

She looked skeptically at Victor, gave him a guarded smile. 'So I heard.'

'I've lost track, Chou.'

'We did the Agricoltore in Penne.'

'Yes, I needed the mountain air of the Abruzzi for my sinus condition.'

'There are other reasons, but why bother?' she noted. 'You're not being hired, Pauli.' She had the businesslike

54

manner of a Parisienne shopkeeper. Her skirt was shorter than women wore in Munich, and Victor noticed that she had gorgeously shaped legs and wore black silk stockings. Her eyes were dark, lambent, carefully mascaraed.

'We lost the Commerciale,' she explained, 'because it was in Naples.' Her face registered disgust and an element of disbelief. 'As a Neapolitan, you probably know a little game that they play with tourists. We stole a Fiat in Rome and naturally parked it outside the bank. One of our tires was punctured with a knife while we were inside and when we came out with the bags of money, two *lazzarone* offered to help us fix it. They thought we had luggage in the trunk and that as soon as we unloaded they could steal a piece ...'

'We left the money on the street,' Salica continued, 'and Chou and I eventually made our way to Cavini's mortuary over the rooftops and he managed to get us on a train. Unfortunately, the destination was Munich. Cavini said you'd look after me till I can make arrangements.' His face softened. 'Just a few weeks, Vittorio. *Clemènza, aver pietà di mio*. You're a *sportivo*, ehhh?'

'A few weeks?'

'*Sì* ... I'm waiting for a contact in Kehl. He can fix it for me to get to Strasbourg.'

'And then?'

'America. There are *amici* there.'

Victor became pensive and considered several possibilities. He dare not bring them to his home. The two of them would cause gossip. Besides, they might endanger Tina and the girls. The bartender at the club had a spare room but he drank off the job and was rowdy.

'How much money have you got?'

'Fifty lire,' Salica replied.

'Talk about living on love ... three days on a train,' Chou said with a twinkle.

Salica snapped his fingers, squished saliva against his teeth. 'You're complaining.'

'Who's complaining?'

He pointed a finger at her as though she were the accused in a criminal prosecution, then presented his case to Victor.

'She worked as a dancing partner at Il Pesco Gatto entertaining lonely men and degenerates who could dance for six-hour stretches ...'

'I was deserted –'

'Who tells you to get involved with a married Italian? You're Parisienne, supposed to be smart, ehhh? I give her a trade, a craft.'

'I'm grateful. I love robbing banks. Six years I studied ballet –'

'Right. You carry yourself terrific. She dresses as a boy and glides past the tellers' window. *Swan Lake*. You should see her.'

Victor raised his hands to end the dispute.

'Basta.' He took five hundred marks from his safe and gave it to Salica. 'You've got to have a place where you won't be questioned about having papers or identity cards. So the commercial hotels are no good.'

'Whatever you say, Vittorio.'

'I have an old friend who has a pension.'

He looked at the two of them, knew that they'd be an endless headache until they left for Kehl, but he had no option. He would honor his word to Cavini. He picked up the telephone and dialed the number of the Pension Weissbeck.

Five

The threats Alex made alarmed Victor. When Alex asked, 'When are we going to stop being victims and defend ourselves?' he had remained mute, preoccupied. They sat in a corner booth, drinking Huber's Slivovitz straight. All around him the club bustled with activity: waiters setting up their stations, the constant ringing of the phone for reservations, singers wandering by, the pianist practicing at the bar. They were all sources of irritation which grated on his nerves while he tried to calm Alex.

'Look, the Nazis aren't infallible ... maybe they made a mistake?'

'Like Heydrich made with your singer?' he returned furiously. 'If the Nazis are beyond the law, then I can stand outside with them. Will you let me have your revolver?'

'No!'

'I'm appealing to you as a friend.'

'And as your friend I have to refuse.'

Alex called for another drink, sat morosely slumped at the table.

'Listen to me, Alex, you're not a criminal.'

'What constitutes a criminal? Is he born that way? Is it a question of being influenced by his surroundings ...?'

Victor couldn't answer him. Each day the Nazis chipped away at their lives until the edifice that once passed for civilized behavior became dust. Humanity was as meaningless as a medieval Scholastic argument. Victor hardly dared survey the destruction. All that remained for him were a series of elusive, disconnected memories he grasped at like an old man recapturing schoolday idylls. Sam had become a prisoner of his boarding-house – nothing more than a navvy who no longer could spare an evening to see his friends. The *Mittwoch* dinners that they used to have had ceased when Judith had died of tuberculosis. Alex, too, had retreated, scrabbling for a living when he lost his matchmaker's license and boxing halls refused to accommodate the bouts he arranged. He had fallen to the lowest level – a man who trained fighters for a pittance. No one of promise would go to Stein's gymnasium, just the drays, elderly pugs with deadened reflexes, their faces a puttied mass of scar tissue.

The two men had met when Victor first arrived in Munich and worked as a sales representative for a vinter of hocks. He had sold wines to Sam who was then employed as an assistant to the wine steward at the Regina Palast. Sam had ultimately worked at the Nachteule for more than a year, helping Victor stock his wines and liquors, organizing the kitchen, and then had stayed on as a waiter. He introduced Victor to Alex, and the two men would drop into the gym several afternoons a week. Eventually they were joined by their wives, broadening the relationship.

It was customary for the Steins to make Rosh Hashanah dinner, the Weissbecks prepared the Passover meal, and Tina had them all in for roast goose for Christmas. No religious differences upset the easy balance of their friendship. They were just six people who enjoyed each other's company, spent summer vacations together. Victor had attended Jonathan's *bris*. He had wet the infant's tongue with schnapps during the circumcision, and Tina had baked the sponge cake and cookies for the party afterward. The three couples over the years had developed that purest of ties – friendship.

Now Alex was remote and intimated that he had been betrayed.

'Alex, we're just individuals. The Nazis have an army – human life doesn't mean a thing to them.'

'I won't let Fritsch get away with this.'

'You won't get the boys out of Dachau by antagonizing Fritsch any further.'

'You sound like Sam,' he observed acidulously. 'Here's my ass, kick it.'

Just then Victor was called into the kitchen by the maître d'. Salica had missed dinner at the pension and so had insisted on staying at the club. The chef had neglected to start the roasts; he was too busy preparing spaghetti ala vongoli for the wily Salica. Paolo had upset the routine. He was snooping around the larder, checking the fish for freshness, cajoling the assistant chef to prepare a vitello tonnato, suggesting that various dishes he enjoyed be added to the menu. He handed out tips to the kitchen staff and was buying them drinks from the bar.

'He's tipping with my money,' Victor protested to Chou who stood back with a wan, tolerant smile, shrugging haplessly at them.

'No fenuch?' Salica asked with disbelief. 'What kind of kitchen is this, Vittorio? How do you expect the chef to create when you don't buy the right vegetables?'

'That's the way he is,' Chou said stoically. 'You're nice to him, he pisses on your shoes.'

Boldly Victor took charge and dispatched Salica and the girl to a table near Alex. He made hurried introductions, then, as the club began to fill up, left them to attend to the mass of officers lined up at the doorway.

Alex ignored the two uninvited guests. It was nine o'clock. He left the table, threaded his way through the heavily made up women, searching for Fritsch. He stood at the entrance. Girls jammed against him as they thrust their way to the bar. A drink was overturned behind him, and an SS lieutenant caused a burst of laughter when he delicately patted with a handkerchief the exposed cleavage of the girl who had been the victim.

Out of the corner of his eye Alex saw Fritsch's face, but then his view was obscured by a massively built lieutenant with perfectly symmetrical features, straight flaxen hair, and large, cherubic blue eyes. The lieutenant stopped so that his superior could whisper something to him.

Alex advanced slowly, uncertain of his intentions.

'Well, here indeed is our champion trainer,' Fritsch said. He extended his hand and the lieutenant moved off into the crowd.

'I have a place where we can talk.'

'Ah, you're a man of influence. Just as I thought.' He preceded Alex to the booth. A bottle of Huber's was on the table and a waiter stood by attentively. 'See, I'm here at your command.'

'How're my children?'

'Excellent. People get a bit confused about the SS, so let me explain what happened. I'm a major in the SD, the political arm of our organization, and my primary field is intelligence in the security service. The Gestapo is one of the divisions in the *Schutzstaffel*, but they function as the criminal police branch. They have a tendency to meddle in political affairs and sometimes our areas overlap. An order

was given to pick up your sons by someone in the Gestapo
... but we'll get to that after we've resolved our business.'

The explanation was too glib and practiced, Alex thought.
'I agree to work with Schmeling.'

Fritsch sipped his schnapps.

'How deep, Herr Stein, is your commitment?'

'I'll do everything I can short of fighting Louis myself to
see that Max wins the fight.'

'Splendid. I knew you were acting unreasonably this morning. You see, the Führer has made it clear that this fight is a
personal test which has engaged him emotionally. In the
political sphere, this fight will highlight our achievements in
Germany. Twenty years ago we were on our knees, defeated,
demoralized, a nation of weaklings threatened by a Bolshevik
takeover. Now we walk with our heads held high. We have
pride. We don't have to grovel at anyone's feet. We've recovered from the stab in the back. The *Dolschstoss* defeated
us and we'll never again allow that to happen.'

He peered at Alex. 'Herr Stein, you as a Jew were offered
the opportunity – an opportunity any German would be
proud to seize – of trying to help a German win the heavyweight championship of the world. What was your response?'
he demanded rhetorically. 'You were totally negative. You
slammed the door in the face of the entire German people.
You categorized us as spiritless, losers who ought to turn tail
and run.

'A generation ago, that would have been the case. No one
would have argued with you. "Yes, naturally we'll quit," a
majority of Germans would have said. Hitler has restored
our will, given us a national purpose, and when he rails
against the Jews, can't you see that he's absolutely right? He
is speaking not merely from his own vast experience with the
problem, but he calls our attention to the unhappy actuality
of our observations. Only a Jew would have said *die* to me
this morning, and corrupted us with his defeatism.'

To Fritsch, Alex realized, any dissenting view constituted
Jewish cowardice.

'Two men get into the ring,' Alex began optimistically,
'and when they're heavyweights who can hit as hard as Louis
and *our* Max, either man can end it with a single blow.'

Fritsch was pleased. He nodded like a schoolteacher approving a bright pupil.

'*Our* Max. That's the very point. He belongs to all of us – Jew, Catholic, Protestant. He's a national symbol. I congratulate you, Herr Stein; you've seen the light. In Der Führer, Adolf Hitler, we have found our salvation. In Max Schmeling we have a living example of the Führer's world view. He will be victorious.' He raised his glass and chinked it with Alex's. '*Prosit.*' Alex despised his own weakness. 'Needless to say, Reichsführer Himmler will be delighted that you're going to help. He mentioned that the two of you had a productive conversation this morning.'

'It dealt with leeks and mineral water. I don't recommend the SS diet for Max.'

Fritsch smiled conspiratorially. 'Well, I won't be the one to contradict Himmler.' He rose, carefully straightening the creases on his perfectly pressed trousers. 'If you'd like to accompany me to my car, you can see your sons haven't been harmed.'

There was a black Opel limousine parked by the curb. Alex's eyes filled with tears when he saw the faces of his sons pressed against the window. David waved buoyantly at him, but Jonathan held back reproachfully, and when he got out of the car he said defiantly to Alex:

'Papa, they wouldn't fight like men.'

'What a boy,' Fritsch observed. 'You see how generous and understanding I am? Pure psychology. I realized that you couldn't give your best efforts if you had a gun to your head. All you needed was a good scare. You have your sons back.'

Alex nodded in thanks, but his eyes held fast on Fritsch who ordered his driver to take him to The Swan in the old town. The golden giant Alex had seen earlier in the club joined Fritsch in the car. When it pulled away, Alex saw the major coquettishly lay his head on the lieutenant's shoulder.

In the Nachteule kitchen the two boys ravenously ate a steak pizzaiola which the chef prepared under Salica's direction. Victor thought it would be best for Salica and the girl to go directly back to the pension with Alex.

'Take them with you, please. If you're stopped for any reason, you can use Major Fritsch's name. That ought to be enough,' Victor said.

But Alex appeared to have trouble following Victor's instructions. He gazed blankly at his sons and did not respond to their questions.

Jonathan shook his arm and he pulled violently away.

'Papa, what's wrong?'

'We're all right, Papa,' David said. 'It's over.'

Waiters rushed by shouting out their orders.

'Alex, why don't you leave now?' Victor asked.

'All right,' Alex replied in a dreamy, faraway voice.

'Alex, aren't you listening to me?'

'Yes, we'll be going.' He held out his hand and Victor embraced him.

Salica and Chou followed them into the side alley. They walked silently to the front of the club where taxis were lined up. Waves of officers were going into the club and no one paid any attention to them. Alex gave the pension address, then fell silent. His head rested on the cool leather seat and Jonathan pressed close to him, quizzically studying his father's face. David dozed in the front seat.

'Are you going to be a boxer like your father?' Salica asked Jonathan.

'No, I'm too smart.'

'That's the right idea. Just make your money and put it in a bank.'

'Some people buy shares of companies,' Jonathan explained. 'There's a boy at school whose father works at the Böise and he's made millions by buying and selling bits of paper.'

'Ah, a financier,' Salica noted approvingly. 'I'll know whose advice to ask when I have my fortune. Right, Chou?' She sat beside the sleeping David and stroked his head.

'How do you know Uncle Victor?'

'We grew up together in Naples.'

'Uncle Victor's very successful.'

'There was a time when I could buy and sell him like a few pencils,' Salica observed, snapping his fingers. He smiled wryly. 'I was ruined by women and uncooperative banks.'

'You need a good wife,' Jonathan told him. 'Someday I'll have one.'

'I thought the same thing, but I took vows before I left Italy.'

'What vows?' Chou asked.

'To pursue romance as a bachelor.'

'Thank God,' Chou remarked.

62

'What kind of work do you do, Mr Salica?' Jonathan asked.

'I open doors ... a special field of lockwork. When a man doesn't have a key or has lost it, I help him get the door open. Or if he has a safe in his office and misplaces the combination or forgotten it, I offer my assistance.'

'How did you learn?' Jonathan persisted.

'It was a skill or should I say technique that I possessed even when I was a boy. People would be out for an evening, or marching in a parade, and they would forget their keys and I would appear with one of my wires which I'd fit into the lock and I'd play it like a musical instrument. And if it refused I would coax it, talk sweetly to it as though it was a lovely woman who was somewhat shy and had a tendency to walk with her eyes lowered when all she had to do was open them so that the world could see what a glorious creature was hiding there. Then presto, the lock would miraculously open. Pauli *il mago* – the magician, they called me – would find himself with a reward for his talent.'

He lightly touched Jonathan's curly hair with affection. The boy had fallen sound asleep.

'You've been through a great deal, Signore Stein. It will pass. Just don't dwell on it. You've got your sons back, so rejoice, drink some wine, hold your wife's hand, pray to God, give a beggar a few coins, and go on living.'

'If I were a different kind of man, it might be possible.'

When the taxi stopped at the pension, Alex told the driver to wait. He and Paul carried the boys in their arms. Sam greeted them at the door and told Alex that he had fed Miriam some potato soup. Alex's face was lighted with a triumphant candescence.

'Put the boys to bed for me,' he said, 'after Miriam sees that they're well.'

'Where're you going?' Sam asked as Alex strode out into the garden. 'Alex!'

'I'm fine, Sam, really I am. I just have to go to the gym for a few hours to prepare for tomorrow. There's nothing to worry about.'

The taxi wove through the tortuous, narrow cobbled streets of the St. Pauli District. In this nether world of workmen's bars, prostitutes who shouted out of windows, trembling drunks who fell into the gutters, beggars, panhandlers, strip clubs, the Nazi regime had met its match in obduracy. It had brainwashed millions, but had failed to eradicate vice. Alex regarded this life of the streets with its petty criminals, its illicit trade in cocaine, as a healthy reaction. He had the driver stop at the Nymphenburgerstrasse.

He walked lithely on the balls of his feet and with a slight roll of his hips ... a hunter on the prowl. A row of cabarets lined the street. Jazz and Dixieland blared out of speakers above each entrance. Attractive young men loitered under the canopies and Alex heard shrill whistles and catcalls trail him. Falsetto voices crooned *'Liebling,'* and perfumed boys hawked prices at him. He reached The Swan.

A shill-doorman winked at him when he paused to look at the photographs displayed in gilt frames. Above him a pink neon light flicked SIEBEN AKTE – KUNSTLERIN VON BERLIN. Men in décolleté evening gowns, wearing long, ringleted wigs, earrings and necklaces, imitated shy girls frozen at that moment between promise and fulfillment, leered out at him from the photographs, offering whatever forbidden fantasy a man might conceive.

Inside he crept to the bar. The room was dimly lighted. A band played a lisping rendition of *Clair de lune* while a female impersonator wearing a white satin gown seductively tugged at the fingers of his long black gloves as he began to strip on the small box stage. The audience was hushed. Alex was approached by an eagle-eyed bartender with a pencil-thin flashlight who asked him what he wanted to drink. He ordered a brandy. In the darkness it was virtually impossible to see anyone's face, and he realized that he'd been foolish to risk another encounter with Fritsch.

A pompous comedian dressed as an army officer appeared. He carried a riding crop and prodded the stripper, ordering him to stop.

'An unfortunate breach of etiquette, *Mein Herren,*' he said. 'This young lady thinks she's at the officers' mess.' Raucous laughter filled the room and Alex was aware that the cabaret was packed. Cigarettes flickered at the tables. 'We cannot have officers of the Third Reich walking around with stiff peckers,' he continued as the stripper covered pubescent girlish breasts in mock embarrassment. 'Punishment?' he asked the audience. There were shouts of *'Ja'* and

'*Nein,*' so the comedian swatted himself on the rear and flounced off. The stripper continued until he was down to a pair of lace panties. Then as he threatened to remove the panties, the stage was blacked out and the voice of the comedian came over the microphone.

'The Swan cordially invites you all to dance. We remind our patrons' – he gave a hoarse, growling, lascivious laugh – 'that no more than six SS men may occupy the same water closet at any given time. We are a cabaret, not a barracks ... Captain Röhm need not have died in vain. In his memory the management offers free spankings to anyone caught puckering his lips, exposing himself to a woman, or pissing on the toilet seats.'

A salvo of high-pitched cackling, foot-stamping, and applause accompanied the last remark. The band drooled sentimental fox-trots. The lights – imitation Roman-style torches – lifted the room out of darkness. Alex watched the men pair off, glide to the dance floor. From his corner of the bar he could not be seen unless a match were held to his face, but he was able to make out the faces of those dancing and the features in the cluster of tables on the lower level. There was a mixture of army men and civilians. He still had no idea why he'd gone after Fritsch or what would happen if the two came face to face. Some impulse stronger even than his desire to live drove him. He could leave safely, but thoughts of how Miriam was beaten and kicked – his sons taken to Dachau – brought out a state of wild, irrational anger. Fritsch must not be allowed to get away without paying a price.

He leaned over the rail separating the bar area from the tables and through bleary eyes scanned the dance floor. In a corner beside the pianist two men were locked in each other's arms. The tall blond officer held Fritsch's face up to his own and kissed him passionately on the lips. Fritsch's hand touched the young man's earlobe, then his fingers rushed through the thick hair.

Alex returned to the bar and called for another brandy. It was almost midnight when the two lovers left. From the lobby, Alex watched the lieutenant wave good-bye to Fritsch who was driving away in his car.

Alex followed the lieutenant. A group of men called out the officer's name. 'Erich, how can you be sure Fritsch isn't playing around with you?'

The lieutenant held up a signet ring on which a hawk had been carved. 'He gave this to me ... it's his university ring.'

'Why aren't you with him now?' a slender, beautiful young man with somber eyes asked. 'You could come to my room.'

When the young man made a move to touch him, Erich dodged him and announced that he was going home.

The night air had become heavy with chill dankness. Erich took the route along the Isar River. Flat barges made their way north, waves in the river flapped hard against the embankment. Alex was touched with a fine mist of spray as he followed Erich. He felt feverish and confused.

Erich crossed a footbridge and was swallowed by the darkness. Alex began to run, his heart pumping rapidly. The lieutenant turned when he heard the footfalls on the cobbled bridge. Alex stopped.

'Who is it?' Startled and unsure, Erich walked back toward him. 'Identify yourself. I am an officer of the SS.' The voice was commanding, strident. 'Did you hear me?' He was now no more than two feet away from Alex, their faces hidden in the black night, their bodies ill-defined.

'He loves you!' Alex cried. 'Jew! Jew ... Jew ... Jew ... Jew ... *Ich bin ein Jude*,' he shouted in a frenzy.

'*Was haben sie gesagt ...?*'

Alex's left struck hard into Erich's stomach. He felt the flesh yield, separate, as the big man gasped in shock. Alex cleaved a right into his solar plexus, and Erich's mouth foamed with spittle as he jackknifed in anguish. His head was low now, and Alex's left hook caught him sharply in the eye. He sagged backwards against the stone wall of the bridge. Alex struck with a right cross which crashed into Erich's nose. Erich raised his arms and held his elbow close to his sides to defend himself, but Alex ripped through with punch after punch into the stomach. Erich's arms dropped as he attempted to cover, but Alex flailed at him methodically, first to the eye, then the nose, then the mouth. Erich's left eye was closed, and Alex pumped his hook in a series of blows to the right eye until again there was the sound of bone mashing. Blood spurted from Erich's mouth and nose, and Alex felt himself growing stronger, more dangerous. Erich's head rested on his shoulder; Alex stepped back and fired a blow at his nose. The big man's knees gyrated crazily under the relentless barrage. Alex held him by the throat and pounded the point of the jaw, then the cheekbones in a tattoo as though he was holding the heavy bag. When he let Erich fall, the body sank to the ground and lay motionless on the cobblestones. Alex lit a match and held it up to Erich's face. It was anonymous, featureless. He stooped down and removed the signet ring from Erich's left hand and put it in his pocket.

In a low, pained sigh, he muttered incoherently, 'Love,' then staggered away.

* * *

Jonathan slept in a small downstairs room by the kitchen. He kept the door ajar in the hope that he would be sure to hear his mother if she called. He had remained awake until well past midnight, urging his tired body to fight against the exhaustion which numbed his mind.

The knowledge that he and Lenore were under the same roof and that he could not see her tormented him, bringing out a streak of rebelliousness which Sam was hardly a match for. They had argued from the moment he'd arrived until Sam had lost patience.

'She's been upset and crying, worrying about your mother. Do you want to make her worse?' Sam threw his hands frustratedly into the air under Jonathan's disapproving stare.

'Lenore'll feel better when she sees me.'

'The answer is no. She's sleeping. When I tell your father the way you're behaving, he'll take a strap to you. I don't know what's the matter with you . . .'

The boy stood his ground, thwarted, eyes blazing furiously, strangling in the yoke of childhood. He watched Sam pad down the corridor, then pressed his face against the cold, dank, greasy wall. He heard a snapping voice behind him.

Salica held a pack of cards in his right hand and cut them. 'Watch, ehhh?' With his left hand he pulled an ace of hearts from the center of the deck. He beckoned Jonathan to join him. His room had a sour odor of neglect, peeling paint, old clothes in camphor. At a washstand, wearing an oversize robe, Chou examined her skin. She had taken a bath and wrapped a tattered towel over her hair. She plucked an eyebrow with tweezers and smiled at Jonathan.

'Company?' she asked Salica.

'Right. Who's this Lenore?'

'My friend,' the boy returned suspiciously.

'Them women'll ruin you every time,' he averred. 'The way you're carrying on, it'll be the crazy house for you. Where'd your papa go?'

'I don't know.'

'It's good for a boy to develop a taste for the ladies. When I was your age I fell in love every week. Wasn't a maid who could pass me on the stairs I didn't pinch.'

'Paolo, that's no way to talk.'

'Ehhh, I wish my father had given me some advice when I was his age. Now you listen, Jonathan. You're after something, well, you can't take it whenever you feel like it, so you plan, scheme, till there's no suspicion. Then when everyone thinks you've lost interest, you go in and grab it. But you've got to have patience and a plan. Sam says no, then you agree. You act reasonable – always a gentleman. But the way you fought, he'll be wary. He won't trust you. Understand?'

Jonathan's eyes flickered in assent.

Salica dealt a hand of casino and told Jonathan to watch his movements. Even though he concentrated he couldn't detect Salica's method of pulling aces out of his sleeve. The sleight of hand fascinated him. Salica shuffled slowly, made no untoward motion, didn't try to divert his attention, and yet he continued to pull aces.

'How do you do it?'

'I started with them before you came in.'

Jonathan observed how he concealed his cards in his long tapered fingers and was able to shift those he dealt himself with others up his sleeve.

They had played for another hour. Jonathan could barely keep his eyes open but he insisted on remaining up till his father returned. He fell asleep in the chair. Salica carried him to his room. Jonathan sensed that his clothes were being removed but he could not resist the strong hands which lifted him and placed a blanket over him.

Salica touched his forehead and Jonathan opened his eyes.

'Please leave the door open. She might come down later.'

'You never quit, do you?' Salica said, cuffing him affectionately.

In a dream state Jonathan imagined he saw Lenore's image. The queens flew out of the pack, shimmering across the screen of his subconscious. Her face blended into that of the four queens. When he reached out to touch them they dissolved. In a fit of frustration, he lurched off the unfamiliar bed and awoke. Disoriented, he tried to trace the events that brought him to the pension. He left his bedroom to get a drink of water. A dim night-light was on in the kitchen and he heard the scrape of a dull pencil over paper. He entered on tiptoe. Lenore sat barefoot at the table. She was wearing a pale yellow nightdress and writing in a notebook.

'I watched you sleeping,' she said.

He sat beside her and rubbed the sleep out of his eyes.

'Why didn't you wake me?'

'I hated you.'

The remark astonished him.

'Why ...? I didn't do anything.'

'I thought you were dead and I'd never see you.'

'Lenore, that's not fair.'

'If you were dead, I'd be with you. All the people I cared for are dead. So it can't be so terrible.'

'Don't talk that way.'

'Why?' she asked distrustfully.

'We're going to have a summer holiday together ... a trip on the Rhine. I had to be with you. No one could stop us.'

She shook her head affirmatively. Her long hair fell across her mouth. He pushed her hair away and ran his finger across her mouth and cheek.

'We'll always be together.' He leaned over and looked at her homework book. He was revolted by what he read. He turned the pages and saw that line after line carried the same bitter sentence. It leaped out, striking him, and his outrage was so overwhelming that he picked up the notebook and was about to tear the pages out.

'Don't!' she implored him.

'Why are you writing this?'

'The teacher punished all the Jewish children again.'

He shook his head furiously. 'We're not criminals.'

'Frau Hoffman and the other teachers say we're guilty of the *Dolchstoss*.'

Alex stood at the kitchen entry. 'It's a lie.' His clothes were blood-spattered. The two children were startled by his

69

appearance. Jonathan rushed up to him and Alex clutched the boy in his arms.

'What happened to you, Papa?'

'Somebody picked a fight with me. Now go to bed, children.'

Six

Alex trotted alongside Schmeling and his trainer, Machon. The Englischer Garten was swathed in mist and the early sun burned away the low clouds. From time to time he turned around to check on Fritsch who was riding behind them in an open staff car. Fritsch was unnaturally pale and gray pouches sagged under his bloodshot eyes. He looked as though he were in shock. Alex raised his fist and exuberantly shouted to him.

'Victory, Major! Cheer up, Max is going to tear Louis apart.'

Schmeling wore a heavy gray sweat suit and weighted boots for his daily six-mile roadwork. Sweat trickled down his brows, but he was not breathing heavily. He was training diligently and had paced himself well. If it weren't for the Nazis, Alex would have taken a professional pride in helping Schmeling prepare for the heavyweight championship.

When Machon dropped off, joining Fritsch in his car, Schmeling turned to Alex.

'I get along with Jews ... I don't really have anything against them,' Schmeling said. He had a smile on his face. 'The joke is that my American manager, Yussel Jacobs is a Jew, and Mike Jacobs, the promotor is Jewish. It's all madness ...'

'Then why let yourself be used this way?'

'Do I have any choice?' He paused and seemed to reconsider his statement. 'I don't mean that I'm being forced ... You see, what more could an athlete want? I fought through the Depression when Germany was on her knees. To see her rise up again under Hitler makes me proud to be a German. We've got dignity. Could any man spit in the face of his country's leader when he's backed by him, invited to his home ...?'

Behind them the car horn tooted and the driver informed them that they'd done six miles. They continued for another hundred yards in a wind sprint, then both paused by the river to catch their breath.

'Do you think I have a chance?'

'When two sluggers get into the ring, anything can happen.'

'Alex, you didn't really answer my question.'

He was pleading for support, and in his dark eyes, Alex saw uncertainty and the fear that assails a man who realizes he is past his prime and can only look back to his springtime.

'We'll look at the Farr fight.'

'I've seen it six times.'

'Not with me you haven't.'

Schmeling nodded hopefully, sighed, and signaled the car to pick them up.

'It's odd the way my destiny is linked with Jews.'

'I'll see you at the gym at eleven. No workout or shadow-boxing until we talk.'

*   *   *

There was a charm, a mystique, a quaintness, and a nobility about banks that Salica found completely irresistible. In his amorous gaze, historical continuity had formed one of those enchanting romantic meridians in which a man and his fate are united in a time continuum.

Yet, nobody in his right mind would have found anything sacred or aesthetically uplifting in the austere, pompous, gray pseudo-Ionic columns or its dismal portico when passing the München Bund Hypotheken-und Wechelbank. What could the spiritual heir of Dante and Petrarch find to rhapsodize about, or how could his eyes grow misty as though in the presence of holy reliquary when confronted by a mere Bavarian Mortgage and Discount Bank?

Money, Paul thought.

He had borrowed Sam's elderly Linhof box camera and was photographing the exterior, using Chou as a model to avert suspicion that he was anything but a tourist. Like a beautiful woman, a bank needed understanding, respect, caution, until her secrets could be learned. Paul possessed the necessary tools of seduction, invariably approaching this period of courtship with ardor and a quickening of the pulse. Was it possible, he asked himself, that the Nazi pomposity, the arrogance of their power, would persuade them to forsake the safeguards that any sensible burgher would take in his small shop?

72

Surely, a bank such as the Munich Bund would engage elite armed guards, all of them sharpshooters, the latest alarm system, and crack Gestapo surveillance teams to monitor the bank's daily activities? The Germans were a nation of security-minded wizards, or so he thought before he and Chou walked through the marble vestibule and were greeted by an elderly guard who wore a hearing aid and was reading the *Münchener Post*. They exchanged '*Guten Tagen,*' and Salica strolled around with a grin on his face, nodded at customers and tellers. He stopped at the central desk which contained deposit and withdrawal slips.

Chou was dispatched to the vaults. She would check out security there by applying for a safe-deposit box. This was their customary working procedure. Once inside the bank they did not communicate, pretended to be strangers.

Salica stood at the desk and drew a quick sketch of the floor plan of the bank. He counted the number of clerks, secretaries, and noted the executives sitting at desks behind a wooden rail. He visited the men's room, pushed open a window, and was startled to see that the bars were warped, rusted, with considerable play. He could not get over the carelessness of the Germans. Why weren't there a rash of bank robberies?

'It's a sardine can,' he muttered to himself, taking a seat on a bench reserved for customers waiting to see the assistant manager. His name was taken by a secretary and in a moment a beaming man by the name of Max Nolde walked from his desk with an outstretched hand to greet him.

'Rome ... the women there are magnificent,' Nolde declared. 'I had my holiday there last year. Talk of art treasures at the Borghese ... me, I'd prefer a stroll down the Via Veneto.' Chou sidled by and Nolde's attention immediately wandered from Salica to her backside. His eyes lit up. 'That's an entrancing sight, no, Herr Salica?'

'Adorable.'

It was evident to Salica that the assistant manager was one of those insufferably giddy, flirtatious bachelors. He had his mustache waxed, and didn't so much as comb his hair with a parting down the center but rather folded it tautly like a hospital sheet. He wore beige-colored spats and a striped brown suit. He gave Paul coffee, a sweet roll, and a tour of the bank. While financial institutions all over the world were having a difficult time, the München Bund was solvent. Germany, Nolde explained, was experiencing a wave of prosperity as a direct result of Hitler's fiscal policies.

'The Führer has wrought an economic miracle. Just a few years ago the country was on the verge of collapse ... the mark was worthless, the streets were filled with anarchists and Bolsheviks demanding a revolution ... Pfft, Hitler put a stop to that with the SA.'

Salica nodded approvingly and studied the portly banker who jangled a set of numbered keys on a long gold chain with a swastika charm.

'Formidable. In Italy we were fortunate to have found a leader comparable to Hitler. Il Duce and the Syndicalists changed the face of the nation. All the trains run on time now.'

'Yes, I've heard they're a marvel,' Nolde observed.

'One of the wonders of the world.' He paused and for a moment a cloud of vexation passed over his face.

'Is something wrong?' Nolde asked as they sat down at his desk.

'Naturally as a businessman I am concerned about your security. In Italy, we're still plagued by brigands and Mafia who think they own the country. They laugh in the face of our *carabinieri* and Prefect Mori ... robberies continue to unsettle commerce.'

Nolde burst out laughing.

'My dear Salica, you're in Germany. The SS is at our disposal.'

'I don't see them in here.'

'The thought of them is enough to stifle the impulse of a thief. They are relentless in their pursuit of criminals and subversives.'

'You've never had an incident?'

'Good God, no.' Nolde clasped his chubby hands together. 'Incidents regarding the bank are simply unthinkable ... beyond the realm of possibility. This is a country with laws and citizens who respect them.'

Nolde proffered a blue account card to Salica which he proceeded to fill out.

'Salica Importing and Exporting Company,' Nolde read. 'Will you be making a deposit today?'

'There'll be a letter of credit sent to you from my bank

74

in Milan.'

'Splendid. I look forward to your future prosperity. Welcome to Munich.'

When they joined up on the corner of the bank, Salica was in that fever of excitation that Chou recognized as trouble.

'Your ass put us in business. When you walked by he literally stopped breathing.'

'Paul, it's crazy. We just can't go in. This needs to be planned.'

'You're the plan, my love. I'll try to get hold of Bastia in Kehl.'

'What for?'

'Guns.'

She had thrown in her lot with him and there were moments such as these when she regretted her decision. He was too mercurial and unstable. Sooner or later she knew that they would run out of luck. When she hesitated, he took hold of her and asked:

'Don't you trust me?'

'I wonder.'

'I'm not going to America without a penny.'

'Then wait till we get to France.'

'The security in their banks is too good.'

'But, Paul, we're in Germany; if the SS catch us, they'll shoot us.'

He raised his somnolent eyes and brushed back the hair the wind had blown in her face. He stroked her like a puppy.

'Listen to me. Except for that old fart at the door, there aren't any guards. They haven't got a chance against us.'

'I'm afraid.'

'Since when?'

'Since the Commerciale. We need an organization. A good one and not pickups.'

'Believe me, Chou, this one will work.'

'What makes you so sure?'

'He's got keys to every lock in the place and he carries them with him.'

'But how do you know he takes them home?'

'You'll find out for us.'

'How?'

'Pick him up.'

'What do I do afterwards?'

'Play him ... we're trout fishing.'

'And if that isn't enough?'

'*Ciao, cuòre mio*, you're my woman. ... I'm not going to let him touch you, ehhh?'

She believed him.

'Incredible, but you're absolutely right, Alex,' Schmeling said in his office at the gym. Alex had a curious elation. He coaxed a smile to Fritsch's bloodless face. Machon grabbed hold of Schmeling and the two did a little jig around Alex's desk.

'Louis *blinks* before he throws a punch,' Schmeling said. 'It's incredible that with all the people working with him, nobody noticed it.'

'Farr did,' Alex said, sipping some coffee. 'But it didn't really help, even though he took the fight to Louis and slugged toe to toe with him.'

'Farr can't punch,' Machon noted sarcastically. 'He's game, but he hasn't got Max's power.'

Schmeling went through his exercises, light bag work, and shadowboxing like a man given a last-minute reprieve, but Alex wondered whether Louis's style of telegraphing his punches would actually help Schmeling. Louis punched so rapidly and with such awesome power that he could drop an opponent before the man could take advantage of his flaw. With youth and punching speed on his side, Louis appeared invincible.

When Schmeling got into the ring with a sparring partner and Machon started his stopwatch, Alex felt Fritsch's eyes probing him.

Alex turned away and headed back to his office. If Schmeling lost he was a dead man. He had to think ahead and formulate some plan.

Lenore had agreed to meet Jonathan after school by the lake for a boat ride. Jonathan had rushed back to his apartment, scattered his books in the living room, kissed his mother who was being looked after by Tina Conte, then bolted down the stairs two at a time to the basement for his bicycle.

He cycled past the railway siding, pausing to wave at David sitting on top of the hill as he did every day after school.

Coming out of Munich's Bahnhof the great expresses of Europe were switched at this junction to the outside track by the switchman who sat in his wooden booth above David. From his post, David shouted, 'I saw the Rosenheim Express. It was an hour late and won't get to Vienna till midnight. They've painted the engine red.'

Jonathan never fully understood the mysteries of trains, nor the place-names his brother recited. David's sense of adventure puzzled him. Jonathan was too deeply rooted in Munich. It would always be the center of his world.

He turned off the Bolkerstrasse and took the bike path across the Parkplatz. Some young soldiers were sitting on the grass playing chess. Nannies pushed their prams by the lake and some old women were feeding bits of bread to the swans and ducks. An organ grinder cranked music while his monkey leaped among small, twittering children.

Jonathan set his bike in a stand beside the boathouse. The boatman, wearing hip-boots, waved at him, and Jonathan was relieved to see the wooden red canoe still tied to the dock. The canoe gave him an inscrutable serenity. When he sat in it and held the slickly honed varnished paddle, he became a conqueror who could safely navigate rapids, explore uncharted territory. A new world opened for him. He grasped the paddle and touched enchantment. Summer and her silken recondite mysteries possessed him, fixing his destiny.

He saw Lenore cycling toward him, her ponytail dancing in the rush of wind. He stood up in the canoe and called out, 'Lenore, I'm here.' His reedy voice echoed. In his excitement the canoe veered from side to side. He shifted his weight to the center. She walked along the dock. Her small, black, patent leather shoes gleamed in the sunlight. She was wearing a black-and-white checked gingham pinafore. Her face was flushed with nervous excitement. He stepped back on the dock and took her hand.

'Step in the middle,' he instructed her, taking hold of her cool, slender fingers as she got in.

'Papa almost didn't let me come. He's always so worried about something happening to me.'

Jonathan handed a mark to the boatman, who made a note of the time on a sodden piece of paper that he kept in the pocket of his rubber apron. There were only a few rowboats out on the lake. Jonathan knifed through the water with a strong, practised J stroke that his father had taught him the previous summer when they had taken a camping trip in the Black Forest. He kept them moving rapidly until they reached a small sand cove which was concealed by a mass of overgrown cypresses. He was out of breath from the exertion.

They always came to this small cove; it was wild and the fragrances of the grass and the pine trees onshore were carried by the wind and funneled through the cypresses. Several times before, they had heard music from the apartment house just beyond the park. Four musicians playing string instruments used to practice. Although Jonathan did not know the names of any of the works, he would sit spellbound in the canoe with Lenore, his eyes never leaving her face. This afternoon she threw her hands up in excitement as they drifted.

'I know the piece ... Mama used to play it ... Debussy's Quartet. We still have the recording.'

She leaned back, her head pressing against his knees, and the exquisite composition of her face made his heart thump. The music floated out over the water, mournful, swanlike in its evocation of eternal childhood, an endless summer stretching before them. They would always be together, he thought. He ran his fingers tenderly along the ends of her hair, and she stirred slightly then turned her head. She smiled at him and ran her index finger along the back of his hand. Frogs croaked, idly rippling the water among the water lilies, and salamanders scurried in the brush behind the canoe.

'I want you and I to have our *own* red canoe,' she said, blushing slightly, aware that she was on the verge of confessing what she knew must remain private. But she couldn't stop herself. 'I thought you'd die in Dachau ... and if you did, I couldn't live. I'm not sure how to die, but I would have found out so that I could die and be with you.'

He held her head in his hands and lightly, with trepidation, touched her lips with his, then he pulled away, realizing that he had committed an unpardonable offense. It was forbidden.

'I'm sorry,' he said with agitation. He seized the paddle and was about to head back but she stopped him.

'Why?' she asked. 'I didn't mind ...'

78

The musicians stopped for a few minutes. Jonathan pressed his lips against her ear.

'What was it like?' he asked.

'I'm not really sure. You did it so fast.' She closed her eyes and offered her lips to him. 'Don't rush this time.'

He moved his mouth to hers and their lips joined. He ran his tongue along her lips. Then he opened his eyes.

'You've been eating cinnamon,' Jonathan said.

'I stopped at Rumplemeir's. That's why I was late.'

She held both his hands and pressed her cheek against his. 'Do it properly this time and don't taste me.' He dutifully pecked her cheek and she threw her arms around his neck. She took a deep breath and held the air in her lungs. Her face turned red and her lungs felt as though they would burst.

'Jonathan, I love you.'

★　　★　　★

Alex stopped at the Munich Bund Bank. He had decided to remove his savings bit by bit and make arrangements for Miriam and the boys to leave the country. He was reasonably sure that Fritsch had called off the Gestapo. Yet when he entered the bank an involuntary tremor racked his body. Was he imagining the stares of the clerks, the disapproving glances of the executives who sat behind the highly varnished wooden rail? He swabbed sweat from his forehead. The bank was airless, a tomb. He could hardly catch his breath as he presented his passbook and a withdrawal slip for three thousand marks.

The clerk gave him a blank look, then turned to a large red ledger on the shelf behind him. He scanned the pages, ran his finger along endless columns. The finger paused and Alex leaned over the cage.

'It's Alex Stein . . . one fifty-seven Franz-Josef-Strasse. Stein's Gymnasium. I'm the owner.'

The clerk nodded and walked leisurely down the aisle.

'I'm aware of that, Herr Stein.'

'Where're you going?'

'I'll just be a moment,' he called out.

Alex tracked with him, like a horse performing a dressage exercise. The clerk stopped at the desk of an elderly, plump bespectacled man. He leaned down and whispered.

'I don't understand what's going on here,' Alex charged. 'I've been a depositer for eight years. My account has never been overdrawn.'

'Please, Herr Stein, you're in the bank. We have a great deal of business to transact. Just be patient.'

'Well, then, explain what's happening.'

'I'll just have to see the assistant manager for a moment. Why don't you have a seat?'

He rolled back on his heels and supported himself on the rail behind him. The great glass dome above him thrust sharp fragments of sunlight into his eyes and motes of dust floated crazily around him like a squadron of insects. He pursued the plump man who now leaned over the desk of Nolde. Alex attempted to open the wooden gate and a secretary curtly said:

'You can't come in here, *mein Herr*, without consent.' When Alex remained there with both hands on the rail, she raised her index finger and the elderly guard plodded forward. 'Please show this gentleman to the waiting room.'

'What if I refuse?' Alex demanded.

'Refuse?' the secretary echoed him. 'There's no such thing. You do what you're told in the bank. That's the law.'

Nolde and the head teller strolled calmly toward him. Nolde's brows were raised. He shook his head disapprovingly and stood with his hand resting on the rail.

'What's the problem?' Nolde asked severely.

'I presented my passbook and a withdrawal slip' – he indicated that Nolde was holding them – 'for three thousand marks. They're in order.'

'We'll see ...'

'What do you mean? You're holding my savings.'

'I'm aware of that. And you're receiving interest of seven percent compounded quarterly. 'There is no irregularity at the bank. You can be certain of that, Herr Stein.'

Alex threw up his hands in despair.

'Give me my money ... my wife's ill. I need it for medical bills.'

'I'm sorry to learn of your wife's ill health, but there's nothing we at the bank can do about it.'

'Why can't I have my money?'

'You should have received notice –'

'– Of what?'

'The Interdiction Protocol.'

'What does an interdiction mean?' he implored, his voice cracking. He felt he was sinking, losing his balance.

'Your funds are frozen.'

'What kind of conspiracy is this?'

'That's a very serious accusation ... we could take legal action against you for such an inflammatory remark. Outrageous.'

'You, *mein Herren*, are the outrageous ones, the conspirators, who steal a man's savings without offering him an explanation. Is the bank failing?'

'Guard, get this man out of here,' Nolde commanded.

'You have to tell me what's going on.'

'When the government discovers some irregularity in a client's account, they take steps ...'

'What irregularity?'

'How do I know? It could be taxes, or any number of things. No reason need be given. Your account is frozen – the funds are blocked.'

'Who ordered it? I have a right to know ... please. If I've done something wrong I would like to appeal it, but who do I see? How can I prove that I'm innocent of whatever charge has been brought against me? You see my point of view, surely?'

Nolde stepped back and huddled with his chief clerk for a moment. He seemed unwilling to offer any assistance, but then returned to his desk and took out an envelope and handed it to Alex.

'I was told to give you this if you had any queries.'

Alex anxiously tore it open. The stationery was imprinted with a border of black swastikas and in a formal, sweeping Gothic script the note glared at him.

> *Dear Stein:*
> *You're a very dangerous man.*
>
> Wilhelm Von Fritsch (Major SD)

Alex was dazed, and he gulped the air when he reached the busy street. From behind him his arm was taken and Salica embraced him enthusiastically. His eyes sparkled mischievously.

'Beautiful, Alex. Nothing could have been more perfect. I saw everything that happened to you. I've got an erection. It never fails when I get close to money,' Salica observed. Alex peered at him uncomprehendingly. 'We'll strip them of every penny they've got in five minutes. Let's have a drink.'

Chou was sitting at a table at an outdoor café sipping a Pernod. She feigned not to notice them as they took a table. Flustered, Alex looked from one to the other. Salica expansively ordered a bottle of Piper-Heidsieck.

'Alex, your problems are over. Chou's going dancing with Nolde tonight.'

Seven

Alex sensed that he was sinking. There was no way he could get out of Germany without money. For a few days Victor advanced him money, but then Victor called him at the gym and insisted they meet so he could explain why he was unable to continue.

Victor was unsettled when he picked him up at the tram stop on the Leopoldstrasse. In the back of the car Salica sat with an open bottle of Moselle which he offered to Alex. Victor kept glancing in the rearview mirror and he shook his head dispiritedly. Alex's eyes were pocked with crow's-feet and he seemed drained of all energy. The mere suggestion that Victor was having problems disconcerted him, for Victor seemed untouchable, an Italian, a Catholic, with friends in the police.

'How could anything happen to you?'

'Alex, from the moment Heydrich picked my little place, I've been inundated by SS men. I've had no choice but to take them as patrons. Since I'm a foreigner they now feel that they can drink, eat and not pay their bills. They tell me that they want charge accounts. Can you believe it? The other day when I complained to the police about what was going on and how the club was infested with prostitutes, I was told that there was a serious problem about my liquor license. If I wanted to remain in business, I had to contribute half my daily proceeds to Himmler's special SS fund to show good faith.'

Salica belched loudly and put his feet up on the seat.

'See, Vittorio, I told you that you'd be better off with the Mafia. It's all the same in the end. When someone stronger than you comes along, you have to pay him or he pisses on you.' Salica turned to look out of the back window. A dark blue Mercedes sedan was behind them. 'Are they still watching your family, Alex?'

'I don't think so.' He didn't trust Salica. The man was a criminal who spent his time working out elaborate plots which Alex thought indicated an unbalanced mind. His scheme to enlist Alex – and Sam, of all people – to rob the Munich Bund Bank could have occurred only to a lunatic. Victor had told him that he was paying a debt to his father-in-law by helping Salica. Several times Alex had warned him that Salica was dangerous and he ought to keep away from him. Yet there was a secret bond of loyalty between the two men that troubled Alex, since it placed his friend in constant jeopardy. Salica was not discreet. He wandered around the city as though he owned it. He spent his nights in bars, and Sam, too, was afraid that he'd be picked up by the police and traced back to the pension. Yet Salica's manner betrayed no uncertainty.

He rolled down the window and whistled at a girl walking her dog. He crooked his finger, beckoning her to come to the car. When the girl ignored him, he swore at her in Italian.

Victor could not help laughing.

'What was so funny?' Alex asked.

'He asked her if she was saving it for Hitler! Paul, you'll get us all thrown into jail.'

Alex asked to be dropped off at the next corner.

'I was under the impression that you had guts, Alex,' Salica said captiously. 'You don't walk away from a fight, but you're frightened to take chances.'

'I'm not a thief . . . I've had no experience.' Alex gestured in frustration to Victor. 'Can't you explain to this crazy that people don't rob banks in Germany? It just isn't done.'

Salica squinted at him and cocked his head to one side in a sardonic manner.

'Why not? In Italy it's an industry and in the United States they've made an art of it. Dillinger and other experts select a bank, study its routine, and walk in with guns and remove the cash. It's really quite simple.' There were two essentials for a bank robbery: a plan and desperate associates who would do what they were told. Salica was convinced that the combination was perfect. 'Alex' – his voice was wheedling, persuasive – 'what've *you*, of all people, got to lose? After Schmeling gets chopped up by Louis, you're a dead man. Fritsch'll wear your balls as earrings.'

'It's worth the risk,' Victor shakily declared. 'My position is hopeless. And if there's a war with England we'll be trapped here. I'm prepared to make a run for it.'

'The Bund?' Alex repeated incredulously, 'I don't see how it's possible.'

84

Victor parked his car at the Briennerstrasse. Along the wide street artisans were setting up their stalls for Auer Dult, the huge flea market sale which would begin in a few days. Trucks were lined up at the curb and porters with dollies lifted crates off them. They were enveloped by a swarm of bustling men and women humping everything from farm plows, sofas, saddles, lamps, paintings, kitchen pots, crockery, to their stalls which were decorated with multicolored bunting. The noise level was intolerable, and the three men dodged from side to side to avoid the sweating loaders who roared 'Pab Auf!' as they hurtled through the crowds with their wares.

Suspiciously, Alex peered over his shoulder.

'Relax, you've lost the Gestapo.... In a crowd they're helpless. I'll give you an education yet,' Salica asserted.

They burrowed through legions of wagons, barrows, one-wheeled carts. Bare-chested, sweating men threaded their way through narrow openings from the side streets, holding bureaus and armoires over their heads. Enormous raw-boned farm girls in blue-striped milkmaid aprons bellowed, staggered, groaned under the weight of heavy steamer trunks filled with every conceivable form of detritus which they had accumulated before making the pilgrimage to the city to sell their wares.

'What's the point in coming here?' Alex barked over the din.

'To meet a friend of mine,' Paul said, standing on tiptoe and waving to someone Alex couldn't see. 'You've got to learn to believe in me, my dear Alex. I didn't manage to evade half of Mussolini's security service just to be picked up by a few fat-assed Gestapo agents.'

In the distance, Salica directed his attention to a stall on which a yellow silk handkerchief was strung. He elbowed his way through the crowd. Lying on a wooden stall pell-mell was a heap of ancient, rusted rifles, with battered stocks; chipped broken pistols and revolvers were stacked alongside.

Alex took Victor aside and whispered:

'Are you really going through with it?'

'You're a dead man and I'm broke, so why ask questions?'

The man behind the stall was a round-faced, stocky Corsican with curly blond hair, a straight nose, and a lazy left eye which wandered over them listlessly.

'The finest antique weapons from every country in

Europe.' He reached out and picked up a rifle. 'An English flintlock. Shine it up and it'll decorate your wall.'

'I like birds,' Salica said.

The man ferreted through his stock without comment. 'What kind?'

'Falcons.'

'I admire them myself,' the man said, extending his hand. *'Mi chiamo Marc Bastia.'*

'Paolo Salica ... fratello. Mi amici Vittorio e Alessandro.'

They shook hands warmly, and Bastia pulled out a gunny-sack from below the stall which he gave to Salica.

'I can't get you across the border until after the twentieth,' he informed them. 'My people are on holiday till then.'

'Do we need papers?' Alex asked.

'No.'

For the first time in weeks Alex relaxed.

'We'll try for June twenty-third,' Salica stated.

'Any reason?' Bastia asked.

'A business opportunity. That's why I needed the mer-chandise. What condition is it in?'

'Almost new. Two Walthers, a Luger, a Mauser, and three twenty-two Barettas.'

'What's the price?'

'We'll discuss that when you get to Kehl,' Bastia said vaguely. 'Use them in good health.'

'No price?' Salica insisted.

'It depends. The Unione Corse does you a favor. Maybe there's a service that you can do for us. Money doesn't always have to change hands, Paolo.'

'Grazie!'

'Prego, fratello.'

Women, no matter what their dependence on a man, don't like to be pushed around, and Chou was no exception. Paul was a brilliant, ingenious thief but she was disappointed in him. He lacked the residual tenderness she had come to ex-pect. When he was on a job he demanded nothing more than information and squeezed her like a lemon, coaxing her to develop a close relationship with Nolde whom she found unbearable. Yet she preferred to go along with Paul rather than chance abandonment. In the year that they had lived together, he had been faithful, but he had always held something back, unwilling to make a true commitment. She had no illusions about him. He cared for her so long as she performed. He was using her, but she was carried along by the powerful momentum he generated. At bottom she was aware of her position. She was the mistress of a professional criminal and she passively clung to her role. At twenty-four her past was a red-inked column of emotional insolvencies which marked her failed enterprises as a kept woman. She occasionally wondered how much she could tolerate, but such scrutiny only made her unhappy and she banished the grievances that floated to the surface.

Situated on the Max-Joseph-Platz on the right bank of the Isar River, the Fatima Ballroom, a mock Oriental dance palace given over to cadaverous widows, lecherous bachelors, husbands whose wives were away for quack water cures, was the favorite stomping ground of Max Nolde. An indefatigable dancer, he had been out with Chou no less than six times. His technique on the dance floor was a fricassee of styles ranging from quasi-Valentino tangos to Hussar pyrotechnical displays performed with handkerchief between his teeth to energetic Bavarian *Volk* polkas during which the taps on his heels and soles jangled spastically on the crippled wooden floors. He sweated like a stallion all the while.

To Chou's horror he never sat out a dance. He had given her a selection of painful corns and an incipient bunion.

'Dancing exalts the soul, Chou.'

With her eyes closed, she dreamed of his keys, of vaults, of safes, and sleeping on a mattress made up entirely of crisp marks.

He was also a virulent gossip, utterly schizophrenic in his parsimony. When a bill was presented to him, he invariably shrieked for the owner and threatened him with dire credit reports. At the Fatima he never paid a penny.

'Max, my ankle's giving way . . .'

'Well, maybe we've had enough for the night.'

He had a cleanliness fetish about his elderly Opel, keeping a feather duster in the back seat. The car had ruptured springs and he never drove it faster than twenty kilometers an hour, terrified that he'd hit a bump and damage the car. On a normal thirty-minute ride, she would doze off, knowing that it would take him over an hour. He had a poor sense of direction, constantly got lost.

Each date would end with them sitting in the car outside Sam's pension. He was an inveterate stroker. At traffic lights he would attempt to jam his hand under the skirt for a *kitzeln*. She staved him off, pleaded an extended monthly which was driving her and her eminent medical specialists crazy. It stopped, it started, always without warning. Never knew when it would burst out, preventing intercourse. He was hysterical about hygiene and he changed the subject when she claimed cramps were upon her. She invariably held out hope, future prospects.

'A night with you, Max, when we're free of fear ...'

'It will come,' he said optimistically. 'Passion has its season.'

She would leave the car, staggering on her swollen ankles, and head for the paradise of a hot water soak. She had reached the point where she no longer cared about robbing the bank, just wanted to shoot Nolde.

In the pension, Salica would be waiting, half asleep, sexually aroused, and she would order him to get her a basin of hot water.

'I'm becoming a porter, not your lover,' he would protest, grumblingly throwing off the bedclothes and hopping on the cold, damp floor.

'You wanted information and I'm getting it for you.'

'You're walking like a cripple. Where's he keep the keys?'

'Sleeps with them around his neck.'

'Tell the truth, Chou. Are you giving him a little bit?'

'What would you do if I was?'

'Cut your throat.'

'What about the money?'

'You got a point. Be honest with me. What's going on?'

'You sound jealous.'

'I'm walking around all the time with a hard-on thinking about you.'

She closed her eyes.

'I'm sleepy. Pauli, get the hot water.'

'What am I supposed to do about my cannon? It's smoking.'

'Tomorrow.'

'What about now?'

'Bang it against the wall. *Bonne nuit, chéri.*'

*   *   *

Life for Alex settled back into a familiar routine at the gym. Fighters scheduled for provincial bouts at working-men's clubs and beer halls trained halfheartedly. Alex patiently instructed them, kept the locker room clean and supplied with fresh towels. He tried to ignore the teams of Gestapo agents keeping him under surveillance. He waited for Fritsch to make a move.

Although Paul had not pressured him, there was a tacit understanding between them. Either Alex had to take part in the robbery or Paul would not help him escape from Germany. To demonstrate his compliance Alex took possession of the guns which Paul had wrapped in oilcloth and layered with a film of bacon grease he had taken from the pension kitchen.

Schmeling and his entourage had already left for the United States and were lodged in a training camp in Speculator, New York, where he found the mountain atmosphere of the Adirondacks similar to his surroundings at home. Photographs of Schmeling showed him posed with Jack Dempsey and promoter Mike Jacobs outside the Osborne Hotel. Dempsey had predicted a victory for him.

Nightly radio reports by Arno Helmers from the camp told of the thousands of Bundists throughout the United States supporting Schmeling. Torchlight parades along Eighty-sixth Street in New York's Yorkville section were shown in cinema newsreels. Gigantic photographs of Hitler and Schmeling were displayed by the German-Americans as they proudly strutted in paramilitary formations, wearing swastika armbands and singing 'Deutschland Deutschland, über alles.'

To avoid compromising Alex, Victor was assigned the task of purchasing railway tickets to Kehl. Neither man had told his wife that they would be leaving the country. They knew that Tina and Miriam would insist on making preparations for the trip and this would arouse suspicion among their neighbors.

The next thing to be done, the friends agreed, was to enlist Sam in the enterprise. Victor took it upon himself to coax Sam out for a drink.

Salica and the mysterious girlfriend who kept odd hours had already set off Bauer's curiosity. Now Victor's presence intensified Bauer's interest. From the sitting room he eavesdropped on the conversation the two men were having.

'I can't leave just yet,' he heard Sam say.

'I'll watch the roast, Papa,' Lenore volunteered. 'You haven't been out for days. It'll do you good to spend a little time with Uncle Victor.'

'There, she's smarter than you are. A child sees the light.'

'But what's all this about?' Sam insisted.

'I just wanted to see you for a while. You haven't been down to the club for months and Tina's offended because you haven't accepted a dinner invitation since Easter. Come on, Sam, don't be stubborn. Get your jacket and we'll have a drink.'

Salica entered the kitchen from the back garden door.

'Here's Pauli – he'll join us, won't you?'

'Why not, Victor?'

Innocent enough, thought Bauer. These new lodgers kept to themselves and were out most of the time. There were nights that Salica didn't sleep in his room and would return just as Bauer was leaving to make his morning calls. Perhaps he had some kind of night job. A number of Italians came to work in Munich. This man might be employed by some foreign firm. He'd heard a vague reference to some kind of exporting business at dinner one evening when one of the other boarders asked Salica how he liked Munich.

When Sam finally gave in, Bauer rose from his chair by the door, parted the curtains and watched the three men get into a black Citroën. Except for an elderly traveler in dental supplies who had a back room on the ground floor next to the Italian's, the pension was empty. Bauer had waited for days to get Lenore on her own, but he was repeatedly frustrated by Sam's refusal to leave her alone.

The car drove away. He folded the newspaper and placed it in the community basket. On tiptoe he walked soundlessly down the hallway. Lenore was sitting with her back to him at the kitchen table shelling peas and she did not hear him until he was upon her and his wet mouth was pressed against her neck. Startled, she leaped up from the table, upsetting the bowl of peas.

'All this time and not a single word to me, Lenore.'

'I say good morning and good night whenever I see you,' she replied, her eyes large with an unnameable terror.

He placed his hands under her arms and lifted her up.

'Please, I have to stay here to see the dinner doesn't burn.'

90

Bauer opened the oven and breathed in the bouquet of the breast of veal. He lowered the burner and wagged his index finger at her in a peculiar obscene gesture. His finger looked like a white worm.

'*Komme, Mädchen* ... your little vest is still in its wrapping paper.'

He carried her up the stairs and she quavered helplessly in his tight grip.

* * *

On his third glass of schnapps, Sam relaxed and forgot about the pension. The bock beer he used as a chaser was still on his lips, and he brushed it off with the back of his hand. How he'd missed the camaraderie of his close friends, pleasant afternoons like this spent with them, swapping stories, discussing one another's problems and the prospects for the future.

Despite Salica's presence, the reunion delighted him. It would enable him to settle the vexing problem of Lenore's vacation. Sam would not be accompanying her this year, since it would mean closing the pension when summer visitors came to Munich. He couldn't afford to lose transient business. For most of the year he had been living on his savings, and if he hoped to survive the coming winter he would have to make the rounds of the big hotels, tipping concierges so that when they were full they would recommend his pension.

'I'll probably be too busy to take a holiday, but I'd appreciate it if you took Lenore with you on the Rhine.' His request was met with an unfathomable silence. 'No one will miss me ... and the children will enjoy themselves. I'll let you have my camera. You'll take photographs and we'll spend an evening looking at them when you get back, eh, Alex?' He caught the waiter's eye, signaled for another round of drinks. He opened his cracked leather billfold and placed ten marks on the table. 'My turn, gentlemen.' Disconcerted by what he considered a certain unusual evasiveness from both Victor and Alex, he asked:

'Have I said the wrong thing ... is Lenore the problem? You know she won't be any trouble, but if you don't want the responsibility I quite understand.'

'We're getting out,' Victor said.

'Out? Where? What's this all about?'

'My club is finished and it looks as though the Gestapo are waiting till after the fight to pick up Alex.'

'But how can you leave with nothing?'

'No one said we were going without money,' Salica interjected. 'We're going to have lots of money.'

Sam leaned forward, perplexed, and drank the rest of his beer.

'I don't understand. Why, Alex hasn't got a hundred marks to his name since they blocked his money at the bank ...' In a fluster he turned to Victor: 'What happened to the Nachteule? How could you think of giving it up?'

'The Nachteule is under new management. The SS,' Victor told him.

'And Alex's money is about to be unblocked,' Salica noted smugly.

'How do you propose to do that?' Sam asked.

'We're going to take it,' Alex replied.

'You can't take money out of the bank just like that.'

'It's known as bank robbery,' Salica said.

'Madness!'

'Lower your voice, Sam,' Alex ordered him. 'Our only chance to live is to get out of Germany. In three days that's exactly what we're going to do.'

'How? You don't just cross a border. You need passports. There's no way –'

'Paul's fixed it,' Victor said.

'The Bund ... robbing it? Incredible! We're all drunk. Yes, my head's spinning.'

Salica moved his face close to Sam's and spoke as though to a child. 'Sam, you took me in without questions when I had nowhere to go ...'

'It was for Victor. He's my friend ... he'd do as much for me.'

'The fact is that you saved my life. You've taken an enormous risk by having me in your pension.'

'Well, you're a strange man, Paul, but I've grown quite fond of you and your girl. Lenore likes you both very much. All your tricks with cards and sleight of hand.'

'Sam, listen to me,' Salica said. 'When the Germans go into the Sudetenland and who knows where after that, there'll be another world war. All the Jews in Germany will be killed.'

'But I have my pension – and a child at school. Everything I have is here in Munich.'

'Don't you want to live?' Victor asked. 'Will you sacrifice yourself and Lenore because of bricks? They'll take the pension away from you sooner or later. It doesn't matter that your father-in-law holds the deed. They'll kill him if necessary.'

'Judith is buried in the garden ... leaving my wife. No, please, I can't. I'm not a thief. I can't go with you. One day, Hitler will be stopped and you would have left your own country for no reason. Don't go.'

'I'm a marked man,' Alex said. 'Whatever happens after the fight, they'll pick me up.'

'But if Schmeling wins, you'll be a hero.'

'Sam, those men sitting on the bench' – Alex inclined his head to the window where two men were reading papers at an outdoor café table – 'are Gestapo. They're with me all the time.'

'Oh, God,' Sam said, lowering his head and letting the tears flow freely. 'It's terrible. I feel helpless.'

'Come with us, please,' Victor implored him. 'They'll kill you and Lenore. If we have to die, we'll know that we fought.'

'I can't.'

If only he could explain what property symbolized to him, the loyalty it inspired. No matter what the Braukeller did to make life difficult, they wouldn't drive him out. He'd rather be dead than homeless. The years of struggle, saving to buy the pension, would have made his efforts meaningless. He was a captive of his past and he could not renounce it.

Shakily, he got up from the table and his figure was crumpled; he was a man yielding, defeated by circumstances. He crossed the street and took his place on the orderly queue waiting at the tram stop.

Eight

Lenore shivered from the cold in Bauer's room. She had been standing naked, wearing only the black leather vest while he touched her. He had promised not to hurt her if she listened to him, but another threat he made guaranteed her silence. He had showed her a long, black-barreled pistol in his bureau drawer and told her that he would kill Sam if she uttered a word of what happened. She had submitted without protest as he probed her body with his fingers, but he was careful not to inflict any pain on her, and when she squeaked from time to time he had cautiously withdrawn. He repeatedly cooed soft words of endearment and asked her if his touch felt good, while he explained that he was preparing her gradually for another encounter when there would be no great hurry. He would acquire more gifts for her, buy her dresses and high-heeled shoes. He knelt at her feet and said:

'I worship you ... this is a holy rite. We'll be together always.'

'You won't shoot Papa?'

'No, indeed not. I'll protect him so long as we can have our moments. He'll find a defender in Karl Bauer – not an enemy, *Liebchen*. Rely on me. Come to me with your problems and I'll make them vanish like a magician.'

He got off his knees, stood by the mirrored wardrobe, and unbuttoned his fly; she saw something emerge from his trousers, a swollen, veined, muscular wand. He massaged it with his thumb and forefinger and it grew larger as he emitted a low whine of pleasure.

She stood transfixed, immobilized by dread. She could no longer hear what he was saying, but she pulled back her hand when he tried to make her touch it.

'It's poison,' she heard a voice, not her own, reverberate through the room.

'Nonsense,' he said. 'God blesses this moment or else He wouldn't have allowed it. We'd be dust,' Bauer insisted. 'Struck down in our tracks. Plagues would destroy us,' he

94

raved. 'It's an act of God ... mysteries ... a miracle.'

Bauer wrenched her by the wrist. Tears fell on her cheeks and she licked them, tasting the salt. Her teeth dug into her lip and her mouth filled with blood.

'What've you done?' Harsh, guttural, outraged. 'Dripping everywhere!'

'I ... can't, Herr Bauer.'

He raised his fist close to her face. The hairy, clenched fingers blocked her vision.

Bauer's hand moved to the pulsating hard mound of flesh. It spat out a creamy, milky fluid which shot on the mirror. Bauer gripped her neck.

'Touch me!' His eyes were wild.

She shied away. Blood sprayed over her hand.

Bauer suddenly became ebullient and he sat down on the bed, cleaned himself with a towel.

'Impotent, that's what the doctors said for years. But what the devil do they know?'

Her skin tingled and the taste of blood made her sick to her stomach. She didn't know how to escape. The door was locked and he had the key in his waistcoat pocket. From somewhere in the house came the sound of her name. Bauer jumped to his feet.

'Take off the vest and run into the hall bathroom with your clothes.'

He unlocked the door and picked up her panties. He poked his head out and she banged her head against the hallway wall.

'There's been a little problem,' Bauer called out. 'Down in a moment.' He thrust her into the bathroom. 'Clean yourself up. I'll be carrying my revolver when I see your father. One word from you, and I'll shoot him. It's up to you if he lives or dies. Do you understand me?'

She nodded dumbly and fell into the bathroom, scraping her knees on the rough, uneven tile floor. Bauer closed the door behind her and fixed his clothing. He had time. Sam was unsteadily climbing the stairs, his eyes bloodshot, a dull, worried look on his face.

'Fortunately you've got an attending physician on the premises,' Bauer said.

'What happened?'

'She fell and cut her lip and became hysterical. But Dr.

Bauer to the rescue. My firm gives each of its travelers a course in first aid. I can point with pride to the fact that I was the prize student. I received my certificate with honors.'

'Is she all right now?'

'Naturally. She's in the bathroom, cleaning up. I prescribe two Bayers and she'll be perfect. I took the precaution of turning down the dinner before attending to her. Stuffed breast of veal! Since our little chat you're outdoing yourself in the kitchen, Herr Weissbeck. The kitchen now rivals any pension in Munich. When our sales conference takes place later this year, I'll be sure to engage rooms for other members of the firm. My word carries weight.'

Sam, ashen-faced and breathing heavily through his mouth, held onto the banister.

'Thank you for your help, Herr Bauer. I've been with some friends ... I'm quite tired and think I'll lie down for a bit.'

'Just the thing. An afternoon on the town with your comrades, a forthright exchange of ideas is valuable. I speak from direct experience. The mind takes flight ... we leave such encounters with a clear vision.'

'Too much schnapps,' Sam said with a sheepish smile. 'I overdid it.'

'Excesses ... a man after my own heart. We define our boundaries by straddling them, extending ourselves to gain deeper insight into our personalities.'

'You're a philosopher, Herr Bauer.'

'Leave Lenore to me.'

*   *   *

The whole expedition struck Jonathan as peculiar but he had not demurred. How could they afford new summer shorts and swimsuits when his father had no money? His mother had cut down on meat and they were now eating herring and potatoes or chicken every other night. Then, to make it stranger, Jonathan saw the Contes coming from another direction in the Tietz Department Store. He never recalled seeing Victor shopping with Linda and Georgie. He also wondered why his father had accompanied them. Still, he and David circled the camping department, examining penknives, portable stoves, canteens, and sleeping bags. He picked up a small compass and walked around the

96

counter with it. David was casting a fishing rod and pretending to be hauling in a catch.

'Isn't it going to be exciting?' David said. 'Just think of us fishing along the Rhine and then cleaning the fish and cooking it for dinner. I can't wait to leave Munich.'

'Who's paying for the holiday?' Jonathan asked.

'As long as we're going, why ask questions?'

David waved at Linda Conte, a dark-eyed little girl with fine alabaster skin, coal-black hair and the delicate features of the miniatures one saw on cameos in jewelry store windows. She wore small, gold-cross earrings in her perfect ears. David thought her exquisite. She was eight and always hiding shyly behind her mother. Her head would dart out and she would give a dainty little smile, then giggle. Her older sister, Georgie, was eleven, David's age, and he admired her accomplishments. She could paint and also play difficult classical pieces on the piano. On Christmas Day, he had spent an hour in her room posing for his portrait. She had drawn a remarkable likeness of him in charcoal and Miriam had the sketch framed.

'Aren't we supposed to be going with the Weissbecks?' Jonathan asked.

'I'm not sure,' David replied.

The prospect of being without Lenore alarmed Jonathan. He rushed over to Miriam and both she and Tina admonished him. He could see the look of concern on their faces and he realized they were having a confidential discussion. He looked around for his father but now couldn't locate him or Victor. A wave of panic set in, and he considered leaving Tietz's and going to the pension to find Lenore and ask her if there had been a change in plans. He decided to test his mother in order to discover what was going on.

'Can I have the compass?' he asked.

'No, we can't afford it.'

'Well, if you haven't got the money, why'd you bring us here?'

'Jonathan, go talk to the girls,' Tina said peremptorily. When he hesitated, she added, 'Right now.'

He sensed that his nightmare was coming true. It was upon him, twisting him, trapping him. He and Lenore were going to be separated. In bewilderment he searched the department for his father. There had to be an explanation. Why hadn't he been asked what *he* wanted? 'It's unfair,' he muttered.

'What's going to happen?' Georgie asked him. She, too, was troubled by this singular shopping expedition.

'Have you spoken to Lenore?'

'No, not for weeks.' Her plump face creased indignantly. 'They're not going to put you all in concentration camps, are they?'

'I hope not.'

'Why're our parents so funny? I saw my father come in and then he went out with yours.'

'Where?'

'He just disappeared. I mean, he behaved as though he didn't know us.'

The pinched faces of their mothers alarmed them. Both women seemed to be caught by some emotion that was slowly shattering the air of calm they had affected in public. He and Georgie watched from behind a large yellow tent as Tina threw up her hands and then she and Miriam embraced.

At a signal from their mothers, the children gathered together and silently followed the two women to the food hall. Woodchucks, pigeons, and rabbits hung over the butcher's counter. In the delicacy showcase there were rolls of wurst, gelatinous boar's head, imported salamis, giant hams, smoked cheeses, and pâtés.

The women were buying loaves of packaged bread, cold chickens, and pieces of sausage. Jonathan couldn't for the life of him understand why Miriam would buy such food. Although they ate *trafe* when they went out, Miriam kept a kosher home and would never buy liverwurst. When they had finished making their purchases, he took hold of his mother's arm and demanded to know what was going on.

'Stop asking questions. Just do what you're told!'

They were all hustled into a taxi and given a signal to remain silent. They looked at each other in consternation when Tina told the driver to take them to the Bahnhof. Jonathan was about to protest, but Miriam put her hand over his mouth and threatened him with her eyes. He implored his mother to tell him where they were going. Her mouth tightened and he felt himself lose control. At a light,

98

he put his hand on the door handle. As he was about to turn it, Miriam slapped him across the face and he fell back, stunned, lapsing into speechless outrage. She had never before hit him.

'Mama, don't ...' David protested. The two Conte girls wept in sympathy as Jonathan gritted his teeth and defiantly glared back at his mother.

'Mama, I can't go ...'

Tina backed up Miriam. 'When we see your father, he'll give you the beating of your life.' She turned to Miriam and held her hand. 'What's wrong with him?'

'I can tell you,' Jonathan interposed. 'If we don't take Lenore with us, she'll die here in Munich. The Nazis will kill her. It's horrible ... how can you do that to her when she has no mother? Mama, you were Aunt Judith's friend.'

The accusation hung in the air, naked, irrefutable. The veins stood out on Miriam's white neck, throbbing. She lowered her eyes, averting Jonathan's. He clenched his fists in frustration and pounded the leather jump seat.

'The Nazis stick together ... maybe they're right about us – that we only care about ourselves. *Dolchstoss! Dolchstoss!* he screamed relentlessly, out of control. 'I don't want to live if they're going to murder her.'

'Miriam, what is he saying?' Tina asked, beside herself. She slid the partition glass so that the driver wouldn't hear them. 'Jonathan, listen to me ...' Her voice was broken and her chest was rent with shared anguish. 'Samuel won't leave. Your father begged him. He's frightened. They'll take his pension. He doesn't understand. Lenore doesn't even know we're leaving. Please stop. Look what you've done to your mother. Don't you think we all feel for Lenore? We wanted to take her – to save her. But Samuel refused.'

Spumes of acrid gray smoke spiraled through the air by the station and the sounds of train engines grinding over the tracks filled the taxi, shaking it as it stood waiting for the express to pass. Sparks flew crazily off the rails. In the windows, Jonathan could see men and women in the dining car eating, calmly drinking glasses of wine, men with their noses buried in papers, women rolling balls of yarn, children with their faces pressed to the glass waving to strangers. A whole life passed by in a flash. Families united and separated.

99

'I can't — I won't let her die,' Jonathan cried, then bolted out of the taxi. He ran through the weaving cars like a dervish on a collision with destiny.

* * *

Alex hardly knew how to react. Jonathan sat by his side at the communal dining table in the pension. The boy was intractable, a law unto himself. Although it was clear that he had to punish him, he was overwhelmed by his forcefulness and he could not help but admire him. Truculent, silent, unyielding, Jonathan had said:

'I had to do what I believed was right.'

What impressed Alex about his son was his fearlessness. Although he never consciously played favorites between his sons, he knew that Jonathan was a replica of himself, formed in his image, with his determined spirit.

Yet the boy had endangered the enterprise and he must be disciplined, Alex thought. He pared an apple skin into a long ribbon then handed the apple to Jonathan. The boy took it uncertainly. He looked across the table at Lenore whose behavior puzzled him. She had not given him the welcome he had anticipated. She was moody, withdrawn, and he felt betrayed. He wondered if she were holding back, afraid to commit herself under the scrutiny of her father, Alex, and the boarders. The atmosphere crackled with unspoken intentions which he could not comprehend.

He abruptly rose from his place and said:

'I'd like my punishment now, please, Papa.'

'When I'm ready,' Alex said, pulling him down.

'I don't want the apple ...' He offered his plate to Lenore who stared dreamily at her untouched food. 'I know I should have listened to Mama. I'm sorry. It's just that I didn't want to leave you,' he said, fixing his gaze on Lenore.

She lifted her eyes from the plate and he couldn't quite explain why her presence was disturbing. Was it the circumstances of his running away or some injunction of Sam's which prevented her from responding to him?

'Parents have their reasons for asking obedience from their children,' Alex said. 'You're here, so we'll make the best of the situation. But next time, Jonathan, don't question my motives.'

His defenses were crumbling and he was on the brink of

tears. This public rebuke in front of Lenore infuriated him. The tyranny of adults was intolerable. He would have preferred the strap – quick, final, decisive, providing an incontestable purge. He had been unprepared for psychological warfare and he was ill-equipped to handle it.

'Everyone respects people with minds of their own,' Alex continued, 'but the good of the family has to come first.'

Jonathan choked back a sob, clenched his fists under the table, and his anger focused on Sam who had cowardly refused to leave Munich and was responsible for endangering Lenore's life. What could possibly hold Sam in this city? This dank, drafty rooming house with its filthy garden and its greasy travelers?

'I wish this house would burn down,' he said sharply to Sam.

'The boy's impossible, Alex. He has no respect for anyone,' Sam charged.

'More than you do,' Jonathan said.

'You're eating at Uncle Samuel's table! What's wrong with you?'

'Lenore,' Jonathan said entreatingly, 'tell him you want to leave Munich.'

She looked away, not daring to side against her father. Bauer passed by the table and nodded to them on his way to greet the hulking, swaggering, drunken figure blocking the doorway. Geisler had come for a visit, carrying a large pail of beer. The two embraced.

When Bauer was out of earshot she said:

'I want to stay here with Papa.' She watched Geisler take a seat at the other end of the dining room. His small, porcine eyes were like blood-red stones, and he wore a stained swastika armband.

'All right, you can have your punishment,' Alex told his son.

Jonathan's anguish rose to the surface. He clung to his agony. The warm, sweet taste of defeat filled his throat with bile. He mentally repeated – I must not cry. Such a show of weakness would have rendered his sacrifice meaningless. He had made the choice consciously to return to Lenore and he despised her for compromising him. What prevented her from speaking out? He pointed his finger at Lenore and said bitterly:

'Liar! You *don't* want to stay here,' then he followed his father into their room. He was tempted to ask for an explanation for their flight with the Contes, but he decided not to give Alex the satisfaction of trammeling him again. He kept his eyes open and gripped hold of the wooden footboard. He bent over so that Alex's angle would be unimpeded. There would be no last-minute pleas for a reprieve or an admission of guilt. He longed for the punishment. It would demonstrate that his motives were pure and that he had the courage to accept responsibility for his actions. No, he could never be a weakling like Sam who worshiped this ugly house, nor two-faced like Lenore.

The moments passed with harrowing slowness. His back was becoming cramped from the unnatural position. The mental torture he experienced shattered him, and he heard involuntary infantile gurgles rip through him. That Alex did not strike him altered the entire character of the debasement he anticipated.

Alex sat on the edge of the bed and rubbed his hands through his curly hair.

'Jonathan, tell me what's wrong?'

'Hit me!' he shouted.

'I want to understand you.' He eased him up from his stoop and held his son securely in his arms. 'I'm not going to touch you.' He rubbed his rough, bristly skin against the boy's face. 'What is it?'

Jonathan's face was seared by a rush of tears. His chest heaved in a torment of frustration, lost hope, and despair.

'I love her, Papa. I love her,' he cried with arms outstretched. 'I thought I'd never see her – that she'd die and I couldn't be with her.' He crumbled into Alex's arms.

When the thrust of the pain had run its course, Alex sponged his face with a wet cloth.

'It's a dangerous love, Jonathan. When you love as a child, you can't accept disappointment.'

*　　*　　*

Salica had a floor plan of the bank spread out on the bridge table in his room. He went over each man's job with an air of supreme calm. Victor and Alex had followed his scheme to the letter, drawing the Gestapo into Tietz's by apparently shopping with their families, then when a crowd of people had surrounded an assistant demonstrating a new English toaster on the market, they had rushed down the fire stairs unnoticed and returned to Sam's pension. Salica was a marvel at deception, possessing an intrinsic astuteness. Yet, for a man in hiding, he took extraordinary chances, parading around in public places as though he had nothing to fear. Perhaps this was just the right tack: to act contrary to rational expectation. If he had stayed put, kept to his room, avoiding any contact with the other boarders, he might have aroused suspicions, for Munich was a haven for SS spies and informers who bartered information for future favors.

His knowledge of Nolde's habits and precise schedule was remarkable. He had spent all of his time trailing him during the day, observing him at lunch, at his local tavern. He even followed him to the cinema with Chou one night. What Salica had not learned about the man was provided by Chou.

'We'll go on the morning of June twenty-third, after the fight. People will be coming into work late. No matter who wins, they'll be discussing it, ehhh? Nolde leaves his apartment on the Burgstrasse at exactly seven thirty. He stops for coffee and a roll at his *hofbrau*, checks to see if there are any bargains in wines which are being unloaded. He scans through his paper searching for sales which he sometimes goes to on his lunch hour. At eight o'clock he walks here' – Salica pointed to the street map – 'to Schlosser's, his tobacconist. He buys six Uppmann Havana coronas.

'He then picks up his car at the garage. He sometimes bribes the mechanic to give him a few free liters. He pulls out of the garage and makes a left turn. Chou will be waiting for him. She'll flag him down. He'll be surprised but he'll stop. The moment she gets into the car I'll be with her. I'll ride in the back seat. Victor, you and Alex will follow us to the bank.'

'What time will that be?'

'Approximately eight fifteen. Nolde will reach the bank at eight thirty. He'll park in his usual spot in the back lot. Victor, you park your car here in front of the bank. At this point, Alex and you come down the alley to the rear and Chou will get into your car.'

'Can she drive?' Victor asked.

'She's an animal behind the wheel. Is everything clear?' Both men nodded.

'The guard will come on his bicycle at eight forty. Sometimes he's late. He and Nolde have keys which they have to insert in the lock at the same time to open the door. We'll go in with them. At eight forty-five, the tellers, cashiers, and secretaries begin arriving.'

'How many are there?' Victor asked. He was becoming a bit queasy.

'Twenty-eight,' Salica smiled at him. 'You're accustomed to large parties, Vittorio. You'll be their host and seat them.'

'Where?'

'On the floor. Then you'll join me at the safe with Nolde.'

'What do I do?' Alex asked.

'You'll guard them. One look at that face and with a gun in your hand, you shouldn't have any trouble.' He reached for the bottle of wine at his elbow and poured himself a glass. 'Once we've got the money sacks out of the safe, we'll put all the bank staff behind the gates in the safe-deposit area. From what Chou and I've seen the only alarm is behind the clerk's desk and he won't be sitting there.'

The discussion excited Alex. The prospect of recouping his savings and striking back at authority was intoxicating.

'At nine thirty the bank opens. The shades are raised at nine twenty-seven, so that gives us half an hour. The manager arrives at nine forty-five and the Direktors at ten.'

Victor caught Paul's eye but was reluctant to pursue the question troubling him.

'What is it, Vittorio?'

'I'm worried about Nolde. He could refuse to cooperate.'

'I'll persuade him. Believe me, I will.'

'What happens if one of the staff manages to trigger the alarm?' Alex asked uneasily.

'Well, you make it very clear to them that the punishment for that is death, won't you?'

'You'd actually shoot?' Victor was astonished.

'Without a second thought,' Salica replied.

Alex's sense of security increased as the plan was laid out step by step. He was in the hands of an expert. Each minute was accounted for and their positions during the robbery were repeatedly explained. With his palm cupping his chin, Victor's attention was riveted on every word of Salica's.

Alex studied the route they would take through country dirt roads. Farmers would be harvesting hops and he hoped they would not attract attention. He hardly knew how he would explain all this to Jonathan. It was bad enough that they were on the run, but how could they keep the robbery from him? What kind of example was he setting for the boy? Once when David and Jonathan had stolen penknives from a sports shop, Alex had severely punished them and then exposed them as common thieves to the owner. He had cut out their pocket money for a month and restricted their playtime.

'What are we supposed to do about my boy?' he asked.

'When I was his age, I used to go along with my father when he collected money from the tavern owners,' Salica said.

'And you followed in his footsteps,' Victor said smiling sardonically.

'Vittorio, you'll never understand the Mafia way of thinking, ehhh?' he said reproachfully. 'It's only when people need protection from the law that they accept us for what we are.'

'What's that?' Alex asked.

'The only court the ordinary man has.' He had lost his carefree manner now and he closely examined the street plan of the neighborhood.

'We'll have to come back to the pension for him. It means altering our route.' He ran his finger along the Isar road. 'Jonathan will wait for us at the corner of the Braukeller at precisely ten fifteen. And, Alex, he'd better be there.'

* * *

It was 3.00 a.m. in Munich but the lights in every house and apartment were still on. It was the morning of June 22, 1938, and Germany waited with cool assurance for Max Schmeling to bring the heavyweight title back to the nation. Their inexpensive Volksempfanger, 'people's receivers,' which Goebbels had recently introduced, were all tuned to Arno Helmers who was broadcasting the fight live on the Nazi network. Behind his steely tone were the sounds of Louis's Harlem supporters singing 'Flat Foot Floogie.' The voice of Sam Taub, the American announcer, stationed close to Helmers, could also be heard.

'Ladies and gentlemen and our beloved Führer,' Helmers began, 'I must sadly report that at this moment a conspiracy led by the Jewish governor of New York State, Herbert

Lehman, is under way. Yankee Stadium has a crowd of seventy thousand people, many of them black as night, who have been given free tickets by the millionaire governor to cheer for Louis. There have been threats of a riot if Louis does not win.

'In our hearts we know that Max Schmeling is the superior fighter. Even Jack Dempsey, the greatest fighter who ever lived, has predicted a victory for Max. Let me comfort you with the thought that there are others – our countrymen from Germany who live in Yorkville – who have come in smaller numbers than the Negroes – to support Max. The emblem of our fatherland is prominently displayed by our fellow German Bundists who are proudly wearing their swastika armbands.'

Alex and the others were in the pension sitting room listening to Helmers's description.

'He hasn't got a chance,' Salica declared.

'Who do you mean, *mein Herr?*' Bauer indignantly demanded. He wiped the beer foam from his lips. Sitting beside him on the sofa was Geisler, a pail of beer at his feet and a paper bag of pretzels on his lap. Even with the windows open he sweated through his shirt and his collar was a sopping rag.

'Louis will take him in a few rounds,' Salica replied.

'That's disloyal,' Geisler informed him. 'You're a traitor to Germany.'

'I'm a sporting man, so let's bet.'

'The odds at ringside according to Sam Taub have increased,' Helmers noted bitterly. 'Max is now a thirteen to five underdog. A pity that our nation is not represented here to even things out. Those of you at home in Germany, Austria, and our loyal suffering friends and relatives in the Sudetenland, follow my advice: if anyone is foolish enough to offer you those odds, take them and don't ask questions.'

Bauer opened his worn leather purse and counted out five hundred marks:

'Well, are you one of those men who just blows air out of his mouth or do you want to wager?'

'I don't want to take your money,' Salica said blandly.

'Just like a foreigner . . . or a Jew' – Geisler glared at Alex – 'to make these cowardly statements and back down. The Führer has identified you November Criminals who stab the nation in the back when they need support. Why Himmler let scum like you work with our Max is a mystery, Herr Stein.'

Alex whispered to Sam who left the room for a minute then returned with several thousand marks which he handed to Alex ruefully.

'Twenty-six hundred to a thousand,' Alex said, placing the money on the table in front of Bauer.

'You should get out of our country and live with Jew lovers like Roosevelt and his pack of Zionist animals,' Geisler said sharply. He stood up, towering over Alex. 'I've got a good mind to take you outside and teach you a lesson. It's a pity you're not my size.'

'Do you want to bet on that as well?' Salica asked.

'I would, believe me, it would be a pleasure to take your money and burn it after I won, but I've been laid off work.' Spittle gathered at the corner of his mouth and he stretched his hand out. '*Sieg Heil, Heil Hitler*,' he chanted.

'In Yankee Stadium it is humid and there is a possibility of rain,' Helmers continued. 'But Mike Jacobs, the promoter, believes the weather will hold for the fight. The weigh-in was this morning and Schmeling was a trim, fit, one hundred and ninety-three pounds. Louis weighed one hundred and ninety-eight and three-quarter pounds.'

Drowning out Helmers's voice was a thunderous, deafening ovation when Max Schmeling appeared.

'Max is in the ring and he's brimming with confidence. Not a nerve in his body. I would like to take this opportunity to read you a telegram sent to Max from our esteemed Reichsführer and war hero, Hermann Göring: "May you return the championship to its rightful place in Germany. Heil Hitler. With good wishes, Hermann Göring." Another has been sent by Dr. Josef Goebbels. It reads, "Dear Max, your victory will confirm in all nations' minds the truth of Aryan supremacy. Win for the Fatherland, cordially, Dr. Josef Goebbels."'

Geisler stalked around the room, a mastodon, lumbering from side to side. Victor was concerned that he might cause trouble and, ever diplomatic, attempted to placate him. The crowd's tumultuous sound from the radio drowned out Helmers's voice.

'I'm not a German, but I live here . . .'

'What does that matter to me?' Geisler said morosely.

'Everyone in Germany wants Schmeling to win – including my friend,' Victor declared.

'If you'll permit me to comment as a man of the people but whose profession allows him entrée to the haut monde,' Bauer interjected, noticing Geisler clenching his fists, 'our beloved Führer has worked tirelessly to generate and utimately instill a sense of purpose and national pride in the Fatherland and your friend's remarks cut us to the soul. Max Schmeling represents the flower of German manhood. He personifies Siegfried – the sportsman as warrior – and he symbolizes our hopes in this match. This is not simply a boxing bout, but something deeper and more precious to those of us who love our country. It is a statement of our destiny.'

Alex held his nose and moved toward them like a bantam cock.

'Balls. Two men in the ring don't represent anyone but themselves.' He sidled up next to Geisler. 'If you want to increase the wager, now's your chance.'

Geisler became flustered and turned haplessly to Bauer.

'Done. Double the wager,' Bauer announced, pulling out a thousand-mark note which he handed to Geisler.

'Fine, now let's listen to the fight,' Alex said. As he was about to return to his wing chair by the radio, he had second thoughts. 'Herr Bauer, I may be smaller than your guest, but if he calls me a traitor once more, you'll be scraping him off the wall. So let him support his man and cheer as loud as he likes, but for his own good tell him to keep his mouth shut.'

The volume was turned up by Sam who looked with pride at Alex. He had wanted all his life to give vent to the fury which welled up in him when he was humiliated, but he had backed off, retreating with his tail between his legs. He went to the sideboard and opened a bottle of schnapps, then poured drinks for his three friends and himself. As they raised their glasses in a toast, Sam's loneliness became overpowering. He had grown to like Salica. He preferred not to think of Victor and Alex leaving Munich. Perhaps they would call off this mad robbery. Since the afternoon he'd had with them, they hadn't brought up the subject. There had to be another way for Alex to survive even if Schmeling lost the fight. It was irrational for the SS to hold him responsible. Yet he agreed that it would be best for him to leave Munich for a time.

'Louis is moving around the ring shadowboxing,' Helmers said. 'He's wearing a blue silk robe and now he's taking it off. He has a flannel robe underneath. He's going back to his corner and sitting down. His trainer, Jack Blackburn, is lacing his gloves. They're using eight-ounce gloves ...

'Max is smiling at me and I've just waved to him. Good luck, Max. Beside him is his American manager, Yussel Jacobs, and his faithful trainer, Max Machon, who is leaning down and giving Schmeling some final instructions.'

During the playing of the German and American national anthems, Victor pleaded with Alex to ease up on Geisler.

'Referee Arthur Donovan is informing the fighters and their trainers of the rules governing the fight which is sanctioned by the New York Boxing Commission. Louis is wearing black trunks with a white stripe and Schmeling is in dark blue solid trunks.

'There's the bell! Louis moves out in a crouch. He's being cautious. He looks like a giant panther about to spring. Schmeling sends out a long right which is just off target. Louis begins to circle Schmeling. He's feeling him out, remembering their first fight.'

'Catch him when he blinks,' Alex said aloud. 'Come on, Max!'

Bauer was stunned by Alex's about-face.

'They're in close. Now Louis is jabbing. One, two, three jabs.'

'Cross with the right now,' Alex shouted.

'Schmeling lands a right but it was on the head ... Louis is jabbing him at will. Four in a row, and he twists his glove viciously. Louis crosses a right and he's stunned Max. Max's face is white ... he's hurt. He's against the ropes. Schmeling's turning to avoid the punch. Louis catches him as he turns. A kidney punch! Max is in terrible pain from this foul blow ... Schmeling's hanging onto the ropes to support himself. Referee Donovan is waving Louis to a neutral corner and scoring it as a knockdown even though Schmeling's still on his feet. He stops the count at one ... Schmeling lurches gamely to the center of the ring. Louis is boring in ... a left, another, a short right. Max is being lifted up into the air. He's falling on his shoulder. He's trying to clear his head ... He's up at a count of three. He should have stayed down till nine. He's groggy and his knees are buckling. Louis is after him like an animal. Louis hooks him to the jaw, then again crosses with the right. Louis is hitting him at will – nine punches to the jaw. Max is down again on all fours. He's struggling to move. Schmeling doesn't know how to quit. He's up at two. Louis is on top of him with another hook and a right and Schmeling goes down for the third time.

'Max Machon has thrown the towel into the ring, but Referee Donovan continues to count. He's at five, six, seven, eight ... Donovan waves his arms apart. He's stopped the fight. Schmeling is being helped to his corner by Jacobs. Jacobs is protesting to the referee that Louis fouled Max ...

'My God, loyal Germans, we've been stabbed in the back again. They're calling it a knockout. Two minutes and four seconds of the first round. It's a disgrace! Schmeling is sitting on his stool with his head bowed. He's in terrible agony and he's angry. The kidney punches at the beginning of the round paralyzed him. Illegal, foul blows. The people in the stadium are out of control. The hysteria in Yankee Stadium is beyond belief ...

'Max, we sympathize with you – all of Germany does. You lost as a fair sportsman against a wild animal who only understands the law of the jungle. Even in defeat you fought with courage and honour and you will always be a great champion to your nation and the Aryan race. Good night, Mein Führer and Germany,' Helmers said emotionally.

Tears ran down Geisler's face as he strode to the door. He raised his fist at Alex and in a garbled, drunken voice, breathing heavily, he said:

'It's only the beginning. One day we'll settle the score with you people for good.'

Nine

Sitting in the middle of the circular living room in the Berg-hof, his alpine redoubt, Hitler and his entourage shared Geisler's sentiments. It was four in the morning. The Füh-rer's sensitive stomach had betrayed him during the long night. He had vomited four times, continually coughed, sput-tered, changed handkerchiefs every hour and was constantly administered to by his personal physician. Dr. Theo Morell, an habitually unkempt skin specialist whom Hitler believed to be the greatest doctor in Germany. Assortments of pills had been pressed on the patient all evening – Mutaflor and Gallestol – to relieve his gastric pains and cramps. However the only medication that seemed to quiet his condition of meteorism, an affliction characterized by virulent seizures of machine-gun-like farts, were the small, black, antigas tablets provided by Morell. They had fallen from the Führer's pill-box and were scattered on his side table like bird droppings. That they contained seed of strychnine and belladonna was unknown to both physician and patient.

Now that the fight was over, the others waited for the ashen-faced Führer to speak. He was worn, with sagging ocher pouches under his luminous blue eyes which traveled over the faces of Himmler, Göring, Rosenberg, and Goeb-bels.

'Who was responsible for this farce?' he shrieked, rising and beginning to pace. The question galvanized the aides and secretaries surrounding him.

'The task was assigned to the SS, Mein Führer,' Himmler ruefully admitted. 'I in turn asked one of my aides, Major Wilhelm Von Fritsch, to oversee Schmeling's training pro-gram.'

Hitler's voice snaked through the room. 'The *Jew* you located in Munich ... didn't he have a hand in this?'

Fritsch nodded mutely.

'Did the Jew sabotage your efforts?' Hitler demanded, staring glacially at him.

'I'm convinced that he did. He deceived Machon and

Schmeling, who know more about these things than any of us.'

'They're germs – poison. From my earliest days in Vienna I personally isolated that fact. The Jew by his nature has always perverted society. He knows nothing else but to be devious, to twist what is healthy so that he can exploit it.'

'What is the SS going to do with this Jew? Give him an Iron Cross? Reward him? Pay him a pension for life?' Göring inquired sarcastically.

'We'll institute a *ratissage*,' Fritsch observed. 'I myself will see to it. He won't be given an oportunity to go to ground. You can rely on me, Mein Führer.'

*   *   *

Alex woke Jonathan at six in the morning and told him to be at the Braukeller corner at ten o'clock sharp. He made it clear that he would not tolerate any disobedience. He was to say his good-byes to Lenore and Sam without causing any difficulty. 'I'm putting my trust in you, so don't let me down. There'll be a time when you'll see her again,' he said reassuringly. Jonathan did not believe his father but he no longer had a choice. He watched Chou and the three men get into Victor's car and drive off.

Victor stopped at Ringer's Hofbrau, a small tavern opposite the Nachteule. He looked across to his creation. He had built it up over a period of years. Little by little he had expanded it, broken through the wall of an adjacent empty shop which became an annex to the dining room. He had nursed it along like a loving parent, only to lose it now.

Yet, in spite of his loss, he forced himself to regard the enterprise with some detachment. The character of what he had conceived had been altered so radically. He could never be comfortable as the owner of an SS brothel. He was thirty-two and the prospect of beginning anew might have daunted another man, but Victor believed in his stars. Another opportunity would eventually arise and he would seize it. Convinced that he possessed an unusual combination of business acumen along with the capacity to handle people, he felt sure he would rise to new heights one day. If only they could get to America . . .

They had a breakfast of baked herring, potatoes, and scrambled eggs, which they pasted on large hunks of buttered pumpernickel. The tavern filled up with taxi drivers, beer haulers, truckmen, and delivery boys. The only topic of discussion was the fight. Occasionally, Victor caught a glimpse of an SS patrol passing by and he inclined his head to the others to indicate that this was unusual. They spoke in muffled voices, so as not to be overheard by the drivers sitting close by idling over their coffees, angrily giving their opinions for Schmeling's defeat. Their faces were carved in shades of sullenness, disillusion, and in their red, haggard, bloodshot eyes there was a spirit of deadly, unbridled belligerence. Schmeling's loss was theirs, a triumph of beast over man, another venomous insult thrust at Germany by her enemies.

An SS man poked his head through the door and scanned the room.

'They're looking for me,' Alex whispered.

'If he comes over, get ready to move,' Salica said.

The SS man ambled over to the counter and stood by the cash register talking to the owner. He had a photograph in his hand and he showed it to him. There was no response from the owner and the SS man told him to keep the photograph. They waited until he'd driven off, then they paid the waiter and left. Victor took a last look at his club.

The Citroën crawled along the curb of the Burgstrasse, a wide boulevard of pseudo-Italianate apartment houses indented by small food shops, courtyards and tailors, laundries and cafés. Its ground-floor concierge peepholes had a burgher vigilance. Poplar trees lined a plaza where some early risers sat on benches reading their newspapers and discussing the latest liver cures. It was seven fifteen. Salica left the car to buy a few bottles of Vichy water. The herring had made them thirsty. He stuck his head in the Weinstadl and observed a few customers sitting at the bar. A grouchy waiter in a clean, crisp, long white apron was accusing referee Donovan of dishonesty for having stopped the fight without having given Schmeling the benefit of a full count.

'He would have come back – there was less than a minute to go.'

'Louis might have killed Max,' a grease-stained mechanic said.

'Max's a great boxer. Look what he did in the first fight.'

Paul caught the waiter's eye and asked for two bottles of

Baden water. He waited nervously while the waiter took forever to go to the cold room. It was seven twenty-two. Should he walk out? When the waiter finally reappeared carrying the bottles, Paul took out a hundred-mark note.

The waiter had to return to the bar for the change. Salica cursed Victor for carrying only large notes. The waiter unlocked a metal strongbox and laboriously began counting. 'I don't want to confuse the manager. This is yesterday's takings.'

Paul's watch showed seven twenty-eight. By the time he had his money and dashed out the door, Nolde was down the street, heading toward him, Paul tore across the road to the car and flung himself inside.

'Shit, don't ever give me herring for breakfast.'

'I wanted to go there ... a sentimental journey,' Victor said.

'When we're out on business?' Chou asked shortly. 'This isn't a nightclub rehearsal.'

'There he is,' Alex said with disbelief. 'Just like you said, Paul.'

'Time?'

'Seven thirty-three,' Chou replied. 'He's three minutes late.'

It was going to be another hot day. The four of them sat in the car sweating nervously, gasping for air from the partially open window.

The waiter fastened the front door back and greeted Nolde. They had a clear view of him. He spread his *Münchener Post* on the table, slowly sipped his coffee, then broke off a piece of roll and dunked it. By eight oh five, he had eaten a second roll, settled his bill, stretched, and placed the paper in his dark cowhide briefcase. He squinted in the bright sunlight and took a few steps to the cigar shop next door. The tobacconist was in the window, sticking a yellow, filmy sun-block paper to the glass. He crawled out. He and Nolde spoke for a moment. Cigars and cash were exchanged. Nolde carefully cut the tip of one cigar, took a light from the gas burner above the counter, and savored the first few puffs. It was eight sixteen.

The garage was some sixty yards down the street. Victor started the Citroën. He drove a few feet past the entrance to let Chou and Salica out of the car. He pulled ahead and kept the motor running.

'We can call it off,' Victor said.

'What happens to our families if we get caught?' Alex asked.

Victor's reply froze as he caught sight of a dull gray Opel nosing out of the garage. Nolde inched forward, gave a hand signal for a left-hand turn, and in that moment, Chou waved to him. Nolde blew his horn, craned his neck out of the window, turned out of the garage, drove a few feet, and stopped. Chou opened the passenger door and got in. Paul sprang out from behind a parked car and lunged into the back seat of Nolde's car. It was eight twenty-three.

They were eight minutes late.

Nolde remained double-parked, sure that this was some kind of mistake. Then Salica pointed his Walther at Nolde's head.

'What's going on?'

'We're driving to the bank,' Chou said brusquely.

'Of course I am.'

'To rob it,' Salica informed him.

'What? The bank ... But that's impossible. The bank is burglar proof.'

'You've got the keys that open everything,' Salica told him.

'Yes, but –'

Victor was now closing in behind them.

'The car behind us has more men,' Salica said. He jammed the gun behind Nolde's ear. Nolde gave a little grunt.

'Drive!'

Nolde shifted into first and crawled along to a stoplight. 'What do I tell the authorities?' he asked. 'Chou?'

'Who cares?'

'They'll find out about you. People have seen us out ...'

'Lie to them,' Paul said.

'Lie to the Gestapo investigators? In Germany, that's not done.'

Chou slipped a Baretta out of her purse and rammed it into Nolde's ribs.

'Pauli, let's shoot him now, take the keys, and leave him here.' She dug her heel into Nolde's toe.

'I'll do it. Just don't hurt me.'

*   *   *

115

As a concession to Jonathan, Sam gave in to the boy's pleas. After all, he might never see Lenore or Sam again. A farewell at the communal breakfast table, Sam agreed, was so bleak that he knew he would reproach himself for the rest of his life if he did not allow the children a few more hours together. Lenore could miss one day of school.

When his boarders departed for the day, Sam sat at the long table overlooking the rear garden, peering up every now and then while making bookkeeping entries. The children played on the swings beside the high bower of climbing roses blooming on the back wall. Sam thought again about his friends. How could they possibly rob the Bund? It was impossible. He should have stopped them somehow.

He wrote out a bank deposit slip, placed the bills in a brown envelope, then he tied on his apron. It was time to make the beds. He sighed and climbed the stairs.

Jonathan could not keep his eyes off the church clock in the square across the street. It was eight thirty. In ninety minutes, he would have to leave Lenore. He could not reconcile himself to never seeing her again. She struggled on her swing, and he got off his to push her. She rose higher and higher. Her long, sinuous legs splayed out so that it appeared as though she might fly over the fence beyond. But she acted as though she didn't know he was even there. He grabbed hold of the swing's rusted chains, brought it to rest, then stood in front of her.

'When I took you out in the canoe, you told me something –'

'I don't remember.'

'Lenore, what's wrong?'

'Nothing,' she insisted.

'I don't believe you.' He touched her face and she pushed him off. He dropped to his knees, pulled some blades of grass out, and chewed on one. 'I'm going away.'

She swung slowly, oblivious of his presence.

Sam listened to the radio while he made the beds. Schmeling was indeed injured. He had been taken to the New York Polyclinic Hospital where it was discovered he had suffered damage to his lower vertebrae. Sam turned to a station which was playing *Tannhäuser*. The booming chorus enthralled him and he hummed along as he swept the corridor.

He stooped to collect the dirt in the dustpan, then lost his balance, falling over flat on his back He had been kicked in the rib cage. He gripped his stomach as the pain filled his body. Struggling to his knees he shielded his eyes. A man's angry, twisted mouth formed the word 'Jude' before a boot struck him in the temple.

Geisler pinned him to the floor. 'You're not so quick to defend your friends now.' His fist sprang out and caught Sam in the eye. The ring on Geisler's finger gouged a strip of flesh out of Sam's eyebrow.

'Leave him now' – Bauer's voice vibrated with excitement – 'let's get started.' Sam lay in the corridor. Breathless from the exertion, Geisler heaved himself up and reached for the liter of schnapps that Bauer held. He took a long pull from the bottle then handed it back.

Bauer crept into Sam's room, lowered the volume on the radio, then stood behind the curtains, surveying the garden. He signaled to Geisler to be quiet. They left the room, tip-toed down the stairs.

'Go in through the garden door and bolt it,' Bauer said. I'll lock the front door and follow you from the kitchen.'

'We'll show them Karl, eh?'

'– Yes, of course,' he said, thrusting Geisler outside. He had never been so thoroughly aroused in his life.

Lenore was still on the swing. Bauer savored the vision.

The gate door swung open suddenly. Geisler staggered forward. Jonathan turned but did not move. He'd heard about these drunks who plagued Sam. He fixed his attention on the sulking face of Lenore. Geisler stopped several feet from them, then slid the door's metal bolt.

'Why'd you do that?' Jonathan called out.

Geisler stalked toward them, reached out, and yanked the chain of Lenore's swing, causing it to jerk crazily. Lenore lost her balance.

'Stop it,' Jonathan insisted. 'She could've hurt herself.'

Bauer broke out of the kitchen door. Sweat streamed in his eyes. 'Come here,' Bauer ordered Jonathan.

Jonathan ran alongside the wall and picked up a stone. Bauer attempted to corner him at the wall, but he darted out of the way.

Lenore was being dragged by the hair. She was scream-ing.

'Don't hurt her!' Jonathan warned. Bauer closed in on

him and Jonathan raised the stone. But Bauer stood his ground, shunting him against the rose trellis.

'If you know what's good for you, you'll come into the house,' Bauer shouted.

'Let her go!'

Bauer sprang at him and Jonathan threw the rock, hitting him on the shoulder. Cursing, Bauer chased him along the wall. Jonathan got his foot into the wooden trellis and started to climb. Rose thorns cut through his fingers. Bauer yanked him off and flung him to the ground.

He pulled the boy to his feet and with a closed fist hit him flush on the left cheekbone. Jonathan fell flat on his back. Fragments of light scattered in his head. Bauer raised him by the neck, setting him against the wall. Jonathan could hardly open his eyes. His reflexes were gone, his cheekbone felt broken. The fist twirled at him again and this time it landed in the pit of his stomach, knocking the wind out of him. His mouth filled with vomit and he dropped into a flower bed. In the distance, far away, from other galaxies, he heard Lenore crying.

'Please, please, Uncle, don't hit him any more ...'

Jonathan was numb from the pain of the blows. Blood streamed from his mouth. He sensed that he was being dragged. He raised an arm to protect himself, but Bauer's fist crashed into his forehead, lifting him off his feet. He collapsed among the flowers by the fishpond.

'Get her upstairs.'

'You should have fought Louis,' Geisler roared.

Geisler's jagged nails dug into Lenore's arm as he carried her up the stairs. Bauer unlocked his door and Geisler threw her on the bed.

'Where's the schnapps?'

'It's downstairs,' Bauer said. 'You get it.'

Her head was on Bauer's pillow. He forced his mouth on hers. The sour, bitter smell of his breath sickened her. His fingers probed between her thighs and then he tore off her underpants. In her panic she passed water.

'Good ... pee. I like to see you pee.'

He licked her neck and his tongue was hard and grainy and rough on her skin. He ripped off her blouse and ran his fingers along her nipples. He made her raise her arms so that he could pull off her undervest. Then he pushed her back down on the bed and dropped his trousers. He was raving, using words she didn't understand. He lay on top of her, his weight crushing, smothering her.

His finger was inside her and the pain became excruciating. She winced and twisted her head from under his arm.

'It hurrrrrts. Please, Uncle, don't keep hurting me.'

He didn't hear her. He was in the height of his frenzy and he shoved, pushed, battered at her. She began to shriek with agony as he thrust harder.

She fainted, but was awakened by his slaps across her neck and face. 'Let me in. In! In deeper,' he groaned.

'I can't.'

He pulled her off the bed and carried her to his tattered armchair. He sat on the arm, and spread-eagled her on top of him. Blood trickled on his hairy thighs when he bounced her up and down, his nails gouging deeply into her buttocks.

She sensed something hot and fetid . . . a foul odor press against her cheek. Her mouth was yanked open. Geisler stood over her with his trousers down to his ankles. Rocking back and forth, he slid the tip along her tongue.

They came at her in waves, forcing their way into her. Her mouth was filled with a sticky goo from Geisler. She choked on it. Then her head fell forward on Bauer's chest. She felt his body shudder and he shouted —

'Aiiiiiiiiii . . . . ?'

'Fantastic, fantastic!' Geisler cried. 'Now change places.'

'Let her rest for a while,' Bauer said, holding firmly onto the child. He looked down at the empty schnapps bottle. 'I'll go out and get us something to drink. I need a walk.'

Ten

'Look where you're going, damnit. You almost hit that man at the crossing,' Salica barked from the back seat of Nolde's car. Sweat dribbled under Nolde's eyes and his glasses were fogged.

'The gun ... it makes me so nervous.'

A policeman directing traffic stopped them at a corner, a block from the bank.

'Give me your glasses,' Chou said. Nolde slipped them off and she wiped them on her skirt. 'Enjoy yourself, Max. Pretend we're dancing at the Fatima.'

The policeman signaled them to move. Salica warned, 'No heroics. Just pull into your regular place ... nothing different.'

Nolde turned off into an alleyway running beside the bank. It was eight forty-nine. They had gained four minutes. But if the guard had arrived on time it might still cause problems. His bicycle wasn't there.

'Good old Willie,' Salica said, 'consistently late.'

'I'll finish him for good this time,' Nolde announced.

Chou chucked him under the chin.

Nolde drove to the spot marked with his name. They all left the car. Salica shoved Nolde behind a pillar so they couldn't be seen by the guard when he arrived. Chou walked down the alley.

'All this time you've been following me?' Nolde asked Salica.

'Everywhere. I almost lost you at the cinema the other night. How can you watch the same Western three times, ehhh? I found out why. You're a bad boy. Paying an usherette to relieve you. Ehhh?'

Salica's knowledge of his personal life distressed him as much as the robbery. Nolde drew back, threw up his hands when Victor and Alex came toward him.

'Morning, Herr Nolde,' Alex said. 'Is it all right with you if I withdraw my money?'

'You — Stein!' He began to snivel. 'I'm only an employee. What can I do when the SS orders me to block an account?'

'Why'd you let me sweat?'

'Major Von Fritsch told me to,' he protested.

A sound of humming came from the alleyway. A moment later Willie came into view. He had a lunch pail in the wire basket of his bicycle. He parked the bike, attached a combination lock to it, and ambled to the door.

Alex and Victor cornered him by the rear door. The guard asked what was wrong.

Shoved by Salica, Nolde bounced forward.

'Get your key out, Willie,' Salica said, pushing his gun under the guard's chin.

'Listen to them,' Nolde said, executively.

Nolde and Willie inserted their keys into the Schlage lock, turned them simultaneously. A set of metal gates with a padlock was the next barrier. Finally a dull, heavy steel door.

It was eight fifty-five and they were inside. As Salica had predicted, all the tellers and clerks were late.

'Do you check them in?' Salica asked the guard.

'Yes.'

'Well, my colleague will assist you.'

Victor held the gun pointed at the guard. It became heavier by the moment, alien and unnatural in his hand.

At Salica's command, Nolde was trotting in the direction of the safe.

Victor heard voices outside the door. The doorbell was rung and half a dozen people trooped in.

'What's going on?' the head teller asked Willie.

'A robbery.'

'Not possible. This is the bank. The Führer said it was a criminal offense,' he said with disbelief.

'Take a seat here –' Victor shunted them into a staff room where there were benches and tables. A woman began to cry. 'Quiet down in there.'

'How many in so far?' Alex shouted from the safe.

'Fifteen.' It was nine oh five.

Nolde led them to the strong room and with another key opened the gleaming tracked steel gates. The safe had a combination lock. Shaking, Nolde clumsily spun the tumblers. Behind them they heard voices, some raised in shock, others quiet and passive as the clerks were greeted by Victor.

Salica gripped the two metal handles of the safe. The doors came open, revealing shelves bulging with bundles of marks.

Salica thrust a sack at Nolde and told him to fill it.

'We're one short ... only twenty-seven,' Victor shouted from the other end.

'Someone out sick?' Salica asked.

'I don't know,' Nolde replied.

They had three sacks filled by nine twenty.

Chou kept the car engine running. People had started to line up outside the front door. She lit a cigarette, stared at her watch. They had to be out in three minutes.

'Get them into the strong room,' Salica said quietly. Alex marched the group single file over the mosaic tiled floor. They raised their eyes to Nolde. He was about to collapse but held onto the metal gate for support. Salica picked up his keys and locked the gates.

Groaning, the three men carted the heavy sacks across the floor to the rear entrance.

'Get the shades ...' Salica said irritably.

Alex rushed to the front windows, skidding on the slippery floor. He raised the window shades and saw dozens of people at the entrance. He raced to the rear door. Chou had backed the car into the alley and had opened the trunk. She revved the engine while the trio loaded the thick sacks. When they were in the car, she put her foot flat down on the accelerator. The Citroën squealed onto the main street.

'Slow down, we're right on schedule,' Salica said.

'How'd it go?' she asked.

'Better than the Commerciale,' he replied. 'Women never let you forget.' He opened a bottle of Baden water and took a long drink, burped, and passed it to Victor.

'Here's to the Italian heroes,' he said.

It took just twenty minutes to reach the Braukeller. When there was no sign of Jonathan, Alex left the car at the street to search for him. If the boy had disobeyed him again, he wouldn't be let off lightly. The car crept along the curb, keeping up with him. He avoided looking at his friends. He crossed the street, looked into shops, called out the boy's name repeatedly. A sense of nameless dread took hold of him. Jonathan had given his word. The boy knew how important it was to be on time. The church clock across from Sam's pension chimed ten fifteen.

He ran back to the car.

'I can't leave him. Please, let's go to the pension.'

'If he's not there, we'll have to leave, with or without you,' Salica said.

Alex had his head out the car window, looking in every direction for his son. When they reached the pension he bolted out of the car and to the front door. When he found it locked he signaled the car. Victor and Salica spoke for a moment, then rushed out. They were both angry.

'It's locked. Sam never locks it.'

Salica looked at his watch.

'Let's go through the garden,' he said.

He pushed the garden door. The bolt moved barely an inch and the padlock jangled on the chain.

Chou switched off the car engine, and joined them.

'Where is he?' she asked.

'We don't know.'

Alex asked to be boosted up along the spiked pillar of the gate. He jumped down to the grass. He slid the bolt and opened the lock with the key attached to it. Silently they all walked into the garden. Salica motioned for them to enter the house through the kitchen. The stillness inside was unnerving. They took out their revolvers. Salica waved his gun for them to check the downstairs. Salica's eyes roved through the empty rooms. He placed Chou at the front door and beckoned the others to follow him upstairs. The men cautiously climbed the stairs. At the landing they heard a distant groan and quickened their pace. Sam lay motionless on the floor. Alex stopped to take his pulse. His breathing was shallow and the purplish bruises on his face and head were oozing blood.

'Waaaaaa——waaaaa——waaaa————'

The sound grew louder. They reached the door from which it was coming. It faded, then gained intensity. Salica turned the doorknob. Alex and Victor had their guns pointed behind him.

A man's voice. '*Komme ... Komme.*'

Salica burst through the door. For a moment the three

men were mesmerized. The room was an abattoir. Lenore had bled everywhere. Stripped naked, his bellies rolling, Geisler straddled her naked, blood-spattered body.

Geisler stopped abruptly. 'It's not my fault,' he protested; 'Bauer, Karl Bauer did it to her first. Then he left.'

Victor called out for Chou who came rushing up the stairs. Salica bent down and picked up the girl and held her in his arms.

'Get some bandages,' Victor said.

'Who's hurt?' Chou asked.

'Lenore.' Alex was inches away from Geisler. 'Where's my boy?'

'He's all right. In the garden. Bauer slapped him and he had the wind knocked out of him. Please, this wasn't my fault. I'm unemployed. Really, I don't want a fight . . .'

When Chou came into the room, she raised her gun. Salica pushed her hand down. He helped her wrap Lenore in a blanket.

Geisler had not moved from the armchair. He winced as though he had been struck.

'I'm an honest workman . . . I drink sometimes. Bauer got me drunk. It's the truth. I passed out –' He raised his hands.

'She's a child,' Victor said in a hushed solemn voice, overcome by the horror of the scene.

'It was done already. Bauer . . . Bauer.'

Alex's fist lashed out, hitting Geisler squarely on the lip.

'Don't!' Salica ordered him. 'He's not going to get away so easily. Get up and show us where the boy is.'

Weeping, Geisler rose, walking ahead of them, pleading, cursing Bauer. He led them to the rosebed where Jonathan lay. The boy was still unconscious but his legs jerked when Alex lifted him. Alex took him to the well and pumped water over his head. Jonathan's bloodshot eyes flickered. His mouth had a bad gash.

'Papa –' He shuddered when he caught sight of Geisler kneeling at Salica's feet. 'They were after Lenore.'

'I know . . .'

Alex brought him out to the car. In the back seat Chou was swabbing Lenore with wet cloths and alcohol. Sam, semiconscious, slumped in the front seat. With an effort he raised his head. 'Lenore, what happened?' he muttered, gazing dimly at the girl whom Chou was holding. 'Lenore!'

he cried plaintively. Alex walked back to the garden and blinked as Geisler crawled on his hands and knees like a giant turtle.

'Bauer went for schnapps,' Victor informed him.

Salica removed a stiletto from his jacket pocket. He touched the button. The blade flicked out. It was nine inches long and gleamed in the morning sun.

'No, don't!' Geisler pleaded.

Salica bent over the knife.

'There's a way to deal with rapists. Hold his mouth, Vittorio.' Victor clasped both hands tightly around Geisler's mouth. Salica slashed off his scrotum and penis. The writhing Geisler, in a paroxysm of agony, thrust off Victor's hands and screamed. As his mouth opened, Salica jammed the scrotum down his throat.

They waited for several minutes in the car outside the Braukeller for Bauer. When he did not appear, Salica motioned Victor to start the car.

'Someday ...' Sam began, then halted, breaking into a fit of hysteria. He touched Lenore. 'God help us. *Adonai ...*'

The men bought bottles of water at a small roadside grocery stand on the outskirts of Munich. Jonathan was dehydrated, in pain, and the only thing that helped was the cold water bottle he pressed hard against his cheek. They were hot and cramped in the car and rode with the windows open. Lenore was wrapped in a blanket. Chou held her in her arms. She had applied direct pressure to stanch the bleeding, but it was evident that both children needed a doctor. When they were outside Tuttlingen, a small town in the Swabian Jura Mountains, she beseeched Paul to stop at a local hospital. Lenore regained consciousness but her eyes were blank, vacuous, devoid of any comprehension. She gave no sign of recognizing any of them.

'We can't take the chance,' Salica said when they stopped at a station for gas. They had been fortunate to avoid patrols on the dirt roads which wound through dairy country. Spotted holstein cows moved behind the fences of emerald-green leas. The car was covered with a heavy sheet of brown dust and the windshield had layers of mud-caked insects squashed on it.

A sleepy-eyed mechanic came out of the corrugated iron

shed and filled their tank with gas. Alex took over the driving. Jonathan was shifted to Victor's lap. The heat and humidity had become intolerable. A bit farther along they stopped at a roadside stall. They bought a block of ice, brandy, and fresh fruit. Chou chipped off pieces of ice from the block and passed them around to be sucked. It was impossible to feed Lenore. Chou poured brandy on the ice and pressed it against Lenore's tongue. When she saw Lenore respond, she lifted her head and made her drink from the bottle. If she could get the child drunk, the pain and shock would diminish. She placed drops in her mouth and in a while Lenore's eyes closed and she slept.

The roads furled around the Rhine countryside, revealing a tapestry of gulls, swallows, teals, finches, and thrushes. A plague of sparrows flew over a scarecrow without descending. Bleary-eyed, Jonathan shunted himself to the window. Fisherman cast their nets from boats; ferries drifted across the Rhine; a boy stood on a pier with a wooden rod. Hands in the fields puffed at their pipes and regarded the lone car with dim curiosity. The air was filled with a sweet pungency of hay and straw. Overhanging blueberry bushes flailed at the speeding car. A heat haze rose fiery orange from the hop fields. Jonathan was disorientated, still in shock.

By four o'clock they were only at Feldberg, the entry to the Black Forest. If they continued along the Rhine route, they would run the danger of being stopped by patrols. They shuttled over dirt tracks, and rickety wooden bridges fording streams. Massive pines cut off the sun, thrusting them into darkness. Sudden gusts of wind shattered branches to the ground. The drive became so treacherous they could cover only twenty-five kilometers an hour.

Out of nowhere from beside a mountain stream an SS motorcyclist with a sidecar screamed out onto the dirt path, cutting them off. The two soldiers approached the car. The driver raised his goggles, craned his neck inside the car. The soldier in the sidecar drew his Luger and pointed it at them.

'Everybody out for a search,' he said, wagging the gun at them. 'Your keys and papers ...' The man left the car. 'You, too, Fräulein.'

'We've got two injured children and we're lost,' Chou said quickly. She turned Lenore so that he could see her battered face. 'Please don't make me wake her.'

'Where are you going?' the other demanded. He was a tall, reedy boy with a sparse stubble of beard. He wore the insignia of the Hitler Youth.

'To Kehl,' Victor replied.

'Why?' the soldier with the gun asked.

'To meet our wives.'

'What happened?'

'The children were climbing with me and our rope gave way,' said Sam.

The two soldiers huddled for a moment, looked carefully at the car, and were about to walk off when the younger one took a cloth from his sidecar and wiped the mud-spattered license plate. He seemed troubled.

'Where are your tents and camping equipment?'

'We left them,' Alex answered nervously.

'You must have a lot of money to abandon expensive equipment,' the young man persisted.

'Getting the children to a doctor was more important,' Salica said. He sensed that his answer did not satisfy the SS men. They stood their ground and once again demanded their papers and the car registration. When Victor hesitated the other soldier drew his gun.

'Quick now . . . and you, out of the car with the children.'

Alex opened the door and lifted Jonathan out.

'Why don't they ever leave us alone, Papa?' he blurted out.

Alex shrank back, pressing Jonathan's mouth against his shoulder. Chou gently placed Lenore across the seat. The moment she was on the running board she fired her Baretta into the face of the young SS man. The other one, stunned by the shot, reeled around and was about to shoot when Victor grabbed hold of his arm. He wrestled him to the ground and wrenched the gun out of his hand. Salica dove down and cut his throat from ear to ear. They threw the bodies into the creek, then pushed the cycle and sidecar down the embankment into the water.

'I should have listened to you, Alex,' Sam said. His eyes bulged. 'Next time, let me kill one of them.'

It was past midnight when they reached the silent, deserted town of Kehl. They were by the Rhine again.

They pulled into a darkened service station where they had arranged to meet Bastia and their families. Emerging from the car stiff-legged and chilled by the night air, Jonathan did not follow the others into the weather-beaten, ramshackle house behind the station. He stood at the river embankment and gazed through the darkness at France. Tugs tooted their horns and flashed their lights to show their position.

His mother called his name and he ran to her. The touch of her lips on his forehead reawakened his grief.

'I'm sorry I left you ...' he sputtered, losing control of himself.

'You did the right thing after all. But what's right in this world?'

The group waited, huddled on straw pallets in a dank shack beside the garage, until three in the morning. Marc Bastia had his truck in the workshop, the money sacks in the rear, covered with canvas. The men had been drinking Calvados, a rough apple brandy which Bastia had supplied. Red-eyed and exhausted, Alex leaned on a splintered wooden horse at the far end of the shack. A flickering candle beside him threw grotesque shadows on the wall. He chewed on the short nub of a pencil as he scratched a letter on a grease-stained piece of brown wrapping paper.

Dear Major Fritsch,

I am not by nature a dangerous or violent man. I am sorry for what I did to your young friend. In future, however, you Nazis should be careful about who you push around. I am returning your university ring, the one you gave to your lover. I would like to add that I wanted Max Schmeling to win against Joe Louis as much as anyone in Germany.

Alex Stein

He sealed the letter in an envelope and addressed it to SS headquarters in Munich.

Lenore's cries were unbearable to listen to. Tina and Miriam had taken turns ministering to the girl. Only one thing helped to quiet her. Miriam grabbed hold of Alex outside the workshop.

'Ask Bastia for more ... she needs it.'

He nodded and entered the workshop. The truck's engine lisped. The carburetor pinged. Overhead, a dim light struck a collection of tools, spare parts, worn tires. Attached to the ceiling were sheets of ragged flypaper which were blown by a droning fan.

'Carbon in the plugs,' Marc Bastia said.

'I thought it was the carburetor,' Salica said. Stripped to his undershirt, his torso smeared with grease, his muscles gleamed.

'Lenore's crying again. Can you help?' Alex asked.

Bastia wiped his dirty hands on a smock hanging by the door. His lazy eye wandered over Alex. He had an eerie nervous habit of smiling no matter what the situation. He regarded Alex with a certain distrust.

'What weight did you fight at?'

'Lightweight ... one thirty-six.'

'Bet you were fast.'

'Not very. I could punch. It's the way it goes. The good boxers have speed. The hitters don't work hard enough. I was like that.'

Salica, he observed, had withdrawn from the conversation and he was puzzled by the sudden restraint.

'I'm taking a lot of chances for you people, right?'

Alex agreed.

'Do I ask for money?'

'No.'

'Paolo and me came to an understanding. I brought you guns when you needed them because Paolo would do it for me. You, you're all strangers. Do you ask maybe I need something?'

'What do you want?'

'You think I like Germans or Germany?' he demanded. 'No, it's just business. I've got connections here ... they supply me with morphine base. Now what do I want? I want you, and your two other friends and the boys and the women to bring some to America if I can get you to France.'

'I thought you knew the guards.'

'I keep the wheels greased but I don't give guarantees. I see that they let you through, you take the base with you.'

'We'll do it,' Alex said.

Salica looked up. The truck engine sounded smoother.

'It was the plugs. Marc, please get a syringe and give the little girl a shot.'

Alex thrust his envelope on Bastia.

'Would you mail this for me?'

Bastia squinted at the address, then laughed. 'I'm a postman now ... You've got friends everywhere, Alex. You're a good man to know.'

The border was a half mile from the hotel and the truck lumbered slowly through the sleeping town. There was a light on at the wooden hut on the German side. A large sign advised them that they would be searched and that they required passports.

Alex reached over from the front seat and gripped Miriam's hands. They sat in silence. Marc left the cab and greeted the guards. Jonathan raised the canvas. The two guards were laughing as they shared a smutty joke with Marc. The guards shook their heads and everyone in the truck relaxed for a moment. Then they came toward the rear and shone their flashlights inside, holding them on each face. They returned to their hut and brought out a sheaf of papers which they flipped through.

Chou heard the guards squabbling. 'What's wrong, Marc?' she whispered out of the window.

'I don't know. They should have let us pass ... we agreed.'

'Papa, will they let us go?' David asked. He gripped hold of Jonathan when there was no response.

The guards signaled to Marc and he followed them into the hut. The door slammed. The long, warped wooden barrier rattled in the wind. Marc was the first to come out.

'They've got a photo of Alex sent out by the SS. They want to take him. They'll let the rest of you go through.'

'Alex, no,' Miriam cried.

Everyone in the car began to babble and shout.

'Damnit, keep quiet,' Paul said, climbing out of the back. 'Marc, do you think they know that we've got the bank money with us?'

'No. The price would have gone up. They're already talking about the promotions they'll get for capturing Alex.'

'Offer them my share,' Victor interjected.

'And mine,' Chou said.

'It's crazy,' Alex protested. 'You've got nothing. Take the

money and just let Miriam and the boys go with you. It's the only way.'

The guards spoke with Marc for a moment, then trailed him to the back of the truck. Salica tossed out two of the large bags stamped with the name München Bund Bank. Each of the guards seized hold of a sack. Straining, they lugged them into the hut and closed the door. The chill night air was sour with fumes from the barges spitting geysers of dense smoke, passing below the bridge.

'Let them take the money,' Chou said.

Miriam shivered and clung to Alex. Salica stood outside, jittery, cupping his hands over a match to light a cigarette.

It took them a moment to react when the barrier, whining on its wire cable, cranked slowly up. Bastia rushed to the cab and started the engine. He inched along the wooden bridge at five kilometers an hour. Tires thudded on the metal struts.

Jonathan sucked air, tasting it, savouring it. Money was the universal language. He had never actually understood its value, but it leveled all opposition, *bought* life. In all the excitement, the singing and the kissing, he moved closer to Lenore. Her eyes were open and he wanted her to rejoice with them. He squeezed her hands and whispered in her ear.

'We'll go out on a lake again – in our canoe ...' Held by the dumb, empty expression on her battered face, he released her. Her eyes closed.

He knew it would never again be the same with them.

BOOK TWO

Eleven

They had taken passage on a rotting freighter, the *Ile du-Rhône*, a listing tub out of Bordeaux moiled with rust, carrying a cargo of adulterated wine from the Dordogne as well as Bergerac tobacco which would be blended with Virginia into an aromatic pipe mixture favored by émigrés. Aboard ship Jonathan heard seamen play the harmonica, sing French bistro airs, and swear in a dozen languages. And once he had witnessed a grimy, coal-caked stoker take another passenger's wife in his arms.

He avoided Lenore, preferring to eat late at the greasy seamen's mess. Listening to their chatter, a babble of French patois, Italian, and English, he began to pick up words and expressions which he introduced to the others who struggled with their English grammars and phrase books. Mr. Creel, the second mate, a bald man in his forlorn sixties from London, was engaged as a tutor for a dollar a day, and when he was off duty, Jonathan would play chess with him, coaxing further hints on English pronunciation.

Yet the thought of Lenore never left him, and he would watch her sitting alone on a deck chair, her face in the sun, squinting into space or peering vacantly at the vast expanse of water while she fed oil-spotted birds of passage trailing the boat. She had ripened like a melon, seemed older, mature – he couldn't explain it – more composed than the Conte girls or even himself. She seemed to need neither stimulus nor human companionship.

One evening through the porthole he overheard some women discussing Lenore as they sat on deck. The word they used to describe her angered him.

Idiot . . . .

In the small close cabin he shared with David, he leaned down from the upper bunk.

'They'll have doctors in America to help her.'

'She'll never talk,' David observed with finality. 'That's what the French doctor said.'

'But it's impossible. She knows how to speak,' he protested. Her silence was monstrous, an affront to logic.

'Well, if you believe in miracles, anything can happen.' David checked a word in his pocket dictionary. 'English is crazy. "Steal ... Steel." Every other word sounds alike and you spell it differently. No masculine or feminine. It's all the same. Do you think Americans ever know what they're talking about?'

'She's not an idiot but a *victim*.' He sounded like a lawyer.

'What?'

'*Das Opfer* ... Mr. Creel explained it to me.'

'Jonathan, you worry too much. We're free from the Nazis. Does anything else matter?'

Money, of course, and it was an unending subject of speculation to the men. In the middle of a game of hearts, Sam would sullenly look up from his hand in consternation and ask his companions if he'd be better off looking for a boardinghouse outside of New York in a resort area or investing the two thousand dollars that he had in some city property. He always had a map at his elbow on which he made notations.

'Liberty, New York, has a musical sound, doesn't it, Alex? Nature, freedom, fruit trees. Lenore'll love the country.'

'Sam, *spiel*, please,' Victor, his patience warped by Sam's constant stalling, pleaded. 'And for Christ's sake, hold your cards away from Pauli.'

'You saying I'm looking at his hand?' Paul demanded.

'He's waving them in your face,' Alex returned.

'The man can't play. It's a good thing that just pennies are involved, ehhh? Chou, take my hand,' Paul said, getting up in disgust. 'I'm going for a walk. Three weeks on a boat ... To think that some Italians fish for a living.'

Sam immediately laid a heart on Chou's spade lead, compounding the injury of slow play by going void in hearts.

'What's got into Paul?' he asked. 'I need advice.'

'He's worried about customs,' Chou explained.

'But Mr. Buchalter said in his letter that he'd be able to fix things so that there won't be a search,' Victor said, paling. The prospect of being arrested on their arrival in New York gnawed at him; he dreamed often of being placed in leg irons by beefy policemen.

'Well, you know Pauli ... he doesn't trust people he

hasn't met,' she replied.

Alex raised his gnarled left fist and struck the air.

'Believe me, we can handle any trouble,' he assured them.

Visas had been arranged in France by an obliging sympathetic consulate in Bordeaux who carried out Roosevelt's policy of welcoming immigrants in flight from the Nazis provided they were not anarchists or Chinese. Yet it became apparent to Jonathan that some other force paved their way.

Money does not whisper, rather it emits a gargantuan bellow which even the dimmest immigration official can hear clearly. Thus, the stop at Ellis Island's way station went with unusual smoothness. While thousands queued on python-like lines, the fugitive bank robbers were treated like aristocracy. They had prudently decided to deposit their money – two thousand dollars was each man's share – while still in France in the Morgan Guaranty Bank as evidence of their solvency. Although such an act was antipathetic to Paul, he eventually succumbed to the blandishments of his partners in crime. He would case the bank as soon as he stepped on American soil. Wall Street, he had read, was filled with such institutions and he would, he told Chou, gather interest on his principal after a few weeks. A passbook would be a formidable instrument for entrée to vaults.

The women and children waited in an anteroom cooled by a fan. Their vaccination forms were found to be in order and all that was holding up the stamp of approval was one of those trivial disputes among the four men that the Italians regarded as a matter of honor and the Jews one of expediency.

'Mind your own goddamn business. It's my name and I can do what I like with it,' Alex told the indignant Italians.

'You're a traitor,' Salica howled.

'You're not going to be shipped to a pogrom,' Victor told Sam and Alex. 'It's a free country.'

'A Jew is always tainted. More Gentiles than Litvaks here,' Sam replied, turning fuchsia in the humid, windowless room of the inspector. 'Why do I have to spend my life in a new country with people pointing their fingers at me ... "He's *one* ..." They'll say, "West is a region." You can spell it, read it on a map. What kind of name is Salica in any case? It sounds like a sausage.'

'I'll die Salica.'

'And the Contes go back to the Rennaissance.'

'There was such a thing in Naples?' Alex asked half-humorously, since, he, too, had designs on a new name. 'I thought the Contes pissed on the streets and stole spaghetti from garbage cans. STONE. Not Stein, my friend. Americans only know from power. My boys have been insulted enough. Somebody at school will call them yids and we'll be back where we started from.'

'Don't do it, Alex,' Victor implored him.

'Why not?' Sam interjected. 'They're our names. I don't want to be reminded of the past, have people spit on my head. A Jew I'll always be, but West is geography. I embrace half of America.'

The inspector, his bald sweating forehead shielded by a green visor, lost his patience.

'I've got hundreds of people to see today. Now what the hell do I write on your entry cards?'

'West,' Sam answered.

Alex followed: 'Stone.'

'Your heritage!' Victor cried.

'Europe can keep it,' Alex responded.

Thus the Stones and Wests were officially born on Ellis Island while the city swooned under a broiling summer sun in late August.

*   *   *

Sandor Kofsky chomped on a cold liver knish which he had bought from a discount deli near the docks. His dull-brown, bloodshot eyes were, however, riveted on the pilgrim party disgorged from the Ellis Island ferry. A mistake might be fatal at this most important moment of assessment and he might pick out a group of *mockies* who would dray him around all day and pay him nothing. A dollar maybe, plus carfare, and that only after he'd rung his hands, shrieked curses at them, and told them that he was the father of two blind children, girls, identical twins, and that his wife was stricken with spinal tuberculosis which had passed to the lungs and now she was spitting blood. As for Kofsky himself, a burly chap of two hundred pounds, five six, his hair tangled, spiderweb fine, his stomach a roiling forty-four-inch balloon, his mustache graying at the edges and flecked with hardened bits of kasha, well, he'd already had three and a

138

half heart attacks, so what more could a cruel existence, the Furies, the dybbuks, hold in store for him? Just death and the prospect of leaving the widow to sell herself on the streets to a Nazi harem in Yorkville.

Hitching up his thick worsted trousers, then tightening the massive nodule of his Windsor knot, he crept forward during this urgent moment of *schmecking* out his party. A belch growled at the back of his throat and he pounced on Linda Conte.

'Shirley Temple,' he said, seizing the child's arm. 'I swear on my wife and the lives of my twin daughters. Such a *mitzvah* to meet you, Miss Temple.'

'He's crazy,' Tina barked. 'What's he talking about?' she asked Alex.

'Who knows?'

'Allow me, allow me, please, kindly a moment to make the proper introductions' – his eyes roved over them, all together, twelve, including the children – 'I am Sandor Kofsky, chairman and president, elected democratically, I might add, of the Williamsburg Greeters' Society and allied to the Brotherhood of Delancey Street Landsmen which embraces the nations of Poland, Rumania, Russia, Austria, Herzegovina also included, and provinces no longer found on the map and absorbed by Austro-Hungarian Empire, they should *plotz*, at your service.'

'We're from Naples and Munich,' Salica advised him.

'Give me a chance to finish, Signore ... Italy, its plains, islands, Corsica, Sicily, and its diaspora.' He already had four suitcases under his arms and was denouncing other greeters blocking his path. 'Not to mention, *mein leiben Herren*, Schleswig-Holstein, Greater Germany, Danzig, and the Sudetenland.'

'What are you doing with our things?' Sam asked.

Kofsky was humping the cases into the back of his Chevy jitney.

'I'm your guide to New York. Have you got an apartment, a hotel? Food for the children?'

'No, not yet, we just arrived,' Miriam admitted.

'That's why God' – Kofsky squinted at the celestial residence obscured by the sun – 'in his wisdom and charity appointed me to oversee your arrival and settling down. My purpose in life is to carry out his holy work.' Kofsky hustled them inside, heaved cartons on their laps, and handed out sacks of melting jelly beans and gumdrops to the children.

'Now where are we going?' Alex was growing alarmed.

'*Where* are we going? To your apartment, of course. First we'll stop at Katz's Delicatessen for lunch. The boychiks look like they're starving. Your friends, the Italians,' he hissed in his Balkan manner, 'I'll take to a pizzeria parlor, not for us that *chozzerai*. Pastrami on club and celery tonic, kishka that purifies the soul, French fries, latkes, now I'm talking. My mouth's watering already.'

In confusion, Alex joined the others on a jump seat, his knees were squashed, and he listened to Kofsky babble about connections he possessed to perform ceremonies in *Mikvahs* on untainted women, food and rent prices, crosses, watches, Stars of David, clothing, and furniture he had for sale.

On Eighth Avenue he made a frenzied U-turn and almost killed a mounted policeman's horse eating oats from a sack. He spat out venomous curses when the cop whistled him down and demanded his license.

The men listened with amazement as he reviled the cop, wished his family death from hernias.

'I'm on God's mission,' he screamed, 'escorting these people to their new homes after they escaped from the Nazis, and you've got the nerve to give me a ticket. Who told you to park a horse in the middle of the street? Since when did Eighth Avenue become a restaurant for *ferds*? Wait, wait, Mayor La Guardia will hear of this. This is not the end. Forget your dreams of being a detective, riding in a car. You'll be on that horse till your *kishkas* hang out for insulting Sandor Kofsky!' The cop never uttered a word but simply wrote the ticket and returned to his animal.

'You can speak to the police like that and not be arrested?' Victor said as they all buzzed about the argument.

'What, it's a free country and Sandor Kofsky is a citizen two years now. My money goes to pay that Irishman's beer bill. I smelled his breath. He was drunk, you all saw that. What can you expect from a man who rides a horse for a living and hands out tickets to respectable people? Commissioner Valentine gets my report.'

Kofsky drove like a man possessed, passing lights, narrowly missing pedestrians, honking furiously at any vehicle ahead of him. He stopped for a dollar's worth of gas which his clients advanced him.

'Fine, I like to know that I'm appreciated,' he said, grasping the bill from Sam's hand. 'Mechanic, check the oil while you're at it. Okay, another fifteen cents, Mr. West. Mechanic give me the bottle, not from the can,' he bawled. 'From the can I can't see what's pouring. Could be empty and I'll have another fire in the crankcase.'

They were on Delancey Street, which was choked with pushcarts and peddlers. At Katz's Delicatessen, he thrust his way ahead of others waiting and seized a table.

'My family just arrived from a year on the high seas, they're hungry,' he cried to meat slicers sweating over briskets. 'Immediate seating or, believe me, God will make a fire here.' He led his charges to a long table in the rear, pulled menus out of the waiter's hand, and stopped to argue with someone he claimed owed him a fortune. On his return, he presented his case to Salica. 'He owes me two hundred dollars for a fire I made.'

'What fire?'

'His furniture store was in trouble, so I got him insurance, then I made a fire, you could see it for six blocks. Four alarm.'

'If his store burned down,' Sam logically suggested, 'he has no business.'

'Before he had no business. Now he's got cash! Imagine, you do a favor for some people and they tell you to sue them.'

It was slowly becoming apparent to the men that they had fallen into the clutches of a lunatic. While Kofsky was arranging a takeout order to be charged to them, they agreed they would have to lay down the law to him. They had to keep the appointment arranged by Bastia. It was dangerous to continue walking around with the morphine base.

'Don't short-weight me, *gonif*,' Kofsky raged at the counterman.

'Could we have a word with you outside, sweetheart?' Salica asked, gripping him by the back of the neck.

'Anything you say, Signore.'

The frenzy of commerce charged unabated outside Katz's. Hawkers cawed demonically, offering services and goods ranging from knife sharpening to burial arrangements. Men wearing heavy sandwich boards lumbered forward, stricken by the heat. Beggars pleaded for pennies. Elbows resting on bedclothes and pillows, sucking in the fetid air, housewives haggled with pushcart vendors from open windows. Chicken flickers with Bunsen burners blistered their fingers as they scorched the *penkis* off defeathered chickens while feather collectors stuffed their sacks. Rabbis gloomily marched through the traffic in processions, wearing full black coats, pleading for alms, and warning of catastrophes to the ungenerous.

The alleyway beside Katz's was littered with rancid garbage which invalids flung from their kitchen windows. The pandemonium of humanity in search of survival set off fusillades of noise. Kofsky's mosaic of gold teeth formed a smile.

'Do I know, months on a boat, well, Kofsky understands. The Lord forgives these occasional transgressions. He's not always a God of wrath. Women ... ? A nickel a *shtikl*.'

Salica shoved him against the wall and the cowering greeter raised his arms defensively to ward off an anticipated blow.

'Listen, my friend, we got out of Germany when half the Gestapo were chasing us, so don't play games with us. You'll pay for the food you're taking with you. Lunch, you're our guest, understand? You find us a place to stay. The women and kids need some rest, then we have an address in Brooklyn to go to. You take us, you get paid. Fuck around with us and your twins'll be eatin your balls for dinner *Capische?*'

Kofsky nodded sulkily. The sussing-out process had not been successful, he told himself. Stick with his own kind and keep away from Italians. Murderers all of them.

'Landsmen and Signores, you misunderstand me –'

Alex pushed close to him and seized him by the windpipe.

'Do what the man asks, schmuck. Take somebody else for a ride. We're smarter than you.'

*   *   *

The families settled in two furnished apartments on the same floor on Havemeyer Street in Williamsburg. The Seamen's Bank was on the corner, a harbinger of good fortune in Salica's mind. Although the furniture was moth-eaten and tattered, reeking of camphor, the women were jubilant, and set upon the rooms in teams, scrubbing floors, walls, lining the cupboards with newspaper, and polishing the rickety bureaus and wardrobes.

Arriving with groceries, flanken, soup greens, and lima beans for dinner, Alex saw Miriam smile for the first time in months.

'It's home, Alex. Not perfect, but we can stop running,' she said, her face suffused with color. The Steins had agreed to share with Paul and Chou. Even though Lenore had not reacted to the change in surroundings, they all hoped that being close to the Conte girls might restore her confidence.

Cooking smells wafted strongly from the kitchen and the men all had a drink before they left for their appointment. Kofsky had grumblingly accepted five dollars for his services and was promised another five after he escorted them to the Parkway Cafeteria on Pitkin Avenue in the Brownsville section where the drop was to be made. He was shunted into the toilet while the morphine, still packed in its oilskin sheets, was transferred to a suitcase. Chou passed out revolvers, and when Victor shied away, she said, 'Just in case, Vittorio. Strangers, you never know ...'

'What's the fire that you got to go to on Pitkin Avenue five minutes you're off the boat?' Kofsky asked at an intersection.

'Business,' Salica replied, 'with a merchandise man named Mr. Louis Buchalter and his associates, Mr. Reles and Bugsy Siegel.'

Kofsky repeated the names silently a number of times like a hypnotic prayer in Hebrew, then stopped the car.

'Ho – no – my breath. I'm not breathing. I'm *chaloshing* ...'

'Fainting, why?' Alex inquired.

'No further,' he yelped. 'I'll call a cop. You're so lucky you met with Sandor Kofsky. On your knees you should fall to me, saving your lives. Lepke Buchalter. You visit him and nobody ever sees you again. Not even God. Merchandise business he's not in. The disappearing business is his *gescheft*. You don't read a *News* or *Mirror* a day goes by that they don't fish a body out of the river which Lepke, Reles, and the Italian Anastasia buried there.' He pointed at the cracked roads. 'The sidewalks and the gutters they can't fix in Brownsville because of all the concrete Lepke uses for his murders. Shoes he makes with them. The river's so bad you can't buy a piece of chicken carp that doesn't taste of cement. More bodies in there than fishes. You give a listen to Walter Winchell's radio program and you'll hear plenty. You want to live, use the mail with Mr. Lepke. Send him a package and no return address. That's twenty dollars' advice you got for nothing.'

Salica nodded thoughtfully and handed Kofsky a five-dollar bill.

'Keep talking,' he suggested, 'while you drive.'

'While I drive? You're on Saratoga and Pitkin. Take a walk ... stretch the sea legs from the ocean trip. It's a few blocks. You see blood on the sidewalks, follow it, and you'll find Abe Reles. Me, I'm going to Doc Gitlin for some bicarb and his son, the lawyer, for advice.'

'What's the story with Lepke and these people?' Sam asked.

'They stick together like *voncen*. Winchell calls them the Combination – Murder Incorporated. It's a business. Someone you don't like, you give Anastasia a call, he'll disappear them. For a hundred dollars, he'll kill the President. Every day Dewey, O'Dwyer, all of them are in the papers telling the public how many they killed for the week.'

'Then why haven't the police arrested them?' Alex inquired with astonishment.

'The cops is, first, ascared of them and, two, Lepke pays them off. Other day, right in the middle of Seventh Avenue and Thirty-eighth Street, Lepke threw acid into a big manufacturer's face. Five hundred witnesses, nobody saw who did it. Lepke's picture is in the newspaper in the centerfold of the *Mirror*, smiling, his silk shirt shining, and the manufacturer lays like a dog in the gutter. Smart you think you are, well, my clients, I'd go back to the Nazis if I was you. Don't play with Lepke. He doesn't know from *chachmas*, believe you me ...'

'If you're afraid to drive up, then wait here on the corner,' Sam, emboldened, advised him. He leaned out of the window. 'Hopkinson Avenue. It's another ten dollars. Eat a piece of kishka and purify your soul, my friend.'

'Sacrifices I make for my family,' Kofsky cried, reaching into the bag beside him.

* * *

144

Although every cop in New York theoretically pursued Lepke for having jumped bail on an extortion charge, he calmly sat with his colleagues in the Parkway Cafeteria nibbling on an appetizer of brains, chopped liver, swamped in chicken fat, radish, and onions. Squat and jowly, his dark eyes were unforgiving and rancorous. On the back of one of the Wanted posters sent out with his photograph, Lepke was scribbling a series of demands that he expected his associates to enforce. He had the sensibility of a tiresome accountant and the manners of a freeloader.

At his table sat Abe Reles, beetle-browed and unsmiling, biting the skin around his nails so that his fingers appeared uniformly flesh raw. Beside him Bugsy Siegel, in a silky gray mohair suit, nervously pecked at his watch and worried about the trousers creasing. He was late for a date. Stirring his coffee was Charlie Workman, the doe-eyed killer who had followed Dutch Schultz into the men's room of the Palace Chop House and shot him in the back of the head while he was at the urinal. Charlie's spiky hair stood up, resembling the antennae of a hungry grasshopper. Rounding out the quartet was Lepke's closest friend, Albert Anastasia, heavyset, his thick features doughlike as pasta, his ears the size of turnips. He'd caught a case of crabs the previous week and he scratched his balls reflexively.

When the four shabbily dressed foreigners entered the cafeteria and looked around the tables, Lepke rose and motioned to them. Salica, carrying himself erect and dignified, was the first to reach the table. Lepke introduced himself and his confederates.

'Mr. Buchalter, I am Paul Salica and these are my friends. Can we discuss our business privately?' His manner was courteous but firm.

'Let's go for a walk,' Lepke replied. 'My head's fuckin splitting.'

The two groups eyed each other suspiciously and jockeyed for close position behind their principals when they left the cafeteria. Salica, almost a head taller than Lepke, ambled lazily, studying the area, and forced Lepke and Siegel to slow down and keep pace with him.

Pressed for time, Siegel grew irritable. He didn't like the look of this deliberate Italian with his arrogant smile.

'Let's go, Salica,' he said, 'hand over the merchandise.'

'*Lento*,' Paul replied. 'We went to a great deal of trouble.'

'What's this bullshit?' Siegel exploded.

'Relax, Bugsy. Give the man a chance.' Lepke resented the fact that Siegel had the run of the city while he was skulking from one hideout to another.

'Mr. Buchalter, my friends and I need your help and guidance. We came straight from the boat and we have no money —'

'Are you trying to badger us?' Siegel asked.

'I don't know what you're talking about,' Salica replied, scowling at Siegel. 'What business have you with this?'

'He's my associate.'

'Well, he should know that we brought four million in morphine and nothing has been touched from the shipment. It was very risky.'

'Listen, enough with the stories,' Siegel said.

'How much money do you want?' Lepke asked.

Paul thought of an enormous figure.

'Ten thousand dollars,' he said, extending his hands in supplication. 'We're poor immigrants.'

'This I don't believe,' Siegel cut in. 'A dumb, greasy wop like you trying to juice us. You can get your head opened in five seconds.'

Salica ignored him and continued to stroll with Lepke, taking in the surroundings and conscious of the men following him. 'Bugsy, give him ten Gs.'

'Like hell, Lep. How can you let this cocksucker pull a number like that on you?' Lepke's face remained stolid and ultimately Siegel yielded and counted out ten thousand-dollar bills.

'Thank you, Mr Buchalter. You're a generous man. Mare Bastia told me that we would find you accommodating. Now can I ask your valuable advice? I have connections in California and I thought that would be a good place to set up a business.'

'What kind of business?' Lepke asked. He was enjoying playing the two men off against each other.

'It's something like yours . . . on a smaller scale of course.'

'That's Bugsy's territory.'

'Perhaps we can share it,' Paul insisted. 'I'm willing to reach an agreement.'

'It's closed, guinea,' Siegel snapped. 'Man, either you're

just plain dumb or you want to get iced.'

'I think you better stay out of the West Coast,' Lepke said. He had not collected his narcotics and he sensed that the two men might go for each other at any moment. 'Miami's a free city. Just a few Cuban locals and they're not wired to us in any way.'

'Thank you. If I need any assistance, can I discuss it with you?'

'Sure.'

They were beside Kofsky's jitney and the greeter dropped the hunk of salami he was munching and placed his hands on his chest when Lepke's piercing eyes fixed on him.

'Heart attack number four!' he groaned.

Paul opened the rear door and pulled out the suitcase which he handed to Lepke.

'Now, *paisan*,' Siegel began, 'what's to stop us from welching on you?'

'Your employer is a man of his word. If I had to deal with you, I would have used this.' Before Siegel could react, Paul had his revolver out and held it against Siegel's head, then with a casual smile, he put it back in his pocket. 'You're very bad mannered. If I were you, I'd learn some respect, especially with a stranger.'

'You got a point there, Paul, and for a greenhorn, you got the balls of a burglar,' Lepke said with admiration. 'When you hit Miami you might want to shoot over to Havana. An associate of mine runs the Nacional Hotel. His name's Meyer Lansky.'

Paul grasped Lepke's hand. 'One question . . .'

'What's that?' Lepke asked expansively, his good humor restored by the fortune in narcotics he would soon distribute through the city.

'In my country, men like ourselves live quietly, obscurely. In New York everyone knows about you.'

Lepke grinned like an adolescent.

'I'm a star. My name's in the papers and on the radio every day.'

'I know that, but is it a good thing? It would worry me.'

147

Twelve

It was inevitable that the families would separate. For weeks they had been living in each other's pockets, and in spite of the affection they all felt, the four men began to grow uneasy with their living conditions and progress. Petty quarrels broke out among the women about who would cook and clean and were relayed to the men who were struggling to find out how they could establish themselves in their giant new country.

At the end of September, Sam had to make a decision. The city oppressed him, subways made him nauseous, and the assortment of doctors and hospitals he visited with Lenore offered sympathetic interviews but no hope of a cure. The girl was in deep shock and might remain in this suspended state for the rest of her life. He no longer attempted to communicate with the child, merely coddled her, kissed her, fed her, and cherished her. Institutions and sanitoriums were recommended, but that would mean giving her up to strangers. Various charitable refugee organizations offered to take her in, but he realized that this would be tantamount to abandoning her.

After an examination by a psychiatrist at Bellevue Hospital, he learned that her condition was becoming more serious each day.

'What if we got out of the city and lived in the country?' he had asked.

'It's worth trying,' the doctor replied. 'It might just be that living with your friends reminds her of what happened. Neither she nor they realize that it's happening, but a mechanism is set off and she can't control it. She's got a deep psychic wound and since you're not prepared to institutionalize her, then make the break.'

Sam hastened back to the apartment to tell the others of his decision. He found Chou packing. Salica was on the telephone. It was Chou's turn to make dinner, and Sam dreaded this rotation system the women had agreed upon since Chou merely flung hot dogs into a pot of boiling water

148

until they split and shrank.

'Are you going, too?' he asked with relief, since he did not want to take responsibility for breaking up the union that had been formed.

'I'm afraid it's time,' Chou replied distantly. 'I like Tina and Miriam, but I'm not a housewife. We upset them. Whenever they want to clean, Pauli's sleeping, and they complain that he's holding up the housework.'

'He keeps late hours,' Sam said.

'He's a criminal. How can he live a normal life? He's up half the night stealing.'

'Unfortunately, that's true.'

'Nothing unfortunate about it. You've all got an extra two and a half thousand because he stood up to Lepke. Accept him for what he is.'

'If not for Paul, we'd be dead.'

'What about us? Listen, Sam, we'll always be friends in good and bad times. We just can't live together.'

'I know that. It's funny that being in a free country makes us all so different.'

'That's why we came here, Sam,' Paul said, still unshaved and walking around in his underwear. He looked with affection at Sam. 'I just got Chou and me train tickets to Miami.'

She was exhilarated and embraced him.

'When do we leave?'

'I'll pick up the tickets tonight at Umberto's Clam House.'

'Not the station?' Sam inquired.

'No ... they belong to a guy who had his last steam bath and someone's delivering them to me.'

'A dead man's tickets?'

'Well, he's not going to use them. He owed money and he was late once too often.'

His casual attitude toward life and death horrified Sam. In their flight from Munich, there was a justification for killing. It was a matter of survival. But ... in the United States, a democratic society with no secret police, no army persecuting them, wasn't it wrong and willful to bilk innocent people? The new nation which had accepted them all deserved better treatment.

'Why're you giving me such a funny look, Sam?'

'Was I? Lots of things on my mind. I suppose I'm upset that I'm not getting anywhere in the city. All I've seen were

149

small hotels and boardinghouses that have been foreclosed
... nobody can afford to pay for a room.'

Lenore sat listlessly staring out of the window. Chou
picked up a hairbrush and ran it through the girl's hair. She
was precious to Chou.

'Are you going to leave?' Salica asked from the bathroom
while he finished shaving.

'I've been thinking about it. I want to visit the Catskill
Mountains and look around up there. It's a vacation place.'
He shrugged apathetically. 'Maybe I can find what I'm looking for there. When we got here I felt there was a chance the
doctors might be able to help Lenore. But I've been told
wherever I take her won't matter.'

'Get yourself a good woman,' Salica advised him, parting
his hair a la Valentino. Chou handed him the trousers she
had just pressed. He examined his shirt for creases, then put
it on. Why, Sam wondered, did Paul take such elaborate
pains with his toilet and clothes? Who did he see apart
from other thieves?

'What have I got to offer a woman?' Sam asked.

'You're an attractive man; don't sell yourself short. Some
woman'll grab you,' Chou said.

'You'll wake up one morning and Lenore'll be herself,'
Paul added hopefully.

'I don't believe that. If I did, I'd drive myself crazy. I
accept ...'

They sat at the kitchen table and Sam poured himself a
glass of strong tea. He sucked on a piece of lump sugar
while drinking it. Salica mixed himself a strange concoction
known as a Manhattan which he had grown fond of. More
than any of the others, Salica had adapted himself to the
American way of life, following baseball, attending movies.
He mourned the death of Jean Harlow and demanded that
Chou bleach her hair platinum. He himself became a fashion
plate, wore shoulder-padded, broadly striped, double-
breasted George Raft suits which he filched at Howard
Clothes Stores. He adjusted the snub-nosed .38 in the shoulder holster he habitually carried. Salica, the American.

'I hope you don't mind me speaking my mind ...' Sam
began. The intensity of their gaze disconcerted him. They
both possessed that reckless sensitivity to criticism fostered
by being outside society and beyond the law.

'Well, what is it?' Paul said harshly.

'There's a lot of good in the two of you, don't spoil it. America's your parent, don't treat her like a victim. You've got a new start here, no problems with the police. Don't dirty your hands with dope and robbery.'

'Ehhh, Sam, what's so hard to understand that not everybody is like you? I don't want a job or a business working year in and out for what? Money? Well, Chou and me'll make money, lots of it. Lepke's been a friend to me. Giving me introductions to people. I'm in his business, for Christ sake. Now's the time for me to make my move in a new territory. I mean, what would you like to do, pass a law against people like us? But what does it mean? I'm an outlaw ... I'm free –'

'And the gun you carry?'

'That guarantees that nobody takes my freedom from me. Come on, Chou, throw on a dress and let's go get our tickets.'

Sam rested his head in his hands. Why couldn't he get through to them?

'I haven't explained what I mean and you're angry with me.'

'Angry, no,' Chou replied. 'We just can't hear you.'

* * *

Alex was beginning to discover, much to the torment of his thin-soled sneakers, the sprawl of Brooklyn. His mastery of buses, subways, trolleys and the transfer system had been achieved with the assistance of Jonathan, who developed a profound skill at screaming, 'I'm lost, help me!' whenever they entered a public conveyance, which enabled Alex to slip through turnstiles and wait with arms open to receive the despondent boy. So far so good, they had never been caught. A nickel saved meant a juicy five-cent hot dog at the Nedick's stands and an orangeade which the two shared.

Frum Bushwick to Bensonhurst from Flatbush to Coney Island, the boy and his father scoured for a location for a gym. Alex was determined to establish himself as a matchmaker. They found church halls that were too narrow, armories too large, and Knights of Pythias sanctums too holy to be given over for use as a gym. They visited Stillman's Gym and Alex spoke to fighters who traveled from all of the five boroughs to work out there. Alex would have fighters lining up around the block to use his facilities if he could just find the right place.

They followed up newspaper leads to dank lofts, and finally when they had run out of patience, they came upon an American Legion Post which was moving to larger headquarters. Alex did not much like the area, a junction at Saratoga Avenue and Eastern Parkway, since it was on the perimeter of Brownsville, and he was afraid that it would attract the hoodlums he had met on his arrival. It would also mean moving from Williamsburg, and he had grown fond of the area.

But the moment the real-estate broker turned on the lights in the hall, Alex had a feeling of exaltation. There were benches, hundreds of wooden fold-up chairs, the lighting was excellent – which would save him money on fixtures – and there was a kitchen and a large bathroom. He could install showers and lockers in the storage area and he could rearrange the seats and buy a secondhand twenty-by-twenty ring at an auction.

'How long has it been on the market?' he asked.

'A few months,' the broker replied. 'I've got a funeral chap interested in it.'

'What kind of rent are you asking?'

'One-fifty a month on a ten-year lease.'

'That's high,' Alex said, mentally working out a layout which would be similar to the one he had in Munich. The concrete posts could support heavy bags and the floor was tongue-and-groove. He wet his finger and cleared the dust on a floorboard. It would take a marine varnish that would prevent slipping.

'Would you take a hundred and a percentage?'

'You're breaking my scullions.'

'Well, should it be a funeral parlor or a place where athletes can work out?'

'The owner doesn't give a shit if it's a morgue.'

'That business is pretty popular in this neighborhood.'

Jonathan whispered to his father.

'Papa, with the kitchen here you could get someone in to make sandwiches and meals for the fighters so they don't have to go out to eat.'

Alex touched his face affectionately. The boy had a point, and Alex had grown to respect his instinct. Through the window Jonathan watched the foot traffic. Hundreds of people passed by every minute and the sidewalk was so crowded that people walked in the road and dodged cars. If only his father could think of something to sell that they wanted, they'd be rich overnight. But he couldn't imagine his father running a store.

'One twenty-five,' Alex offered.

'Okay, first and last month's rent and a month's security. That's three seventy-five.'

Alex pondered. It was an enormous sum and he'd have to invest money in equipment and work out time payments. Carpenters and painters would have to be hired. He saw his small stake vanishing, himself destitute in this strange country.

Jonathan tugged at his sleeve as he wandered indecisively around the empty hall.

'It's the best one we've seen, Papa. Take it before someone else does.'

What made the child so sure that he would succeed? Could he see something that escaped Alex's notice? The idea of selling food to the fighters was a good one. Miriam could come in and prepare sandwiches. He'd have soft drinks and juices in a cooler. There'd be a profit in that. Why was he hesitating? If only he could discuss it with someone who could give him sound advice, but neither Victor nor Sam understood his business.

His voice quavered when he said, 'Okay, I'll sign the lease.'

Jonathan leaped into his arms and kissed him.

'What do you want it to read?' the broker asked.

'Stone's Sporting Club.'

He stood in a daze outside, staring at the redbricked building. People hurtled past him, rushing back to their offices and stores.

'If they were fighters, business would be wonderful,' he told his son.

'Maybe they'll want to watch them train ... and you could charge a nickel for them to get in.'

'That's crazy. Who's interested in fighters? It's boring unless you're in the business.'

'It's not boring when they fight. People pay for tickets and come from everywhere.'

'Jonathan, you're too young to understand. They only

153

come when there's a boxing card. The gym is for training.'

'Does it have to be? Can't you get some of them to fight?'

'Everything he thinks he knows,' he said fondly. 'The problem is you have to be a promotor, and I've had no experience.'

'You're a smart man, Papa ... you'll learn if you want to.'

Alex could not explain the thrust of confidence he felt when he looked at the smiling boy tightly grasping his hand.

*   *   *

Victor knew he was through with nightclub business. It was far too complicated in New York, requiring a liquor and cabaret license, and as a foreigner he could not qualify for them. Furthermore, the financial investment was beyond him. Besides, he was fed up with running a club; he longed for a life which would ensure him greater regularity.

He had gravitated to the musicians' union and spent most of his time sitting in the Automat around the corner gossiping with them and listening to their endless complaints about crooked bookers and indolent agents. He had bought *Variety* each week and studiously examined all of the ads for performers. He noticed the vaudeville calls for novelty and specialty acts week by week. The circuits seemed not to be able to get enough child performers and magicians. Every booker was searching for another Shirley Temple or a Jackie Coogan. And so he had come up with his idea.

His had always been a musical family. He, Tina, and the girls all sang and played the piano, and little Linda had an especially fine melodic voice. If they could form some-kind of family singing act they could play theaters throughout the country.

Tina was bringing the children after school for an audition he had arranged with a booker for the Orpheum Circuit. Victor anxiously waited outside the Automat for them, listening to the chatter of the musicians loitering at the entrance. Jimmy Petrillo, the head of their union, had told them that one day they would get royalties for music on records and radio plays. It struck most of them as fantastic, but Victor listened carefully at the meetings Petrillo spoke at. Why should the stations and record companies have a license to print money at the expense of musicians and performers? The public paid for records and sheet music. It was unfair for the stations to play popular music hundreds of times without compensating the performers. The suggestion touched a deep chord in Victor's mind and he believed he saw a way of protecting the performers. If initial contracts with publishers and record companies signed by performers demanded a royalty, then the companies would naturally pass on the buck to the networks and their affiliates.

The girls appeared and ran to him. They were dressed in matching yellow tulle dresses with flounced hems, stiff petticoats, and shiny patent leather Mary Jane shoes. Tina had on a dark brown gown, and she carried a rented midnight-blue tuxedo for Victor and black pumps. Boldly he hailed a taxi. A subway ride would leave them with soot on their clothes. Besides, the heavy humidity threatened rain.

'Don't be nervous,' he advised them. He himself experienced flutters.

'They'll be fine,' Tina replied.

'Papa, on the *Barber of Seville* chorus,' Georgie began, 'you start a little too soon and it throws us off.'

'Oh, I've got a music critic here . . .'

'She's right,' Linda agreed. Her dark brown eyes were serious and her attitude wonderfully professional for a child of eight. 'If Mama gives us all a cue at the piano, we won't come in late.'

'I'm the conductor,' he observed defensively. 'Now, we'll begin with the Schubert lieder and then move on to Rossini. Georgie will introduce the selection in German and, Linda, you translate it to English. And with the *Barber* we'll reverse it, with Linda speaking Italian and Georgie in English.'

'I don't see why,' Tina said.

'Why? I'm the impresario . . . it's what they call a gimmick, a novelty that two little girls can speak three languages. Americans are always amazed when children can use a foreign language. Especially the Irish, and they're the most dedicated fans for singers . . .'

The audition was to be held in a skyscraper on Broadway and Fortieth Street. Victor slipped into the men's room to change his clothes and a few moments later he emerged resplendent and commanding in his tuxedo.

'Now when your mother and I sing the duet from *Aïda*, don't drown out your mother in the harmony. No high notes, Linda, okay?'

The Contes presented themselves in a stark office with a few stools, and an elderly piano presided over by Phil Parks, a balding, gaunt man with hollow eyes and brown pouches. He drank milk mixed with Scotch, smoked his cigarette down to the nub, and waved his nicotine-stained fingers by way of greeting to Victor. They had met at the union hall and Victor had told him about the family quartet.

He nodded lugubriously to Victor.

'I just had to get rid of Nero. I hate firing, but dogs and magic don't mix,' Parks said dolefully.

'What happened?' Victor courteously inquired.

'The dogs jumped off the ramp while Nero was pulling a hankie out of his ear and one of 'em ran into the audience and bit a lawyer. We got a lawsuit with so many zeroes in it that I'm dizzy.' He eyed the children suspiciously. 'They don't got any hamsters or mice?'

'We're singers, not animal trainers.'

'Nero's dead in the business. Exiled ... Maybe he can find work in South America.'

'Where was he working?'

'The Orpheum in Philly.'

'You have an opening?'

'If you can sing, you'll have his spot from there to the Coast.'

Victor raised his hands. The impresario was about to go to work. Tina tinkled at the piano, found a problem, and pumped the pedals furiously.

'The E's flat and there's a dead G,' she noted plaintively.

'Don't worry about the piano,' Phil said, grimacing at one of the poky windows behind him. In the airless room, the Contes went through their repertoire. They roved from Rossini to Puccini, airs from Schubert, a rendition of 'Irish Eyes Are Smiling.' After thirty minutes they were sweating and waiting for some response from the despondent booker.

'I can see that you're quite taken with us,' Victor began confidently.

'I'm thinking,' Phil replied. 'Something's missing.'

'What's missing ... a seal?'

'No, a seal won't work, but it's not a bad idea. I never heard of one that bit.'

'Then what?' Tina asked. 'I assure you that I play the piano a lot better than this.'

'Piano's fine. A twist, a highlight, a specialty. Can the kids stand on their heads?'

'No, absolutely not,' Victor said furiously.

'All Italians can do somersaults and walk on wires,' he informed them.

'We can't.'

Pensively Phil topped up his milk with a slug of Scotch.

'I've got it!'

'What?'

'Hoops.'

'What are hoops?' Tina asked.

'Wooden hoops. Let the girls wiggle wooden hoops around their hips while they sing.' He got up, shook Victor's hand, and congratulated him.

'You're in business. Sixty a week and expenses.'

'Impossible,' Victor replied. He signaled to his women to leave. 'Insulting.'

'That's top dollar for a new act.'

'Phil, thanks for your offer, but we've got another audition with Loew's at five.'

'Seventy-five.'

'Eighty. And we keep any record rights and you get only ten percent if we do radio on the tour. If the act is a success we move up to a hundred by the time we get to Chicago.'

'They'll fire me!'

'Well, go to South America with Nero.'

'You're unreasonable. We're taking a chance.'

'So are we. Where are you going to find two Shirley Temples?'

'They're nothing like her.'

'They sing and dance.'

'They ain't in the movies.'

'They will be.'

'You're all alike, you Italians. You, Petrillo, and the rest. You're killing us.'

Victor bowed and told Tina to pack the music. Phil followed them to the elevator.

'Okay, you catch the train to Philly tomorrow morning.

'We get on the train when we sign the contract.'

'I'll be out on the street.'

'When you have the contract, make sure that there's a ten-week guarantee even if you cancel.'

157

'You're worse than an agent.'

Victor nodded.

'I hope so.'

*　　*　　*

Fueled by enthusiasm for the future, the families had agreed to dine out on their last evening together. They settled on the Kaiser Hof, a German émigré restaurant on Eighty-sixth Street in the heart of Yorkville.

They rode the trolley across the Williamsburg Bridge. The children rushed up and down the aisle, elated by a dinner out in a real restaurant with their parents. Lenore joined in the game and Jonathan studied her in the midst of it. She was robotlike, a doll which had been wound up and responded automatically. Sam, too, watched her and called Alex's attention to what he considered this remarkable display of animation. Alex was convinced that she would eventually recover.

'Doctors don't know everything. When you're living in the country away from all this noise and dirt, she'll be better off.'

'We'll keep in touch, won't we, Alex?'

He grasped Sam's hand and held in firmly.

'Of course ... We'll come to visit and there'll be times when you'll want to get away and come to the city.'

'I can't believe we're not going to see each other after tonight,' Tina said. The pain of separation was intolerable. Could she ever feel such a close attachment to people again?

Victor leaned over and kissed her on the cheek.

'No regrets, Tina. We're starting over and the traveling won't last forever.'

'Couldn't you and Alex or Sam work together?'

'No, we're too different. I'm not interested in a hotel or spending my life in a gym.'

'Then what are you interested in?'

'Money ... a position of respect. I've got ideas, so trust me. I'm still learning the business. ... The theater, vaudeville, music ... something's missing from it. People here don't really know what they're doing. It's hit-and-miss. The booker who hired us could never work for me.'

'You're working for him,' she said.

'Now I am. But it's not forever. Everybody I've met connected with the business is a greasy slob. There's room for a gentleman, but first I have to learn the tricks.'

It was dusk when they reached Yorkville. The German signs, the delicatessens with familiar food displayed in windows, touched off a yearning for the Germany they had fled. Even the people trooping past them looked German. The language was spoken in the streets, Sam noted with excitement. The butchers carried goose, ham hocks, sides of Westphalian ham, bratwursts. Pennants advertised a local Oktoberfest ... 'Bockbier from Munich.' Shop windows carried placards of the Hamburg Bremen Line and gave the dates of voyages.

Only Salica was ill at ease and irritable.

'I would've preferred Umberto's downtown,' he told Chou.

'It's majority rule, Paul. Just one more night.'

'I know, but these drunkards coming out of the bars don't look any different from the Nazis.'

'Don't spoil it for the others.'

'Why would they want to come back here and be reminded ...?'

'It's a sentimental evening.'

'I don't see how people can be sentimental about concentration camps.'

The Kaiser Hof bar was crowded with beer drinkers who were volubly discussing Hitler's blitzkrieg in the Sudetenland. Alex walked by quickly, afraid that he would hear something that would upset him and culminate in an argument. After all, he was in a free country. People could say or think what they pleased.

The headwaiter escorted the party to the dining room and two busboys shunted together some tables on a raised level overlooking the dance floor. Musicians dressed in lederhosen were enthusiastically playing a medley of polkas. Dancers, sweating already, thumped energetically to the music. Waiters bustled by with trays filled with large steins of beer. On the wall were washed-out pastoral murals of the German countryside peopled with shepherds and blond milkmaids.

'It's *gemütlich*,' Miriam said, coaxing Alex to the dance floor. David took turns dancing with Georgie and Linda and Victor asked for bottles of Liebfraumilch to be chilled and ordered a round of Dortmunders for the men and Cherry Heering for the women. When the music slowed to waltz-

159

time, he led Tina from the table, wrapped his arms around her, and gracefully swirled her through a series of waltzes. The waiter brought hors d'oeuvres, trays of klops, rollmops, and Bismarck herring in a mustard sauce.

Jonathan and Lenore had been standing by the bandstand watching the dancers. He held her hand and swayed with her to the music.

'You're not an idiot,' he whispered. 'In a little while, you'll be yourself again.'

Unendurable, the thought of her leaving, but there was nothing he could do. Thwarted by his reliance on adults, he had no idea how he could see her again. He held her close, barely moving to the music, and her body seemed welded to his. There was no response, and he could detect nothing more than a dreamy, vacuous expression on her face. Yet he was convinced that she understood him.

A hand pushed him away from her. Georgie seized hold of him.

'Dance with me, Jonathan. I'm better than Lenore.' Before he could break away, she had her arms wrapped around his waist and was whirling him around the floor while Lenore stood in the corner motionless and unaware of what had occurred.

'Please, I don't want to dance.'

'But Lenore's no fun.'

'I can't just leave her there.'

'Why not? She'll be fine. We can see her.'

Reluctantly he let Georgie lead him around the floor, and he waited for her to tire, but she was inexhaustible. He kept an eye on Lenore over Georgie's shoulder and suffered because Georgie had eaten herring and onion and her breath was rank. Georgie chattered about the train trip to Philadelphia and how she and Linda were eventually going to be in the movies. She was full of herself and he found her tiresome, a braggart filled with self-importance.

'Ask David to dance,' he said finally, breaking away from her.

'David's eating.'

'I don't care.' He turned his back on her and retrieved Lenore who had not moved.

Paul excused himself from the table. He looked at his

watch. It was eight fifteen. He slipped through the customers lining up at the doorway and jumped into a cab parked at the curb. If things went on schedule he'd be back in less than half an hour.

'First Avenue and Sixty-fifth Street,' he said.

The cab caught every red light and Paul became edgy. The trip had taken fifteen minutes. He was dropped at the corner and walked to a dark blue Chevy parked on the corner. He got into the back seat.

Paul had met Happy Maione and his partner, Frank 'The Dasher' Abbandando that afternoon at the Luxor Baths. The Dasher was an acid thrower and stinkbomb specialist who had developed a talent for outrunning his pursuers.

'Where the fuck you been?' Happy asked.

'Traffic.'

'Bugsy didn't think you'd show.'

'Was it his idea for me to do this?'

'Yeah,' Happy replied. 'He don't think you're for real. You got a pick or a sticker?'

'No, my gun.'

'Paul, we don't wake up no neighborhood. This ain't Brooklyn, so we don't use heat.'

He handed Paul an ice pick.

They left the car and walked toward the candy store where George 'Whitey' Rudnick, one of Lepke's loan sharks, sat on a stool, scanning the early *Daily News*.

'Why does Lep want him taken out?'

'Whitey's a bad adder. He's been shorting Lep,' The Dasher explained. 'Paul, you bop the candy store man soon's we walk in.'

As they entered the store the owner was stooped over a pile of magazines he was sorting on the steps of the storeroom. Paul quickly slammed him across the back of the neck with the butt of his .38.

Before Whitey could make a move, Happy whipped a garotte around his throat and The Dasher was stabbing him in the neck and chest with the ice pick.

'You don't know arithmetic,' Happy was shouting. 'You make minus signs when they should be pluses, scumbag.'

The Dasher broke the ice pick and reached for a switchblade which he jabbed into the dying man's stomach.

'He don't like dying,' Happy said, crushing his windpipe

with the wire.

Rudnick was released and his legs twisted off the counter seat. His face was bloated and he fell against a stack of *Liberty* magazines. Happy wiped his hands with a counter rag then handed it to The Dasher.

'See the way it works, Paul. Nice and quiet and clean. We walk to the car like gentlemen. No cops or sirens and no neighbors sticking their heads out of the window because they think they heard a "boom-boom." '

It was nine by the time Salica returned to the restaurant. He found Chou standing at the table, searching the sea of faces.

'Are you okay, Paul? I was worried about you.'

'I just had to get a little fresh air.'

'Sam ordered a schnitzel for you. If you want something else one of the kids can eat it.'

'Schnitzel's fine,' he said, wiping the sweat beads off his forehead with the back of his hand. He was unhappy with the part he had played in the murder of a stranger. But it had been necessary to prove himself to Lepke and Anastasia. He needed their support in Florida. They were his sponsors in the Combination, against Siegel's wishes.

'Pauli, where'd you go?'

'Don't ask.'

'A contract?' She glared at him. 'Why?' She turned away from him, hurt and deceived.

'Chou, I had to make my bones again.'

He unloosened his tie and stared at his dinner. He had no appetite.

'I'm not important enough to be taken on trust.' His dark eyes moved restlessly over her face. 'Not yet.'

'We'll take a few banks in Florida, then they'll respect you.'

'Chou, that's finished,' he said patiently. 'You don't understand. That's for strong-arm *balordos*. I want to run a business. Banks ... I want them to be my friends ... to lend me money. You steal from one of them and Hoover's agents spend years looking for you. No, I don't need that. They don't know I exist ... I keep it that way.' He paused and reflected for a moment. 'The boss is Luciano and he is in prison. But there's one man Luciano trusts, a smart Jew who runs his finances. Lansky ...'

Empty bottles of wine formed a locus at the center of the table. The men had been talking in raised, ebullient voices about their future plans. Sam tipsily walked through the aisle, a beatific smile on his face, and bowed to Chou.

'With the permission of your man, may I have this dance?'

'You attract dancers, eh, Chou?' Salica said with a loud laugh.

'It's been a long time. I might be a little rusty,' Sam apologized as she followed him. He placed his hand around her waist and felt her cool fingers resting on his neck. Eyes closed, he led her smoothly in the waltz. 'The Blue Danube' was one of his favorites. He and Judith had danced to it at their wedding.

'It's a good feeling to be holding a woman again.'

Chou smiled. 'I thought it was against your religion.'

'When I lost my wife, I thought it would be disloyal to her memory to go out with other women.'

'That's when you started to die,' she said.

'I realize that now. It's a new life in a new country. I don't want to think about what happened.'

'That's the right idea.'

'I won't offend you if I tell you something?' She nodded. 'You smell good.'

'You're an attractive man,' she said fondly, kissing him.

'Chou, you tell Paul that I didn't mean to preach to you the other day. You're both very precious to me and I don't like to think that you'll ever be in trouble.'

She turned her head to the direction of the bar. A group of rowdies splashing their steins of beer barreled through the dance floor, jostling people. They were hoarsely chanting 'Sieg Heil ...' A red-faced, thin man wearing a striped polo shirt raised his hands. The musicians stopped. Sam opened his eyes and saw the man wrest the microphone away from the band leader. Sam blinked nervously. The man had swastikas tattooed on his arms. He bellowed over the microphone.

'Bundists and fellow Nazis, now is the time to demonstrate against the Jew-lover Roosevelt who has insulted our Führer by condemning his take-over against the criminal Czechs.' The men with him spontaneously began to sing 'Deutschland, Deutschland, über alles.'

Sam broke away from Chou, rushed to a table, pulled a bottle of wine out of an ice bucket, and leaped onto the platform. He slammed the wine bottle over the head of the Bundist at the microphone. Alex and Salica darted from the table and climbed to the bandstand. Women caught in the crossfire of fists and bottles shrieked for help. Sam had his opponent pinned to the floor and was choking him. Victor yanked him off.

'Let me kill him,' Sam protested. He struggled free from Victor.

Sam was hit from behind by someone and he rolled to the floor. As he was about to be stomped, Alex got to his assailant and struck him with a solid punch in the eye, then he helped Sam to his feet.

'Come on, let's get the hell out of here.'

Salica signaled to the women and children, pushed them out a rear fire door to the alley, then returned to look for the others. Sam had again climbed to the bandstand and was still swinging wildly. He was lacerated and he was being pounded by a Bundist. Salica stepped between them and held his .38 against the man's head. He politely said :

'Sam, say good night.'

Reluctantly Sam allowed himself to be led out.

He was breathing heavily and his nose was bleeding but he felt elated and triumphant. He had proved himself, demonstrated that he could defend himself without help.

Through his puffy lips he smiled at all of them.

'That's what we should have done in Germany when all of this started.'

'Absolutely, Killer,' Alex replied. 'Maybe you want to fight on my first card. A little training and you'll be ready for Joe Louis.'

Thirteen

No matter how often Sam saw the squat, dented, brown and tan Short Line bus, he would stop whatever he was doing, go out to the wooden gate to welcome personally each of the guests whether they had booked for a weekend or a month. Perhaps this human touch accounted for all the regulars who in the three years since he had gone into the hotel business would not consider their summer complete unless they had spent some time at West's Hotel just outside of Monticello, the unofficial capital of the Catskills. The music that played over the loudspeaker system was the kind that people could hum to: Paul Whiteman, Harry James, or Guy Lombardo. Sam would hand out the Activity Letter and take the names of all his guests so that he could mention them, their businesses, their children and grandchildren in the next letter. People of no import never forgot the pleasure of seeing their names in print. Even newcomers were treated like old family friends, put at their ease and asked if they wanted anything special from the kitchen. Bellhops would wait for the driver to open the bus's kidney-shaped luggage section. Busboys in white ducks would be behind buffet tables on the lawn, offering lemonade and hors d'oeuvres to the travelers who had ridden five hours on the bus. As the guests checked in, Sam would stop the music and take over the PA system.

'Welcome to West's Hotel ... tonight we have our Champagne Dance Contest with Yolanda and José for your entertainment. Prizes are awarded to the three winning couples and you are the judges. Enjoy, my friends. Any problems, come to the desk and ask for me, Sam West, your host. Welcome.'

Hymie, the regular bus driver, said:

'Another full house, Sam.'

'Yes, thank God and why not? My rates are lower than Laurel's; Grossinger's can't touch my food, and at least at West's you don't need a map to find your room like in the Concord.' He clapped his hands cheerfully. 'Hymie, you didn't notice ...'

'What?'

'My new neon sign.'

'But it's not on.'

'I keep it off during the day to save the country electricity,' he said heroically. 'FDR needs it for the airplane factories.'

'So, you got a neon sign that you don't use.'

'The point is, it's there and the war won't last forever.'

It was 1942 and Sam held War Bond rallies during the winter and practiced rationing by observing Meatless Tuesdays and Fridays. Fish was a brain food and his vegetable cutlets had become renowned. He had also discovered that his Jewish clientele paid mere lip service to kosher food. As a consequence, he did not have to invest in cutlery and china for dairy and meat. Furthermore, people on vacation still yearned for meat and he discovered that the only acceptable substitute was shellfish, never mind that it wasn't kosher. Once a week he traveled down to the city and picked up massive Main lobsters, gulf shrimp, scallops, and clams at the Fulton Fish Market which was controlled by Joe 'Socks' Lanza and his Mafia family. No fish could come into New York without Socks's approval; he was paid a toll by every boat and truck which carried fish. Paul Salica had introduced Sam to the fish czar who had seen to it that Sam received the highest quality the market had to offer. It became something of a joke around Manhattan that the best seafood to be had was in a small Catskill hotel called West's.

Guests, no matter how much they were fed, invariably got hungry after the casino entertainment and their card games, so Sam built a coffee shop and snack bar adjacent to the casino and at midnight it was filled. People sat around till two in the morning eating bagels and lox and salami sandwiches. They also liked to dance, and many of them had no idea how to approach the new popular Latin dances, so Sam paid the Levy's – Yolanda and José – a flat rate for group lessons and got twenty-five percent on private lessons that samba and rumba enthusiasts enrolled in.

A day camp at the nominal fee of ten dollars a week per child got the kids off the parents' backs during the day. Private instructions in tennis, boating, riding, and golf were also available at a small additional charge.

Sam spent money where he had to: the chef, stolen from Lindy's, received three hundred in cash a week and all the

Rupert beer he could drink; Stevie Bernstein, Sam's social host, known as Mr. Laffs, was another hundred; and the Gary Kugler Orchestra – five pieces and a singer – pulled out three hundred a week. Victor, who had gone into booking bands and singers, had made the deal for him. Where could anyone hear music like Kugie's? Wasn't his the resident group in the Copacabana lounge during the winter? Furthermore, where could the public watch, at only a quarter a head, such well-known fighters as Solly Krieger and Georgie Abrams train? By arrangement with Alex, he provided free room and board at a cabin by the lake for these fighters.

The shabby boardinghouse that Sam had bought three years before was now entirely remodeled. There were one hundred acres and a lake for the seventy-five guests Sam accommodated.

Sam passed through the knotty-pine-paneled rustic lobby where he was seen smiling in scores of photographs in the West Hall of Fame corner. The hotelier was visible holding up his dukes to a gloved Barney Ross; embracing Menasha Skulnik, the celebrated thespian of the Second Avenue stage; receiving a blessing from Cantor Mendel Kirstein; smooching with the black Cotton Club songstress, Dora May Ruby, the singer who introduced in perfect Yiddish 'Bei Mir Bist du Schoen' to the shock and delight of West's sophisticates.

Yet not every aspect of life at West's was perfect. Busboys and waiters, the dreaded dining room staff, caused Sam endless problems, transported him to new heights of grief.

The staff were mostly college students. Sam had a weakness for young men who were pre-anything – med, dent, law – and recruited them from the labor exchange in Manhattan. They were given free room and board, paid ten dollars a month. Many of them earned a hundred and fifty a week in tips which were tax free. Stan Hovitz, the maître d', looked resplendent in his maroon dinner jacket and matching bow tie. But he had lost control of his staff and had reports from the kitchen that there had been a virulent outbreak of *loxing*. The term was a kindly euphemism for spitting in milk, coughing on cream cheese, rubbing one's penis on a slice of cantaloupe, the adding of nose bogies to raisin Danish, unspeakable practices in many dining rooms through the mountains. Hotels rumored to be subjected to loxing immediately lost their trade. Three such establishments, through no fault of the owners, had that year already gone into receivership. Loxing was a weapon devised by those who depended on tips and were stiffed.

'We'll nip it in the bud, eh, Stan?' Sam declared.

'I sure hope so, Sam.' Stan was applying a thin coat of Vaseline with a Q-tip to his already gleaming patent leather pumps.

'I have suspicions ...' he had a habit of staring, and Sam thought that he himself might be the object of Stan's scrutiny.

'Like who?'

'Lieberman.'

'The Dental? Hard to believe. He's a year away from his shingle. He wouldn't do such a thing,' Sam said, considering a cherub-faced, draft-deferred NYU Dental School scholar. 'Lieberman has been with me since I started ... three summers now. He worked Decoration Day weekend even though he had exams. No, Lieberman is a prince. He cleans my teeth for nothing at the school clinic. He's a professional man.'

'I heard it was him,' Stan persisted.

'From who?'

'Sam, you're asking me to betray a confidence.'

'What are you, Stan, an attorney? A medical man? You're a trusted employee ... *a caterer!*'

Stan succumbed to flattery, Sam well knew.

'The head dishwasher.'

'He's drunk all the time. Talk about loxing – he's an expert. Last year he came in so loaded, he puked on the dishes he was washing. Next case ...'

'Well, then I don't know.'

'Okay, close the doors. I'll talk to them.'

The staff were brought in from the kitchen and grouped around Stan's table where pairings of new arrivals were being arranged on the maître's chart. A red chart for a married couple, blue for a single male; maidens received yellow so that they could, as Sam insisted, 'sit with their own kind.'

'Mr West wants a few words with you ...' Stan said lamely, then resumed his pairings.

'Gentlemen, friends, scholars ... *boys,*' Sam began, his face crinkling in a friendly smile, his arms open to embrace the ten waiters and busboys who manned the dining room stations. 'In other hotels you've worked, you know of the kind of food that is served to dining roomers. Reheated *dreck* which tastes lousy and gives trots. Here the chef serves you the same menu as the guests. Cheap is dear. Look at you all, suntanned, healthy, well fed. Your bunks get maid service. Nothing is denied you. You want to socialize, dance with the ladies, you can.' His luminous gray eyes rested on each face in turn. In a whisper he resumed: 'Sexualities, do I say a word, ask a question? Romance, am I saying no? Be careful, take precautions, don't get caught by the husbands, and no trenning with ladies at your station because dining-room-service tip time can get confused with bedroom activity. At every other hotel, boys get fired for relations with guests. They can't use the lake, or play tennis. But here, my friends, except for your work in the dining room, you're guests.'

There was a muttering of approval and broad smiles from the boys.

'So how come somebody is resorting to loxing, which is a sin, not to mention against state health codes? What have I done to deserve a loxer among you?'

In unison he heard the word, like an inspirational coda from a cheering section:

'Stiffs!'

'Stiffs?' Stan repeated. 'This season we've got guests you could chew chopped liver for them they don't put a hand in their pocket. Fifteen, twenty specials I'm running for every dinner and I get a thanks.'

'It's wartime. FDR is telling all of us to conserve,' Sam noted, head erect, the picture of a patriot. 'People aren't spending. Democracy is fighting for survival against the Japs and Nazis and you're worried about a tip here and there. With Stan, I'll discuss his situation privately.

'Now the rest of you hear me good. This is a four-and-two house. Any busboy or waiter who doesn't get that minimum tip for a weekly guest, he comes to me. I take him at his word and he gets the money from me right in his hand. Cash!'

'It's not fair to you,' Lieberman, the semidentist observed.

'Fair, where are you going to find fairness or justice? That's God's department. Here you get stiffed, I'll pay.' He raised his index finger, wagged it in admonition. 'But no farting in the borscht, or spitting on tuna salad' – he heard a few nervous giggles – 'or attacking with your dicks, fine, expensive melons which I get on a quota from the Washington Market. Understand?'

Applause, he walked with head high, refusing to acknowledge the boys' endorsement. He made his way to the range to discuss the addition of lamb shanks to the Sunday lunch menu. Chef Emil Cardoza was standing there, his neckerchief sopping, his bloodshot eyes running rivers of beer, as he shoved lobsters under the grill in preparation for the Friday Night Siege. Sam took a shortcut into the freezer and counted fifty lobsters which would go into the salad later in the week. He smiled at Lorenzo, the salad man.

'Lorenzo, what would happen if we cut lobster salad this week?'

'I'll tell ya,' the vulpine-faced, yellow-toothed employee began, 'I'd save my fuckin hands from the claws and they wouldn't get so torn up that I'd have to wear them surgical gloves. You know how I feel about pickin meat outa those motherfuckin cocksuckers' asses.'

'How does shrimp strike you?'

'Shrimp, them slimy, scabby, rubber little dicks I can live with. For shrimp salad, Sam, I'd kiss your ass in Macy's winder.'

'No, don't kiss my ass. Just don't make the chopped liver so greasy. Schmaltz must nurture the liver, prevent dryness, not swamp it so that it slides off a fork.'

'You fuckin Jews don't know how to eat.'

'Oh, Italians are great cooks? Where in America is there an Italian hotel, huh, Lorenzo? You want somebody killed, they stick a knife in you and' – he burst into laughter – 'they can hold up banks.'

Sam repaired to the grill. Emil hated the broiler. It brought the range temperature up to two hundred and fifty degrees.

'Sam, how do you expect me to drink beer that's warmer than piss?' Chef Cardoza asked.

'Well, I'll put a refrigerator behind the range for your private use.' Since he would be responsible for stiffs, he had to cover himself. 'Emil, you're the prince of chefs ...'

Emil cast a murderous glance at Lorenzo.

'Lorenzo, you guinea snot, you touch my knives again, I'll slash your balls off.'

'Who wants them? Listen, Emil, if you could cook, you'd be in a restaurant. Kiss Sam's feet he hires you.'

'*Enough!*' Sam said. 'Emil, we've got two hundred and six lobster dinners.'

'Don't remind me,' he said, waddling on his tiny feet which supported two hundred and fifty pounds of solid fat, parched white skin, blue-veined, scarred hands.

'I got fifty more in the freezer.'

'I can't handle it. Not enough broiling time and you know it.'

'Am I crazy or did I bring up the word broiling? Let's say I take fifty more reservations and we run out. Can't we offer them boiled?'

'They're too small ... one-pounders.'

'So how about adding a few fried shrimp with them?'

'Could do.'

'Emil, you won't just throw them in the pot. You'll devein, please. For poisonings I'm not covered.'

'He poisons wherever he works, that suck Emil ...' Lorenzo called out like a wild man. 'His knives. I seen them shitty knives. They're for butter.'

Sam gently approached Lorenzo and rubbed the back of his neck paternally.

'Lorenzo, when I'm in the kitchen, take it easy on the language. I got to talk to guests when I leave and I don't want to use foul words. Other day, after leaving you, I told an old woman she was full of shit.'

'Sam, you got a prick?'

'I believe so.'

'When it reaches your ass, go fuck yerself,' he said with a cackle.

'Fine.'

Everything was beautiful. You just had to know how to handle the natives in the kitchen. He returned to his cottage which was built on a small inlet beside the lake. It had a sandy beach and offered total privacy. Sylvia Kane, the book-keeper and his mistress, had run a bath for him and laid out his midnight-blue gabardine suit, black shoes, Lew Bregman polka-dot bow tie, and white-on-white shirt. She was in her dressing gown, a rounded, handsome woman with eloquent curves and a diffident smile.

She was blond, thirty, a spinster from Brooklyn who had come up to West's two summers ago in search of friendship and new faces. She had long since given up any hope of marriage. Engaged at twenty-one to an accountant, Sylvia had faced the tragedy of his death a month before the wedding.

He had gone out to a liquor store for Passover wine and had walked into a robbery and been shot to death.

She was quiet, did not mix with the guests, and often took a rowboat out alone with a picnic lunch to spend the afternoon in solitude. Sam would watch her from outside his cabin. He could understand her loneliness. He had had to face the loss of Lenore. He had placed his daughter in a private hospital outside the town of Liberty. Sam visited her once a week, brought her dolls which she did not play with, games she never opened, books she was unable to read. But he bought her a small victrola, and the nurses told him that Lenore listened intently and with apparent concentration to music. Nevertheless, she remained mute, apathetic. Lenore, according to Dr. Green, her psychiatrist, was secure in the dark world of her wound. Communication would endanger the tenuous structure and expose her. At least now, Sam felt, she was no longer vulnerable.

So, shared tragedy was the basis of the relationship Sam and Sylvia formed. He courted her with dignity, inviting her to stay for an extra week at the hotel. The week became months and at the season's end when Sam and his room clerk could not handle the paperwork and were behind with guests' charges and bills, she moved into the office and brought method and order to the chaotic situation. After New Year's, when Sam closed for the winter, he went to Brooklyn with her and moved her out of her parents' apartment on King's Highway. Her parents were not told of the arrangement. Sylvia simply said:

'I like the life better in the country. I'm not stuck in an office all day ...'

She had saved five thousand dollars and placed it at Sam's disposal with no promissory note or attempt to solicit a marriage proposal. For all she knew, Sam might have been a fortune hunter, but she took the chance. They had not yet been intimate.

She moved into Sam's cabin and became his mistress.

She accepted the fact that Sam could not marry her ... for years.

'Lenore won't understand and it might affect her condition.'

Sylvia might have forced the issue. How would Lenore know if she weren't told? Even if she learned of the marriage, would she actually understand what had taken place? But Sylvia was not pushy and it was this very lack of aggression which made her so totally feminine to Sam. He thought of her as a true woman, faithful, trusting, and reliable. She never brought up the subject of having a child with him, and the maternal qualities she possessed were profligately spent on Sam.

He was fortunate to have encountered her at a critical moment in his life. She not only stabilized him emotionally but forced her savings on him. She helped finance the casino, the small hall which was used for entertainment and dancing. Construction on the casino began immediately after the first Labor Day. Sylvia had secured a bank loan and developed a friendly association with the manager of the Monticello bank.

'It's important always to have a bank on your side.'

He smiled sheepishly and allowed her to take charge of the building program. A year later came the annex to the main house for the overflow of guests.

'Someday I hope we'll have a dozen buildings like this.'

'Just be patient,' she cautioned. 'It takes two seasons to pay for each room.' She showed him a chart with rows of figures which indicated the cost of each additional unit. 'You want to grow but you have to be able to control it.' She told him about the local custom of naming new buildings after family members. At her suggestion, the annex was christened Judith House in memory of his wife.

The soul of prudence – a virgin when she came to him – she nonetheless grew increasingly passionate when they were alone, and he responded like an adolescent with his first girl. She had reawakened his taste for life, stifled for years in Munich. Memories of his marriage grew dim. At West's he was king, a benevolent despot.

Running late now, he dressed hurriedly and she tied his bow tie. He ran his hands over her bare waist, then cupped her breasts.

'Sam, you're making me sexy.'

'Is there time?'

'Later. Maybe tonight you'll give your bookkeeper a dance?'

'More than that.'

She slipped into a short black theater dress which sparkled

173

with multicolored jet beads. She straightened the peplum over her hips and tied the straps of her platform shoes.

'No stockings?' he asked. She had painted her legs with makeup to create the effect of stockings.

'I ran my last pair and I can't get any more.'

'I'll drop Pauli a line. He can get you silk.'

'It's not necessary. I can live without them.' She touched her forehead reprovingly. 'With all the check-ins I forgot to mention that Victor phoned from Los Angeles when you were down at the dairy in Ferndale.'

'The phone bills he runs up . . .'

'He said to call him collect. It was about a singer you should hire. Victor thinks the boy's going to be a star.'

'Everybody Victor handles is going to be a star.' Sam looked at his watch. 'I don't know if it's three hours earlier or later there.'

'Earlier.'

They strolled out and paused by the lake. The sun was setting over the mountain and the water was still, a harmony of steel-blue light. They held hands when they walked up the path to the main house.

Someone was playing 'I Hear a Rhapsody' on a jukebox.

'We're beautiful,' Sam said, embracing her.

Fourteen

Even though his office had *three* telephones, Victor needed more lines to take the calls that bombarded him every Friday afternoon. In his two-room office on the corner of Gower and Hollywood Boulevard, he employed three agents and a girl Friday. On weekends he worked on the books and got out his checks, but he still managed to squeeze in a round of golf at Lakeside, the most exclusive country club in Los Angeles. Rubbing shoulders with Bing, Bob, shooting the breeze in the locker room with George Brent and Coop, playing poker with Bud Abbott, Frank Morgan, Beery, and Ward Bond, and getting a line on Selznick's plans and what Spencer had thought of a script were absolutely essential.

The golf course was merely an extension of his office, and Victor lived for his business. He was an elegant, conservative man in a business known for its brash, rude, uneducated slobs. He insisted on his three men wearing dark suits and inconspicuous ties. His boys were college graduates who spoke softly and comported themselves like gentlemen. The Victor Conte Agency people were different and indeed noticeable. They took clients to lunch at Perino's and discussed business, not women.

The secretary buzzed him as soon as he put down the phone. The entertainment booker of the Chez Paris in Chicago had been holding on.

'Victor, don't I count any more? You keep me waiting like I'm a nothing.'

Like most bookers, Larry Karp was vain, a 'starmaker' of chorus girls, and indispensable to agents who wished to push established talent.

'Dr. Professor Karp, my favourite human being, my teacher. If not for you, I'd be in Cleveland or Pittsburgh.'

'Exactly, Victor. My balls are frying. It's a hundred and six and I have to sit in my office for an hour, waiting to get connected.'

'What's the problem?'

'The band and the singer you sent out.'

He checked his index file and pulled out a card. Barbara Sherill and the Les Austin band had played a number of clubs in Los Angeles. This was their first tour through America. He was trying to get Barbara a record contract with Decca and he was close to making the deal.

'Victor, listen, we get people in here who when they see a girl like Barbara and invite her for a drink ... they expect her to join them.'

'Which people.'

'Torrio and Nitti.'

'Barbara's Les's girlfriend.'

'That's not relevant. She was rude to Nitti. That doesn't help my health or my business.'

'She's a singer not a hooker. The girl's got pipes and she'll be making a record after the tour. You got her cheap.'

'Victor, that doesn't matter and you know it. When she's *approached* she has to respond.'

'I've got the contract in my hand' – Victor switched on the fan, his office was broiling – 'and it doesn't contain any clause about socializing or sleeping with customers.'

'Speak to her, Victor.'

'Larry, when I worked for you, did we tolerate shit like that? You're a pro and you take pride in running a first-class establishment with a national reputation for food and entertainment. Frankly, you come on like that to any other agent in town with important clients and they pull the act and shit-list you.' He was angry now and he refused to give in. 'Look, nobody's pushing anyone around in Hollywood any more. Bioff tried and strong-armed the studios pretty good for a while and now he's on trial. This is a clean industry.'

He heard raspy breathing at the other end. Karp became asthmatic when nervous.

'I'm into Frank Nitti for a hundred big ones,' Karp's voice squealed. 'We did a total revamp because business was good. He'll turn off the juice if I cooperate. Please, Victor.'

'I'm not a pimp.'

'Victor, one day you'll need a favor ...'

'Hey, I always need them, and I do them for people who are late payers or want to get on their feet. But I've busted my ass to build a name and reputation. This kind of favor I can't do. If the girl likes him, then fine. What she does is her business. But I'm not getting my clients to put out if they want to work. That's not my kind of operation, Larry. I'm an agent, not a whoremaster.'

He hung up and walked through the main room where his men were talking on phones to studios and radio stations.

He sat down on the edge of the receptionist's desk to take a call from Sam. His face relaxed as he picked up the phone. His relationship with Sam had been good for both of them. Victor had been able to act as the entertainment booker for West's from the hotel's opening. Both men had been beginning their new careers: Sam was his first client. As a consequence of his own travels through the Orphèum Circuit, Victor was able to handpick comedians, magicians, singers and dancers who were looking for work and would not command fees beyond Sam's modest entertainment fund. West's had become his showcase for new talent.

'Victor, when are you going to come east and stay with me?' Sam asked.

'I only wish I could ... Listen, the invitation goes both ways. You and Sylvia aren't busy in the winter, so why freeze to death upstate? Get a little sun on your body out here and be our guests.'

'Maybe we'll try to this year. Alex'll be coming up next week. It'd be wonderful if we would all get together. But what about this singer you picked for me?'

'He's a young black kid. I caught him at a jazz club in New Orleans last month and I signed him.'

'What's he sound like?' Sam said, a bit doubtfully. 'Jazz isn't too popular here.'

'Velvet, Sam. He's really a ballad singer. I want you to give him a shot.'

'Let me check my schedule.'

'His name's Billy Davis. The women'll go crazy about him.'

'How about the weekend of August twelfth?'

'You got it, and if you like him I'll give you an option for Labor Day, okay?'

'What'll he cost?'

'Seventy-five for three shows.'

'Sold. Give my love to Tina and the girls.'

Victor hesitated for a moment, then overcame his reluctance. Although the reports seldom varied, he felt compelled to ask, 'Is there any improvement in Lenore?'

'She's been taken over by a new young doctor and he thinks there's a slight change. She still doesn't talk, but when she looks at me, I feel there's some recognition.'

'I'm glad.'

He hung up and left the office. He was on his way to a meeting at RKO. He walked down to the garage under the building and pulled out the light green prewar Buick sedan. It was low on gas. He opened the glove compartment. Paul had sent a large envelope filled with gas ration stamps. Even though he only qualified for a B sticker, he had been well supplied all year by Paul.

On his way to the studio, he stopped off at Pink's for a chili dog and chatted with several out-of-work actors who subsisted on chili seven days a week. Victor studied the faces and paid careful attention to their voices. He had learned that you never could tell where you'd run into someone who had star potential.

His eye wandered to the face of a young man with sleepy eyes and drooping lids. He was tall, broad-shouldered, and he was wearing chino work pants and a grimy vest. He was leaning against the rumble seat of a '34 Ford and eating a hot dog loaded with onions. Victor had seen him around a few bars, drinking beer and listening to other actors talk about their careers. There was a street look about him and he smelled strongly of sweat. His face was rough-hewn and somewhat expressionless. But just leaning there he gave off an aura of powerful masculinity. Victor introduced himself and offered to buy him another hot dog. The young man nodded casually. His movements were indolent.

'Can you act?' Victor asked.

'Way I'm tryin to make my livin,' he said lazily, slurring his words. Even breathing seemed to be an effort.

'Have you done anything?'

'Uh-huh ... You remember that scene in *The Grapes of Wrath* when the cops come to the Okie camp lookin for Fonda?'

'Yes. I saw it three times.'

'Well, then you must've seen me. Hank was runnin outa camp and he run right past me ...' He smiled ironically. 'Three times.'

'No speaking part.'

'No, but I shouted pretty good – "rhubarb, rhubarb." '

He took out a tightly rolled cigarette, lit it with a wooden match which he snapped with his thumbnail.

'What the hell are you smoking?'

'Little weed, want a drag?' He offered the spiff to Victor.

'Reefers?'

'So.'

'You can get arrested for something like that.'

'I'd make the papers.'

'Are you high all the time?'

'Mister, you got it.'

'What's your name?'

'Ronnie Flynt,' he said languidly, rounding his lips and blowing a smoke ring.

'Are you represented?'

'Do I have an agent? Naw. I went around to most of them when I first got here. They weren't much interested. Anyway, the ones I saw are full o' shit.'

'How do you live?'

'Bekins off and on movin furniture.'

'How'd you beat the draft?'

'I'm a Nazi.'

'Seriously.'

He stamped the reefer out on his thumb and placed it in the cellophane of his Old Gold pack.

'Thanks for the dog.'

Flynt intrigued Victor. He had a latent strength that would appeal to women who dreamed of being ravaged by a beefy, good-looking truck driver or mechanic. He had presence and a different look about him. Victor took out a business card and handed it to him.

'VCA ... Victor Conte.' Flynt looked surprised. 'Are you interested in me?'

'I could be if you weren't hopped up with reefers.'

'I don't smoke on the set.'

'That's not good enough. If you want to make it, you can't be seen like this in public. Studios and producers in this town worry about their image. They don't like actors getting headlines behind bars. Immoral behavior gives them seizures. So smoke all the weed you like at home, but not in the street, not in front of executives. You'll make them nervous – and they'll blackball you. Let me know when you decide to have a bath and smoke only your Old Golds. Then we'll discuss what I can do for you.'

Flynt shook his head, lazily blinked his cornflower blue eyes, and smiled slowly.

'Mr. Conte, you're a fuckin schoolteacher.'

'You want a lift?'

'Where you headin?'

'Melrose to RKO.'

'I'd take you out your way. I'm due up in Beverly Hills.'

'Moving job?'

'Uh-huh. You could say so. This lady wants me to take her and her bed apart.'

'Dressed like that?'

'That's the way the lady likes it . . . with onions.' He lethargically lifted his muscled arm and saluted Victor.

There was no question about it. Flynt was Peck's bad boy, a loner, but he possessed the essential quality that was necessary for a star.

Ronnie Flynt had sex appeal.

RKO was a headache. Run by the crazy millionaire pilot Howard Hughes, but no one ever seemed to know where the man was. Romancing an actress, playing golf, or, as a practical joke, buzzing the Bel Air Country Club with his airplane. Occasionally he was in Washington. And Victor knew that when Hughes was away, no matter how his executives talked about their power, titles, total freedom, they were merely Hughes's office boys.

Joel Freed was the one Victor was waiting for now in the RKO reception room. Freed had been an accountant with Hughes's tool company in Houston and had been drafted to the studio to keep costs down. He had found a novel way, Victor thought; he said no to every project presented to him. If you didn't make movies, Freed reasoned, how could you lose money?

Victor had been waiting more than an hour when Freed pried himself loose from the telephones. He was a short man with bushy red eyebrows, owlish, horn-rimmed glasses, and the furtive manner of a purse snatcher.

'Victor, my apologies, but I was just on the line with H.H.' Victor looked at him skeptically. This was Freed's standard line. 'The Chief's at his bungalow at the Beverly Hills Hotel and he wants to *see* you.'

'Does he know I'm not a woman or even a chippy?'

'Victor, when you meet him, don't shake hands or breathe near him and please no jokes. He has an aversion to comedians.'

'Is it yes or no?' Victor asked. He would be late again for dinner and Tina's cannelloni had to be eaten while it was moist and not dried like bark. 'Joel, he had a hit with *Hell's Angels* and the script and the girl are perfect for a sequel.'

'The girl bears an unholy resemblance to Jean Harlow.'

'That explains Hughes's interest.'

'H.H., please.'

'Okay, then I'm Signore Conte.'

They drove in two cars to the Beverly Hills Hotel. Hughes's bungalow was a large double hidden behind palm fronds. Freed knocked on the door gently, frightened he might wake his master.

'It's open,' a twangy Western voice called out. Freed tentatively tried the knob. Hughes was seated at a bridge table, shuffling a pack of cards. On the table was a slab of cream cheese which he was eating with his fingers. There were three girls in attendance, a blonde, a redhead, and a raven-haired beauty with a marcelled widow's peak.

The four of them were completely nude.

The blonde nestled at Hughes's ankles and was blowing him. No wonder he doesn't shake hands, Victor thought, watching the lanky eccentric recluse pick at the cream cheese with his long fingernails. He had unkempt dark hair, patched with gray, a saddle-tramp, untrimmed mustache. Victor noticed he was not entirely naked. He wore grease-stained canvas tennis sneakers. Hughes pointed but did not offer the cream cheese.

'The Philadelphia company makes this especially for me with nonfat milk,' Hughes began. His dark eyes wandered from Victor's face to Freed's. He seemed truly unconscious of the effect he created. 'Fatty foods are poison,' Hughes informed him.

'No one would disagree with you.'

Hughes raised his index finger, described a circle with it, and indicated through this sign that Joel Freed could depart. Freed moved from the sofa and vanished. Victor munched on a grape from a silver bowl.

'Are you in a hurry?' Hughes asked.

'My wife won't leave me if I'm late.'

'Well, then let's play gin for a while,' Hughes said, motioning him to a chair at the table. 'I go on retreats, Mr. Conte, not the religious sort. But I abstain from drink, women, and life while I'm working. I've just spent a year in Long Beach working on a new plane. I didn't see anyone but engineers and draftsmen.' He dealt out cards to Victor and told the blonde to desist and for the redhead to take over the commitment. His cock was flaccid, and he seemed detached but patricianly indulgent of the girl's efforts to bring him to some form of conclusion. Victor won the first hundred-point game and Hughes asked for a return match. The stakes were a dollar.

'You've got a fine way of running your studio.'

'I've lost interest in the business,' Hughes admitted. 'It took up too much of my time.'

'Then what do you want with Rita Sanders?'

'To sign her to a contract ... for seven years.'

'And loan her out to other studios?'

'If the property's right for her.'

'Who decides that?'

'I read the scripts ... all of them.'

'When do you find the time?'

'That's not your worry.'

'Mr Hughes, Rita is my client. I agreed to handle her because I'm convinced she has talent and can become a major star. I don't think it's fair to tie her up all that time.'

Hughes knocked with five and did not come back to the subject for a few minutes. He beckoned the third girl.

'I'm ready,' he said. And indeed he was. He had an enormous erection and his penis quivered although he himself was anything but excited. He rose from the table and they went into the bedroom.

'Come with us. I can still talk, Mr. Conte,' he called out when Victor appeared ready to leave.

'You're a remarkable man, Mr. Hughes. The first I've met who can negotiate and fuck at the same time.'

'I'd like to meet Miss Sanders. I gave this a great deal of thought after Joel sent me her pictures.'

'She wants to act. I have no idea what her sex life is like. I think you ought to read the script she wants to do.'

'I did. "The Devil's Chariot." It's a mistake. The critics

182

will kill the picture. It's a steal of *Hell's Angels*. Jean Harlow's an immortal. The public'll resent a new actress imitating Jean. The picture won't make a dime and Miss Sanders will die a short, painful death just like Mary Dees.' He switched from one girl to the other, mounting or being straddled. He settled on the blonde, patted her rump, and noted factually, 'Blondie, you stay, you've got the tightest pussy.' He looked up to Victor. 'Trial and error, whether it's an airplane or a woman. I'll guarantee Miss Sanders a hundred thousand a year for seven years whether she makes a picture or not.'

This was the biggest deal Victor had ever had in his hands. His commission would be seventy thousand and he'd have a share of his client's points if a film went into profit. Hughes was watching *him* while the girl swiveled her hips, then got on her toes and rode up and down. Her crescent-shaped breasts flapped against her chin.

'It's an attractive offer and I'd do you less than justice to suggest otherwise, Mr. Hughes. But I'm in the talent business. Most agents sell flesh. I don't want Rita for an annuity. I try to guide a career, build it, so that apart from money we can take a certain pride in the work.' He closed his eyes and contemplated the headlines in *Variety* and the *Reporter*—'VCA and Hughes Deal Set for Rita Sanders.' It would help the agency's reputation and make the big boys like the Morris office take him seriously. 'As Rita's agent, I will in good faith report the offer to her promptly. But I'll advise her not to accept it. She can then legally break our agency agreement. In fact, I'll release her. But I feel strongly that she expects me to sell her talent, not her ass.'

The blonde continued pumping away, her face screwed up tautly as she had multiple orgasms. Hughes finally reached a climax, withdrew, and the girl wiped his member with a towel.

'I don't like to be too late getting back to Encino,' Victor said. 'It's Friday night and I always have dinner with my family on Fridays. So please excuse me.'

'You've made a mistake,' Hughes said.

'I've made them before. But this isn't one that I'll personally regret. I'll let Joel know how my client feels about your offer. Good-bye.'

The Contes lived in a spacious Spanish-style house in the Encino hills at the fringe of the San Fernando Valley. After six months of touring with his daughters and Tina through cities that even now set his teeth on edge – Cleveland, Pittsburgh, Philadelphia, Chicago, Indianapolis – Victor had realized that America's Midwestern heartland did not suit his tastes. Tina was constantly washing, cooking canned food on a two-ring burner, and the girls had a series of childhood illnesses. They needed an education and stability. Besides, he didn't believe in the trouper's cliché about the show going on when performers were starving and being hounded out of their hotels by irate managers who were choking on unpaid bills.

He had been fired for refusing to work when his pay was late in coming. He and his family had traveled the Far West in an old Dodge and reached Los Angeles, broke and confused. It was Paul Salica who had lent Victor a thousand dollars to rent office space and start a theatrical agency.

But first Victor returned to Chicago alone to learn the booking business as Larry Karp's assistant. The six months he spent with Karp, added to the time he had put in on the vaudeville circuit, gave him a sure knowledge of what theaters and clubs required and, even more, a real understanding of the performer's life. He took under his wing an assortment of musicians, singers, band leaders who had been unhappy about their representation. When he opened his office at the end of 1939, he had seventy-odd clients.

During his first year, Paul had advanced him another three thousand. In five months he paid Paul back and in a year he was secure enough to buy the house and four acres in the Encino hills.

It was nine thirty and his daughters had the radio tuned to the Kraft Music Hall. He felt tired and at the same time restless. He joined Tina in the living room and poured them ponies of Strega.

He looked across the room at the dark-haired woman he had loved so passionately. Her figure was still good, but that quality of reserve he had admired in Europe seemed alien in this new country where people were open and outgoing. They were seldom intimate. Victor invariably took home work; contracts to check and a pile of scripts layered his night table. His deepest desire remained below the surface.

He never discussed it with Tina. He wanted a son, and Tina could no longer have children. He roved around the room, stopping at the fireplace.

'What's wrong, Vittorio?'

'Nothing,' he replied sharply. 'It's just the pressure at the agency. I used to be able to shut it out when I came home ... but now I feel like I'm suffocating.'

'Then hire some more people.'

'It isn't that easy to find qualified people with the war on.'

'As long as everything is okay with us –' she faltered and her mouth tightened.

'Tina, what's upsetting you?'

'I wouldn't like to think that you'd revert to the old Italian ways.'

'Which ones?' He threw back the Strega in a single gulp.

'Oh, you know, come to an understanding. The woman just shrivels up.' She lowered her eyes. 'It happened to my mother. A woman looks sixty for her whole life when her husband stops touching her.'

She lapsed into silence, then left him. He welcomed the sound of the telephone. He picked it up in his study which overlooked the rear garden. The palms were illuminated by multicolored floods. Below the redbrick decking the pool was an aqua frieze.

The connection was poor and it took a moment before the crackling stopped.

'Can you hear me, ehhh?' Salica asked.

'Pauli?'

'Vittorio. How're you, Tina, and my girls?'

'Couldn't be better.'

'I'm planning a secret trip to Arizona and California ...'

'My house is yours.'

'I can't see you this time.'

'Pauli, everything's fine with the agency.... Is there anything I can do?'

'If you hear anything about Siegel's activities, let me know. Don't try to weasel information. Just listen.'

'I see him at parties and around the studios.'

'Keep an eye on him.'

'When are you arriving?'

'I'm not sure. Victor, don't mention this trip to anyone.'

He remained in his study for a few moments, skimmed

185

through a script, but his mind wandered. He had to leave the house. He embraced Tina affectionately while she dried the dishes.

'*Amore*, I have to go out. One of my clients is having a problem. He just punched the director. Tina, no more silly thoughts. You have no reason to be insecure.'

'I just feel cut off at times. Don't be too late.'

'I'll see if I can settle the problem and be back soon.'

He drove across Ventura Boulevard and turned up Laurel Canyon. He shot into Woodrow Wilson Drive and parked in the driveway of a small ranch house cantilevered on wooden stilts. He took out his key and opened the door. The anteway led to a small living room filled with shabby second-hand furniture. Clothes were strewn everywhere. The bed had not been made and a radio was tuned to a station playing Sammy Kaye. He took his jacket off and threw it on a chair piled with bras and panties. He removed his tie and headed for the bathroom.

The girl in the bathtub had long auburn-red hair and she smiled at him.

'I didn't hear you come in, Victor.'

He pulled her out of the tub. Her breasts were enormous but firm and the buds of her nipples were a deep pink. She smelled like a wild violet and he began kissing her.

'Should I get the soap off?'

'No, wet, just the way you are.'

They walked entwined into the bedroom. Her hand flicked at the buttons on his fly and they both fell down on the bed together. She pulled down his trousers and seized hold of his cock and began to kiss it. Then she put it in her mouth and moved her head up and down with a rhythm that drove him crazy. She eased her mouth off and got on her knees with her pink backside to him. She wiggled her backside, and when she felt the trickle of his come begin, she turned around and put his cock back in her mouth and swallowed until he was completely dry.

'God, Rita, we're like wild animals,' he said.

'Isn't that the way it's supposed to be?'

Rita Sanders had been his mistress for six months and he could no longer imagine living without her.

She leaned over the side of the bed and reached out for a reefer. She lit it and passed it to him. She sensed that some-

186

thing was worrying him.

'What's wrong?'

'Howard Hughes offered you a hundred thousand a year on a seven-year contract.'

'Victor, you're my career. I wouldn't fuck him if my life depended on it.'

'Well, wouldn't you like to think about it? I mean, look at the way you're living, Rita. In this dump.'

'Hey' – she ran her long nails along the small of his back – 'do you hear me complaining? I don't give a shit about my career. I just want you to be mine. Nothing else matters. I'm your woman. Tina's got your kids and your name, but I've got your cock and that means I've got everything.'

She lay back in his arms. Her eyes were filled with joy and they passed the reefer back and forth until they had smoked it down.

'Rita, I love you,' he told her for the thousandth time. Somehow the sound of the phrase only had a reality when he was with her. 'Someday I'll get a divorce.'

'Don't rock the boat. This is a community property state. I'm happy the way we are.'

'But you have to want more,' he said as though negotiating on her behalf against himself.

'Honey, to have you love me is enough. Why ruin what we have by being greedy? Your success belongs to me as well. Victor, listen to me. I'm happy, happy, happy with you. Does it really matter that I'm your secret?'

Fifteen

The Salicas enjoyed hotels: messages were delivered, room service was constantly available, no housework was involved, they could come and go as they pleased no matter what the hour. The Roney Plaza was the most prestigious address in Miami Beach. Walter Winchell, the most powerful newspaperman in America, spent his winters there and Paul had the adjoining penthouse. The two men had met the previous season. Paul had been instrumental in persuading his benefactor Louis Lepke to surrender to Winchell and J. Edgar Hoover.

It was Lansky who had sent Paul to Lepke to convince him that a deal could be made guaranteeing that he would serve only a year or two at Dannemorra. Lansky wanted the pressure off. Lepke's violent activities had caused federal and state officials to bear down on the Combination's business. Numbers banks had been raided, bookmakers closed down, loan sharks rousted. Everyone who had any connection with the Combination had been dragged in for questioning.

'If we can't operate in an orderly fashion,' Lansky had told Paul, 'without police interference, we might just as well look for jobs.'

Paul had been nervous about the assignment, but he had to cooperate with Lansky. Lansky controlled many of the organization's financial investments and was Luciano's most trusted aide. What Paul did not realize was that he was being used as a stalking horse. Lansky was out to trap Lepke and he did. Lepke was convicted in federal court for extortion and sentenced to thirty years, then claimed by New York and successfully prosecuted for murder by Burt Turkus, the assistant DA. Lansky had guaranteed Paul protection against retaliation by Bugsy Siegel, but Paul knew that Siegel would come after him. So he would make the first move, he told Chou when they were on their way to a cocktail party at Winchell's.

'Pauli, why can't you be satisfied with what we've already

188

got? We're living like millionaires – we've got almost three hundred thousand in the Bahamas.'

'Babe, I'm hungry.'

'But why go after Siegel? It'll just be trouble.'

They were on the balcony of their penthouse and Paul gazed out at the yachts cruising along Indian Creek. He wore a crisp white linen suit and he was deeply tanned. Chou was in a creamy silk dress and she toyed with the eight-carat diamond ring Paul had given her as an engagement ring. They had married when they first reached Florida.

'Bugsy's not the real thing. Every day he's in the papers bullshitting with some actress or socialite. Siegel's not a heavy hitter. I hate self-promoters like him. A man in our business has to be dignified, keep out of the news. Listen, Chou, out of nothin in Miami Beach – a desert – I made something. But who knows about me except *mi compari*? The public does not know I exist which is proper. I'm like a shadow. I have the respect of Lansky and Frank Costello and they're my line to the boss. He appreciates what I'm doing.'

The entire Combination knew and admired the job Salica had done in Miami Beach. In three short years with Lansky's backing, he had taken over the gambling in the city. Every bookmaker got the betting line from him. The national wire service was hooked to his office. Independent bookies paid a hundred a day for the service. All those who played the numbers were assured a fast payoff from his runners.

Tourists who wished to gamble were chauffeured out to Fort Lauderdale where they shot craps, played roulette and blackjack at Paul's Peacock Club. He ran a clean club and chased the hookers out. He was afraid of prostitution—many Combination families gave up the business after Luciano's conviction on white slavery charges—and he abhorred the narcotics traffic.

Paul fervently believed that he was performing a valuable service. Gambling and sports were as closely tied as a husband and wife. He took care of both: he had a thirty percent interest in the dog track and he was sole owner of the Miami Fronton Corporation which ran jai alai games every night during the winter season.

Paul had established close ties with all of the major figures in the business. Whenever any of them came down for a winter holiday, Paul made it his business to see that they received the best accommodation at the Roney or the Shelborne. He managed to get them on golf courses like La Gorce; Chou took their wives shopping on Lincoln Road. He entertained lavishly, sparing no expense to please Frank Costello or Joe Adonis. It was an investment in his future. Nightclubs, accurate tips on the horses at Hialeah, a night out at Ciro's or the Copa where the best ringside table was always reserved in his name. He was a diplomat and he had ideas. He also possessed a singular European charm which the women loved. He was gallant, amusing, respectful, and courteous ... and he was more ambitious than any of them.

The hotels on the beach were supplied linen by his company. His service stations sold recapped tires, his agents came up with gas ration stamps. Did it matter that the stamps were stolen from a federal depot or counterfeited by his ring of Cubans who operated out of a small cigar store?

It was nearing seven. Paul and Chou left their suite and walked the few feet down the corridor to Winchell's place. They found him out on the large terrace showing off his latest acquisition – a putting green the hotel had put in at his request. The small dapper man waved at Paul through the crush of show girls surrounding him. Slight and wispy, he preferred long-stemmed roses who were prepared to do him favors. They knew that a squib in his daily column in the *Daily Mirror* guaranteed instant celebrity, that if he was their enemy they were virtually unemployable. His power extended to all areas: entertainment, politics, and the stock market. A tip in his column or on the radio program would lead investors to buy thousands of shares: it didn't matter what the product was; Winchell's endorsement meant that it was hot.

'Hey, neighbor, how're you and your lady?' Walter Winchell's staccato voice sounded like a ratchet. 'Paul, get yourself a drink ... I want to talk to you.'

Paul took two glasses of champagne from a waiter and joined his host. Winchell shoved two girls out of the way to make room for him. 'Listen, my man, an old personal friend of mine from New York has a problem.'

'How can I help?'

'Paul, Mike Jacobs and me go back a long time – even before he was a promoter. He doesn't like the way your friend

190

Alex Stone is grabbing all the new young fighters just coming up.'

Salica had heard of the rivalry that had developed between Mike Jacobs's Madison Square Garden and Stone's Sporting Club. But he didn't understand it. The Garden was a colossus; Stone's was a local neighborhood place with no reputation. How could Jacobs regard Alex as a competitor? It was true, though, that Stone's was packing in fans who were desperate to see a fight. Most of the major fighters were already in the service, and the Garden had to feed from the same pastures as Alex.

'Alex has a right to be in business, doesn't he, Walter?'

'He's a poacher and he'll wind up with the short end of the stick if he continues to get in Mike's way.'

Paul laughed easily and turned to Chou.

'It's hard to believe Jacobs is taking Alex so seriously.'

'You listen to me, Paul ... we're on good terms,' Winchell informed him. 'But just remember that I've got a line on what you're doing.'

'That sounds like a threat,' Salica said.

'Me threaten?' Winchell melodramatically feigned astonishment. 'I don't threaten, I bury.'

'What do you suggest I do?' Paul had become a master of conciliation, at least in public. 'We have a good relationship and I'd like to keep it that way.'

Winchell smirked. 'That's the kind of response I expected.' He looked past Paul and waved at some guests coming toward him. 'I know you're on the way up in the organization, and naturally I want to keep things on a friendly basis. Personally I like you, but I have loyalties to other people. You tell Alex to stick with amateur promotions. That way everyone's happy. Jacobs doesn't swallow Alex ... there's enough for both of them. But once he brings in pro cards, he's eating out of Mike's pot. Got it?'

'I'll speak to Alex ...' He felt his temples throb; drops of sweat collected under his arms. But he controlled his anger, kept his face relaxed and expressionless.

'You do that, pal.' Winchell dismissed him.

Paul was silent on the drive down to Joe's Stone Crab Restaurant on First Street. He didn't want Winchell climbing on his back, but at the same time, he resented his interference.

'He's a cockroach,' Chou said.

'But he's dangerous. He thinks he can get to Alex by putting pressure on me. I'm going to let him think he's succeeded.'

'Does he know that you're sending fighters up to Alex?'

For a year now, Paul and an ex-trainer who worked for him had been scouting promising young Cuban and South American fighters and supplying them to Alex. Because of the shortage of talent, Stone's had been drawing enormous crowds for their Wednesday night bouts.

'No. I've covered myself. I use Carmine Demarco as my connection to Alex. Alex doesn't know which of the boys I control.'

'Shouldn't you tell him?'

'No, Alex might think I'm fixing fights.'

Although Joe's was mobbed, Paul was immediately shown to a corner table. All of the Combination people frequented Joe's whose stone crabs were world famous.

Paul tasted the cold, dry Verdicchio and signaled the waiter to pour it for Chou. She reached across the table and clasped hold of his hand. The two of them lived for each other; she never had any doubts about his fidelity, but she worried constantly about his drive for power. She feared that one day a contract might be put out on Paul.

'Why do you want to go to California?'

He looked up at her in surprise.

'What makes you think I intend to?'

'When you were sleeping the other night, a long-distance operator called and said she was ready with your call to Victor.'

'Oh, I'd already spoken to him. What's so unusual about me speaking to Vittorio?'

Her lovely face was screwed up as though shot through with pain. He studied the perfectly structured features and the flow of blond hair which she now wore like Veronica Lake over one eye. She had styled it to please him.

'Pauli, *amore*, we're always truthful with each other.'

'I didn't want you to begin worrying.'

'But why go to the Coast ... it's not your territory.' She shook her head and pushed her plate away. 'If this was a social visit, you would have mentioned it to me.'

'I heard through Costello that Bugsy's planning some kind

of hotel in the Nevada desert. Gambling's legal there and he's got support from the Commission.'

'It doesn't concern you.'

'I have to find out more about his plan. There'll never be legalized gambling in Florida. And Havana's been closed up because of the war. Bugsy's got the whole West Coast and he's a bad organizer. Out West, I could turn a whole region around. They need more sports action on the Coast. The people out there are crying for it. When the war's over, I want to be there, running California. The fact is, sooner or later Bugsy'll make a mistake and open his big mouth once too often and then they'll come to me because I've got the resort experience and they'll give me the Coast on a platter.'

'Have you discussed this with anyone?'

'Not even Lansky. It's best right now that I'm his errand boy. When I'm ready to make a move, I'll get Meyer's backing.'

After dinner they decided to go down to the dog track for a few races. Paul was concerned about the weekly take. A few sharpshooters may have drugged the dogs. Too many long shots were coming in, and there had been a twenty-two-hundred quiniela earlier in the week.

Paul had discussed the situation with Carmine Demarco and they had worked out a plan. Their men were stationed at the payoff booths; others were floating around the bars, in the grandstand, and one group was assigned to the clubhouse. Three races had been run when Paul and Chou reached their box. Carmine Demarco was sitting just below them, binoculars around his neck. He was a short stocky man in his forties with a thick mustache, dark brown eyes, and a flat nose. He snorted when he talked and sounded as if he had a permanent cold.

'Anything happening?' Paul asked.

'No, it's quiet. Pauli, what surprises me is that nobody's hitting the bookies with the winning dogs.'

'It's tougher with the bookies. They just stop taking the action and they got a face for us. I think we're up against a ring. They figure that if they job the pari-mutuels we got no way of locating them.' He squinted in the glaring light. The dogs were being led out to the track. 'Have you checked the cages and the trainers?'

'Yeah, they're all clean. Besides, they're our regular people. They wouldn't try to fuck around with us.'

Chou studied the program. One of Paul's bookies leaned forward and gave her a tip in the fourth race.

'Five minutes to race time,' the announcer boomed over the PA system. People strode toward the pari-mutuel windows, gabbling about selections. Rusty, the electric rabbit the dogs would chase, whirled around the track. Chou went down to the enclosure and greeted several trainers. The sleek greyhounds had their wire muzzles removed and yapped with excitement. Their bodies were long and bony, but their legs and hindquarters were powerful and muscular.

The dogs were led into the starting gate. Paul listened to the announcer calling the race, but his eyes were on the field. He had a stopwatch in his hand. He moved his high-powered binoculars around the track and nudged Carmine.

'Why's Rusty going so fast?'

'Is he?'

'Yeah – four seconds faster than usual.'

He put down the binoculars and with a disgruntled expression read the tote board.

'Fuckin long shot again,' Carmine said. 'Shit, Pauli, it's ninety-two and a quarter payout.'

'Look at the place dog . . . seventy to one.'

He and Carmine left their seats and dashed to the pay windows. About a dozen long-shot players were lined up. That was an average payout. One of Carmine's Cuban boxers gave him a blank look, then approached Paul.

'Anything?' Paul asked.

'No, and I checked with the other boys.'

'The fuckin rabbit was too fast,' Paul insisted. 'Carmine, get a urine test on the two dogs.'

'I'll see the starter and ask him what's happening. Could be a mechanical failure.'

The men dispersed and Paul leaned against the soft drink stand, puzzled and angry, waiting for the head teller to report the tally on the race. He watched the line shorten and was about to leave when there was only one grizzly, unshaven man left. But a girl in her twenties got behind the man. She was a tall brunette with a stripper's body, her breasts bulging over her low-cut peasant blouse. Paul couldn't believe his eyes when she fished a stack of twenty tickets from her beaded bag. Legally he could not go near her. If he harassed her and she was a legitimate winner, she could complain to the state racing commission and he'd lose his license. The booth teller counted out thousand-dollar bills and the girl put them into her purse. As soon as she walked away from the window, Paul rushed up.

'What was the payoff?'

'Just over eighteen thousand.'

Paul kept an eye on the girl. She was alone as she headed for the exit. Chou caught his eye and he pointed to the girl. 'Get Carmine and the others. I'll meet you out front.'

Chou left the box and signaled Juan, a bulky, slow-witted heavyweight Carmine had hopes for. She whispered to him, then followed Paul out the turnstile. They kept the girl in view and made their way to the car. The girl hailed a Yellow Cab and waited at the curb.

'Is Carmine on the way?'

'I told Juan to find him.'

'Get the car ...' He looked everywhere but could not find any of his men. 'Fuckheads,' he said aloud. Chou pulled the Cadillac out and he got in the passenger seat. 'It's the Yellow Cab, two cars ahead.' She cut through a barrier and now the cab was in sight. Paul craned his neck out of the window and saw that the girl was in the back seat. 'She's going to make a delivery.' He reached under the dashboard for a switch, turned it, and two fully loaded .45 automatics mounted on a spring plate snapped forward, butt first. He turned around and saw Carmine, Juan, and three other men running around the parking lot.

The cab shot suddenly into the night traffic and made a sharp left turn. Chou cut off a line of oncoming cars as she followed. She switched off the headlights and left on the parking lights. She let the cab get a block ahead.

'There's nobody behind us,' she said. 'I guess Carmine couldn't get to his car fast enough.'

The cab kept within the speed limit, crossed the Harbor Island bridge, then drove through the blacked-out area of single-family houses on both sides of the bay. It turned into a road which overlooked the bay. A shadowy moon provided the only light when Chou switched off her parking lights and entered the street at ten miles an hour. The cab had stopped in front of a large colonial house which had a speedboat tied to a pier alongside the house. Chou pulled the .45 from the magnetic plate and Paul signaled her to cut the engine.

The clapping of the waves in the bay rhythmically stroked the anchored boats.

'I don't get it,' Chou said. 'She isn't moving out of the cab.'

'Could be she's waiting to be picked up.'

Paul peered into the darkness and was about to get out when a car screeched into the street.

'Shit, we're boxed . . . it's a whipsaw.'

The car sped alongside his and Chou started the engine and made a half turn onto a lawn. Bright lights from the car blinded her momentarily and Paul leaped into the back seat. The car roared up to theirs and Paul saw a sawed-off shotgun balanced on the lowered window of the car.

A voice rang out.

'Got a present from Bugsy, you cocksucker . . .'

The street exploded with the report of shotgun fire. The windshield on Paul's side was shattered and Chou threw up her hand to protect herself from the shards of glass. The car moved nose to nose with Paul's Caddy and he leaned out of the window and fired the .45 at the driver's head.

'Chou, stay down . . .'

Her face and arms were cut.

The driver was shoved out of the car and the other man crouched in the passenger seat and fired the sawed-off shotgun twice. Chou cried out in pain.

'I'm hit, Pauli,' she screamed. Her silk dress was spattered with blood.

Lights came on throughout the neighborhood as people rushed to their windows.

Paul pushed open the rear door and used it as a shield. He reached over and seized the other .45, then crawled on his belly through a patch of mud. The man raised the shotgun again; Paul leaned through the opposite window and fired six shots at the back of his head.

Paul drove the car like a wild man to the Beach Hospital. He held Chou's head in his arm and pleaded, 'Don't die, don't die on me.'

Doctors from the emergency room rushed out to his smashed car and placed her on a stretcher. She was breathing, he was told. Her face was cut up and her right shoulder was pulpy, fragments of flesh hanging off.

'What was she hit with, a cannon?' one of the doctors asked.

'I don't know,' Paul replied. 'Is she going to live?'

A doctor rolled back her eyes. The pupils were dull and glazed.

'She went into shock when she was hit.'

A team of nurses cut off her dress and three doctors waited in the operating room. Paul was beside himself with panic. He went to the telephone booth and made the call collect.

'Hi, Pauli,' Frank Costello said. 'Business must be bad. You run outa money?'

'Frank,' he said calmly, 'two of Bug's people tried to hit me. They got my wife. She's in the operating room.'

'Pauli, I'm sorry, real sorry, believe me . . .'

'Frank, there's gonna be a fuckin war.'

He slammed down the receiver and returned to the waiting room. Nurses walked past him. He lighted a cigarette but when he took a drag the cigarette stuck to his lips and he burned his fingers. The clock above the sofa seemed suspended. Chou had been in the operating room for an hour and a half. He fell on the sofa and crumpled into a ball.

A doctor finally appeared and Paul forced himself to his feet.

'She's going to be all right. We cleaned the wounds. She'll have trouble moving her arm for a long time but physical therapy will help. We've had to pick the glass out of her face. She'll have some scars from the sutures but a good plastic surgeon should be able to fix them so you'd hardly notice.'

'Thank you, doctor. Can I see her?'

'She'll be in her room in a few minutes. She's still anesthetized.'

He walked down the corridor. A nurse ushered him into a room where Chou lay bandaged and asleep. Intravenous tubes were attached to her right arm. She smelled of ether and new, wet plaster of Paris. Her face was a crisscross of adhesive strips.

He bent on his knees and kissed her hand.

Sixteen

Jonathan had spent a great deal of his free time working out at the gym with his father's boxers, and he had developed into an extraordinarily powerful fourteen-year-old. He was fascinated by all the activities of the club and there were moments in his relationship with Alex when he seemed to be in control.

He was tireless in his attempts to find new ways to use the place. It offended some deep commercial instinct in him to close for an evening. It was at his insistence that Alex bought a job lot of roller skates and had new flooring installed so that on Sundays Stone's became a roller skating rink. On nights when there was neither a boxing nor wrestling card, Jonathan persuaded Alex to rent it out to local churches for bingo evenings. During election periods, Jonathan got his father to send out mailings to candidates offering the club for speeches and political rallies. When this proved successful, he went through the Yellow Pages and built lists of charitable organizations who could rent it for fund-raising functions. He suggested that they offer these charities special rates – a flat fee against twenty-five percent of the take.

He pointed out to his father that what each event – whether church bingo or a political rally – had in common was food. Spectators got hungry and thirsty and didn't want to wait for their order. In the club's first year, Alex applied for a beer license and after a few well-placed bribes he received it. Jonathan had a section at the rear outfitted with luncheonette equipment and a large grill which could handle a hundred hot dogs at a time. He had got the idea from Nathan's in Coney Island. He even persuaded Alex to buy Hebrew National hot dogs, put up a sign, 'Strictly Kosher' to entice the Jewish spectators, and suggested solving the problem of fast service by precooking the hot dogs, then placing them in an oven. He himself made the salami sandwiches and placed them in wax paper bags so they'd remain fresh. There were ice-cream sandwiches and pops, but the most profitable item was beer. On a fifteen-cent bottle the profit was ten cents. The supply of beer was essential to the operation of the food business.

Lately there had been problems with deliveries and Alex told him to visit the distributor to find out why his order had been cut by fifty cases. It was a blistering hot, humid day and Jonathan's polo shirt was a sopping rag when he got off the bus on Bushwick Avenue.

On his way to the beer depot, he noticed kids coming home from summer school. Boys and girls grouped on street corners chattering and making plans to go to the beach. He stopped in a candy store, bought himself a Pepsi and a pretzel, for he had forgotten to eat lunch. He sat at the counter under the fan, wiping his forehead with his handkerchief, and watched beer trucks pulling out of the driveway across the street on the way to their weekend deliveries.

He left the candy store, crossed the street, and wandered into the loading yard. The dispatcher had left his post. Jonathan skimmed through the order forms and located the one for Stone's. His father had ordered two hundred cases.

'Goddamn it, they've cut a hundred,' he called out to a passing driver.

'Watcha lookin for, kid?'

'The dispatcher.'

A small man in a grimy undervest came out.

'Who you?'

'Jonathan Stone – Stone's Sporting Club.'

'Oh, yeah. I catch a fight down there a couple a three times.'

Jonathan glared at him.

'Who do I speak to about our order?'

'Joe Profaci.'

'Where do I find him?'

The man's brown eyes narrowed and he pulled from a bottle of beer, then lighted a cigarette, and blew the smoke in Jonathan's face.

'You're talking to him boy. Now I'm busy, so you give me a call.'

'Mr. Profaci, why're you cutting our order every week? We pay promptly.'

'Promptly, huh? So's everybody else and they pay a little extra to get a name beer. You gotta come up with a little more for us and look after the drivers.'

'How much extra per case?' Jonathan asked.

'Listen, I tol' you I was busy, now get lost.'

'Look, Mr Profaci, we're losing sales and we need the beer.'

'So does people which are close to us and our own family.'

'If my uncle was here, you wouldn't treat us like shit.'

'Who's your uncle?'

'Paul Salica in Florida.'

Profaci's long ferret face revealed interest.

'You people is Jewish, so how's Paul your uncle?'

Jonathan took out five dollars and placed it on the crate Profaci used as a desk.

'Call him in Florida. He lives at the Roney Plaza.'

'Don't get so excited, kid.'

'We all escaped from Germany together and my father helped to save Uncle Pauli's life. Ask him if you don't believe me.'

Profaci nodded uncertainly.

'I met Paul a couple times in Miami and he showed me and the missus a real good time,' he said warily.

'If you're selling beer to other people at a higher price, then we'll pay it and raise the prices to our customers.' He paused and waited for the offer to register. Profaci was eyeing him respectfully.

'You got a lot of balls for a kid.'

'Listen, we can sell all you can supply. We've got people lining up ten deep around the counter on fight nights. You've been there, so you know.'

'So calm down awready ...'

'You're a fight fan, right, Mr. Profaci? Why do you have to wait on line and buy a ticket? From now on, you just call me anytime you want to go to the fights and you've got two ringside seats. What do you say?'

'I call you?'

'Uh-huh. I run the box office, too.'

Profaci flipped through the orders and found Alex's. He studied it for a moment.

'Now, you wouldn't shit me about your family and Paul bein so tight? Cause I find out yer lyin you never get another case of beer from here.'

Jonathan extended his hand and Profaci shook it.

'Yer a tough little fucker, huh.'

200

'Just trying to run a business like you. Remember, just ask for Jonathan whenever you want the best house seats.'

'Ringside, ehhh?'

'Fifth row so you don't have to strain your neck looking up.'

'Okay, you gotcha beer.' He flagged down a driver loading his truck. 'Ehh, Sal, Stone's on your route ... you give 'em tree hundred cases. What bouts you got comin up which look good?'

'A Cuban by the name of Kid Machado. He's got a new punch called a bolo, a sort of combination uppercut and hook. He hits like a mule. He's fightin a Mexican welter.'

'When's this fight?'

'The Tuesday after Labor Day. It's our big fall card.'

'Okay, Jonathan, you got a deal.' As he was about to leave, Profaci called after him. 'Hey, should I bring a gallon of olive oil for your mom? It's liquid gold these days.'

* * *

He had not seen Lenore for more than three years. The letters he had written had been returned with a note from Sam explaining that she had been placed in a hospital. Jonathan had put the letters in a shoebox at the top of his closet and made an effort to shut Lenore out of his mind.

He was sitting on his bed, going through his clothes with his mother and deciding what to take for the two weeks he was spending up at West's.

Miriam pulled down the shoebox, set it on the bureau, and found packs of baseball cards tied with rubber bands.

'Do you want these cards thrown out?'

'I'm saving them.'

'What for?'

'I'll trade them in a few years, Mama ... they'll be worth lots of money then.'

Miriam stroked his hair, kissed him on the forehead.

'You never stop, do you?'

'Well, I want to be a millionaire and look after you and Papa.'

'Your father's doing just fine,' she said defensively.

'I just want to make us rich.'

They had moved twice and now lived comfortably in a bright, two-bedroom apartment on Eastern Parkway and

Troy Avenue. The rooms were large with high ceilings, the furniture new and comfortable, the refrigerator filled with smoked salmon, cold chicken, fresh fruit and vegetables. Canned goods from S. S. Pierce were stored in a walk-in closet because the pantry wasn't large enough to accommodate the cartons. What was more, Miriam was able to buy her stylish dresses and suits from Best and Company and Peck and Peck on Fifth Avenue. 'What more could you want?'

'A fortune,' he said earnestly.

'Jonathan, the trouble is your eyes are bigger than your stomach.'

'You and Papa don't understand me.'

Miriam's eyes widened in amazement. He had a point, but she was reluctant to admit it. She and Alex frequently argued about Jonathan. He was a loner, indifferent to school, seldom completed his homework assignments, stayed out late hours. But he had a sure instinct for business opportunities and in an odd way he bullied both of them.

David was her prize – the prince of the household. He made Arista with a 94 average and was active in student government at Erasmus High School.

He and Jonathan went their separate ways. Miriam was distressed by what she regarded as her failure to coalesce a relationship between the two brothers. It wasn't that Jonathan didn't care; he simply had other things on his mind. When the family planned a Sunday at Coney Island, Jonathan declined to join them because he had other commitments: a teenage B'nai B'rith tea dance at the club at a dollar a head.

'What's this?' Miriam held up a black velvet pouch.

'Mama, please, let me have it.'

She had already shaken it and the letters spilled to the floor. He held his head in his hands, covering his eyes. She sat down on the bed beside him.

'What are you doing to yourself? You're torturing yourself ...'

'That's my business.' Surly, refusing commiseration.

'Jonathan, you have to trust me. Darling, you keep your secrets in a dark closet. It'll poison your life. We have to talk about it.'

'What's there to say? *Das Opfer!*' He spat the word out. 'You think Lenore's an idiot. I don't. One day she'll be cured

202

and I'll marry her.'

She took her head sadly. 'All these years you've been writing to her and she never received any of your letters.'

'It doesn't matter.'

'Of course it does. You're being twisted with your suffering. You have to face facts. Lenore will never be normal. Those men in Germany hurt her so badly that she had to retreat into another world. Don't you think I care? Her mother was my closest friend. She's the daughter I never had. But when someone becomes ill, you have to accept it and not let it destroy you.'

He rose from the bed and walked to the window. His body tensed. 'You don't have faith.'

'That's not fair.... Faith I have, but miracles I don't believe in.'

'Money ...'

'What's money got to do with anything?'

'If I spend enough money on her, get doctors, she'll be cured.'

'That's your idea of faith? Jonathan, dollars and cents aren't going to cure Lenore. Sam's spent thousands on her. New doctors, sanatoriums, different types of treatment. There hasn't been any improvement. She's a beautiful child, but she's insane.'

The word crushed him and his face was spattered with tears.

'Get it out of yourself,' she pleaded, her eyes filling. 'Cry, purge yourself, darling ... let it come out.'

He kicked at the wall violently.

'She loves me ... she told me she loved me.'

'Jonathan, that was in another life.'

*   *   *

On the ride up Route 17 to the Catskills, Jonathan's parents and brother were jubilant. They had not had a family holiday since arriving in the United States. There had been an occasional weekend in Atlantic City and day trips up the Hudson to Bear Mountain and Indian Point. But this was the real thing – two weeks out of the city in a proper hotel. David chattered happily in the back seat. He had brought his sketch pad, charcoals, a set of oil paints, and a number of canvases. He marveled at the landscape as they

passed dairy farms with large red silos. The smell of freshly
cut hay filled the air.

'It reminds me of Germany,' David said.

'Without soldiers,' Jonathan retorted.

'I can't wait to see the hotel. I'm going to get up at five
every morning so I can paint with the first light.'

Miriam smiled at him. He was so different from Jonathan.
He embodied the cultural interests and sensitivity of her
family. She had more in common with him than with either
Alex or Jonathan. Somehow this son was above the hunger
for money; she could have conversations with him that had
nothing to do with cash receipts, ring records, or the ail-
ments of boxers. She found herself attempting French re-
cipes – coq au vin, caneton bigarde – to please him. At least
it was a change from the meat and potatoes that Alex and
Jonathan demanded every evening. She and David never
discussed the war. It was something out there away from
them; an ocean protected them from the Nazis. Alex never
tired of going over the war casualties; he listened attentively
every night to Gabriel Heatter's news broadcasts and Ed
Murrow from London. To Alex the war was tangible, but
she closed her ears to the reports of savagery.

In David she saw herself fulfilled and she nurtured him,
sharing Saturdays with Milton Cross and the Metropolitan
Opera on the radio, or Toscanini leading the NBC Symphony Orchestra. Occasionally they would sneak out to concerts in Prospect Park while the others were at the club.

At Monroe, David pleaded with his father to stop the car.
He wanted to take photos of the lake that ran through the
town. Swans and mallards floated on the water. Alex refused, irritated.

'We're trying to make time so that we can get there for
dinner.'

'I'd like to stop,' Miriam said.

'Since when do you take pictures?' Alex asked curtly.

'I've got a stomachache. Must've been the French fries.'

He pulled off, muttering under his breath. Miriam went to
the ladies' room at a Socony station and David lined up
pictures with the Kodak box camera Miriam had given him
on his birthday. When she emerged, he insisted on photographing her by the lake.

'Two weeks you'll have for pictures,' Alex grumbled, 'so

204

why're we stopping now?'

Jonathan calmed his father. 'Give them a few minutes.'

Alex shrugged. He couldn't understand what they found so remarkable about a lake with swans.

'I got the beer, Papa. Three hundred cases.'

'Who's going to drink it all?'

'After the fans see Machado fight, we're going to be drawing better than last season.'

'You really like him.'

'I've seen him train every day after summer school.'

Alex smiled. 'After school? Since when are you going? I've got a stack of letters from the principal about your attendance. If you don't stop cutting school, they'll send a truant officer, mister.'

Jonathan ignored the reproof. 'You've signed Machado for only one fight after the Labor Day bout.'

'So, how many should I sign him for?'

'At least six.'

'You listen to me, my friend ... that's a five-hundred-dollar guarantee per bout, and you're asking me to tie up three thousand? What if he's a stiff? A fighter training is one kind of animal. When it's a real fight and he's getting hit, it's another story. I've been there, I can tell you.'

Jonathan stared at his father. 'When Machado's welter-weight champion and getting five thousand from Mike Jacobs at the Garden, you'll kick yourself.'

Alex raised his fist defiantly.

'Five minutes alone with Jacobs I'd like. I'd break his head.'

'So they'd arrest you and you'd lose your license.'

'Don't be such a smart aleck with me.'

'I'm just trying to explain that if you've got a potential champion tied up at the club, like Jacobs has Joe Louis, then you'll always draw. The bookies have the fight even money now because they don't know one from the other. As far as they're concerned, two spics are fighting.'

'You really have that much confidence in Machado?'

'I see the people who come from Manhattan to watch him work out. They know him from Havana. He was fighting middleweights and light heavies there. He murdered every welterweight he ever fought. And he's never been knocked down. He doesn't cut. His skin's like horsehide.'

Alex strolled down to the riverbank. David was inserting a new roll of film. His father unnerved him and he dropped the film spool.

'So, enough with the pictures. Sam's waiting for us. He'll think we had a crack-up.'

Miriam beckoned her husband.

'Let him take a picture of the two of us, please, Alex? It'll be something to remember. Our first trip to the mountains.'

Reluctantly Alex stepped over some rocks and, with a martial glare, posed.

'Pop, you look like a Jewish Napoleon. Smile, for heaven's sake,' David said. 'You love this lady by your side. Put your arm around her.'

Alex brandished his fist at Jonathan standing above him by the car.

'I've got things on my mind. You, *bonditt*, got me all worried. It's enough that I'm taking you on vacation out of the hot city. You've got to cost me three thousand dollars.'

Miriam turned to him in puzzlement. 'What's wrong now?'

'Oh, Jonathan's driving me crazy.'

Jonathan struck a boxing stance, thrust his left and right into the air, and then looped his left in imitation of Machado.

'That's the bolo,' he called out. 'Jacobs'll say he invented it.'

'Son of a gun. How am I going to get in touch with him now?'

'Please, Alex, stand still for the picture.'

Frowning, then forcing a smile to his pugnacious mouth, he placed an arm around Miriam.

'When we get to Sam's you can call him.'

'Where should I call him? I'm walking around with a phone book?'

'Hotel Theresa, room three fifteen, or if he's out you can try the Chateau Madrid. He likes to go dancing there. Says it helps with his footwork,' Jonathan replied triumphantly.

'*Momser*,' his father shouted, 'if he's not champion, you're out of my will.'

'You haven't got enough to leave me.'

'Such a big mouth,' Alex said, flicking a left out at him which the boy blocked. He clinched with his father and pressed his palm against his stomach.

'You're getting soft, Pop.'

It was late afternoon when they reached Monticello, the gateway to the Catskills. The town was filled with women in cotton pinafores, clutching their shopping bags. They bellowed at tradesmen about stale food, clamored about the prices of chicken, complained of the salty belly loxes that hung like flags in the store windows. During this furious bartering they warned the merchants that they'd make reports to the OPA about black market prices.

'They're disgusting,' David said, put off by the sight.

'They can't afford no better,' Alex said.

'Any better, Pop. Double negative.'

'Oh, you're giving me English lessons now?' he replied angrily. 'Next time I hand you a Washington or a Lincoln, ask them how they speak.'

'Don't take offense so easily,' Miriam interposed.

'Then you stop taking his side.'

'Papa, I didn't mean to hurt your feelings, but people judge you by the way you speak. Why should anyone think less of you . . . ?'

'Listen, big shot, when you go out into the world, let's see what kind of success you make of yourself with all your fancy words which half the time nobody understands. You never come down to the club – you let your brother do all the work. Once you should ask if we need to be relieved – to go out to a movie or even shop for a pair of shoes.'

'I don't like the smell there. It stinks,' David answered, losing his temper.

'Pop, let it alone already,' Jonathan said. 'Why does David have to be interested in the club?'

'My head's exploding with all this bickering,' Miriam cried. 'This is supposed to be a vacation for me, too.'

In the back seat, David leaned over and whispered to Jonathan, 'Thanks, but I can fight my own battles.'

Jonathan shook his head from side to side. 'Dave,' he said in a whisper, 'at times you're a little prick.'

David shrank back. He resented Jonathan's dominance and felt threatened by his physical prowess. He knew they could never be close friends, that they both paid lip service to their blood kinship.

David longed for independence. The brutal, scar-faced men with their foul language surrounding his father repulsed him. They didn't understand anything about the beauty of the world.

West's Hotel didn't add to his happiness. The sprawling, low-level buildings struck him as graceless, an architectural eyesore. What was worse, he had counted on having his own room, somewhere in a castlelike turret. But he was assigned an attic room with his brother. He folded his clothes neatly and hung up his Saturday-night blue gabardine suit. He tested the two beds and settled on the lumpy one because it was beside the window. He let the others go on the tour with Sam, promising to join them shortly. He went out in the corridor and saw a dark-eyed young maid in the room opposite, making it up.

'Is there any way I can get a reading lamp?' he asked.

'Isn't there a light in your room?' she asked.

'Yes, but it's on the bureau and it's not bright enough. If I could have one of those lights that attach to the bedpost. They hook on ...'

The girl came toward him, wiggling her hips. She was small, with a firm, supple body, and she gave off an odd feminine odor which tantalized him. He realized she was perspiring. He had never smelled sweat on a woman and it was different from the bitter, alkali wetness of a man.

'I'll see if I can find one.'

She stooped down in the large cupboard and rooted through several old cartons where everything from irons to clothespins were lodged. He leaned over and looked at the back of her dark rayon stockings. He could see black garters and a peninsula of white flesh at the top of her thighs. He felt aroused and uncomfortable. She brought out a scratched metal lamp and he took hold of her elbow to help her up.

'Thanks,' he said, staring at the rise and fall of her breasts.

'How long are you here for?'

'Two weeks ... until Labor Day. What about you?'

'I live up here.'

'At the hotel?'

'No, I just work the season. I'm from Ferndale. My father works in a hardware store there.'

'Are you in high school?'

'Yeah, I'll be a junior.' She sounded bored and restless.

'Me, too ...' He had skipped a year but did not mention it. She must be at least a year older than he and he knew that girls of that age preferred eighteen-year-olds.

'Where are you from?'

'We live in Brooklyn. Do you get down to the city?'

'Once a year if I'm lucky. I stay with my aunt in Coney Island.'

'Hey, that's not far from us.'

Her name was Ellen Berg. She said his family must be fabulously wealthy to be able to afford such a long vacation and he did not contradict her. They agreed to meet after dinner but first she elicited a promise from him.

'There's lamb chops on the dinner menu ... will you steal a portion for me?'

'Sure, no trouble.'

She seemed concerned that she had asked for too little.

'Get them well done.'

'Okay.'

'I'll meet you behind the casino at eight o'clock.'

* * *

At the end of Billy Davis's rendition of 'That Old Black Magic,' with the audience in the casino clapping and stomping their feet as the elegantly dressed black man took bow after bow, Jonathan slipped out of the back row without anyone noticing. He passed David, who was hidden in a corner of the snack bar talking to a dark-haired girl, and he headed to the main house. The lobby was deserted and the partition behind the check-in desk where the office was located was darkened.

He crept into the office and switched on his flashlight. Boxes of files were stacked up against the walls. He hardly knew where to begin. There were so many index cards scattered everywhere. The safe was locked. He opened desk drawers, careful not to disturb any of the folders. Everywhere he looked, there were names and addresses of guests, lists of food, menus, stencils for the hotel newspaper. His task was futile but he kept at it, fighting a battle with the clock. The show would continue for another half hour.

He searched through Sylvia's desk and located a large book of hotel checks. He flipped through the stubs: accounts to the Monticello Dairy, the Ferndale Meat and Provision Company, the Fulton Fish Market. He squinted under the sharp light. His hands trembled, but he was determined to continue the search. He continued going through the check stubs. Toward the end of the book, he found what he was looking for: a check stub made out for three hundred dollars to Dr. Leo Green. Below it he read: ('Lenore – psych, New Liberty Hospital'). He replaced the book, scanned the office with his light, and closed all the drawers. As he left, he bumped into a bellhop who asked him what he was doing inside.

'I needed some stationery,' he replied in a quavering voice.

The bellhop led him to the writing room set in an alcove in the lobby and he awkwardly thanked him. 'By the way, have you got a local phone book?' he asked. 'I want to look up a friend of mine.' In a moment he was handed the Sullivan County directory. He skimmed through the pages and located the address and phone number of the hospital. He debated calling, then went to the phone booth and dialed the number. A woman's voice answered.

'I'd like to send a present to a friend of mine,' he said, 'and I'm afraid of it getting lost. I've got your address, but can I have Lenore West's room number to make sure that it gets to her?' He waited an eternity and then the woman responded.

'Room four fifty-six.'

'Thank you very much.'

Jonathan rejoined his parents in the casino, took his mother out to the dance floor, and did a slow, well-timed foxtrot with her. Alex was so impressed that he implored him to enter the Champagne Hour Dance Contest.

* * *

The boat was damp and David took off his jacket and spread it on the seat for Ellen. Then he tentatively put his arm around her shoulder. He had never been this close to a girl and he was giddy with anticipation. ' "She walks in beauty like the night." '

'Me?' the girl exclaimed.

'It's Byron.'

'Oh?' She didn't know what he was talking about, but something about him appealed to her. She hoped Billy Davis would come down soon and catch her. He had dropped her after a week for a married woman guest and she was vindictive and angry. She saw in David a young man of means who could rescue her from the tedium of a small town. She had learned that he was the son of Alex Stone who owned the sporting club in Brooklyn. Her future lay with someone like him or out in Hollywood with a star of Billy's magnitude. Whichever way, she had to escape.

David groped between her legs. She pushed his hand away but sighed and blew her hot breath in his ear. His temples were throbbing and he reached out to kiss her breasts. She stared at David's mooning face and drew him close to her.

'It's too damp in the boat.'

'Where do you want to go?' he asked, totally compliant.

'In the boathouse ... there are some blankets inside.'

He held her hand as they went. The boathouse was dank and smelled of sodden wood. He switched on his flashlight, and the two crept like conspirators over leaky rowboats and warped oars that were strewn on the floorboards. In a locker in the back she found a khaki blanket and opened her arms to embrace him.

'David, please don't hurt me,' she pleaded.

He clutched her in his arms.

'I swear I won't.'

'I don't want to lose you after you go home.'

'I'll write to you, Ellen, I promise.' The prospect of a romantic correspondence – actual love letters – appealed to him.

'But when can we see each other again? A letter isn't seeing someone.'

'Well, you'll come to the city to visit your aunt.'

'Where'll I get the money? Every penny I make goes to my people.' The sulk of discontent played on her moist lips and her voice became low with the bleat of poverty. 'We're poor, don't you understand?'

Her breasts swirled before his eyes like quicksilver.

'The Short Line bus fare isn't that much ...'

'To you maybe.'

'Hey, I'll pay ... I've got an account in my own name at the East New York Savings Bank. My bar mitzvah money.' The thought of losing her over money distressed him. He had almost five hundred dollars in the bank. 'Don't worry about the fare.'

She lay down on the blanket, yielding, soft, and seemingly defenseless. He kissed her, then felt himself losing control when she opened her mouth and slipped her tongue into his mouth. He grew dizzy, molding into her body. She spread her thighs and he gasped as his fingers penetrated the soft sticky hairs.

'Oooh, play with it,' she groaned, undulating her hips and positioning his untutored hand.

His fingers were wet with her juice. He unbuttoned his fly and she helped him pull down his trousers. He leaped on her, smothering her breasts and face with kisses. Her strong fingers gripped his member and she shoved him inside. She groaned and writhed like a wild animal under him, calling his name. 'David, David, David ... oh, give it to me. Give it to me good. I'll never forget —'

'I'm not wearing any protection,' he said, remembering warnings he had heard all his life. 'What'll I do?'

'Pull it out. Don't come inside me!' she insisted.

By sheer force of will, he pulled himself out. Her fingers clasped around him and she tuggged at it. 'Up and down, up and down,' she said, skilfully wrenching him.

'I'm shooting,' he exclaimed triumphantly.

'I'm a man, he told himself. A man in love with the most beautiful girl in the world. His mouth lingered on hers.

'I'll never let you go,' he assured her.

'We'll always be together,' she said, continuing to grope and knead him. There were visions of trips to New York in her dark eyes.

*   *   *

Jonathan was careful not to wake his brother when he opened the dresser and removed the Kodak box camera. He crept out of the room and counted the money he had brought with him. Twenty-six dollars and forty cents. He walked to the rear of the kitchen and stood behind a clump of bushes. A large refrigerated truck was backed against the kitchen and two men with grapple hooks unloaded huge sides of beef covered with a thin veil of frost. Sam stood beside a scale in the kitchen, clipboard in hand, weighing the meat. Sam signed the receipt and the men closed the door and returned to their truck. Jonathan waited for them to start the engine, then he waved them down.

'Are you going anywhere near Liberty?'

'Yeah, want a lift?' the driver asked.

'I'd appreciate it.'

He was dropped off at the slaughterhouse on the outskirts of town and he walked the rest of the way. He had breakfast at a diner, then went into a drugstore and received directions to the hospital. He bought a bunch of flowers outside a vegetable store and strode through town, breathing in the optimism of a new day. He followed the signpost on the road to the New Liberty Hospital. He had expected bars and gates with guards, but he saw instead people of all ages sitting on the broad lawns, an occasional nurse carrying a tray. Patients were playing cards, reading, listening to the radio. After a few moments he realized that this was not a madhouse but a general hospital, and that the people on the lawn were either injured or recuperating from an illness.

He spotted some children with broken arms and legs in a playground where an elderly nurse on a beach chair dozed.

Behind the swings, sitting on a bench peering at the children, was Lenore. Jonathan's pulse quickened. Furtively, he approached her, then dropped to his knees by her side. She was deeply tanned, taller, and her body had filled out. Her silver-blonde hair had been cut short. She was exquisite.

'It's me, Jonathan, do you remember?' he whispered.

Her stolid face became animated with comprehension. He handed her the flowers, but she dropped them on the bench.

'Baaaaaaaaaaa – Baaaaaaa . . .' she stammered.

She placed her arms round his shoulders and she fixed her gorgeous clear gray eyes on him.

'Jaaa –'

'Don't try to force it,' he pleaded. 'You know who I am.'

She nodded and rose, and he entwined his hand with hers and they walked out of the playground. The nurse was still sleeping.

'Do you want to go to town?'

The question puzzled her for a moment, then she lowered her eyes and gestured to the building behind her. The hospital. 'Come on, they won't miss you for a while. It'll be okay.'

They strolled out of the rear gate down the road. Cars whipped past them and she appeared apprehensive. The noise troubled her.

'You look wonderful, Lenore. You're getting better.'

She attempted to get a word out but was only able to

sputter and breathe heavily.

He took her to an ice-cream parlor and ordered two chocolate floats and long pretzels. She sucked on her straw and occasionally smiled at him. She watched him scoop out the ice-cream with a long frappé spoon and she imitated him. She had chocolate all over her mouth and he wiped her lips with a napkin.

'You'll always be my girl,' he told her, but her concentration had wandered. She broke the pretzel into small chunks and dipped it into the float, eating contentedly. They left the ice-cream parlor and explored the other stores in town. She stared in windows and was held fast by women's clothes and shoes. He noticed that she was wearing soiled canvas tennis sneakers and took her into the shop. A salesman measured her foot and Jonathan asked him to bring out a selection of bedroom slippers. She picked up a pair of sealskin slippers trimmed with black leather and rubbed them against her face.

'Try them on, they're beautiful.'

The salesman put them on her feet. She stood up and walked to the mirror. There was childish glee on her face. She turned and looked at him over her shoulder. She shook her head. Jonathan took out his money and paid the salesman four dollars.

'I've missed three of your birthdays, so you've got two presents to go. What next?' As they passed a lingerie shop, he spotted a dressing gown in the window. 'Right, a bathrobe.' She tried on several and he settled on a black velvet one which matched the slippers. 'Now something really personal,' he said, stopping at a jeweler's. In the display case he saw a cameo locket on a chain. 'You can wear this all the time and then I'll be with you.' The locket was seven dollars, heart-shaped, and it had a clasp which opened. Inside were pockets for small photos. He snapped the catch around her neck and was embarrassed when the jeweler scrutinized him. His hands lingered on the warm, soft nape of her neck.

He picked up some film at another shop, loaded the camera, and stationed Lenore under the marquee of the local movie theater. He focused the lens. 'Smile.' She didn't understand so he went toward her and with two fingers gently pushed the sides of her mouth. 'Are you ticklish? Yes, you must be. All beautiful girls are ticklish.' She was like a statue and he raised her arms and ran his fingertips along her ribs. She began to giggle. 'Right,' he said, returning to the edge of the sidewalk. 'I can't have you looking like you're at a funeral.' She continued to laugh and there was a hint of something uncontrollable and peculiar in the shrill noise she made. 'Okay, stop, that's enough. I've got a real actress on my hands.'

He stopped a passerby and asked him to take a photograph of the two of them. The man was amused and suggested that they embrace. Jonathan solemnly placed his hand around her waist, and she opened her mouth slightly and looked up at him.

'When's the wedding?' the man asked, returning the camera.

'In a few years.'

Kids had lined up at the box office and had begun to jeer at the two of them, and Jonathan moved away with her.

'Haven't you yokels ever seen somebody from the big city?'

The title on the marquee was *How Green Was My Valley*. Lenore pressed her face against the stills of the actors. She seemed mesmerized by the mystery of the photos. He looked at the starting times and said, 'Have you been to a movie?' She shrugged haplessly. 'Well, it's about time. Come on.' He picked up the shopping bag with her gifts and took her by the hand and joined the line.

After buying their tickets, he went to the candy counter and in a wild splurge he bought a Chunky, a Clark Bar, Mounds, Raisenettes, Goobers, licorice, two Hershey bars, and a bag of popcorn. They found seats in the back row and waited for the movie to begin. He put his arm around her when the lights dimmed and the titles began.

'Walter Pidgeon, Maureen O'Hara,' he exclaimed. 'Uncle Victor's out in Hollywood and he knows all of them.' Her eyes were on the screen and she clapped wildly when Welsh miners began to sing in a chorus. He restrained her, and gripped her hand tightly, then when she understood, he released her and peeled the paper off the Chunky and put it in her mouth. All through the film, he studied her reactions.

She was paying close attention to the dialogue and the story, so he reasoned there had to be some intelligence which had not been damaged. It was becoming increasingly clear to him that she understood English, but her illness prevented her from speaking. She would recover, he was convinced, if she were allowed to live in a normal environment. Sitting beside him in the dark of the movie house, gnawing away at a candy bar along with the hundred-odd other children, she seemed as normal as any of them. She needed patience, kindness, and not that awful banishment in order to regain her speech.

He had to speak to Sam about her. Surely Sam would respond to reason? The woman he lived with was friendly and warm. Why couldn't they rescue her? Tears of anger seared his cheeks. You couldn't just imprison the girl because she was an inconvenience.

Her fingers groped at his, and her palm was wet and sticky. He kissed her fingers, tasted the salty sweetness of her flesh. Her chest heaved when the men in the film were down below in the coal mine and apparently trapped. When the wooden roof caved in, she shuddered and groaned with the other spectators. It was clear that she understood what she was seeing.

'Lenore, you're my sweatheart and I love you,' he said in a low pained voice.

Her eyes turned to him and she nodded slowly, closed her eyes, and held up her face which he kissed. He thought his heart would burst with the emotion that swelled up inside him. She leaned her head on his shoulder and he stroked her hair, and when he pressed his face against hers, her eyes were wet and doleful. He held her tightly to him. If it were up to him, he would sit in the theater forever, protecting her.

It was late afternoon when, blinking, they left the theater. The sunlight lashed at them. They'd be worried about her at the hospital and, for all he knew, would have reported her missing. But he couldn't let her go, and he clutched at her arm, refusing to yield.

'Come on, let's go and have something else to eat.'

They walked to a sandwich shop across the street. As they reached the curb, a police car pulled up and two cops got out. Behind them was his father's dark blue Oldsmobile. Sam and Alex rushed from the front seat. Sam seized him by the shoulders.

'You little bastard, I'll break your head,' he stormed wildly.

'Are you outa your mind?' His father's voice.

'Give me a chance,' Jonathan protested.

Sam's hand lashed out, striking him viciously across the cheek. He dropped the shopping bag, shoved Sam away, and raised his fists.

'We'll take him,' one of the cops said.

'She's not crazy. She understands everything,' Jonathan cried, looking at Lenore's frightened face. She was shaking, cowering, and uttering jibberish sounds.

Sam struck him again.

'Do that again, you fuck, and I'll kill you,' Jonathan said. He rushed over to Lenore who was being led by the hand to the police car. 'I'll never leave you.'

She was crying bitterly and he picked up the shopping bag which had fallen into the gutter. He thrust it inside the car. 'I'll send you the pictures.'

The car was moving away from the curb and a crowd had gathered and watched with curiosity.

He walked toward his father with his head lowered, striking the air with his fists, crippled by his anguish. Sam turned away from him and Alex shook his head disconsolately.

'What in the name of God are we going to do with you?'

It was too painful for Jonathan to remain at the hotel. With Alex's consent he returned that evening to the city by bus. It was four in the morning when he arrived at the deserted Port Authority building. Geysers of smoke spewed from the sewers and the humidity clutched him, bringing him out in a sour sweat. Dragging his battered suitcase, he rode the IRT back to Brooklyn. When he reached the apartment, he fell onto the sofa without removing the dust sheet Miriam had covered it with. Silently he took his wound to sleep with him. In the dark recesses of his mind, he saw an image of Lenore smiling at him.

Seventeen

Paul did not feel comfortable in the dimly lighted nightclub. He was not in the mood for raucous drunks or the high-kicking Copacabana show girls thrusting themselves at the ringside table he occupied with Frank Costello and his partner in the club, the sleekly handsome, exquisitely tailored Joe Adonis. It was at the urging of these two men that Paul had come to New York. Costello had arranged for a noted plastic surgeon to operate on Chou and he had personally guaranteed Paul's safety.

'Look, these things happen and it's nobody's fault,' Costello said. His voice was naturally gravelly and had a limited range. Often it sounded as though he were beveling wood with a file. 'Bugsy's been spoken to –' He looked to Adonis who was carving his steak.

'He claims he don't know anything about what happened in Miami,' Adonis said.

'I don't have to believe him.'

'Agreed,' Costello said. 'But Bugsy has the support of the Commission. You, you're isolated.'

Adonis sipped his drink and tried to soften the blow. He was diplomatic and a gentleman.

'Pauli, everyone knows you're doin a fabulous job in Miami. It was dead as Kelsey's nuts till you were brought in by Lep and Meyer. It's profitable – t' ings is quiet, under control. You're a comer. You're gonna be very important. It's clear to Francesco and me. We are behind you one hundred percent.'

Paul had yet to touch his steak. He knew he was being boxed in. As a relative newcomer, he had to rely on the goodwill of the established members of the Combination. He wasn't strong enough yet to go nakedly after Bugsy.

'Now nobody's starting any wars within,' Costello observed authoritatively. 'There's too much involved. Black market, gambling, numbers, the waterfront. The FBI is busy looking to catch saboteurs and spies. We don't need no attention. No war.'

Paul had learned from Lansky that showdowns were to be avoided. No single man could stand up to the Commission. Lay back, keep a cool head, and lull the opponent to sleep was the only way to survive.

'*Compari*, look at my position. Lepke gives me introductions. He arranges for me to stake out a new territory. I work my ass off and after a time, I do the job. I have the respect of the Commission. Thirty-five percent goes to them. I don't hold out. There's never any question of my loyalty or that I'm capable.'

They both nodded in agreement.

Adonis patted his hand like a proud uncle.

'You're a first-class man, no question,' Adonis said, battering his steak with ketchup. 'Nothin but good reports on you, Pauli.'

'*Grazie*, Giuseppe. I appreciate that from you. So why do I get myself in the shit? Lepke is wanted by every cop in the country. My benefactor, right? To draw him out, the Feds and the cops begin to put pressure on everyone in town. Numbers banks are raided, hookers are scooped off the street. Your Piping Rock Club in Saratoga gets heat. People get arrested. Bookies are locked up. It's trouble. Everybody is worried because of one man.'

'Right,' Adonis said. He lifted his glass and sucked an ice cube, then looked up at the line of dancing girls. 'See that redhead, second from the left.'

'She's over six foot.'

'You like 'em big? Man she wrap her legs around by my ears the other night, I thought I'd come up deaf.' The girl wiggled the pony tail covering a small section of her buttocks and winked at Adonis as she danced by.

'Joe, we got time to talk about cunt later.'

Paul waited for the act to change. Two singers came out and boomed a medley from *Pal Joey* and Adonis's attention returned to Paul.

'Meyer comes from Havana to see me and says that Lep trusts me, and he explains the problems.'

'Meyer doesn't consult us on this,' Costello noted icily.

'How am I to know? Should I start making phone calls to everybody to ask permission? Meyer tells me what to do. I've got no scores to settle, so Lepke will listen to me and respect that I'm acting in his interests. Meyer says I have to convince Lepke to give himself up to Winchell ... that a deal has been made on an old rap. He'll do a year or two at the most. I visit Lep. He's living like an animal in Anastasia's basement. He's crazy with suspicions because of Reles naming people to O'Dwyer. He can't trust a soul.'

He glared angrily at the two men at the table. 'I'm a patsy. I didn't know that Winchell is going to bring Hoover along and that they're going to bury Lepke in federal court, then let New York State nail him on murder charges. I did what I was told. Meyer does not act without Charlie Lucky's approval, so it is important that I do it right. Charlie is watching me, counting on me.' He raised his voice – 'Suddenly all the problems are solved! You, Joe, Tommy Lucchese, are back in business. And I wind up with a reputation as a shitheeler. Anastasia and Siegel believe I'm responsible. Nobody tells them otherwise. I'm alone. No one takes my part – explains that I've been *ordered* to do this thing.'

Costello pushed his plate away and finished his highball. He looked uneasy and dismayed.

'The problem is, as I told you, Meyer didn't inform us.'

'We're in the dark, you understand,' Adonis backed him up.

'Well, how am I supposed to know what's in your mind and Meyer's? Besides, who profited by Lepke being taken out of circulation?' He pointed a finger at Costello and Adonis. 'The two of you more than anyone else. You were both feeling police pressure. I should've come out of this a hero – not a rat's ass which a cocksucker like Bugs can take shots at, and leave my wife lying in a hospital with her face scarred.'

'She won't have a mark on her when the doctor takes the bandages off,' Costello said sympathetically. 'I don't like her getting hurt any more than you.'

'It's not right to touch a man's woman,' Adonis added.

'Tell that to Bugsy. From the minute I met him – and I'm delivering four million worth of drugs – the man gives me a hard time. He gets jealous. Maybe because my operation is throwing off more money than his is in California? If he wants to change territories, I'll be happy to do it.'

Costello nodded solemnly.

'You've got right on your side, Pauli. But now it's time to talk about peace.'

'Peace! How? Do I go out to the Coast and take a shot at Bugsy's woman? What happens to me and my business? I've lost face with my people. Why should they put out for me when they think I'm walking around on borrowed time?' He threw up his hands in despair. 'My operation's falling apart. If any shitass can shoot me down and my wife, what's my power? Francesco,' he pleaded, 'would you give me loyalty? Giuseppe, would you have any respect for me? If you were the one sitting out in Duke's in Cliffside and a car comes by and people shoot at you and your wife, what's your Family going to think if you don't fight back? Are your soldiers going to put their asses on the line if you lay back? Come on,' he said forcefully, 'I don't stand up, they know I'm finished.'

The two men regarded him silently and paid scant attention to Joe E. Lewis, the comedian, who made his entrance tearing up racetrack tickets and bolting to the closest table for a Scotch highball.

'What do you suggest?' Costello asked fretfully.

'You can't just reinstate me. You have to prove that I not only survived, but I got more power.'

'Where's that supposed to be?' Adonis asked, walking into the trap Paul had laid. 'The cities are a closed shop – what's the use talking?'

'I have to go back with Arizona.'

Both men looked at him as though he had lost his mind.

'Arizona? What's there? It's desert ... dry climate for TB and asthma cases.'

'It's got potential and it'll take the right man to develop it,' Paul said ingenuously. 'It's a vote of confidence from you and the Commission,' he added.

'I got no objections,' Adonis replied. 'Do you, Frank?'

Costello's puzzlement increased and Paul knew that he sensed something.

'No gambling. Just local clubs. Far as I know, no important track.'

In time, Paul thought. It was at the border of Mexico and had direct access to both California and Nevada. It was his gateway to the future.

'If it's a desert, then I'll irrigate it. I want it.'

'Pauli' – Adonis began to laugh and caught Joe E. Lewis's attention – 'they don't have an Italian restaurant in the whole fuckin state.'

'Then I'll have to eat steak.'

He rose and explained that there was only an hour left to visit Chou in the hospital. Costello signaled the captain and asked that a bottle of iced Dom Pérignon be brought wrapped to the table.

'You give Chou our regards,' Costello said. 'Okay, Pauli?'

'Sure, when do I hear?'

'We'll make our recommendations to the Commission. By Labor Day you'll have yourself a new state,' Costello said with a frozen smile.

Chou's room resembled a florist shop. The most prominent floral arrangement was a giant horseshoe of mixed roses placed against the wall beside her bed. A large, heart-shaped card was signed:

With love,
VIRGINIA and BEN

Paul sat down on the side of the bed and took her hand. Her face was covered with bandages and he bent over to kiss her forehead.

'How are you, Chou?'

'Pauli,' she cried, 'I want him dead.'

'Soon ...'

*   *   *

Victor had carefully arranged a private luncheon in the garden of the Beverly Hills Hotel with Hedda Hopper to discuss plans for his New York trip.

Heavyset, with flabby arms, a Kewpie doll's painted lips, and helmeted in a large black hat embedded with a variety of tulips, Hedda was talking with her mouth full. A piece of asparagus clung to her front tooth. She disapproved of his signing Ronnie Flynt.

'I hear he's a dope smoker and fools around with young girls.'

'He's reformed,' Victor assured her.

'Well, he's attractive in a kind of sweaty way,' she noted contemptuously. Victor smiled ironically and coughed into his fist.

'Aren't you eating your salmon?' she asked.

'No, I can't keep food down before I get on a plane.'

He passed his plate over to her. She heaped mayonnaise on it from the sauce boat and lost a gob of it on the pink tablecloth. He despised her but she was the most powerful columnist in Hollywood and he was aware that she rather liked him because he had never given her a false story.

'Victor, frankly, I don't think video's ever going to be important. Maybe if you like seeing baseball on a ten-inch screen it's okay. But important people'll never watch it and major stars won't appear on it. Not enough money, no prestige, and it's strictly for the working stiff.'

He profoundly disagreed with her but that didn't matter. He needed an item in her column about his trip to New York, something to pave the way for him. The networks, still in their infancy, regarded Hollywood with awe.

'Hedda, you've always been good to me which is why I feel compelled to give you this exclusive.'

She licked her lips in anticipation.

'I'm going to put together the biggest package of programs ever conceived.'

'Like what?'

'You're right about sports. Until the screens get bigger, a game's tough to follow. But don't forget we live in an insulated town. Screenings and movie theaters are available to us. Movies shape our lives. But outside of New York, Chicago, and L.A. the country is a wilderness. People are cut off. Television isn't just a novelty. It's going to be the average man's means of learning what's going on in the world.'

'What kind of programs do you have in mind?'

'What works on radio ... quiz shows like the Sixty-four Dollar Question,' comedies like 'Jack Benny,' 'Bob Hope,' dramas like 'Lux Radio Theatre,' crime shows like 'Gangbusters,' 'Mr. Keen,' variety shows like 'Hit Parade.' If Crosby or Sinatra could be seen as well as heard, the public will run out and buy sets and switch on. The other thing television can do better than anything else is to sell products. It'll be the most important advertising medium we'll have. Sponsors pay dollars. Don't you see it's the beginning of a cycle?'

Her bulging eyes flickered with interest.

'What do you want from me?'

'I'd like you to give this discussion a big play in your column.'

'On one condition. I want you to confirm or deny a rumor that's making the rounds.'

'If I can.'

'Is Howard Hughes shacking up with Rita Sanders?'

He did not lose his poise. 'Not that I know of.'

'Are they seeing each other?'

'How do you want to play it?' he asked, sensing that an abrupt denial would hurt him.

'Maybe they've been meeting on the QT . . .'

'That's entirely possible.'

'Beautiful, Victor.'

What webs of innuendo she would spin from this ambiguous admission. Photos of Hughes and Rita would be side by side and a vulgar squib linking the two would appear below it.

'Have a good flight, Mr. Video,' she said, 'and thanks for lunch.'

He got up from the table, kissed her hand gallantly. To survive in this business, it was necessary to see that the sharks were well fed.

On the Constellation, he read the trade papers for the first hour. When the captain announced that they were passing over the Grand Canyon, many of the passengers rose and gawked out of the windows. The seat next to him, as planned, was unoccupied, and the lovely, fresh-smelling redhead in her gray knobby Chanel suit said:

'Can I join you?'

He put down *Variety* and smiled at Rita.

'Isn't it nice to be alone for once?' he said, caressing her hand.

'Victor, it'll be like a honeymoon. I'm so excited.'

*   *   *

The holiday passed with agonizing slowness for Alex. He was anxious to return to New York because, whenever he left the city, he was convinced that he was missing something, an event, a chance encounter which would alter his destiny. And he did not want to admit it, but he missed Jonathan desperately. Their plans to go on hikes, family picnics, fish the lake, had ended when he left. Alex became

224

moody, short-tempered. He spent his days playing poker on the lawn and his evenings strolling silently with Miriam along the lake shore. He saw David only at mealtimes and was unaware of his constant absence. He didn't consciously play favorites, but as he complained to Miriam: 'How many times am I supposed to look at the flowers he finds on his nature hunts, or admire his pictures? It's impossible to talk man to man with him.'

'Give the boy a chance,' she pleaded.

'Oh, Miriam, I do, but what's the use?' he replied.

Jonathan called him every day and reported on Machado's training. According to Jonathan, Machado's idea of conditioning involved two or three women a night, half a dozen zombies, and dancing the rumba at the Chateau Madrid till dawn.

Jonathan was maturing rapidly, while David was painting sunsets and quoting poetry. Alex longed to discuss the business with Jonathan, how to bring in other activities around the season so that the club would function as a year-round proposition.

'I should go back . . .'

'You promised we'd stay over Labor Day,' Miriam said, distressed. 'How often do we get away?'

'But, look, I've got three thousand dollars invested in Machado . . . the man's in training and he needs me there. I don't know what's going on with my livelihood. If not for Jonathan keeping an eye out, I'd be in real trouble.'

She clutched hold of his arm and forced him down on a bench overlooking the lake. The cool night air made her shiver.

'When, Alex, when was the last time you held me in your arms and told me you loved me?' The accusation of indifference irritated him. 'When's it going to be *our* time? I remember that you couldn't breathe or think unless I was with you.' Why had apathy like a mysterious virus crept into her marriage? She had visited Lenore, and the girl had appeared to recognize her, but during the entire visit Lenore had been looking beyond her, expectant. Was she waiting for Jonathan to reappear? The passion of the children aroused Miriam's anger, for it reminded her of what she had lost with Alex.

'Miriam, I'm not the kind of man – like Sam – who walks

around holding his woman's hand and leaning on her shoulder for protection. I started something when we got to this country and all my energy goes into it. I know we're living comfortably enough, but I want more – not for myself but for all of us.'

'It's you and Jonathan.'

'He's a part of both of us and he's got a way with the club that's special. Every day he's dreaming up new ideas and I have to listen because he always thinks of something that makes money. It's amazing, genius, if you want my opinion. What happened with Lenore set him off the rails, but I understand.'

'I understand, too ... once that was you.'

'No, Miriam, we were different. He's got a sickness which tears at his insides. No use discussing it with Sam, but I watched Lenore in the police car. She was suffering, and I think that if Jonathan could see her more often she'd become human again.' He held her face in his rough, scarred hands and kissed her. She jerked away violently.

'Jonathan, our own child, flesh and blood, he scares me. He's running away with our lives, Alex.'

'You're wrong,' he protested vehemently. 'It's the struggle I'm involved with in the club, with big people who want to stamp me out like a roach. I won't let them do it to me. I'll fight. Please, Miriam, don't drive me away.'

She snuffled in her handkerchief, distraught, perceiving that she was caught between her son and her husband.

'Miriam, come on, please,' Alex said, forcing her into an embrace, 'let's go to the casino. You'll hear Billy singing, we'll dance, have a drink, you'll feel better.'

From behind a hedge outside the casino, David surreptitiously watched his parents greeted by card friends. They would be inside for at least two hours and he could bring Ellen to his room without being detected. As the time at the hotel grew shorter – in two days he'd be back home – David's panic increased. The thought of losing Ellen tortured him. Would she come down to the city or would she break her promise? The prospect of an entire year without seeing her brought him out in a sweat.

He snuck past the bellhop at the desk who was sunk in the sports pages. His room key was clammy and he squeezed it so hard he had an imprint in his palm.

On the second floor he heard footsteps on the back stairs. In a moment she was on the landing and he rushed down, falling on her, pinning her against the wall.

'Don't let's get caught,' she muttered, her mouth half open.

Stealthily they climbed the stairs and David fumbled with the key. She took it from him, the professional door opener, and slid it easily into the creaking lock.

They had never been indoors with a bed at their disposal. His heart leaped at the convenience of this forbidden intimacy. He pushed his hand under her sweater and she gave a soft moan.

'Wait ... please.' Her dark eyes were serious and, he thought, sad.

'What's wrong?'

'I keep thinking of you leaving.'

'Me, too,' he admitted, pressing her hands to his lips. 'It's awful.'

'I've decided,' she fumbled, 'not – well, what I'm trying to say is that I don't want to live without you, David. I've got my working papers and I'm not going back to high school.'

He was astonished.

'You're going to quit? But what're you going to do?'

'Live with my aunt. Last summer I worked a few weeks as a waitress and I was pretty good.'

'Will your parents let you go?' He fidgeted with a chewing gum wrapper. Suddenly it was all getting out of hand. She would be a responsibility. He had no idea how his mother and father would react if they discovered he was sleeping with a girl and she had come to live near him.

'Ellen, I don't know how much money I can give you,' he said, oppressed by the burden.

'Not a penny. I'll make out, David.' She gripped his arm. 'I love you and want to marry you,' she said with certainty. 'Have kids and maybe eventually come back up here and buy a farm. I always wanted to live on a farm.'

His throat tightened and he thought he would choke. 'I'm only sixteen. I mean, it could be years away. I'm taking my Regents exams later this year and then I'm going to college.' Marriage was unthinkable, frightening. 'How can we get married if I'm at school?'

'If you go to a city college you could work – we both can – and make it.'

'But I've always planned on getting out of New York. I'm applying to California schools.'

'California? That's halfway across the world. Why not China?' she said reproachfully. 'Don't you want me?' Her voice cracked and he sat down beside her, kneading his hands in hers. 'Am I just a lay for you? Someone you can poke, then run out on?' She was shrill with outrage, trapping him with guilt. 'You really thought I was just a piece, didn't you?'

Her anger intimidated him.

'No,' he pleaded, 'I care about you.'

'Say you love me,' she insisted. 'Say it!'

'Ellen, I love you.'

She relaxed and her face softened. 'Put it in me, honey. I want it real bad. And, David ... don't pull out this time.'

She spread her thighs and he rammed himself inside her and pumped furiously as she sighed, groaned, and clung to him. At the last moment, through sheer force of will, he pulled free of her and came on the bedspread.

'Why did you ... ?'

He couldn't allow her to finish the question.

'Goddamn it,' he asserted, 'do we need a baby on top of everything else?'

*   *   *

Victor had given Rita three hundred dollars to go shopping. He'd meet her back at the Waldorf where they had adjoining rooms. In the cab on his way to NBC, he read Hedda's story in the *Daily News*.

DATELINE HOLLYWOOD

Victor Conte, the bright young head of the agency that bears his name, has come up with a revolutionary idea for television packaging. Joined him for lunch at the Beverly Hills Hotel on his way to Gotham. Vic confided to this skeptical reporter that he sees Video developing drama programs with its own stars and that many of the radio programs whose listeners number in the millions will work in this new medium ... Well,

Vic, all we can say is good luck, paesano ...'

He had a full schedule of appointments with television executives, but he had decided to try NBC first, since David Sarnoff, the president, had a reputation for giving new people a chance. If he could make some kind of deal there, other doors would open for him. But he was not prepared for the cold, stony-faced reception from the three men who formed the network's programming arm. He sat with them at a large conference table on the twenty-first floor overlooking the skating rink. Ralph Adams, a thin, wisp of a man with horn-rimmed glasses; Alan Dowling, a muscular, red-faced man who seemed to be suffering from some stomach disorder; and Joel Barrett, a dark-haired, oily man who threw off the pungent odor of Old Spice.

He might have been submitting to an audit from three Internal Revenue killers. He wondered which one he ought to play to. Did they make decisions in consort or was one man calling the shots? It distressed him to appear at a disadvantage. He wasn't even certain that they had read the *News* item, and so he decided to treat them as morons and explain their business to them.

'We're all in the entertainment industry and the question we have to address ourselves to is not what we want to see – whether it's classics or Dodger games – but what is it that those people out there all across America want to see when they switch on their sets.'

'If you could predict that,' Adams began, 'you'd be a millionaire.'

'I've spent enough time in clubs, vaudeville, and as an agent to have a sense of what the public cares about.'

'Give us an example, Mr. Conte,' Barrett asked.

'To begin with, let's look at our audiences. Not many people can afford TV sets – a twelve-inch set runs around seven hundred to a thousand – so we're dealing with a wealthy to upper-middle-class segment of society. Andrea, Philco, Dumont, and RCA have the market, and Dumont has the lock on the industry because they make the picture tube which all the manufacturers buy. Now what do these affluent comfortable people want to see? Boxing? Football? No, they go out to the games. They've got season tickets. Programs have to do one of several things: make them laugh, cry, scare them, or involve them as participants.'

He rose to his feet, paced behind them.

'Your audience today likes comedies, human drama, and they're more comfortable if they can relate and identify with the characters.'

'Exactly,' Adams said. 'No poor people or ethnic groups.'

'They want to hear music and watch pretty girls dancing,' Victor noted. 'Now I can provide concepts and the know-how of putting together shows. We can't get Fred Astaire and Ginger Rogers to do TV, so I'll find two unknowns and make them stars. But dancers can't carry a whole show, so we need a singer, preferably a male. He can't sing for ninety minutes, so a comedian is necessary. And there you've got 'The Victor Conte Variety Show.' Whichever one is the strongest element, we build the show around. We have regulars that the audience can follow week after week, and special guest shots.'

He saw no visible reaction from any of them, just Barrett taking notes and Dowling maintaining his austere silence.

'The audience has children and their kids watch shows. How do parents feel about their kids? They adore them. I have two daughters. To my wife and me, they're beautiful. Most parents have the same attitude, but we know that all kids aren't handsome, beautiful, or talented. Every fifty years we get a Jackie Coogan or a Shirley Temple. But what all parents hope is that their kids are brilliant. Show two is: 'Do I have a Genius?' Parents write in, send in school reports, teachers' recommendations, the kids are screened, then each week we select four of them. And we have a knockout contest. We establish the areas of knowledge. At the end of the year, we bring the winners together in their respective categories and the three finalists get full scholarships to a college. Since it's a charitable contribution, what does it cost the network? Nothing. It's a tax write-off.'

Dowling had begun to hum to himself and Victor feared that he had lost ground, but he continued relentlessly.

'Drama. We develop an anthology series and provide plays that are written specifically for TV. We find ambitious young writers who can adapt themselves to this medium. We use quality short stories that will interest a wide segment of the viewers. Nothing downbeat. No cruelty. One week it's a mystery, then a comedy, then straight melodrama. And we

230

get as host a movie star who doesn't work much but who the public likes.'

Dowling looked at his watch and tapped his pencil on the table. He stood up and stared at Victor.

'Who produces these shows?'

'I do.'

'You're based in California.'

'I open an office in New York and commute.'

'So you have an agency as well as a production company?' Dowling asked, intrigued.

'That's my plan.'

Dowling looked to the other two executives for a signal. Both shook their heads negatively and Victor felt angered by their stupidity.

'If we pass, what do you do with your ideas?'

Victor picked up his briefcase and extended his hand. 'I'm having lunch with some people at CBS this afternoon,' he lied. 'Because of my respect for General Sarnoff, I came here first. I appreciate your time, gentlemen.'

Dowling's face twitched and he barred Victor's way to the door. 'Victor,' he said, 'we can't call every show "The Victor Conte Hour."'

'Name it after a sponsor. Colgate, General Motors, Ford Rinso, the Bell System. It's good advertising for them, especially when the show's a hit. The title becomes a recognition factor which helps them sell their products. In other words, it's simply a trademark, but something beyond that which represents quality.'

'I love it,' Dowling said. 'You've got a deal. The variety show should run ninety minutes, one hour for the play, and the quiz show can start as a half hour. If it catches on, we'll go to an hour.'

By three that afternoon Victor had seen his attorney and formed VCA Enterprises with offices in Los Angeles and New York. As he walked along Fifth Avenue, he had that sure knowledge of having arrived. He walked into Cartier's and picked out a diamond bracelet for two thousand dollars which he would present to Rita that evening when they had dinner at the Stork Club. The world was his that afternoon.

*　　*　　*

'Sonavabitch, how are you?' Paul said, seizing hold of Alex and crushing him in a bear hug. 'I've been trying for days to get a hold of you.'

'We were away at Sam's place. Pauli, it's good to see you.'

In another moment, Victor entered the small bar in Peter Luger's. The three men had arranged dinner at their favorite steak house which was not far from their first apartments in Williamsburg.

'Holy mother of Mary, look at the way that dago's dressed,' Paul said when Victor approached.

'Do I have to wear wide-striped shirts and suspenders like you? Brooks Brothers, gentlemen. I'm an Ivy League model,' he said, spinning around on his brogues and revealing a narrow Palm Beach blue blazer.

'You're a regular movie star,' Alex said fondly. He signaled the bartender for setups of Canadian Club with beer chasers. 'To friendship,' he toasted, and they downed their drinks. They had a small squabble about who was to pay.

'It's settled, my friends,' Alex said. 'You're in my territory. In Miami, you didn't let me put my hand in my pocket, Paul, and in California, you'll be the one, Victor. Here, it's my pleasure.'

They had several more drinks as they caught up with the personal news. Victor and Alex listened with dismay to the story of the attempt on Paul's life. Alex said he would visit Chou with Miriam the following day, but Paul told him to wait until the bandages were removed from her face and she became used to the change in her appearance.

Over massive T-Bone steaks and salads of thickly cut tomatoes and onions, they talked about their futures.

'Pauli, can't you be satisfied with what you've already got in Florida?' Alex asked, a note of caution in his voice.

'No, it's not just making money, but, well – how do I explain myself? – it's something that tears at my guts. I want it all. The respect, the leadership in the organization. I can't just be backed in a corner and let other people step on my head.'

'Ambition's a disease,' Alex said. 'We all suffer from it. But in our cases, nobody's taking shots at us.'

Salica's dark eyes clouded with anger. 'My kind of operation always depends on a show of strength. I'm fighting for more territory. I have to grow until I've got control.'

Victor understood his friend. He himself would never be satisfied with remaining a mere agent. He knew that when he returned to the Coast he would have to run from one bank to the other to set up a completion bond for every program he undertook with the network. The bankers would cautiously weigh the risks of backing a man without production credits. It wasn't going to be easy, but he was determined.

They ate hurriedly because they were going to the Machado fight with Alex immediately after dinner. Every now and again, Paul caught the eye of the heavyset man standing by the dark blue Packard parked outside. Carmine now accompanied Paul everywhere he went.

'If I didn't get to see you in New York, I was going to call you about a little chat I had with Winchell in Miami,' Paul told Alex.

'About Mike Jacobs again?'

'Yeah, seems you're hurting him, Alex.'

'The Garden doesn't have a monopoly on boxing.'

'Hey, relax, it's me you're talking to.'

'If Machado turns out to be welterweight champion, I'll have a lock on every division under middleweight. You and Carmine ought to come into boxing in a serious way, Pauli. If you did, we could break the Garden's stronghold.'

Victor was thinking. Finally he said, 'Alex, maybe you got too many eggs in that basket. Isn't it possible to diversify even more now that you bought the lease?'

'Like what, Victor? We already have charity evenings, bingo ... roller skating for the kids.'

'Suppose I could book big band concerts and singers?'

'Would that type of audience travel to Brooklyn?' Alex asked with irritation. 'You and Jonathan, are always trying to talk me out of my real business. My heart's only in boxing.'

'I think they'd go anywhere to hear a Glen Miller or the Dorseys.'

'Why don't you look for a location in Manhattan You'd have access to the movie- and theatergoers. You could stage concerts of popular music, you could rent it out to different fraternal organizations. You wouldn't live or die on the basis of boxing attendance.'

'I'm making damn good money.'

'Maybe you could make more,' Paul interjected.

Alex could not get through to them. He saw himself as another Tex Rickard, a promoter of classic fights which would live forever in the annals of sport. He did not want to become someone who merely rented or leased his club to anyone who could pay for a night. No, Stone's Sporting Club had to become the mecca of boxing, presided over by himself.

'Look, I don't want to be connected with stag nights that lodges throw ... where they bring in hookers, strippers, and French movies. I'm not a showman like Billy Rose. I'm a boxing man.' His face tightened and the lines on his face grew hard and taut.

'Alex, your big supply of fighters is from Latin America, Cuba, but what happens later this year when Joe Louis, Billy Conn, Sugar Ray, Beau Jack return to the Garden? The papers are full of Jacobs's promotion plans,' Victor persisted. 'You'll be an outpost staging two-bit bouts with stumble-bums. Now's the time to expand into different areas.'

Alex swallowed the last of his beer. It was almost seven. The prelims would be starting at eight fifteen and he had to get back to ensure that the ushers had checked in and that last-minute ticket sales weren't being conducted outside by scalpers. He called for the check and said:

'My friends, we're going to the fights.'

*   *   *

The fans shoved, moving in thick waves in the humid, sweltering night, to reach the entrance of the club. Jonathan sat in the ticket booth eyeing customers at the will-call window. He had put two tickets in an envelope for Joe Profaci and wanted to be certain that his beer supplier came to pick them up. He was tense and jumpy. They had never drawn such a large crowd: more than three thousand had swarmed through the turnstiles.

After the first preliminary started, he spotted Profaci glaring through the grated window. Jonathan left the booth and rushed up to him. He was standing with another man, well built and expensively dressed in a tan lightweight suit.

'My ticket connection,' Profaci said. 'Are they good, Jonathan, cause I brought my friend?'

'The best in the house, Joe.'

'This is one hell of a kid, Francesco,' Profaci informed his companion. 'He can talk the pants off people like you wouldn't believe. Jonathan, say "hi" to Mr. Costello.' A strong, beautifully manicured hand with a massive star sapphire ring reached out.

'Who you like?' Costello asked.

'Machado.'

'I hear Rodriguez can move like greased lightening.'

'Machado'll catch him,' he said confidently.

Jonathan took them through a private door and ushered them to their seats. In the row in front were his father, Victor, and his Uncle Paul. The boy felt a ripple of excitement when Paul stood up and reached over the wooden chair and said:

'Ehhh, Francesco, I didn't know you was a fight fan. I would've fixed it so you come with me.'

Profaci stood up and embraced Paul. 'This here kid told me you was his uncle. I didn't believe him.'

'Sure, he's my boy. Closer than blood.'

Paul introduced his friends, and Jonathan rushed over to a beer vendor and ordered him to spend the evening supplying the group of men with beer without charge. He'd pay for two cases plus tips.

Profaci beckoned him.

'Listen, can Frank and me get down for a few bucks? Just to keep interested.'

'There's no gambling here,' Jonathan said. 'But you see the fat guy by the hot dog stand, he might be able to help.'

'Get me down for two hundred on Machado,' Costello said.

'Frank, let me get the line first.'

Costello's dark eyes hovered on Jonathan's face and he returned Profaci's look.

'I like Jonathan's opinion. Pauli, I was going to call you tomorrow, but if you gents'll excuse us, let's take a walk.'

There was something about Costello that impressed Jonathan especially. He seemed to possess inner hardness, a

235

knowledge of the world that commanded respect.

'Joe, who's Mr. Costello?'

'The prime minister, Jonathan. What he says is law – to everyone.'

Jonathan walked with Profaci to Fat Albert, the neighborhood bookmaker and shylock.

'I got it. Pick 'em,' Albert said.

'Okay, we bet Machado a hundred times – that's six hundred to five hundred with the vig.'

You got it, Mr. Profaci,' Albert replied, making a note on his small scratch pad.

'You're in for two hundred, Jonathan,' Profaci said.

'Where am I going to get that kind of money?'

'It's a finder's fee. Your guy loses, you're off the hook. He wins, you're entitled. You're a nice kid. Next time you got a big bout, you get as much beer as you can use. You give me the truth about Pauli and you come up with the tickets. You got credit cause you keep your word.'

Jonathan suddenly looked up as the crowd roared. One of the prelim fighters got caught with a right cross and crumbled to the canvas. People leaped up and stamped their feet in excitement. Jonathan excused himself and headed for Machado's dressing room. He prayed that Machado wasn't with a woman.

Paul and Costello sipped their beer as they stood at the entrance.

'You missed a helluva lunch Joe threw for a bunch of us at La Polini's.'

'I had to meet my friends for dinner, Frank. We go back from the old country. I see them once in a blue moon. If not for Alex and Vittorio, I'd be dead. They're closer than blood brothers.'

'I spoke with Chou this evening and she sounded real cheerful.' He paused and Paul anxiously waited for him to get to the point. 'I also called Bugsy and told him what actually happened with you. He's sorry he got the wrong end of the stick and he asked me personally to say that he hopes there's no hard feelings. There's a loyalty he felt to Lepke and he lost his head.'

'No hard feelings,' Paul replied in a cold, distant voice. 'I accept his apologies.'

'Good. I'm glad, cause our business is too good now for

important people like you and him with major territories to start a war. It hurts everybody.'

'Frank, I'm your guy.' He pressed his strategy. 'As long as I have your confidence, I'm secure.'

Costello wrapped an arm around his shoulder.

'Pauli, I discussed that matter with Charlie Lucky and other people on the council. Charlie sent us word from Dannemora that you got Arizona. He doesn't know what the hell you expect to do there, but after Florida, you got his vote.'

Paul's face relaxed and he extended his hand to Costello. 'Does Bugsy know about this decision?'

'He welcomes you with open arms. Anytime you're out in California, he wants you to be his guest.'

'Frank, my heart's full of gratitude for what you've done.'

'Come on, let's catch the fight.'

Machado might have been on his way to a date at the Chateau Madrid. He had his portable turned to a Latin music station and was gyrating to a rumba in his dressing room. He was fussily combing his hair in front of a full-length mirror while his manager massaged the small of his back.

'I'm such a beautiful hombre, no, Jonathan?'

'You're gorgeous.'

'That Mexican won't even mess my hair. I go out there and give him a few good shots and we go dancing later, what do you say?'

'I'll be your date.'

Jonathan's hands trembled with anticipation. He couldn't believe that Machado was so relaxed and nerveless.

'Time,' a second said, bursting through the door.

Machado's red satin bathrobe was held by his manager. Machado smiled, winked at himself in the mirror. Jonathan joined the entourage.

'Las night I fuck four times,' Machado said during the walk down the aisle.

As they passed the ringside rows, Jonathan saw Alex's group rise and applaud Machado.

'Just don't tell my father – he'll have a heart attack.'

Jonathan sat on a stool just behind the timekeeper.

Rodriguez was already in the ring, prancing up and down like a high-spirited racehorse. He had close-cropped curly hair and his face was slick with Vaseline and sweat. Machado climbed into the ring and opened his arms to acknowledge the cheers and bowed in every direction.

The ring announcer, dressed in a white formal jacket and black trousers, pulled down the microphone and began his introductions.

'From Mexico City, Mexico, the undefeated Juan Rodriguez, winner of thirty-one fights, twelve by knockouts, fighting his premier bout in the United States, weighing in at one hundred forty-five and a quarter pounds . . .'

There was loud applause and boisterous chants in Spanish. His opponent, hailing from Havana, Cuba, winning twenty-seven fights, twenty-five by knockouts, and two losses, Stone's Sporting Club proudly presents Mario 'Kid' Machado, weighing in at one hundred forty-six. Ten rounds. This bout sanctioned by the New York State Athletic Commission.'

Machado was still gaily smiling and waving to admirers who shouted salvos of '*Vaya, vaya,*' and stamped their feet in a frenzy.

The fighters stepped to the center of the ring and received their instructions from the referee. The bell sounded and Jonathan watched the movement of their feet as resin from the canvas filled the air in thin streaks.

Rodriguez had a beautiful jab and started fast, flicking it in Machado's face. Machado moved in close and went to the body, but Rodriguez was quick and ring-smart and spun him around, so that he looked awkward and lost his balance. Jonathan groaned silently when he turned away and looked at the glum expression on Alex's face.

Rodriguez easily won the first three rounds. Machado's timing was off and he was baffled by the weaving style of his opponent. In the sixth round, he shook Rodriguez with a few left hooks but was unable to press his advantage, for Rodriguez clinched and coasted through the rest of the round. It was the first round the Kid had won and it had been close. At the bell, Rodriguez arrogantly waved his glove in the Kid's face and said:

'*Nada.* You fight like a *maricón.*'

Machado started after him but his handlers and the referee

238

intervened. Rodriguez was warned not to speak and then Machado was told not to punch after the bell.

Jonathan leaned his head in Machado's corner. The fighter was furious. 'He call me a fag!' he bellowed angrily. 'Me!' The seconds were trying to calm him down but he had lost his self-control. Machado spat contemptuously into his bucket and leaned down to Jonathan.

'I finish that motherfucker right now. I been carryin him for six rounds.'

'Get him, kid.' The boy shouted nervously.

As the seventh round started, Machado lowered his head and rushed Rodriguez. He threw a beautifully timed combination – a left hook, a right cross, and a short bolo punch – which staggered Rodriguez, who got on a bicycle and backpedaled so that his head would clear. Machado did not wait for him; he began flicking jabs. Bobbing and weaving, Machado shot a looping bolo into the solar plexus. Rodriguez's face lost its color. Machado was after him like a tiger, battering him to the ropes with a series of bolos thrown so quickly that Jonathan could barely follow the action. A short right to the temple staggered Rodriguez again and the crowd arose, shrieking, 'Kill him.' Rodriguez's mouthpiece fell out and the referee kicked it out of the ring. As Rodriguez came off the ropes, Machado threw a short left hook; Rodriguez, his legs sagging, fell forward, crashed down on his knees, then toppled on his side. His face was ashen and his eyes glassy. At the count of eight he gamely rose to his feet – there were still thirty seconds to go in this endless round. Defenseless, he lurched like a drunk from side to side. Machado measured him and then fired off a series of combinations, one to the body, then to the head and back again to the body. The speed of his punching was unbelievable; the sick, shocked look on Rodriguez's face horrified Jonathan.

Finally Rodriguez crumpled, his body made of paper. There was a bluish cast to his lips. He fell between the ropes, his head outside the ring apron. The referee waved his arms, signaling that the fight was over. Rodriguez's seconds jumped into the ring, placed smelling salts under his nose, but Rodriguez's body was limp and unmoving and a hush crept through the crowd. They stood frozen as statues when the ring announcer gave the time of the knockout. They huddled in small groups around the ring when the commission doctor climbed into the ring with two stretcher bearers.

A worried frown masked Machado's features. His head hung low and there were tears in his eyes. As he threaded his way through the crowd, the fans hissed him. Jonathan took hold of his arm.

'It wasn't your fault.'

'He's hurt bad. Why he call me *maricón*?' he asked, still angered by the accusation.

Standing beside Fat Albert, counting out money to the winning betters, Profaci patted Jonathan on the back. Costello and Paul regarded him with approval.

'One smart little son of a gun,' Profaci said, tucking two hundred dollars in Jonathan's shirt pocket.

'He's in bad shape,' Jonathan said.

Alex brushed past him. An ambulance had been called and the doctor had given Rodriguez an injection of Adrenalin in the ring. Blood had caked on the fighter's gums, his eyes were swollen and tightly closed. He hardly appeared to be breathing. Jonathan was nauseous. The sour smell of spilled beer, slick on the floor, stuck to his heels. He shrank away from the man and Paul observed his pain.

'He's going to die,' Jonathan said.

'Maybe not,' Paul said. 'This is a business, Jonathan. Your father knows it, and in my operation, we get used to people getting hurt.'

He walked outside with Paul and watched the stretcher loaded into the ambulance. The gusts of warm air embraced him and broke him out into a sticky, uncomfortable, nervous sweat.

'If I had a kid, I'd like him to be like you,' Paul said. Curious men surrounded them, muttering about the beating Rodriguez had taken. 'Listen to me, Jonathan. You're going to be very special and this is part of growing up.'

He nodded, restrained his tears, and walked back inside the club. The vendors were waiting for him to check them out and they piled coins and bills on the counter.

Lost, suffering, and on the threshold of manhood, he reached into his pocket for the bills Fat Albert had paid out. Behind the counter there was a solitary case of beer and five uncooked hot dogs.

He addressed the vendors, boys, teenagers, grown men.

'It was a sellout, so here's a bonus for all of you ... ten bucks a man. Go out and celebrate and next week get here on time.'

BOOK THREE

Eighteen

Spangles of light from the mirrored circular globes spun on the ardent faces of the dancers circling slowly to Frankie Laine's recording of 'That's My Desire.' Jonathan sat in his office with the door open, counting the receipts. His Thanksgiving dinner-dance had drawn eight hundred and twelve people. He had taken the weather conditions into consideration when scheduling it. Fortunately he had decided on beginning it at four in the afternoon.

He closed his office window. A wet snow had started at five thirty, two hours ago, then gained in intensity. Now his windowsill was layered with a heavy pack of snow. He finished counting the money – almost forty-five hundred dollars. With the receipts from the bar, he could expect another thousand. He calculated a four-thousand-dollar cash profit.

He locked the money in the safe and looked at the dark, glowering sky and said, 'Keep snowing, baby.' He had a captive audience that would stay late rather than rove to other bars and dances.

He had a rough-hewn face with gray pouches under his eyes from the late nights. He was eighteen, but he seemed years older than the college boys drunkenly lurching up to the bar with their flasks.

He sidled over to Machado who was now solely his troubleshooter.

After Rodriguez had suffered brain damage in their bout, Machado had become afraid to hit or open up against an opponent. Although he won a succession of fights, it was clear to both Alex and Jonathan that he had lost his killer instinct. In quick succession, Marty Servo, Tommy Bell, and Fritzie Zivic battered the inhibited Cuban into submission.

It was Jonathan who persuaded him to retire, and from then on Machado accepted Jonathan as his benefactor and regained his *joie de vivre*. No one else would've paid him a hundred a week, bought him clothes, just for managing these nonboxing evenings.

'Where's Tito's band ... it's enough already with the records,' Jonathan said irately.

'On their break,' Machado replied, a long Pall Mall dangling from his lips and crinkling his eyes with smoke. 'In the locker room.'

Jonathan walked through a cord of dancers and opened the locker door. Tito was sitting on a long wooden bench next to his singer who was in a form-fitting white sequined gown. The other musicians were excitedly honking away in Spanish. There was a strong sweet smell.

'Listen, Tito,' he said, 'what is it with you? You play five and take ten. I got people out there who could've stayed home and danced to their radios.'

'Hombre, we just played a forty-five-minute set.'

'Tito,' he said, lifting up the minuscule sleek man from the bench, 'you want to smoke reefers with your girlfriend, do it on your time, not mine. Everybody, kill your reefers or get the hell out. . . .'

Machado stood silently behind him, his jacket open. He wore a shoulder holster and carried a snub-nose .38. 'Needle's wearing out on the victrola, Tito,' Machado said. 'Kids want to jitterbug, wiggie their asses a little.'

The group, muttering complaints, filed past him and out to the bandstand. The dancers broke into applause. Tito had a melodic sound and he was well known in the Catskills. Dolores, the singer, seized the long microphone between her thighs, flashed a smile at the audience, and roared into 'Green Eyes.' Pimply scholars grouped around her like diamond appraizers.

'Lotsa gash here,' Machado observed, eyeing some single girls around the bar waiting for an invitation to dance. 'I got a lot of numbers awready. Chicks've come from everywhere – Queens, the Bronx, and the city.'

'Let's collect from the bar and make the night deposit at the bank,' Jonathan replied, staring impassively at the hungry faces of the girls sizing him up. None of them interested him. He put on his blue cashmere overcoat, took the money from the safe, then added the cash Machado had taken from the bar registers. He made out a deposit slip for $5900 and left. At the entrance there were still people buying tickets. Cars circled the club looking for parking places. He told the ticket-taker at the door to direct the cars to a nearby garage on Saratoga Avenue.

'Next time we throw a dance we'll charge for parking in the lot,' he informed Machado, looking at the bumper-to-bumper traffic trying to get on the lot adjacent to the club. 'Free parking's for the birds.'

'One of the reasons you're jammed is you give free parking. People get jacked off in the city.'

'Kid, if they like what I'm giving them, they'll pay. It's business.'

The streets were carpeted with mounds of snow. They got into Jonathan's light tan Plymouth. He left his reserved spot and turned into Pitkin Avenue. Snow cleaners from the Department of Sanitation were already out in their trucks spraying salt on the roads. He stopped on the corner and let Machado out at the Manufacturers Trust. He decided that when business slowed up after the first of the year, he'd accept Paul's invitation and go down to Miami for a few weeks. He felt restless and worn. Nineteen forty-six had been a long and difficult year. The competition from the Garden had begun to hurt. Fighters returning from the service had been scooped up by Mike Jacobs. Jonathan had coerced his father to have two wrestling cards, but Alex despised wrestling and gave in only with great reluctance. Jonathan wanted to open an arena in Manhattan: the trip to Brooklyn was inconvenient for the regular boxing supporters; the club's attendance had begun to fall.

Machado made the deposit and hurried back to the car. Jonathan slipped him an envelope.

'What's this?'

'Open it.'

It was a hundred-dollar bonus. Machado reached out and embraced him.

'Hey, man, you don't have to do that.'

'You've earned it,' he said with a smile. They were an unlikely pair, but Jonathan prized Machado's loyalty; he knew this was a man who would lay down his life for him if it ever came to that.

Jonathan headed back to the club and blew his horn at the car in his reserved spot but it had no effect. A ticket-taker rushed out into the street and leaned into the window.

'Where've you been?' he asked shakily. 'We've got a fight going on inside.'

Machado flung his door open and followed the man inside. Jonathan relaxed. The Kid could handle any trouble. He leaned on his horn again, and when the car refused to move, he double-parked and walked to the curb. He jumped over a hillock of snow and rapped at the window. A girl with tears in her eyes looked up at him. A drunken, blond-haired man with red eyes, a pint of Calvert in his hand, was shouting angrily at the girl.

'Put out or get out.'

'Hey, calm down and move your car, Junior,' Jonathan said.

The man leaned across the girl, yanked the door handle, and shoved her out.

'You can walk home, sister.'

She reeled toward Jonathan and he caught her sleeve before she fell into a snowbank. She clung to him. The car, its back wheels spinning, skidded away.

'No one's ever spoken to me like that,' she said.

'You'll live. Next time, don't get into a car with a drunk.'

'He was my date,' she said with disgust, biting her lip.

'Well, look around, and maybe you'll get lucky.'

She trailed after him, catching up with him in the lobby where Machado was shoving two young men, one with a bloody nose, through the turnstile.

'Problem's over,' he shouted, hurtling them out into the street. 'But I better keep an eye out.'

The girl had auburn hair and light reddish lashes. 'Can I ask you a favor?'

'Sure.'

'Could you call me a cab? I haven't even got money for a phone call.'

'You'll never get a taxi in this weather. They're still clearing the streets.'

He liked the look of her, the pert outraged curl of her mouth and the black, fur-trimmed coat which was molded to her figure. She had on fitted boots; her heels made her a shade taller than he.

'How do I get home?'

'Where do you live?'

'Manhattan – Eighty-fifth and East End.'

'What brought you here?'

'I did an aunt a favor and accepted a blind date. Never

248

again.' She looked at her smudged face in a compact mirror. 'God, I'm a wreck ...' She deftly ran a puff over her cheeks. 'Can you lend me a nickel? There's a limo service I can call.'

'If you want to hang on for a few minutes, I'll drive you home.'

She weighed the offer and her face relaxed.

'I don't like putting you to trouble.' A squad car drove past the entrance and she said breathlessly, 'You better move your car or they'll give you a ticket.'

'What's your name?'

'Frances ... Frances Packard.'

'Frances Packard, you worry too much, you know that?' He handed her his ignition keys. 'Now why don't you sit in the car, start her up, and put on the defroster, okay?'

With the troublemakers out, the dance was going along smoothly. The single girls at the bar had found partners. Tito's band played 'South America, Take It Away,' and the dancers were gaily bouncing up and down to the song.

'I'm going to knock off,' he told Machado.

'Nice piece you located.'

'A reject,' Jonathan said.

Machado kissed his fingers and gyrated his stomach.

'Man, anytime you want to give me her number, I'll give her one of my best.'

Jonathan trudged out into the snow, got into the car, and sniffed the air.

'You smell good. What're you wearing?'

'Je Reviens,' she replied, rolling the *r* like a Parisian. 'What's your name?'

'Jonathan Stone.'

'It's your place?'

'Yeah, I run it with my father.'

At a light, she reached out and took hold of his hand.

'It's awfully sweet of you to do this. I hope I'm not lousing up your evening.'

'I wanted to clear out.' She had a slender wrist and fine-boned fingers. There was a small cameo ring on her pinky.

After they crossed the Manhattan Bridge, she directed Jonathan to the East River Drive and then to her town house. He pulled up outside.

'Would you like to come in?'

'What about your parents?'

'They're in Europe. Skiing in Switzerland and then to London and Paris on business.'

He held the door for her and with a half smile said, 'I could get fresh.'

'I'll take the chance.'

He wiped his feet on a thick mat and noticed that the floor of the vestibule was marble. A black Gothic P ran along the border. Overhead, a large crystal chandelier threw off a dim warm glow. She took his coat and hung it up.

'Everybody's off,' she explained.

'How're you going to spend Thanksgiving?'

'With my aunt.' She had on a long, gray, ballet-length skirt and a black satin blouse with a wide neck which extended low across her freckled shoulders. She had a narrow waist, and a sash attached to the blouse was knotted tightly into a bow to accentuate her hips.

She switched on the lights in the living room. Two red velvet chesterfields faced each other in front of a fireplace paneled in walnut. The room was striking and he walked around uncertainly, touching small bric-a-brac on the low side tables and gazing at the walls which were covered with nudes and pastoral scenes. He paused in front of a painting of a nude getting out of her bath. He stepped back, averted his eyes because he was conscious of her standing behind him.

'Do you like it?'

'I'm not sure my mother would hang it in her living room.'

'It's a Renoir,' she said, waiting for him to react, but his mouth was tight, perplexed. 'A French Impressionist.' Still nothing but a slow, embarrassed ruckling of his brow. She realized that he didn't know what she was talking about and she found his naiveté charming. She threw some logs on the fireplace and lit a long-tapered match.

'God Almighty, I've never seen a real fireplace except in the movies.' He held up his hands to the fire.

'Do you go to college?'

He laughed. 'I was so glad to get out of high school that nothing could drag me back to a classroom. I guess you go to college.'

'Uh-huh ... Vassar.'

'Where is it?'

'Arlington, near Poughkeepsie.'

'Hey, that's not far from the city.' He sank into a deep velvet wing chair.

'Can I get you something to drink?'

'Rye and ginger.'

She went to a large breakfront, slid open a door where an armada of bottles gleamed. She pulled out a cut-glass ice bucket, then bent low and took out a tray of ice cubes. He jumped up from his seat and leaned over.

'You've got an icebox in the living room? I didn't know they made them.'

'It was built in.'

'Did it cost a fortune?'

She ignored the question and handed him his drink.

'It's convenient.' She switched on the phonograph and he saw a stack of records on a long spindle. One dropped automatically and from hidden speakers he heard Bing Crosby singing, 'You Keep Coming Back Like a Song.' She sat down opposite him on the arm of a sofa. 'I can play something else . . .'

'No, it's terrific. I just don't know when the surprises are going to end.'

His face had a kind of gladiatorial strength which came from the high cheekbones which virtually triangled to his large greenish eyes which like a lynx focused on people until they turned away. It was a habit, this staring. He had a broad nose, irregular teeth – who knew about braces when he was growing up? – and a solid chin with a sloping mouth. He was not a pretty boy, or even handsome, but just the same, the face evinced a gutsy vigor that had a hint of menace. He was the sort of man people in a crowd took care not to bump or elbow because of the implicit threat of violence which might erupt.

'Can I ask you a personal question?'

'Sure,' he replied expansively, sipping his drink.

'Have you got a girl?'

His eyes twinkled with delight.

'Round one to Stone. Have you got a boyfriend?'

'Not anyone special.' She smiled. Her teeth were small, regular, and she had a habit of rubbing her tongue along the edges. 'My parents are starting to worry about me. Jonathan, you didn't answer my question.'

'I have dates. I don't have a girl and I'm not sure that I

want one – ever,' he added as an afterthought.

'Ever? Why?'

'Sometimes they can hurt you ... and besides I can't imagine myself coming home at five thirty, reading the afternoon paper, eating dinner, playing with a houseful of kids.'

'Something wrong with that?'

'It's not for me,' he replied.

'Do you know what you want?'

'To get ahead. Be big.'

'Money?'

'Of course, money. Isn't that what people's lives are about? I'm making more now than any of the stiffs who came to the dance. They'll be lucky if they come near me by the time they're thirty. But I want something more ...' He faltered, confused by the turn of the conversation.

'Why didn't you go to college?'

'Honey,' he looked at her patiently, like an adult patronizing a child, 'what am I going to learn there?' He gestured to the wall. 'The names of those artists. Is that going to make me a happy man? Nah, never. I operate in the real world. I get excited watching a ball game or a fight, going to a movie, not looking at pictures.' He pointed at the painting. 'See her coming out of the bathtub? I'd bet my life that you've got a better body. Pictures don't have anything to tell me.' She took an English Oval from a tortoise-shell case and he lit it for her. 'I'm sure you learn lots of smart things at lectures, but how does it apply to the two of us right now? Does any of it really matter?'

His specious logic had a powerful ignorance about it which trapped her. She closed her eyes and he pressed his lips on her mouth, kissing her so gently that she couldn't believe they were joined together. The record changer dropped 'All Through the Day' with Jo Stafford.

'Do you think we're going to fall in love?' Frances asked with an ironic smile.

'Anything's possible.'

Her mouth had a flavor of orange, singularly pleasing, and he lifted up her drink and smelled it.

'It's Grand Marnier, want to try it?'

'No, thanks, I'll stick to rye,' he said, retreating from the emotional web she spun so finely.

'Tell me about girls who sometimes hurt,' she said. 'Did

252

she make you suffer?' Her face was intent, a mosaic of concern. He was unaccustomed to candor, at least in his relationship with women. It had been a long time since he had felt quite so exposed – vulnerable. He clung to his secret like a miser. It would never be possible to share the knowledge of his loss, so he dallied with Frances unconsciously, revealing his family background in Munich and how they reached America. It would do for the time being, keep her from probing.

She was puzzled by the fact that he had no accent.

'It was one of the things everyone worked like hell on,' he explained. 'We wanted to be accepted as Americans. You see, when everything you've cared about is mangled so badly, you give up on the past.'

'But there must have been memories which were important.'

'Frances, what's important is that I'm breathing and that you are. Places don't matter to me. What are they really? Bricks, walls, where kids are being born and people are dying. Christ, after the Movietone newsreels and *The March of Time* shorts, I couldn't believe that Germany had ever been real. All you could see was a garbage dump of broken concrete and gutted buildings with people scavenging for food. *Deutschland gestabt*,' he observed in a tone of lamentation, then smiled with embarrassment. 'I didn't mean to get emotional.'

'Nothing wrong with that.' She reached out for his hand and held the back of it against her face. It was an intimate gesture which he had only occasionally seen at home when his mother had wished to convey something deep and loving to his father. 'Sit next to me, Jonathan.'

It took him a moment to decide whether he ought to accept her offer. 'How old are you?' he asked.

'I'm a junior in college.'

'Twenty, then. You're two years older than me.'

'Does it matter? In any case, you act a lot more mature.'

He was flattered by the observation. It never ceased to thrill him to be called older than his years, more responsible, not just a kid.

'Frances,' he asked, nuzzling her neck, 'do you want to fool around?'

'Uh-huh . . . when we get to know each other better.'

253

'You think that's going to happen?'

'Depends on you.'

'You like me kissing and touching you?'

'Would you be here if I didn't?' She held his neck and her stark blue eyes were transfixed on his face. 'If all either one of us is interested in is an easy lay, then let's go upstairs, get it over with, then say good-bye.'

He blushed but liked her for being so direct. 'I understand what you mean.'

She rose and offered herself like a sacrifice. 'Which way is it going to be?'

'Let's wait,' he said, extending his hand to her.

She rushed to him and kissed him with passionate gratitude.

'You took a chance, didn't you?' he asked.

'Jonathan, I think you're worth taking a chance on.'

They sat in the living room till after two; the logs in the fireplace were soft flowing ash and he learned a bit about the Packards. She was an only child born when her mother was twenty-eight and her father thirty-two. She had grown up without rules and made her own on the basis of fitting in with the civilized household she lived in. From childhood she and her parents had always been Frances and Isobel and Charlie to each other. She was the experiment of two loving parents who were determined not to alter their lifestyle because a child was in their midst. Her father Charlie Packard, was in property the way Joe Kennedy was in Scotch, Rockefeller in oil, and Du Pont in chemicals. But the Packards had not subjected her to the upbringing of an heiress. She was never forced to do what was *right* and befitting her station, which Charlie explained was 'nothing more or less than bucks,' an uninteresting subject to all of them when there was a world of museums, opening nights, summers in a villa in Cap d'Antibes, winters skiing in St. Moritz, shopping in Hong Kong and Bangkok, hunting at their farm in Virginia, buying racehorses in Louisville and Dublin.

Unwittingly, she made him perceive how hopelessly provincial he and his family were. Of them all, only his brother David had thrust himself outside their narrow realm, but even David had not realized his hopes; he was attending Brooklyn College part-time and working for an interior decorator after school.

254

He kissed Frances good night at the massive mahogany door. The roads were slick with ice and the snow had begun again. 'Drive carefully. I don't want you having an accident.'

He was rather touched by her concern. 'I'll be okay.'

She stood in the doorway and wrapped her arms around her waist as gusts of air blew her hair.

He drove down Eighty-sixth Street. The slush at the curbs had congealed and frozen into steep banks. He was hungry and cold and he decided to stop at an all-night diner on the corner of Third Avenue.

He bought a paper and found a seat at the counter next to a group of truck drivers who were complaining about the road conditions in Jersey and Pennsylvania. Jonathan looked at the drivers' plates. Thick ham steaks, eggs, and hash browns. He told the waitress to bring him an order. Ice shingles hung from the roof and the cook ordered the dishwasher to go outside and knock them down before they smashed a window. Jonathan turned to the sports section of the *Mirror* and started to read Dan Parker's column. The dishwasher girdled in a tattered navy pea jacket, burled past him carrying a rusted, long-handled shovel with a trident-shaped head. Jonathan glanced at him for a second. The man had red-rimmed eyes, set deep in a bloated face. He released a sour, stale breath of cheap whiskey from a brown-toothed mouth. Jonathan turned away and the man stumbled drunkenly to the door and heaved a shoulder against it, growling incoherent curses.

Jonathan returned to Parker's column, which related that Tony Zale and Rocky Graziano had signed for a second fight. He turned the page in disgust. How many times had he asked his father to give up the club in Brooklyn and find a location in Manhattan so that they could be a viable alternative to Madison Square Garden? The city could easily support another midtown arena. But there seemed no way to move Alex. His last jibe still rang in Jonathan's ears – 'Big shot, you find something in the city for the right price and I'll think about it . . .' Alex just refused to take chances.

Jonathan's ham and eggs were set down, but his attention inadvertently wandered to the dishwasher outside, grinding the shovel along the roof as he dislodged the ice. What a racket the old drunk made. Jonathan could not concentrate on his paper. He gave up reading and waited with irritation for the grumbling figure to finish his miserable work, but the man was taking forever, pulling from time to time on a pint bottle.

The drivers left and Jonathan was the only customer inside when the dishwasher reentered, dredging his heavy boots on the sodden sawdust, bringing with him a flurry of icy air. He stopped behind the counter, sniggered drunkenly to himself, and said to no one in particular, '*Ist kalt.*'

Jonathan looked up. His stomach heaved. He dropped his knife and fork on the plate and stared at the man. For a moment he couldn't speak, then nervously asked:

'How long have you been in the states . . . ?'

'I get out from Deutschland almost two years now.'

'You must've had a hard time.'

'The bombing vass terrible. Nothing to eat. The home poooochhh' – he smacked his lips together imitating the sound of explosions – '*Ja*, ve refugees suffered in the vork camps.'

'Where were you?'

The dishwasher thought for a moment and his dull brown eyes retreated.

'Silesia then Essen in the Kruppwerk. Like animals they vorked us. Vy you ask?'

'I had family there.'

'Vair?'

'Munich.'

'Ahhh, München is no longer.'

New York was filled with thousands of displaced persons, tragic reminders of the past Jonathan had escaped from.

'You were lucky to get out.'

The dishwasher grew pensive and threw up his coarse, chilblained hands, his distress unfeigned.

'Iss hard in a new country . . . no friends.' He scraped some blue plates and flung them into a stream of soapy water behind him.

The cook bellowed 'Engel, get your ass back here!'

Jonathan paid his check and returned to his car. He slumped over the wheel and the cold metal burned his forehead. He must be losing his mind. He switched on the ignition and pulled away but found after an hour that he'd been driving around the block, thinking about Munich. He parked in front of the diner, saw from the clock inside that it was four in the morning, but he could not bring himself to drive away. He fed his wound from the rich, agonized storehouse of the past, a prisoner of his anguish. He sat chilled and numb for hours in the car, sobbing, his mind a gaping, raw, bloodied cripple which would not respond either to reason or his intention. Was it meeting Frances that fed his guilt about Lenore and the memories of Munich?

At seven he forced himself to move. His muscles stiffened, seizing up on him when he tried to walk. He slipped on a snowbank and bruised his knee. He reached out for some soft snow and washed his face with it, then struggled to his feet. The pain shooting up from his knee pleased him, confirmed that he was alive.

Engel shuffled out of the diner in his torn, patched pea jacket and thin, gray checked kitchen pants. Christ, he wanted to talk to the dishwasher about Munich.

Jonathan followed him to Eighty-sixth Street and watched him walk down a short flight of steps into a bar called the Deutschland. Jonathan looked through the window. There were other men, perhaps half a dozen, lined up at the dark-paneled bar, drinking straight shots and chasing them with *dunkel* beer. He had forgotten his gloves in the car and he blew on his rough, freezing hands, clouding the window with spumes of his white, bitter breath.

Engel spoke to a few of the men, sipped a long beer, then rapidly drank three straight whiskies from an oversized shot glass. He licked his lips and lit a cigarette. The light filtering in from the street caught the other men puffing at their pipes and cigars, gesturing coarsely, nibbling on bits of cheese, and they reminded Jonathan of a picture he had once seen painted by some Dutchman in one of David's art books.

Engel paid the bartender, picked up his change, and started for the door. Limping, Jonathan gripped the rail, grimacing, and lugged himself to the street. Engel crossed the street against the light and picked up a newspaper at a stand on the corner. He walked with the paper held up so that he could read, then turned up First Avenue. Jonathan trailed after him past Irish bars, Polish and German restaurants, Hungarian bakeries, until Engel paused at the corner to talk to a barkeep shoveling the sidewalk in front of his place. Engel continued uptown to Ninetieth Street. He stopped at a four-story, yellow-brick tenement with gray fire escapes.

Jonathan waited a moment, then followed him inside. He heard Engel walking up stairs that creaked and whined with age. Jonathan looked at the nameplates. He read: 'ENGEL – 15,' and slowly climbed the stairs, huddling on the landing. He reached the apartment door and pressed his ear against it. He heard the sound of water running. He tried the knob; it wobbled but the door was locked. He knocked.

'Ja ...?'

In a moment the dishwasher opened the door. He was wearing underpants. Dark black swastikas were tattooed on each of his shoulders. Behind him was a large photograph of Hitler. He peeked at Jonathan then smiled coquettishly. His flaccid cock bobbed against the opening of his soiled shorts.

'I thought you like me,' he said. *'Komme,* I vill do someting gutt for you.'

Jonathan went inside the room. There was an old unmade sofa bed with tattered khaki blankets hanging over the foot of it. The place reeked of sweat. A radiator under the window hissed sporadically as though asthmatic. Jonathan closed the door. He felt dizzy and sick to his stomach. He could hardly recognize his own voice. It seemed to come from some phantom body.

'Herr Engel –'

'Ja?' A look of expectation, cynical and aroused, played across his face.

'That's your name?'

The dishwasher sensed some danger and backed away from Jonathan.

'In München sie hab' Bauer gefieren, Karl Bauer.'

'Bauer, nein!' He shook his head furiously. 'You are wrong. I am Engel ... Gerhardt Engel.'

Jonathan moved closer to him. 'Commodes, bidets ... the Pension Weissbeck ... a little girl with blond hair.'

'No, no. Engel! Engel!'

'A garden, a boy fighting with you. I'm the boy. *Ich bin er ...*' The rush of memories horrified Jonathan.

The man retreated, shaking his head, whining. Tears of hatred and fear seamed his eyes.

'Sie sind Karl Bauer ...'

Jonathan shoved him against the wall, then lashed out with both fists, hitting him at will in the stomach, the groin, until Bauer, yelping with pain, sank to his knees, his mouth open. Jonathan seized him by the throat and continued to pound his face. He struck blow after blow until his hands and knuckles were bleeding.

Bauer reeled around the room, his arms outstretched. Then suddenly he rushed to the open window and clambered out onto the fire escape. For a moment Jonathan was too surprised to move, then he lunged after him. He got hold of Bauer's leg. Bauer kicked free and Jonathan threw himself over the window ledge. Bauer was rapidly climbing down the ladder when Jonathan gripped his hand. Bauer released the ladder, swinging dizzily. He shrieked, then plunged down the four stories to the empty street. His body seemed to explode into blood-red particles when he hit the snow-crusted pavement.

Jonathan left the building. The street was still deserted. He looked at Bauer's crushed body. The head had been pulverized and a grotesque hole was all that remained of his skull. The snow around him had been sprayed with blood.

'I'm sorry,' he muttered. The sharp wind coming from the river flayed his skin. 'Lenore ... Lenore ...' he shouted helplessly, lost in his confusion, desolate.

Nineteen

Snapping bits of wet snow lashed Jonathan's face. He turned his head at the shouts of thousands of spectators in the stadium at Morningside Heights. The annual Fordham-Columbia football game was in progress. Frances's voice cut through the sound. 'Did you see the quarterback fake a pass ...?' Her words eddied in the damp wind. She turned her apple-red cheeks to him and snuggled against him.

'Are you okay, honey? You enjoying the game, honey?'

'I love it,' he said.

Below them, fraternity boys in straw boaters and raccoon coats tilted their heads back, spattering their chins with orange blossoms from their flasks. Frances squeezed his hand, but Jonathan drew deeper into himself. He felt damned. Bauer's death had been a horrible accident. It had made his life a nightmare. No demon had been exorcized, and he had been plunged back into a past he wanted to escape from; ghosts which had haunted his childhood were revived. When Frances looked at him quizzically, he was overcome by the guilt clutching him.

He took the chased silver flask Charlie Packard passed to him and hoped the Scotch would drive away his morose mood. Charlie and Isobel had flown back from London just for the game. After the game they were due to have their reunion at the DKE fraternity house. Then a bunch of them would go over to the Stork Club where 'Old Sherman gives us the run of the place for the night.'

There was about Charlie Packard a kind of wanton splendor that Jonathan admired. Everything the Packards did had style. At 5 : 00 A.M., Frances and Jonathan had met them at the airport in a chauffeured, prewar Rolls, then onto Reuben's for giant ham steaks and three-egg omelets. They had reached the house on East End Avenue at seven in the morning and Charlie was immediately on the phone talking to his office about coffee futures, the price of copper, and taking a bigger position in a miracle new company called IBM.

The score was Columbia 21, Fordham 3 in the third

quarter, but Charlie continually bellowed encouragement to the Fordham team, his skin aflame with passion.

'God, I hate to see Charlie suffer this way,' Frances told the collegiate-looking woman beside her. Isobel's blond-streaked hair was in a ponytail, and she wore knee-high argyle socks and black and white saddle shoes. The woman was so willowy and girlish that Jonathan could not believe she was Frances's mother.

'It's the spirit of the thing' Charlie said ebulliently.

'Honey, before he's ashes, he wants the pleasure of knowing he never missed a game,' Isobel said.

Jonathan had been alone with Charlie before the game while the women bathed and dressed. He had marveled at the skill with which the man toyed with millions of dollars. But what really startled him about Charlie was the strangely intent honesty about him. Between calls, he didn't question Jonathan, just strung together a few sentences which set out his point of view.

'I won't ask if you're sleeping with my honey yet. That's your business. But one thing I will ask and insist on . . .'

'I'm listening,' Jonathan said with an embarrassed smile.

'If you knock her up, then do the decent thing.'

'Naturally. Where do you think I was brought up?'

'Do you know what I mean by the decent thing?'

'I wasn't born with the lights out.'

'Well, you're wrong if you surmise it's marriage. I'd like you to tell me about it . . . so we can get rid of it. Marrying a woman because she's pregnant is a lousy reason for ruining two lives if you don't love each other.'

'I haven't slept with your daughter.'

'Why, is there something wrong with her?'

'No . . . I'm waiting for an engraved invitation.'

The Renoir nude hanging over Charlie's head seemed to restrict modesty.

'She's never invited anyone to the game with us, so I assume you're a bit special.'

He paused, examined Jonathan as though he might have been an objet d'art he'd bought at an auction and wasn't sure now that he could use. 'Do I worry you?'

'No, not really. You've just got more money than I do. It's a matter of time before I catch up.'

'You're serious?'

'Sure ... in my circles – I guess you'd call them that – no one kids around about money.'

'Maybe you were right not to go to college.'

Jonathan nodded confident of his ground.

'What it boils down to for a guy like me is spending four years to try to make connections. I've seen these college boys from all the top schools. They can't hold their liquor. They make passes at girls who don't want to know. They're dummies.'

After the game, they attended a reunion of old boys and current brothers of Delta Kappa Epsilon at the fraternity house on the Fordham campus. Charlie winked at girls, chugalugged beer from a pitcher, spoke in obscure code words to the brothers. He seemed to be celebrating some goal he had achieved – immutable adolescence.

It was a game of sorts, the way he and Jonathan managed to watch each other. Charlie kept an eye on the brash, cocksure young man and observed him sitting coiled on the stairs while the brothers rushed Frances. Frances's father conceded that Jonathan, in his gamy, slum-bred way, had a kind of instinctive class and poise that the others lacked. Charlie respected a man who could keep his head and had a clear fix on himself. But what experience had changed this boy into a man so quickly?

A group of them left at eight for the Stork Club. Jonathan found himself among bankers, attorneys, men who owned seats on the New York Stock Exchange. He listened carefully to the talk of money, office buildings. the housing boom that Bill Levitt was exploiting in Nassau County. Sherman Billingsley, owner of the Stork Club. joined them for a drink.

'What do you think of them?' Frances asked him, searching for Jonathan's approval.

'Your father put his ass on the table with me, and your mother's a doll. And I'm still waiting for an invitation.' He sipped his champagne, caught a waiter's eye, and ordered Scotch and soda. 'Do you want to go away with me for a weekend?'

'Charlie thinks you're sharp.'

'I'm flattered. but I don't want to sleep with Charlie.'

She clutched his hand tightly under the table.

'A weekend's not possible.' Her backless. kelly-green taffeta evening gown rustled when she leaned closer to him. The

262

dress was decolleté and she didn't appear to be wearing a bra, and yet her breasts were thrust forward and shaped perfectly. In the canyon between them a large emerald on a heavy gold chain bobbed back and forth with every breath she took. 'Will you settle for a night?'

'For openers.'

'You might not like it.'

'Well, I'm not afraid of taking a chance.' He sensed her excitement. A bead of sweat glowed above her lipstick and she blushed. 'I'm going to do wicked things to you.'

'Jonathan, eat your caviar.'

'I don't like the taste of it. Or the champagne.' He pushed his plate to the side. 'I've reserved a room at the Biltmore.'

'We're supposed to go dancing at El Morocco after dinner.'

'Let's cut out. Then maybe hit the Copa. A friend of mine's headlining the show there.'

'I'll try ... It's just that I don't want to be rude to Charlie and Isobel.'

'Don't they sleep? They've been going nonstop since they got off the plane.'

They were interrupted by one of Charlie's friends, an elderly bachelor in a dinner suit who invited Frances to dance. Jonathan ordered another drink and a thin-faced man with washed-out blue eyes sitting across from him said affably:

'Champagne gives me a heartburn and the next day cannons go off in my head.'

'Then there are two booze drinkers at the table.'

'It's Jonathan, isn't it?' He nodded. 'I'm Bill Gardner. Are you at Fordham?'

'I'm in business with my father.'

'What sort of thing?'

'We've got Stone's Sporting Club in Brooklyn.'

'I've heard of the place. You put on fights like Madison Square Garden.'

'I wish. Jacobs and the Garden have a lock on Joe Louis and all the leading contenders. So we're putting on wrestling and tank town cards.' He grimaced. 'It's a shame because I know how to beat the Garden.'

'How?' Gardner asked.

'If we had a place in Manhattan, I'd get out of boxing and

develop other areas.'

'What's your formula?' Gardner asked skeptically.

'No magic,' Jonathan replied. 'Just give the public what it wants. Sports like Roller Derby, bike races like they have in Europe, one-night concerts, charity drives and movie premiers, dances ... make it a convention center. All sorts of things. The city's big enough to support two places. We'd be an alternative to the Garden. But my father won't listen. He's banging his head against the wall.'

Gardner handed Jonathan a business card: William Payne Gardner III, Executive Vice-President, Morgan Guaranty Bank.'

'You ought to speak to Charlie about it. He knows more about property than anybody in this city. If he can find you something and thinks it's a go, then believe me, Morgan won't sit on its hands. We'll get into the act faster than you can finish your drink.'

Jonathan raised his glass and clinked it with Gardner's.

'I guess I'll talk to Charlie.'

'Are you going to join us at El Morocco?'

'I wouldn't miss it for the world.'

When Frances learned that he had changed his mind and accepted the invitation to El Morocco, her face wrinkled with disappointment.

It was a good thing they went as far as he was concerned. He was convinced that he had made a good impression on the Packards and their friends. It had not been difficult, since he liked them. They put on no false airs, never suggested that the distance between Brooklyn and their world was unbridgeable. And when he and Frances left the club early, no one commented.

'I've never been alone in a hotel room with a man,' Frances said, looking at the unfamiliar furnishings while he spoke on the telephone.

'When's your last show, Billy? Two ...' He looked at his watch. 'Why don't we meet for breakfast? Hanson's ... uh-huh. Around four. Well, look we'll catch you tomorrow night. Sure I'm with a girl.' He laughed. 'You're damn right she's more important than you.' He hung up the phone and smiled at Frances.

264

'That makes me happy.' Her hands were extended, open, offering, and he unloosened his tie. He slid down and kissed her neck and ears and her fingers tightened on his back, but then he eased away from her, unconscious of his withdrawal. Images of Lenore flooded through his mind and he had a sense of discomfort and betrayal. What was wrong with him? The harder he tried to banish the thoughts, the more tactile and powerful the spirit of Lenore became, sitting in the canoe on the Isar. He groaned with the pain of it.

There was a startled expression of incomprehension on Frances's face.

'Jonathan, what's wrong? Tell me, please.' She crept closer to him.

'If you were just a piece, it'd be easy,' he confessed, 'but I'm falling in love with you and that makes it very different.'

'I feel the same way, and I want you.' She held him tightly in her arms.

The room seemed to be spinning around, and he didn't know if it was Lenore tormenting him or the drinks catching up with him. He clung to Frances, kissing her, pressing against her thighs. They moved to the bed, rolled on it. He was inside her, his hips bashing at hers.

'I'm a piece,' she pleaded, writhing under him, abandoning herself completely to him. 'Love me –'

'I do.'

'Oh, baby, you're so good ... my man.' Her face was sweaty, and he licked her mouth with the tip of his tongue. 'Don't hold back. God, I always dreamed it would be this way. I'd die for you, my lovely.'

There was a sense of relief when he dropped Frances at her house. She had not asked for promises and he had volunteered none. It was a strange sensation living in the borderless country between two women he knew he loved.

* * *

Hanson's Drug Store was a popular meeting place for performers in New York. It was open all night, served decent bacon and eggs, and if anybody wanted to cop an oz. of grass, ten-mg truck-driver bennies, or some pure smack, it was easy to get just outside the drugstore.

Still wearing his mohair, coffee-coloured tuxedo, trimmed

265

with dark velvet piping, Billy Davis was holding forth in a booth. He was surrounded by a few Copa show girls and an assortment of what he referred to as 'Star-fuckers.' He shared the singular vice of all good-looking entertainers – ladies. He could not say no, and through the years Jonathan had seen him with both traffic-stopping beauties and scabrous mercenaries who looked as if they were expelled from sewers. It wasn't that Billy suffered from a lack of taste, but as he described it: 'I'm just a hunter and you can't judge cooze by its cover.'

Jonathan slid into the booth and Billy leaned across a girl to hug him.

'Honey, I don't see my friend that often, so why don't you wait outside for the man and cop some reds for us?' he said to the blonde who was as tall as a forward. He patted her behind, shooing her away, and said, 'I love 'em the size of basketball players.'

Billy was a handsomely proportioned man just under six feet tall with a thin, saber-shaped mustache grooming his lip. His eyes were extraordinarily large and the color of basalt. His pinkies flashed two rings – a blood-red ruby embroidered with white gold and a star sapphire as large as a carbuncle. With his brown-suede, leather-trimmed shoes and his fat satin bow tie, he was as noticeable as a neon sign in the subway. During his act, his motile features and undulating body gave the impression that he had an electric eel in his undershorts.

'Man, you missed a great show tonight, I was eeeee-lectric.' A chorus around him chimed, 'Yere,' buttressing his claim. 'How in the name of mother are you?'

'Still shooting for my first million and praying,' Jonathan said.

'How come nobody in your family even called me?'

'You just opened. We thought we'd wait till you'd settled in, then come down.'

Eggs, toast, and sausage patties arrived, and Billy drowned his plate in a swamp of ketchup while Jonathan watched and sipped his coffee.

'You gonna come back to the Waldorf and blast with me?' Billy asked. 'I got a selection lined up, waitin on my call.'

'I think I blew my brains out tonight,' Jonathan admitted.

'Jonathan, when I was your age, I could've gone six times

a night. Just change the car and I step on the gas.'

'Me, I gotta be in love. What can I do?'

Billy chomped on a piece of toast.

'You and David got the same sickness.'

'How do you know about David?'

Billy's caps flashed in a crescent smile.

'I hear from an ex-girl. Man, that boy's crazy. We're brother-in-laws. That cunt Ellen I used to boff when I was desperate up at West's keeps writin me. A week don't pass without me gettin some lame-assed letter from her. "Billy, let me be with you out in Hollywood. I'll do anything to get away from David."' Jonathan was embarrassed and he felt a twinge of resentment. He disliked hearing details about David. 'Jonathan,' Billy continued, 'why in hell's name did David get involved with such an awful twat?'

'This is the first I've heard about it.'

'Man, she's bleedin him dry. He pays her rent and she's got the nerve to keep comin on to me. I want her off my back. So tell David to kick her ass in or get rid of her. I like you all too much to get mixed up in some family problem, but, my friend, if I was you, I'd talk to Dave and get his head straight.'

'Thanks, Billy, I'll do that.'

The tall blonde came back inside, her hair windblown, and bits of it clung to the slick, gooey lipstick on her mouth. She jiggled a bottle.

'Your prescription's been filled, Billy.'

Billy rose and tugged Jonathan's sleeve.

'Come with me ... I can't handle all that traffic.'

'Next time. Look, it's four thirty. I can't sleep all day like you. I've got to haul my ass into the club by ten.'

'Baby' – Billy's face creased with amusement – 'you should've been born a nigger. Now promise you'll come down soon with your folks cause Victor'll think I didn't get in touch with you and he swore he'd use my balls on his boccie court ...'

*   *   *

That afternoon Jonathan waited for his brother outside the main entrance of Brooklyn College. It was almost five and it was cold and damp. He rubbed his gloves together as he saw David leave the lighted Hall of Science Building and

267

walk slowly, his head hung low, his pea jacket open. Slivers of snow flurried into his face as David headed for the bus stop. Other students hustled in front of him, but he made no attempt to elbow for his place on the queue.

'How about traveling like a *mensh*?' Jonathan asked, pointing to the car.

'Jonathan, what are you doing here?'

'I thought I'd come down to see how the family scholar is doing.'

'I wish I knew.'

'Where're you heading? I can give you a lift,' he said, taking David's arm and guiding him to the car. 'We don't seem to see each other much. You've left the house by the time I get up and you're sleeping when I get home.'

David smiled uneasily and reluctantly got into the car.

'Where to, chief?'

David hesitated and glumly stared at the windshield, averting his eyes. 'I've got a date.'

'Man, you look like you're heading for a funeral. I'll drop you.' He placed an arm around David. 'Okay?'

'Coney Island.'

'Not exactly a night for walking on the beach.'

'She lives there.'

Around Sheepshead Bay the wind gained force and blew off the water, buffeting the loose awnings above the seafood restaurants and hot dog stands. Fishermen with raw faces lugged boxes of fresh fish from the pier. Jonathan drove into Coney Island proper and David directed him to a side street across from Nathan's. Overhead the elevated train thundered, flashing sparks off the rails. The street was lined with tenements.

'Are you going to tell me her name or invite me in?' Jonathan asked when he parked beside a run-down two-family house. The garden was filled with litter.

'Her name's Ellen Berg.'

'Well, Mom can't object to anyone with a name like that, huh?' he said amicably.

His brother became flustered. A weak crease which passed for a smile appeared on his face, and Jonathan recognized the mannerism which invariably appeared when he was worried or scared. He looked both.

'I'll just see if she's dressed.'

'What're you doing, going to a ball?'

David held onto a rusted, teetering metal rail as he descended to the basement. Jonathan got out of the car and strolled down the street. A coal truck was parked at the corner, and he watched a group of soot-covered kids with a wheelbarrow lift up the rear panel and greedily seize lumps, then hurry off with their booty. From an apartment across the street, a man in long johns was shouting at his wife. Smells of fried peppers, overboiled cabbage, and burned meat permeated the street from open windows. Jonathan saw David waving him in.

'She's been working all day and hasn't had a chance to clean up,' David explained as they entered the one-room, chill basement apartment which was rank with dirty laundry strewn on the open Murphy bed. There was a metal bridge table, two chairs in front of a kitchen alcove where a tribe of roaches, impervious to cold, had accepted the hospitality of Ellen's grimy gas range.

'What's she do?' Jonathan asked.

'This and that . . . waitress some of the time in a bar around the corner. It's tough as hell to get a good job,' David insisted like a defense attorney. 'She'll be out in a minute. She's just doing her makeup.' David offered a glass of Chianti in a chipped coffee mug.

When Ellen came out of the bathroom, a cheap scent wafted through the room. She had on a low-cut peasant blouse and long woolen skirt and she wobbled on spike heels as she avoided holes in the rug.

'It's about time this dope introduced me to a member of his family.' Jonathan rose and formally shook hands with her, and when he tried to release himself, she was still holding on like a tiresome relative at a wedding. 'You're a real good-looking guy, Jonathan.' David was washing out a mug in the kitchen. He filled it with wine from the heavy wicker bottle and splattered the floor, and she glared reproachfully at him when he didn't bother to clean it up.

'Don't worry about it. I'm sure your roaches can swim,' Jonathan noted acidulously.

'They're not my roaches, mister,' she said bitterly. 'They belong to the animal which calls himself a landlord. Three months I've been waiting for the exterminator. But he sez, "For fifty a month, what do you expect, Eastern Parkway?"'

Like where you and Davie live.'

'I guess he's got a point.'

They clinked mugs and she said something about mud in your eye. When she put her drink down there was a thick lipstick smear on her mug, and she picked up a tissue and blotted her mouth. In her dark brown eyes, which never left Jonathan's face, there was a mean voraciousness.

'Are we going out to eat?' she asked in a whine.

'Have you got a favorite place?' Jonathan asked.

'I got a yen for Italian food' – she shook her head reprovingly – 'but Garguillio's is too expensive.'

'Don't worry about the price.'

'Him' – she fixed her eyes on David – 'he always worries about the price. No matter how often I tell him that Papa Alex is pulling in plenty of *gelt* at the club and won't miss a few dollars, he says no. Davie is so cheap. You got a car, so what's it all matter?'

'I work at the club and my father pays me a salary,' Jonathan explained. 'And since David's a college student, he gets an allowance.'

'He can't live on it.'

'I'm working nights at Shindler's,' Davide spoke up.

She waved her hand over his face like she was swatting flies. 'You go to work with your brother and you'll have everything he's got.'

'I don't want to work there ...'

'Come on, let's eat,' Jonathan said.

When they were seated at the restaurant, David excused himself to go to the men's room. The moment he was out of earshot she winked at Jonathan.

'I wish he'd get lost.'

'You don't mean that, Ellen.'

'He gets me so sore. I mean, you're his brother, so why don't you tell him to stand up to your father and ask for more money?'

'We don't do things like that. My father made an arrangement with us – it's family business.'

'It's a sin to ask if you're running short?'

'That all that's bothering you?'

She leaned over, pressing her bodice hard against the table.

'I don't like the way he treats me. I mean, why can't I

270

meet your parents and be invited for dinner like when you're keeping company?'

'Maybe you're not. I don't see any engagement ring and David's never mentioned you at home.'

'Oh, he's such a *hecht* ... yellow ... no backbone. Why I see him is a mystery to me.'

'Then stop.' He called her bluff and she withdrew for a moment, then tried another tack.

'Listen, I'm not some bimbo he can dump whenever he feels like it. I've taken a lot.'

'From David?'

'I give up my life and my family for him. "Come to the city, Ellen. I love you," ' she mimicked. ' "I'll take care of you. You'll have all the money you need." Meanwhile, I'm working my tail off at Cosmo's Bar and Grill over on Bay Fifteen six nights a week and all day Sunday. Davie gives me my rent and that's it. Always my broke. I'm entitled to make a stink when I havta put up with his kind of treatment. I'm living like a nigger in that toilet. Do you think he's got a brain in his head with all the college bushwa? If he listened to me, he'd quit school, go to work with you, and live like a human being.'

David pulled back his chair and sat. He forced a smile to his face, but the pain of the effort was unendurable, and he said, 'I've got to catch up with you two ...'

Dinner developed into an orgy for Ellen. She insisted on trying everything from squid salad to artichokes. But she was a picky eater, tasting a baked clam, then pushing the plate away. The two brothers watched with astonishment her ability to drink. By the main course they had been through three bottles of Valpolicella.

David remained silent during most of the dinner, for whenever he volunteered a remark to lighten the mood, Ellen cut him off harshly or laughed at him. It was a case of a sensitive, weak boy who had fallen into the clutches of a virago, Jonathan realized. He regretted that David had not confided in him, but confidences depend on trust and David had not trusted him. He had failed his brother by being so wrapped up in himself, smothered in his ambition.

Jonathan was filled with self-disgust, and when Ellen left the table to telephone a girlfriend before dessert was served, he touched his brother's hand with affection.

'How long've you been seeing her?'

'Oh, Christ, Jonathan, it's been going on for years. I met her that first summer we were up at West's. She was a maid.'

'She copped your cherry. And she's been leeching on you ever since.'

'I suppose so,' David replied vaguely, lost in his misery.

'Don't you know?' Jonathan asked incredulously. David shook his head unhappily. 'Well, are you in love with her?'

'I was at the beginning and there are times when I think I still am. She's nervous about meeting you, and she isn't acting like herself.'

'Come on ... I can't imagine her any other way. She treats you like shit.'

'Maybe that's what I deserve.'

'David, you're not trapped unless you want to be.' He looked at the soft features, a study in fear and indecision. 'You could be going to school on the Coast. You always wanted that ... the beaches, the mountains, the light. I haven't forgotten. What've you got here, stuck at Brooklyn College and selling fabrics for a decorator? Don't let her spoil your life.'

'How do you know so much more than I do?'

'It isn't a question of knowing more. I've been involved with the grit and shit since we got here. There was no reason for you to pick the same life. I respected you for deciding to go a different way. I may not understand what you're talking about some of the time, but I know that you've got something special and it sickens me to see you piss away your chances on her.'

David's eyes watered and Jonathan knew that he was close to breaking down.

'Look, why don't you tell her it's all over?'

'She'll start screaming, make a scene. I couldn't take it.'

'Be honest with me, David, would you like to pack her in?'

He nodded reluctantly. 'How?'

She threaded her way to them, jiggling her ass as she encountered interested looks from men at other tables. A triumphant smile played over her fretful mouth. She sat down heavily.

'My friend June told me that there's an apartment we could share in Sheepshead Bay.'

'So move,' Jonathan said.

'That's not so easy without money. You know, Jonathan, you saw the toilet I live in. If David could get his hands on a couple of extra bucks, I could have a decent place.'

'He's not married to you. Why should he support you?'

She prodded David in the ribs.

'Tell your brother, *schtumie*, go on.' When David hesitated, she continued: 'He gets all embarrassed to discuss it, but we're hoping, when he leaves school, to get married.'

'Why didn't you mention it?' Jonathan asked him.

David squirmed and his chin dropped.

'DA——VID!' Her voice reached a crescendo of dissonance. 'Open your mouth, dope.'

'We talked about it,' he admitted.

'Talked about it!' Outraged. 'You promised, you weasel. I been living like a nigger for years just because of you.'

Jonathan took hold of her wrist and held it firmly.

'Ellen, that's the second time you said that about niggers. Have you got something against negroes? Aren't they people?'

'Yeah, sure, it's just an expression.'

'I thought you liked them.'

David was perplexed and looked from one face to the other.

'What's that supposed to mean?'

'Isn't Billy Davis an old friend of yours?'

Her aggressive manner vanished. 'Oooooh, that's dirty.'

'Dirty? Nothing dirty about Billy. But if you think so, then why the hell've you been writing him letters all over the place and calling him? Listen, you were a cheap, easy, convenient fuck for him when you met David that summer, so don't give me any shit. You'd fuck anything that walks. You're a tramp who got her hooks into my brother.'

Her face paled.

'Jonathan – please, don't,' David pleaded.

'How could you let him talk to me this way?'

'I wish I could do this like a gentleman, but with you it's impossible,' Jonathan said. 'Listen, Ellen, I hope you enjoyed stuffing your face because it's the last time you're going to see my brother. He's going to leave the city and go out to California without you, sister.' He tightened his grip on her wrist and pulled her close to him. 'If you give him a hard time or try to follow him, I'll fix you myself. Now get the fuck out of my sight.'

He released her and she fell forward, speechless with rage and panic. She banged her fist on the table, upsetting the tortoni she had ordered. Jonathan threw down a twenty-dollar bill and pulled David to his feet and pushed him out of the restaurant. They walked slowly to the car, David shaking his head all the while. Ellen was at the entrance, shrieking as though possessed.

'Fag! Fruit! I never gave a shit about you.'

They got into the car and David's eyes were clouded with tears, then his chest heaved with emotion as he leaned his head on Jonathan's shoulder.

'Why, why, Jonathan, did you do it?'

'Why didn't you stop me?'

'Why . . .' he asked, his wet face touching his brother's.

'Because I love you.'

Twenty

He had fixed David up with a girlfriend of Frances's for
New Year's Eve. As the brothers dressed in dinner suits,
Alex came into the room and studied them.

'Am I wrong or is this the first time you bums ever went
on a double date?'

'First time, Pop,' David said.

'Well, please take a picture tonight for your mother and
me.' He came close to David. 'You got the suspenders
tangled, let me fix them.' He realigned the snaps at the back,
then turned him around. 'You know, I can't get used to the
idea that you'll be going out to California.'

'I'm still surprised myself.'

'Your mother and I were up all night talking about it. I
hate to lose you, but it's for the best.'

'Hey, Pop, he'll be home for vacations.'

'That's airplane tickets and I'm not a millionaire.'

'Then you'll come to see me,' David said.

'Maybe we will. We don't have enough chances to visit
Victor, so it could work out. Victor asked that you stay with
him till you get yourself settled in Los Angeles.'

'I don't like imposing.'

'David, it would be an insult if you didn't accept his invitation.'

On the way to the Packard house, David hummed with
anticipation.

'It's such a peculiar sensation,' he said.

'What is?'

'Being free.'

'You were your own prisoner,' Jonathan said.

'You don't know what it was like ...'

Jonathan shrugged, nagged by the buried wound which
David had inadvertently touched. On New Year's Eve his
thoughts invariably turned to Lenore. Yet another year was
ending and still she remained locked in a well of silence.
He'd give his soul just to hear her say his name. He no
longer inquired about her or wrote letters. Within him there

275

lived a pain beyond definition, coiled, dormant. Would he ever be able to be happy with Frances or any other woman? The futility of his question gnawed at him.

But he threw himself into the evening with nervous gaiety.

David's date was a sylphlike redhead with a fine aquiline nose, brown eyes, and the kind of fragile carriage he associated with dying aristocrats in costume films. Her name was Alexandra Nicholson, and Frances told Jonathan that she had recently broken her engagement. Alexandra and Frances were sorority sisters in Tau Delta Rho, which meant nothing to Jonathan.

The Packards and their friends were listening to David explain Renoir's circumstances at the time the picture they owned had been painted. David said, 'It was shown at the Salon des Artistes at the first Impressionist exhibition. People hooted him and threw eggs at him on the street ...'

Frances took hold of Jonathan's hand and led him into an alcove in the living room. He had fallen into a moody silence.

'You never told me your brother was an art expert.'

'Yeah, since he was a kid he's been drawing and going to museums.'

'He's lovely.'

'I'll tell him you said so. He's gone through a rough patch. It'll cheer him up.'

'Something bothering you, honey?'

'Not that I know about.'

'Charlie wants to discuss some business with you.'

'I'm always ready.'

'That's why I told him not to. Hey, we haven't got much time together before I got back to school ... and it's New Year's Eve,' she added with a plaintive note in her voice. 'Jonathan, how am I going to live through the semester without you?' Her eyes sparkled, finding a midpath between joy and yearning. The fashionable, black-velvet, off-the-shoulder gown and the diamond necklace made her look older tonight.

'I'll miss you, too,' he admitted. 'But we'll have weekends, won't we? I'll come up to see you.'

'I want you all the time. Damnit, I hate myself for sounding so possessive.'

He touched the nape of her neck with his fingers and she tingled with excitement. Her mouth half opened expectantly

276

and she leaned up and kissed him, thrusting her body hard against his.

'Frances, I do love you,' he said cautiously, caught by her need and the beauty of the moment, fighting to shake free of Lenore.

The Packards and their friends left for the Astor where a charity dinner-dance supported by Charlie was being held.

Rows of Cadillacs and new Lincoln Continentals lined the entrance of the hotel. As Charlie and his entourage made their way through the lobby, David whispered to Jonathan.

'I've never seen so many chauffeurs, and look at the diamonds and mink coats. Who could have believed that such a world existed? And to actually be in a man's home where there are Renoirs and Manets. God, Jonathan, I keep pinching myself.'

'How's your date?'

'Terrific. They've got a house in California in Palm Springs. How'd you meet somebody like Frances?'

'She fell into my lap at the Thanksgiving dance I held.'

'Jonathan. I'll always be in your debt for giving me this chance.'

'David, David, you don't owe me a thing. I just cracked an egg. The future is up to you.'

Their eyes closed, her head on his shoulder, Frances and he danced most of the evening to the soft, romantic music of Freddy Martin. As the countdown to midnight began, champagne corks popped and people threw confetti at each other and noisemakers hooted and men and women in funny hats joined hands and embraced in that make-believe camaraderie that engulfs total strangers once a year. Jonathan pressed his lips against Frances's and they held onto each other long after the crowd had finished singing 'Auld Lang Syne,' welcoming in 1947. Jonathan, in the dark with his thoughts, was afraid to open his eyes.

When they returned to the table, Bill Gardner and a few of the men he had met the previous week, were at the table. Charlie had a gold Parker pen in his hand and was writing figures on the linen tablecloth.

'Believe me, it'll work,' Charlie said, looking up at Jonathan. 'All I have to do is persuade my partner to gamble. Okay, Jonathan?'

'Well, I'm not going to bet against you, Charlie,' he said, staring at the strangely shaped building Charlie had drawn. 'Can I ask what it is?'

'Your Arena.'

* * *

West's Hotel was packed solid with nine hundred guests for the New Year's Eve weekend and Sam had had to put some of them up in small neighboring hotels rather than turn away business. The nightclub was jammed. Drunken guests formed a huge conga line, wiggled their hips to the music, and snaked around the tables. Sam and Sylvia watched from backstage while staff photographers shot pictures of the celebrities raising their glasses to toast the New Year. But despite all the merriment, a disconsolate expression froze Sam's mouth. In two days he had to meet with Dr. Green at the hospital and give his permission for a new course of treatment for Lenore. It frightened him, but the pressure of the group of psychiatrists headed by Green left him no alternative. For years, Lenore had languished in the hospital.

He and Sylvia walked back to the cottage, Sylvia draping her mink over her shoulders. Leafless trees shuddered in the sharp wind coming from the lake, blending in with his morose attitude.

'They want to experiment with my child ... what do I say?'

'If there's a chance that she can be helped, then you have to take it.'

'She's a human being, not a guinea pig.'

'Sam, you've never run away from responsibility. She's nothing but a vegetable now. You can't let her remain that way.'

'What if she dies?'

'She's been dead since you left Germany. She eats, breathes, and sleeps. Even the animals that run wild in our woods have more consciousness than she does. They at least are aware of their surroundings.'

Moments later, they were standing by the cottage fireplace staring miserably into the flames. She held him in her arms. 'Sam, don't be afraid to hope.'

But how could he hope? When he had last seen Lenore

278

on Christmas Day, he had brought her an armload of presents. Dolls, jacks with a ball, a new Philco phonograph, and an assortment of popular records. He had installed the phonograph on her night table, showed her how to work it, guided her hand to the arm, and they had listened for half an hour to Strauss's *Ein Heldenlieben*. Throughout the visit she had remained expressionless; it was impossible to judge if she even heard the music.

All New Year's Day he brooded, remained in a dreamlike state. He even forgot about his guests, avoided his usual table-hopping in the dining room. He and Sylvia had been married the previous New Year's Day, but he could not work himself out of his mood of forlornness to celebrate his first anniversary with her. He had no desire to see people. They kept to the cottage all day and in the evening they had sandwiches on trays by the fire. He drank a glass of champagne with her before they went to bed.

But he could not sleep and spent the night worrying. At five in the morning he was up and dressed and walking around the edge of the frozen lake which gleamed like a steel slab in the first light. At eight o'clock, he and Sylvia drove to the hospital. They waited in Dr. Green's reception room. Sam chain-smoking and poking his head into the corridor every time he heard footsteps.

Unlike most of the psychiatrists Sam had met in connection with 'Lenore's Case,' Dr. Leo Green was not withdrawn behind a wall of professional detachment. He was in his middle forties, tousle-haired, with luminous blue eyes, an informal way of dressing – mostly plaid lumberjack shirts and chino trousers to which lint always clung – and he had about him an ease of manner as though catastrophe were as natural as rain. He was carrying a container of coffee which he had slopped on his shirt in his haste to sip and walk. He was wiping the wet spot with a handkerchief when he reached the office.

'Sam ... Sylvia. How are you?' He waved them into his office, put on his glasses. One of the lenses was cracked and he said, 'I was playing touch football with my kids and their friends yesterday. They made an end out of me and I played like a horse's ass. I really should stick to golf.'

They wished each other Happy New Year and Green had his receptionist bring in some coffee.

'Sam, sit down and relax ... we're hopeful of making some real progress now, so that should encourage you.'

'I've heard that before,' Sam said pugnaciously.

'Not from me, you haven't ... it's all the smart guys you brought up here to do a workup when you lost confidence in me.'

'That's not fair, Leo,' Sam protested.

'He just wanted a second opinion,' Sylvia added.

'Well, he's had ten or fifteen.' He opened a thick chart with many pages yellowed, bent, and ragged-edged. 'Now there's no point in rehashing everything about Lenore or where we went wrong, but when she was first brought here, it did seem that her mutism was related to hysteria rather than catatonia. And we were making progress of sorts — nothing miraculous' — he turned pages until he located a chronological table — 'but a few years ago when she had that incident of leaving the hospital with the boy, her illness took on a new strength and became more deeply entrenched. For almost a year she was confined to bed. She couldn't dress or walk. She had to be fed and it was obvious to me and the staff that she'd entered a period of catatonic stupor. What seems to have happened to Lenore after she saw the boy was that her will had collapsed. The retreat lasted for thirteen months. She continued to decline and then there were shouting episodes because her illness changed course again. She was becoming totally unpredictable ...'

Sam slid back into the sofa and he became hostile.

'Look, she was raped by two maniacs.'

'We know all about that. It's done, irreversible. What happened after is what concerns us. Her mind built certain defenses which we couldn't penetrate. But six months ago, there was another change. She developed negativism. We asked her to eat, she put down her fork. We told her to sit, she stood up. She started to have bouts of impulsive behavior — she broke the windows in her room, which was when we moved her. Sometimes during exercise she would run for the whole period until she collapsed. On some days she would hyperventilate, on others she would sit in a trancelike stupor.

'Lately, whenever I see her and try to establish eye contact she repeats the word "Mutti." She must say it dozens of times a day. "*Mother.*" That's significant because the most powerful psychological relationship any of us have is with

280

our mothers.' Green stood up, lighted a cigar, and sat on the edge of his desk.

'What does all this mean?' Sylvia asked.

'Lenore's trying to communicate now. She wants to speak to us about her illness. In short, she's asking us to listen to her, but she can't do that if we don't help her. The important thing now is to bring her to a stage so that she can at least try to express herself ...'

Sam frowned and looked from Green to Sylvia for guidance. 'What if I don't give my permission and sign a release?' he asked.

'Then you write her off as a human being, and I'd ask you to move her to another hospital ... state or private. Institutionalize her and stop this farce about visiting her, bringing her gifts, because it doesn't matter a damn. I understand that you visit because you feel guilt – you love the memory of her and hate the sight of her. That's understandable, and once she's formally committed, you can pretend she's dead. Lots of people do that who love their relatives, because it's too painful to continue seeing them deteriorate. So maybe it's better for you in the long run.'

Sam winced under what he considered an unjust attack. 'You're really taking me apart.'

'Sam, I like you but you're a stubborn man and you're acting out of some psychological fear which I can appreciate.'

Green drank his cold coffee, looked at his watch, and went to a file cabinet to pull out another patient's chart.

'What fear?' Sylvia asked.

'That's up to Sam to ask, Sylvia.'

'Okay, put it on the table.' Sam said with agitation.

'If Lenore begins to speak and makes some progress, when she sees you, she may blame you personally as her father for not preventing the rape.... It'll be only a stage. With productive, follow-up analysis, she'll be able to reason with herself and understand that you weren't responsible.'

Sam gripped Sylvia's hand tightly and the blood left his face. His eyes were sunken and tearful. 'Can I see what it looks like?' Sam asked.

'I don't think it's a good idea.'

'Before I sign a paper, I have to see for myself.'

'Are you making it a condition?'

'I guess so.'

They walked down two flights of stairs to the basement and Green spoke to the duty nurse. He held the door open for Sam and Sylvia and led them down a long quiet corridor. He stopped at a room and opened the door. Sam recoiled when he saw the table with leather straps on the armrests, leg braces with rubber clamps. Electrodes and wires were draped across it.

'Oh, my God, it's the electric chair,' he said. '*Gott im Himmel*, what are you asking me to do?'

'Just give Lenore a last chance. Look, Sam, it's a lot safer than insulin shock. Besides, one of the side effects of electro-convulsive therapy is that there's a loss of memory which may last a day, weeks, or months. So for a time she won't even remember she was ever raped. Isn't that temporary relief worth anything?'

Sam leaned against the wall. 'Go ahead, Dr. Green.'

The following afternoon, Dr. Green, accompanied by two nurses and a male attendant, found Lenore sitting on the edge of her bed. The baffled, hurt look on her face was caused by the fact that she had not been given any food for the past twenty-four hours. She made a strange growling sound. He smiled at her, but the bitter suspicion in her light gray eyes was a warning. She might become violent.

'Lenore, would you please stand up?' She fell flat on the bed. He had counted on her acting contrary to his request. He rolled up the sleeve of her white gown and injected her with curare, a muscle relaxant which would prevent bone fracture and reduce the possibility of spasms. The injection had hurt. She jerked up violently and spat at him.

'You're going to relax and you won't remember anything that happened.'

She was lifted by the nurses and strapped into a wheel-chair and wheeled to the elevator. When they reached the ECT room, she was shifted onto the table. Her ankles and wrists were strapped in place. The nurse put a rubber tongue depressor in her mouth and secured it with a surgical mask to prevent her from biting her tongue.

Green switched on the Bini ECT machine and placed two electrodes on her temples. Lenore's eyes opened wide.

'We'll use a hundred and twenty volts for five-tenths of a second,' he said to a nurse, who made a note on her chart.

Green set the dials on the machine and turned on the current. Lenore seemed to leap off the table; she was galvanized by the brain shock. Her body trembled and she lost consciousness.

'Excellent response,' Green said. 'She had a grand mal seizure lasting fifty-three seconds,' he observed. 'Let's put her on a regime of three ECT's a week with an optimum of thirty treatments.'

When she was wheeled back to her room, Lenore's eyes opened and she stared at Green. She was disoriented and confused. She was carried to her bed and her eyes roved over the room. She lifted her head off the pillow and her long blond hair splayed across her face. She appeared to be searching for something. She reached out to the bedside table.

'Is there something you want, Lenore? You understand me a little now, don't you?'

Her lips moved, pumping up and down as she urged her mind to form a word.

'Muuuuusic . . .' Her voice was soft and sonorous as she repeated the word.

'Music, what a beautiful thought,' he replied, switching the victrola on to a recording of Brahms's Third Symphony which Sam had brought her. She lay back on the pillow, calm, tractable, and alert, and smiled at him.

Twenty-one

Jonathan was convinced that the trouble with his father stemmed from the comfortable circumstances of their new life in America. At forty-three ambition had faded from Alex's mind in favor of security. 'Why should I take chances, tell me why, big shot? I pull in thirty-five, forty big ones a year. Don't gamble with my stake.' Jonathan listened to this kind of tirade for weeks into the new year. His father was inflexible.

Jonathan decided that the time for diplomacy had ended. He cornered Alex in his office at the club one afternoon in February.

'How about knocking off at four thirty and having drinks and steaks at Toots Shor's?'

'Who's footing the bill?'

'I robbed a bank like you,' Jonathan said, helping the grumpy man on with his overcoat. 'We're meeting a couple of friends of mine. They might grab the check. Feel better, Pop?'

Shor's bar was lined with drinkers and Alex turned from one familiar face to another. 'Hey, there's Joe DiMaggio and look, Jonathan, that's Sid Luckman.' The place abounded with sports celebrities and Shor himself, a plump, smiling Irishman with a bull neck and the voice of a pneumatic drill, was standing at the bar, belting back doubles and shouting obscenities at customers. Jonathan edged through the crowd of drinkers, leading Alex.

He waved at Charlie and Gardner who had a place at the bar. He introduced his father to them and gave Alex the free stool. Alex's head turned from one to the other.

'How do you come to know my son?'

'He's sleeping with my daughter, so I thought it might be a good idea to meet you,' Charlie said with a short laugh.

Alex raised his fist and brandished it at Jonathan.

'What's this all about? If you got her in trouble, I'll take you outside and bust your head.'

'We agreed that he'd be careful, or rather both of them

284

would exert some self-control,' Charlie replied expansively.

'Thank God I don't have a daughter or you for a father,' Alex said, astonished by Charlie's attitude. He had never been with a woman other than Miriam, and he considered promiscuity a curse that hung on the heads of all Gentiles who allowed their sons and daughters perverse forms of freedom.

'Hey, are we here to talk about my sex life?'

'Sounds pretty good,' Bill said, handing Jonathan a whiskey and soda. 'It's a damned sight more interesting than banking.'

'You a banker?' Alex asked, suddenly alert.

'That's why I'm here.'

'A loan I can always use,' Alex said, raising his glass to the men. 'I'm thinking of putting new seats into my club. It could run eight to ten thousand depending on if I use fabric or go crazy with leather.'

'Why not raze it and start again? The property could support a couple of apartment houses or an office building,' Charlie suggested. 'It's a good location with access to buses and subways.'

'You've seen it?'

'Uh-huh. Jonathan gave me the tour a few weeks ago. You could get about two hundred and fifty apartments on the site.'

Alex could not believe what he had heard. He darted an angry glance at his son.

'Is this what you brought me here for? To sell me out?'

'Pop, listen for a few minutes and stop getting emotional. Nobody's selling you out.'

'Buying,' Bill said, ordering another round of drinks.

Alex had no idea of what was taking place. He was hurt, confused, and he had not felt so completely out of his depth since arriving in New York. That Jonathan, of all people, should be the instrument of his humiliation was unforgivable. Yet he knew that Jonathan's business instincts were sure, and, he admitted only to himself, much better than his own.

His friends, Alex knew, had passed him by in the race to the top. Poor, pathetic Sam, with his insane child, was closing in on his first million, and the hotel was worth three times that. Pauli had a stranglehold on gambling and loansharking in Florida and Arizona and lived on a scale that was unknown even among the wealthy in Germany. And Victor ... well, in show business circles VCA was now as well known as AT&T. Where, he wondered, had he gone wrong? Was it true that he had the mind of a fighter and could not take the imaginative leap beyond the ring?

At dinner he listened cautiously to Charlie's plans of building an arena. The banker had already guaranteed the financing.

'What kind of money are we talking about?' Alex asked. He sliced into a massive piece of prime rib.

'I've got a parcel of land – twelve acres – on First Avenue and Thirty-fourth Street,' Charlie said. 'I can sit on it and take a tax loss or chop it up and sell it off to developers. But the big money isn't in that. I'd come out with maybe three million before taxes and that doesn't interest me.' Alex listened with fascination. 'The long-term profit would come from developing it ourselves.'

'Dad, Charlie would make us equal partners.'

'How much would we need to come up with?' Alex asked.

'Whatever your place would bring on the open market,' Gardner said. 'Right now, Charlie estimates you could realize maybe five hundred thousand.'

'At least,' Jonathan added. 'It's free and clear. My father bought the freehold.'

'It would make an ideal apartment complex with a shopping center.'

Alex choked on his food. He looked at the men, then at Jonathan. They were destroying him, eating him alive.

'You could get a million if you leverage it at the bank.'

'What do you mean?' Alex asked with dismay.

'I find investors who want to shelter their money from taxes,' Charlie said. 'You sell off, say, seventy-five percent. You keep a quarter of it. So you get cash from the investors and you take your twenty-five after it's developed and borrow against it from Bill.' Alex shuddered. They were double-talking him. 'You repay the bank over thirty years. You'll be getting an income from the apartments as part owner and after paying the bank you'll still have money coming in. The interest that you pay the bank is tax deductible, so you've got a pat hand. You catch the government coming and going.'

'How do you people get such ideas?' Alex asked, crushed in the vise of a logic he could not comprehend.

'Jonathan came up with this,' Gardner informed him. 'It's a beauty.'

'The object,' Jonathan said, 'is eventually to go public. Charlie's prepared to put in five million. We have to come up with a million.'

'Where's my place in all this?' Alex asked.

'We're fifty-fifty partners,' Charlie said.

'Dad, we may be able to build the new place for less than five million. With all the unemployment in the construction industry, we can be operating in a year.'

'In other words, you're asking me as sole owner and pro-prietor of Stone's Sporting Club to give it up, go in with you, and wind up with just twenty-five percent?' Alex's anger surfaced and he threw down his knife and fork. 'That's a screwing if I ever heard one.'

'Why don't you think it over, look at the facts and figures before making a decision?' Gardner advised. 'It isn't often that a proposition like this with bank support and full outside finance falls into your lap.'

Alex apologized for his loss of temper, but he could not refrain from asking in a sarcastic tone, 'How come I get so lucky ... that all this fortune should be mine for the taking?'

Charlie smiled at him. 'Alex, isn't it obvious?'

'Not yet.'

'We want Jonathan, and believe me, we're going to get him.'

Perhaps with the new setup that Charlie offered, he would have an opportunity to bid for fights, lock horns, and go head to head against the Garden, Alex thought. But that didn't excuse Jonathan for undermining him, forcing him into a corner. Jonathan had sucker-punched him.

'I know you're pissed off at me,' Jonathan said. Alex did not turn his head, but stared at the Irish coffee in front of him. 'The Arena is just the beginning. Charlie's buying up every parking lot and garage in the area.'

'Where are the cars? You think everyone can afford to buy one?'

'In the future they will be, and there's no place to park in the city. Please, let me be your friend.'

'You're my son,' he said acrimoniously. 'Friends don't

stick a knife in your back.'

'I'm not undercutting you, just trying to build something for all of us.'

'Being big is an illness,' Alex said, glowering at the two men who had seduced his son. He excused himself and headed for the men's room.

'It doesn't look like he'll go for it,' Gardner stated.

'Maybe I pushed too hard. All the figures we gave him confused him. He thinks we're taking him for a ride.' Jonathan's mouth tightened and his eyes glowed with passion. 'Don't worry, I'll come up with my share. Frankly, I don't give a damn any longer about where I get it.'

'He'd be a valuable man to have with us,' Gardner observed diplomatically. He knew that as smart as Jonathan was, he lacked the maturity to run an enterprise of that size on his own. Alex's caution and experience were not to be dismissed.

When Alex returned to the table, some of the rancor appeared to have dissipated.

'Alex, please don't misunderstand us,' Charlie said. 'We need someone with your know-how.'

'I'm flattered and I appreciate your offer. It just came as something of a shock and there's a lot to digest.'

Jonathan squirmed guiltily. 'Dad, I thought it would be best if the three of us explained it to you, so that you could see the possibilities.'

'*You* could have told me,' he said sorrowfully but without reproach. 'For a while I was convinced I was being led to the slaughterhouse.' His eyes were friendly now. 'There's an expression in German – "the son buys the suit and the father pays for it." I'm a little uncomfortable being given a suit by my son, but he is, as you've both realized, meant for big things.'

'Alex, so are you,' Charlie said, his voiced laced with bonhomie.

'Thanks, I'm glad you think so. I'm going to give Jonathan his share of the club, but as far as joining you, the answer is absolutely no. Maybe it's dumb or pride, but I know that eventually I'd be working for my son and I'm sure he'd be a good, decent boss, but it's not for me. I'd rather fail by myself than work for anyone.'

Jonathan reflected on his predicament, then came to a

decision. 'Dad, thanks for your offer, but I'll raise the money myself. It'll take a while, Charlie, but I'm only in as an equal partner.'

Gardner squinted through his glasses. 'Jonathan, why's that so important? There's enough for everybody. For Christ sake, look at the shot Charlie's giving you.'

'You're both prepared to make a big investment in me, right? Well, shouldn't I prove I can deliver my share of the investment? Don't we live in a world where money talks and bullshit walks?'

* * *

Clouds, the wind violently threshing the leafless trees, the voice of Martin Block announcing the top twenty songs on the 'Make Believe Ballroom.' Yes, it was Saturday morning and Lenore was aware of all its sights and melodies.

'Are we going downstairs, Dr. Green?' she asked him when he had taken her pulse and blood pressure.

'We finished on Thursday,' he said.

The room had two windows and she enjoyed looking out at the garden and the cars passing on the road.

'I'm not afraid.'

He laughed, dropped some ash on the floor, and she rushed from her chair to clean it up.

'Don't bother, an orderly will do it. Would you like to come to my office so we can talk for a while?'

'Yes.' Her eyes were alert, sparkling, filled with optimism. She walked with the unselfconscious languor of a woman who had no idea of how beautiful she was. 'I like your office. All those books ... I wish I could read them but when I look at the words in a book the letters jump around and I ...' She smiled.

Her mental age, was, he judged, somewhere between twelve and fourteen. If analysis proved successful, she would need to be privately educated.

She had been given twenty-five shock treatments over the course of three months, and there had been a gratifying improvement in her response. Part of the battle had been won – communication had been established – but now he had to determine if he could get at the roots of her schizophrenia. It was one thing to eliminate the wall of silence and another to prevent a relapse into irreversible catatonia. He would bring her along slowly, shielding her from the outside world until she could construct defenses. He was convinced it was worth the effort. She had not evidenced autistic or schizophrenic tendencies before she had been raped so there was every reason to assume that her mental illness had been artificial, not congenital.

Green moved his chair so that he and Lenore were facing each other. She was smiling but not making eye contact. She had on a new brown skirt, a camel-colored cashmere sweater, and brown-patterned argyle socks which Sylvia had brought for her the previous week. Her blond hair shone in the sunlight and was below her waist. It had not been cut in years and there was a wild, sensuous splendor about it.

'Your new outfit's very nice,' he said.

'Thank you.' Her eyes wandered to the shelf of books.

'Are you thinking about anything in particular?'

'I would like to learn to read and write and I like numbers.'

'Well, you're going to get a private tutor.'

Her face froze in displeasure.

'Can't I go to school with the other children?'

'Eventually. You've got some subjects to make up and then of course you'll go to school.'

'Will you tell me the truth about something?' He nodded. 'Am I asleep or awake?'

'You're awake. This isn't a dream.'

'Sometimes I'm not sure about it.'

'Well, you hear sounds, voices, don't you?'

'Yes . . . sometimes I'm afraid to talk.'

'Why?'

'Well, something could happen. There could be a fire in the hospital.'

He noted on the pad he held on his lap: 'Delusions involving forces. Thought contact derived from magical source invests it with excessive power.'

'So at times you're afraid to think?'

'Yes, but not always. Just, oh, I wish I knew the words to tell you –'

'You're doing very well. Try to look at it this way. You've been asleep, in a sense, for a long time. Now that you're awake, the world is different. It's not Germany but America. You speak a new language. You're a young lady, not a little girl, but because of the sleep, there's a lot to learn and new experiences to understand. If you don't rush yourself and remain in control, you'll make progress.'

She withdrew into herself. 'That's it. I've lost such a lot, so much time. How do I get it back?'

'By living in the present. We all lose time. For example, young men sometimes spend years studying a subject – maybe it's engineering – and when they leave school they find that they don't really enjoy their careers and give them up. They, too, have lost time.'

She reached out her hand and for the first time looked directly at him.

'Can I have one of those?'

He laughed.

'A cigar?'

'Yes. I like the smell of it.'

'Have you smoked before?'

'No, but I think I would like it.'

'Women don't usually smoke cigars.'

'Why not?'

'Good question. If you'd like to try one, I'll let you, or maybe you'd rather have a cigarette.'

'Cigar, please.'

He lit it for her and the two of them filled the room with puffs of smoke. She didn't cough and appeared to be enjoying the experience.

'See, I'm just like you,' she said proudly.

'In what way?'

'You're smoking a cigar. I, Lenore, am smoking a cigar. So we are like each other.'

'That's an interesting idea.' He wrote: 'Von Domarus's Principle ... delusional identity of predicate. Paleological thinking patterns emerging. I smoke, she smokes, ergo, we are the same people.'

'Lenore, are there any special words you remember from your dreams?'

She seemed embarrassed and blushed. Again her eyes shifted uneasily and she almost snarled:

'Mutti!'

'Mutti. Do you know what the English meaning is?'

'Maaaaaah.' Her tongue protruded over her bottom teeth. 'Thththththhhh.' Her face was nervous and her eyes closed.

'Mother,' he said. 'Say it.'

'Mo – th – ach.'

'Mother.'

'Motha . . .'

'Father.'

'Papa.'

'Good. Now try mother again.'

'Why?'

'Just so that you can get it right. You told me before that you wanted to read and write. Well, saying difficult words is a beginning. Try it, it won't hurt you.'

She hesitated, puffed on the cigar until the ash glowed.

'Moth – errrr.'

She began to grind her teeth.

'You remember her, don't you?'

'She's very bad . . . very bad . . . she telled lies to me.'

'Not very nice.'

'No!' Her voice boomed. 'Awful to lie to its own child.'

He wrote: 'Mother, repression, source of hostility. Accusatory. Breakdown in grammar. Regression.'

'Yes, it's bad to lie,' he agreed.

'She leaved me. We cry, Papa and me. Cried and cried.' Her body shook with anguish and her chest heaved. Tears pelted down her cheeks. 'Bad to leave child-girl in pension. Mutti bad. If she don't go then . . .' She fell out of her chair, writhed on the floor in agony. He raised her to her feet and he wiped her face with his handkerchief. 'Is horrible what she do to me.'

'Tell me.'

'If she don't leave me alone in pension, then it does not happen.'

'What?'

She sank again to her knees in supplication, sobbing inconsolably.

'I do not . . . I do not . . . they do not hurt me. They go with Mo – th – errr, into her, not me. I am little girl. I am Jonathan's. He is mine. Now he is not here. Also asleep. And I am alone. He is alone. It is wrong to make us apart.'

'You loved Jonathan.'

'Yes,' she said, smiling happily. Her mood swings were intensifying. 'We love each other.'

'You want to see Jonathan?'

'Ohhh, yes, please let me see him. I dream I see him in the

hospital, but I didn't, did I?'

'Yes, you did. It's good that you remember. He came to see you some years ago.'

'When does the teacher come? I want to learn so I can write to Jonathan.'

'Soon.'

'I am happy now.'

When she returned to her room he noted on her chart: 'Catatonic-schizophrenia. Prognosis – good.'

Twenty-two

When he walked down the gangway of the Super Constellation, the humidity engulfed him. In the distance he saw Chou, suntanned, dressed in a pink linen suit, waving to him. He crossed the tarmac and strode to the fence and leaned over to kiss her. She embraced him and rubbed her hand through his hair.

'My little Jonathan ...'

Her eyes flooded with emotion and she walked parallel to him until they met at the gate.

'Pauli's going to be happy to see you.'

'I hope so.'

'He would've been here to meet you, but he's in Phoenix. He'll be coming in tonight.'

'You don't mind a houseguest?'

'Come on, you know you can stay as long as you like. You're the son we never had. Pauli's cutting short his trip just to see you.'

Paul had been traveling and Jonathan had been tied up with the construction of the Arena, so it was not until June that a meeting could be arranged. In the past year, in spite of the low profile Paul Salica kept, his name had often been mentioned in the New York papers as the Combination's boss in Florida. But Paul was also Jonathan's friend, a surrogate father, and responsible for his being alive. So let the papers and police rail against his gambling empire, his loan-sharking operation and land developments in Arizona. As far as Jonathan was concerned, the Salicas were as much his family as his own parents. It had been Paul who presented him with a five-thousand-dollar check on his bar mitzvah day, who had taken him aside and said, 'If you ever need anything, promise you'll come to Chou and me first. Lotsa people you'll find'll turn you down. Never us. And if you decide when you finish with school that you don't know what to do, there's always a place by my side.'

There were periods during his adolescence when he regretted that Paul was not his father. Jonathan was attracted by his strength, loyalty, and the overpowering purpose that governed his life. Paul epitomized to him the struggling immigrant who had come to America, friendless, and had carved out an empire. Yesterday's crime was tomorrow's legal business, he rationalized.

Paul and Chou had moved the previous year from the Roney Plaza penthouse to an astonishing palazzo in Coral Gables. Huge palms and oleander bushes camouflaged it from the road. It was hidden behind gargantuan fountains, massive statues, and grandiose alabaster colonnades. There was something primitive and Neanderthal about the estate, a barbarian splendor. Electric gates opened and Chou drove up the twisting driveway, past carefully tended tropical gardens. A car shot past them on the driveway and three men inside waved to Chou. The car squealed to the entrance and the men got out.

'Since we had that problem a few years ago, Pauli doesn't even let me go for a massage without Carmine and a few boys around,' she explained, chagrined. 'Times I feel like a schoolgirl with an overprotective father ...'

'I'd worry about you, too,' he said, taking her hand. 'You're very precious.'

The men were on the portico now, their weapons in full view: pistols, sawed-off shotguns. Jonathan felt as if he had walked into a brigands' ambush.

Inside the house the atmosphere was gloomy, brooding. From an open billiard room, Jonathan heard the low, subdued voices of men and the rap of balls.

'There are times I wish Pauli never got involved in all this. When I was shot I was two months' pregnant. I didn't even realize it at the time and the doctor had to abort the baby.' The corners of her mouth turned down. 'After that I was never able to conceive. It's a wonder Pauli stayed with me. He had visions of a big family, but now he's resigned to the situation. So we've got this mansion and no kids to fill it with, just Pauli's men. We live in a fortress.'

A swarthy, husky man in a white jacket brought Jonathan's suitcase into the marble hallway. The ceiling must have been twenty feet high, and from the entry Jonathan could see across a fifty-foot living room with floor-to-ceiling windows out to a private dock where an enormous yacht was moored, and alongside it two speedboats.

295

'If you want to learn to water-ski or go fishing, you came to the right place. We spend a lot of time on the boat. But even there we have to travel with a skeleton crew of six. Cook, maid, captain, and three seamen.'

He perceived the vast loneliness of their lives, filled with people they wanted to escape from.

'We do a lot of entertaining,' she said almost apologetically. 'Associates from all over the country come down to stay with us through the winter. In the summer we usually cruise the Caribbean, fish in Havana, or go up to Cape Cod and sail the coast.'

She sat next to him on a long, tapestried L-shaped sofa. She looked younger than thirty-five, girlish in her short, bobbed hair, and immensely vulnerable, like an heiress imprisoned behind her money.

As an afterthought she said, 'I'm some hostess. Are you hungry or do you want a drink? I guess you're old enough. Jonathan, I can't begin to tell you how happy I am that you're here. I took a pill before going to meet you and I can't stop talking.' She rested her head on his shoulder, then rang a small glass bell and a Cuban maid appeared.

'Bring us some old-fashioneds. And tell the chef that we'll have steamed clams to start with and barbecued lobsters for the main course. See, I remembered you like seafood and we get live lobsters flown down from the Fulton Fish Market every week.'

With drinks in hand she gave him a tour of the grounds. A venetian-tiled pool was surrounded by a large patio. There was a bathhouse with hot steam. The boat, christened *Chou*, was a customized Chris Craft and could sleep twelve. Beyond the pool was a clay tennis court with night-lights. The main house had eight bedrooms, each one of them done in a different European motif, and they had names like Madrid, Florence, and Paris.

'West's Hotel comes to Florida.'

'Pauli likes to make an impression, and it's paid off. You know it's one thing to live well in a town house or an apartment in Manhattan, but when you've got twelve acres and a boat that looks like a small *Queen Mary*, even people like Costello and Genovese treat you with respect and admire you. Pauli knows how to grease the wheels.'

She led him to his room. 'Naples,' reserved only for

intimates. The room had a garish baroque splendor, with winged blue cherubs painted on the ceiling, a canopied bed, heavy, oversized bureaus. But the view was breathtaking from the terrace. He could see most of the bay, a fusion of aqua light which melded into the soft cornflower sky.

His clothes had been unpacked and Chou showed him all the buttons beside his bed so that he could get the valet, call the maid, order a sandwich or drink from the kitchen or a car from the garage.

'We got spoiled at the Roney with all the service and Pauli was afraid he'd miss it.'

'No chance of that now.'

'Right, Paul's got the Roney for a home,' she said with resignation.

He took a shower then dozed till seven. He was awakened by the sound of car engines revving, men slamming doors and calling hoarsely to each other in Spanish and Italian. Footsteps thudded up the tile stairs and Paul said:

'Where is he, where's my boy?'

The door to the room opened and standing in the dim corridor light was Paul.

'I'm up,' Jonathan said, hopping off the high, European-style bed and into Paul's outstretched arms.

Over drinks by the pool, Jonathan noticed that Paul's face was sallow, bloated, and there were fleshy, purplish crenulations under his eyes.

They sat alone on chaise lounges, but in the living room a group of men were watching, the same protectors Jonathan had met earlier. They were still armed as they moved to and from the bar. Paul, it was apparent, conducted his affairs as though a state of siege were as natural as the tide coming in.

He had just told Paul about Bauer, confessed that even though the Nazi's death was an accident, he still felt responsible and was tormented by guilt. And he hoped for some form of absolution. However, Paul listened with detachment. His reaction struck Jonathan as superhuman and soulless.

'It's on my conscience. Every night when I go to sleep I think about it. I killed a man.'

'Well, it's time you stopped thinking about it. It was an accident. Besides, he deserved to die, and Christ knows,' he added with a sigh, 'good men have been killed for a lot less.' He refilled their drinks and walked silently along the pool. 'Listen to me and try to understand what I'm saying to you. Whether you wanted to or not you made your bones. A man's dead. A man who haunted you. Somebody fucked your girl, hurt her, hurt you. You're free of both of them. They're outa your system now. It was a just revenge, a just death. You're over it and your wound's healing. It's like taking a knife you stuck in the fire and cleaning the infection, cutting it open and letting the pus drain out.'

Strains of music and distant laughter carried from the boats passing on the bay. Small waves flapped against the yacht moored to Paul's dock.

'No more mysteries for you now, Jonathan. You've experienced life and death, and I feel closer to you than I ever did before.' Paul smiled at the boy he wished were his son. 'See, I knew from the time you was a kid that you and me belonged together. Alex is my friend, but he's small ... he'll hold you back. I said to Chou, there'll come a time when Jonathan will see all of us for what we are. Just give him a chance.'

'I feel better now. I'm glad I told you,' Jonathan admitted.

'Course you are. Nothing like opening up, spilling your guts to someone who loves and trusts you.' He took Jonathan's hand in his. 'We won't talk of this again and you *have* to forget it. About Lenore, Munich, the past. It's dead. You were just kids. You're grown up now. The Packard girl sounds like she's right for you, but wait, be patient, don't let yourself be rushed into anything just because her father's got a lot of money. Never forget that Charlie Packard's strictly business with you. Two people you can trust' – he prodded Jonathan in the chest – 'yourself and me. You give Charlie Packard your trust and open your heart to him and you'll betray yourself. Never let him know what's in your mind. He thinks you're a kid he can control, so let him underestimate you. You came to me for the money, you'll get it. No one will ever know where it comes from because that could hurt you. It's between us, no note, no paper, no lawyers, nothing.'

Jonathan stood up nervously. His shirt was soaked. He and Paul turned and headed down the pier and looked silently at the lighthouse beam above the breakwater.

'Pauli, it'll take years, but I'll pay you back.'

'Did I ask for that or any of your action?'

'No. But you can't just put up that kind of money without any return.'

'Someday the whole thing'll be worth millions and you'll give me what you think is fair. When your Arena – isn't that what you're calling it? – is open I'll have a little ticket broker's office set up in New York. When they want tickets, they get them first. Big blocks. The other thing is that there's a side to this whole business that neither of us understands.'

'Like what.'

'I'm not sure. Some kind of deal ...' He turned his eyes on Jonathan's face and they glinted with shrewdness. 'You come out to the Coast with me in a couple of days and we sit down with Vittorio and discuss it. He'll know the angles on television and make the contacts for you.'

For the first time Jonathan could see his plans assuming a tangible shape. With Paul behind him and Victor's support, he could fill the Arena all year long without competing with the Garden. He would swallow the Garden.

'It'll be good to see everyone again. David's at UCLA now.'

'Don't discuss our business with him or anyone else.' They headed back to the house where Chou and the men waited patiently for them. 'We must make sure never to hurt your father.'

'He won't come in. He thinks he'd be working for me.'

'We must always respect his pride. Eventually, he may change his mind.'

'Are you going out to the Coast just for my sake?'

Paul laughed and his chest was racked with a fit of coughing.

'No, not really. See, I've been waiting years to be able to make *my* move and now it's all settled. You being with me is a sign of good luck.'

* * *

Rested and suntanned, Jonathan was still not entirely at ease when they left the plane in San Francisco and picked up two rented cars at the airport, but he stifled his curiosity. He had learned the hard way that Paul discouraged questions, seldom volunteered information. He had asked why Paul wanted to bother with a small ticket agency when there were obviously more lucrative enterprises he might invest in and had received a brusque, irritated reply: 'Don't concern yourself with my affairs unless you're told to.'

But thanks to Paul, a million dollars had been delivered to Gardner by Wells Fargo men with a slip requesting that the sum be placed in a safety-deposit box in the name of Jonathan Stone. Delivering the money in cash was a powerful psychological ploy to engender respect from Packard and his banker. It demonstrated that Jonathan was a man of his word and could not be pushed around.

Paul had stressed certain principles to Jonathan: he should give in on small points consistently so that when he refused to give ground on something major, he could always point to the fact that he had compromised in the past. The other practical piece of advice Paul gave him, Jonathan was smiling about now as they entered the town of Carmel: 'Don't steal from your partners. Just buy them out as soon as possible. Make sure they don't understand what you're actually doing and haven't a hope in hell of running the show without you. Be vague, mysterious, and make it all look like magic. You have to be ready for Packard to counteroffer to buy you out eventually, and when he does, accept at once and he'll panic, because he'll think he's been outsmarted. The idea is to bait the trap with cheese, then close it on his throat. Believe me, he'll accept your offer in the end and think you're the one who's getting burned. Just let him take this public because with his power in the stock market, everyone'll want to get into it. I mean, when you think about it, it's a natural: the Arena in New York three times the size of the Garden ...'

'But Pauli, he's an operator, and once he forms a public company he'll know every maneuver.'

'Except one that he won't ever think of. When the time comes, I'll show you how it works. It's called "fucking the other guy where he breathes." '

Jonathan did not share Paul's distrust of Charlie, but then Paul was suspicious of everyone these days. Even in repose, while sitting at the bar in the motel, his eyes were fixed on the entrance, scrutinizing each man who came through the door. When Paul had to go to the men's room, Carmine was dispatched beforehand to ensure that no one was lying in wait for him. And Paul warned Jonathan not to make contact with anyone until he gave his permission.

Two days after they reached California, they were still at the motel in Carmel. Paul left his room only at dinnertime, spent most of his time on the telephone. Jonathan passed the time reading newspapers and magazines in the deserted motel lobby. For a change of scenery he strolled along the front, looking at the paintings of local artists. Behind him he sensed someone following him. He stopped and angrily gestured to Carmine.

His pasta gut hanging over his striped trousers, his jacket creased and his shirt collar yellow with sweat stains, Carmine came toward him.

'Can't I take a fuckin walk without you crawling up my ass?'

Carmine reached into his pocket for sunglasses. His mouth formed a vague approximation of a smile.

'I work for Pauli years now,' he said in an incongruously soft and resonant voice, 'and he says that I should look after the kid, which is you. And that's the end of it, *capische*? What's the use in talking ... this is a business trip.' He pointed down at the huge rocks where the surf foamed. 'Pauli asts me to jump, I don't even close my eyes. I'm over in two seconds. You're important to him, then you're important to me is it.'

'Carmine, what are we doing here?'

'We're waitin till Pauli says we're going to L.A. or back to Miami.'

'But why do *I* have to stay?'

'You got business with Pauli, so you're here. Relax.'

They went to a small restaurant with outside service and ordered two beers. The candy-striped canopy flapped in the wind. Around them passengers from a Greyhound bus were having a lunch and photography stop. 'This is a tourist place, huh?' Carmine said, drifting off the subject. Jonathan picked up a newspaper, for it was pointless to continue asking questions. He was Paul's hostage. 'Lookit, Jonathan, we got to take care. Pauli's been a long time planning to move to the Coast and he doesn't want a thing to go wrong. He has to make sure nobody can point a finger and accuse him of making a mess of this.'

'Carmine, I don't know what the hell you're talking about.'

'That's not my fault. I explained the situation more than I should of. Come on, let's get back to the motel and have a snooze.' Carmine took hold of his arm.

There was no arguing. They made their way back to Paul's room. Carmine unlocked the door. Juan and Jo-Jo, two of Paul's bodyguards, were in the bathroom, both stripped down to their undershorts. An electric saw was cutting through a ten-gauge shotgun mounted on wooden slats across the bathtub. A new member of the party, a sallow-faced man with weight-lifter's biceps, wore a welder's mask and had an acetylene torch in his hand. Paul had his back to the door, a telephone clamped to his ear.

'Hang on a sec,' Paul said, wheeling around in surprise when he saw Jonathan. 'Call you right back.' He slammed down the receiver, turned red, and raised his fist as though to strike at Jonathan. His mouth twisted in anger, then he suddenly regained control of himself and snarled at Carmine.

'What the fuck's he doin in here?'

Carmine threw up his hands haplessly. 'Pauli, you tell me he's like your own boy ... What do I do, tie him up or take him out?'

Jonathan stared at the gleaming array of rifles, handguns, and shotguns lying exposed on the sofa and a white light of shock dazed him. He slumped against the wall, his head lowered.

Paul came toward him. 'Jonathan, I have to protect myself,' Paul said, breathing heavily. 'I'm taking control of the Coast ... and there's going to be people looking for me.'

'Do you want to tell me about it?' Jonathan asked.

'I'd rather not. All I ask is that you trust me. Nothing's going to happen to me or you. I mean, you see what's going on, but better you ignore it all. We'll be leaving for L.A. around eight tonight which should bring us in around six, seven in the morning.'

Carmine nodded thoughtfully. 'You heard then?'

'Yeah, he'll be catching an early morning flight from Vegas,' Paul said with satisfaction.

'What about Virginia, the virgin?' Carmine asked with relish. 'What's with her?'

'She won't be going with him. Frank's got a soft spot for her. She'll just fade out of the scene. He's taking care of that. She's already admitted that she was the messenger to Switzerland. They skimmed almost two million dollars off the Flamingo. Frank's got the proof. Carmine, check out all the pieces. I want to see Jonathan on my own.'

Paul took Jonathan out on the small terrace of his room. They faced a stark pink stucco wall, and Jonathan vaguely wondered why there was a terrace in the first place, since the sun could never pass through this alleyway.

'I did you a favour when you needed money. Now I need you to be with me for a couple of days more.'

'Understood,' Jonathan replied, wincing at the blackmail threat implicit in Paul's request.

'You had Bauer in your life. I have a man who did me an injury. He was responsible for shooting Chou up and because of him she lost our baby and things have never been the same with us.' He rubbed a hand over his weary, unshaven face. 'I'm entitled to this.'

'But why do you have to be the one? Couldn't you be fishing on your boat in the Keys while someone else does it?'

'I choose for it to be this way. I'm the cowboy in this one.'

'You know I'll do what you want.'

'That's my boy. If you should ever be questioned about this, you came out to L.A. with me to see Victor about your Arena. See, there's nothing to connect me to this as long as you stick by me. No one'll say you lied.'

'Pauli, you're hurting yourself by getting involved in this,' he persisted.

'I like the odds.'

The night drive to L.A. was interminable. For hours they saw no signs of life, just an occasional one-pump gas station or a diner with a closed sign. They had taken sandwiches, beer in an ice cooler, and thermoses of coffee. It was five thirty in the morning when they reached Victor's house in Encino. Paul directed Juan to a cul-de-sac behind the house and gave him a key to the gate.

There was a guest house adjacent to the pool, and the men carried their suitcases and guns inside. Coming down the lawn in a satin dressing gown, rubbing his eyes, was the tall, angular figure of Victor. His mouth broadened into a wide smile.

'Christ, Pauli, can't you arrive like a normal man? I would've sent a limo to the airport for you.' The two men

303

embraced and kissed each other on both cheeks. 'Jonathan, I didn't know you were coming, too' – he stretched his arms out and hugged Jonathan. 'Boy, are David and the girls going to be happy to see you.'

On the way to the house, Paul cautioned Victor about going into the guest house. The men would not need the maids. They would clean the place up and make their own beds.

'Maybe you'd be better off checking them in a hotel. I could call –'

'It's just for the day, Vittorio. Better that they stay here. They'll be leaving tonight.'

'Okay.' Jonathan detected a strain on Victor's face. The arrangements worried him. 'Whatever you say, Pauli.' It was apparent to Jonathan that Paul controlled Victor as he did everyone else who came close to him.

The Conte women came down after seven and Jonathan felt a true sense of belonging. Their affection was spontaneous, open, and pure. Tired as he was, he joined them for coffee and listened eagerly to stories about David's progress, his brilliance. The girls hardly looked like sisters. Georgie was tall, buxom, with raven-black, luxurious hair and sloe eyes; even at that hour she showed a sensuality and a worldly manner as though there was nothing more for her to discover. Linda was the replica of her mother: petite, dark-eyed, fragile, with ivory-hued skin and a charmingly naive quality. She was a girl at seventeen, Georgie a woman at twenty. They told Jonathan David had an apartment near the UCLA campus in Westwood.

Jonathan waited until the girls left – Georgie for her job as a production assistant at Warner Brothers where she was working on *Key Largo*, and Linda to meet David before class – before he gratefully followed Tina up to the guest bedroom. He and Victor agreed to meet at the office later that afternoon. Unfortunately, he was next door to Paul who had showered, changed his clothes, and was waiting for him in the sitting area.

'I'll be out most of the day. Keep yourself available.'

'Okay. Are you coming to the meeting?'

'If I can. If I don't make it, I'm still there if anyone wants to know.'

* * *

304

The Chrysler, followed by Juan and Jo-Jo in a dark blue Chevy, made its way through Beverly Hills. At nine o'clock the cars met at the stop sign on Whittier and Linden Drive. Bugsy Siegel's white convertible Cadillac was parked outside his house at 810 North Linden Drive. Paul was driving now, and he pulled up at the south end of the street while Juan blocked the north intersection. Siegel could not leave the house without being spotted.

Paul opened a fresh pack of cigarettes, lit one, and wheezed. His mind was alert, remembering Siegel had thrown one obstacle after another in his way, blocking opportunities and advancement. Still, Paul had worked harder than any of the other bosses, for as a new boy, unconnected, he had been forced to demonstrate that he was smarter and tougher than any of them. He had courted allies, made himself available for the most difficult and ugliest jobs. And he always made sure that there was no evidence the police could develop which would lead back to him or the other members.

As a consequence, Paul had built a reputation and a loyal following. Paul had contributed a quarter of a million dollars to the building of the Flamingo in Las Vegas and held five percent in Chou's name. Other investors like Costello, Lansky, and the Profacis supported Paul. They were outraged by Bugsy's flamboyant life-style, his total disregard for the money they had invested, and the way he ignored them when they asked for explanations about the skyrocketing costs of the hotel and the reason why, since the opening, the gamblers had been so lucky. Months before, Paul had dispatched Carmine to Switzerland to inquire about Virginia Hill's frequent trips and Carmine had brought back evidence of numbered accounts she had in four Zurich banks. In January Siegel's partners were still reluctant to move against him, because none of them actually knew how to run a hotel, but as a warning and punishment for overspending, they had stripped Siegel of his majority holding and given him ten percent, take it or leave it.

'He's heading for the car ... alone.' Carmine said.

'No backup, nothing. The man thinks he's God.'

They followed him to Beverly Drive where he stopped at a barbershop, had a shave and trim, read the *L.A. Times*, then left to visit his lawyer on Wilshire and Camden. At one o'clock he left the office, drove to Hollywood and Vine, and met a tall, beautiful blond girl and took her to lunch at the Brown Derby.

Carmine and Juan watched the couple from a table opposite while Paul gnawed at a hot dog in the car. After lunch Carmine described how Siegel had manipulated his hand between the girl's legs while eating his Cobb salad.

Siegel and the girl drove to a small apartment house on Fountain Avenue draped with native vines and diseased palms. Siegel was inside for over a half hour when Jo-Jo came to the car and said:

'She's blowin him. I don't think he's ever goin to get off.'

'Do we go now?' Juan asked, filling his shotgun with thick, ten-gauge cartridges he had rubbed with garlic so that when Siegel was shot, the pain would be even more excruciating and blood poisoning would set in instantly.

'Means we kill the girl too,' Paul said. 'Sucking his prick is no reason for taking her out. I'd like to wait.'

'Pauli, it's a beautiful chance,' Carmine insisted. 'What the fuck does the girl matter? I mean, we may not get this kinda pop again.'

Paul shook his head. 'No, not now.'

'When then?' Jo-Jo asked. Sweat dripped from his pale brow into his glassy blue eyes.

'I want the bastard on his own grounds.'

'Suppose we slam in, bop the girl on the head, and then take him out to the desert?' Jo-Jo asked.

'Jo-Jo, your brains are in a shoebox. Lay off the weed.'

This had to be an artistic killing which would inspire admiration and cause fear among Paul's peers.

'Tonight, at home,' Paul said. 'That's the way it has to be done. Not in some chickenshit apartment in Hollywood while he's screwing. There's something gutless about that. I mean, when you invade a man's home and zap him, then you show you're without fear. You're a man entitled to respect. See, we're not blowing some deadass *goombah* in Cleveland or Atlantic City. We're in Beverly Hills ... movie stars are Bugsy's neighbors. They all live in a dream world, think nothing can touch them. They're secure. Everyone in the organization is going to be watching this one. I want to do it so they can never forget it. I want people waking up in the middle of the night, thinking, did I do anything to Paul Salica? Did I offend him, last time I saw him? Is there some-

thing maybe I can do that'll put me on the right side of
Pauli? Do I owe him a favor that he didn't collect? Shit,
when people think of me or mention my name, I want them
to come out in a cold sweat.... Meanwhile I've got a meeting to go to.'

Carmine dropped Paul off at Victor's office on the Sunset
Strip. Victor had moved into one of the new tower buildings near LaRue's Restaurant. VCA had mushroomed; the
agency had offices in New York, Chicago, London, and
Paris. Paul saw the figures semiannually. Like everything he
owned, he held his piece of the agency as a silent partner.
It amounted to fifty percent, but he never touched his
money, simply plowed it back into the business. He had lent
Victor money when he had begun, and after the agency
became overcommitted in television production, Paul had set
up a complicated completion guarantee company in
Nassau, so that Victor did not need to pay interest to the
banks. It saved twenty-percent annually and was a useful way
for Paul to conceal the profits he made from gambling. Nice
and clean, no questions, he reminded himself on his way up
to the tower suite.

Walking through the doors of VCA, he found himself
impressed with the surroundings. Everything in beige and
muted brown colors, the walls were paneled in distressed
cypress on which hung a number of paintings that Victor
had acquired on trips to Europe. Soutine, Picasso, Braque,
and Matisse. The pictures, Victor had explained, were a
good investment and Paul saw no reason to quarrel with
his judgment.

Victor's office was at the end of the corridor. The door
was dark Brazilian teak, hand-carved, and had no name on it.
It was opened by Victor, who smiled serenely. Jonathan was
standing by a window.

'You done yourself proud,' Paul said, his face aglow.

'Well, it took you a year to get up here. See, I couldn't
really describe it. You had to come and make up your own
mind.'

Two of the walls were of glass which ran from floor to
ceiling, framing Victor's French Provincial desk. On the
wall behind the desk was a painting which struck a dissonant
note amid the plush surroundings. It showed men in the

Depression eating in a Salvation Army soup kitchen.

'I can tell you don't like it,' Victor said.

'It's got the stink of poverty.'

'That's why I bought it, Pauli. Because every morning when I walk in here, I see something that Soyer, the painter, is telling me. 'This is how it was.' And that makes me realize how far I've come.'

Victor instructed his secretary to hold all calls.

'Pauli, do you want a drink or some coffee?'

'Straight bourbon.'

Victor pressed a button and a bar slid out of a walnut breakfront. He poured a drink and then joined Paul on the sofa.

'I almost fell out of my shoes when Jonathan told me he was involved with Charlie Packard. For weeks I've been reading in the *Wall Street Journal* about a new Arena that Packard's behind. And this little *momzer*' – he pointed at Jonathan – 'is Packard's partner. That, my friend, is high rolling.'

'What's your opinion, Vittorio?'

Victor rested his chin on the palm of his hand and looked thoughtfully at his friend.

'The possibilities are unlimited.'

'You think Jonathan's going to have his balls cut off?'

'I doubt it. He's put up minimum equity for a fifty percent piece. I wish something like that would drop into our laps. You know what'll happen. For at least five years there are going to be millions upon millions in tax write-offs. Then, when they turn a profit, they'll have all that in tax credits. From a financial point of view, it makes sense for Packard.'

'The question is, how to become profitable?' Jonathan said. 'You know what I think about boxing. It's a one-night shot and you have to have a major fight to really pull people in.'

Victor's eyes filled with consternation.

'I just wish to hell that Alex was involved. I feel like we're cutting the ground from under him.'

'My father passed, Victor. He turned Charlie down flat. You both know that if he changes his mind he's in with me. But my father never likes to gamble. He's strictly meat and potatoes, and I'm not saying anything about him that I haven't told him to his face.'

'The important thing at this stage is to proceed cautiously with a minimum of press buildup,' Victor said. 'Whatever you do, you don't want the Garden to get nervous and start signing up other sports.'

'They've already got the college basketball play-offs,' Jonathan observed. 'But suppose we have a tournament of our own before theirs?'

'Who plays?' Paul asked.

'The small colleges. We could use the NIT and NCAA publicity and build around them.'

'That's a possibility,' Victor agreed. 'The public is crazy about basketball and the idea of the little schools might catch on. You get a small school as national champion, then fans are going to wonder if the big teams could beat them.'

Jonathan had other ideas. 'Victor, there's this crappy sport called the Roller Derby which the Garden won't handle any more. The teams run from one armory to the other. Women teams as well as men. Even my mother watches it on television.'

'Television's what it's all about,' Victor observed. 'If we can make some kind of a deal with NBC or CBS for a fixed number of events over a three-year period, whatever you take in is gravy.'

'What would make them bite?' Paul asked.

'I could. If you were to play one-night concerts with some of my clients, you'd be in good shape. You don't televise it live, but sell the kinescope for another night so that you don't hurt your gate.'

'Name acts only,' Jonathan stated. 'No tryouts.'

'Hey, what's the matter with you?' Paul interjected. 'Would Vittorio hurt you?'

'All I want is to get the ground rules straight up front.'

Victor was smiling at him, aware that Jonathan was attempting to manipulate him. This boy was certainly different from Alex, more cunning and with the foresight of an adventurer.

'Naturally, name acts.'

'Like Billy.'

'Provided there's no conflict with the clubs that want him.'

'Victor, give a little ground,' Paul insisted. 'He's beginning ... he's our own.'

'You two are like gangbusters. I'd have an easier time

making a deal with Sam Goldwyn and Harry Cohn.' He saw from Paul's manner that he would have to yield and so he gave in gracefully. 'Okay, headliners. Big bands, name singers, comedians, the works. Every club and theater in town is going to scream blue murder, but I'll deal with it.'

Jonathan knew he had found an ally, but he did not want another partner.

'Eventually I want my own professional basketball team. If New York can support the Yankees, Giants, and Dodgers, then two basketball teams can make it in the city.'

'That's out of my province,' Victor responded courteously. Jonathan's attitude was becoming oppressive and he would have begged off if Paul hadn't been there.

'Victor, I'll find a way to program the events, but one thing's bugging me. What if the networks aren't interested in televising our events?'

Paul laughed raucously.

'Leave it to Vittorio. The man's got clout with these people.'

'Wiill you come to New York and introduce me to them?' Jonathan insisted.

Victor hesitated. He had a business to run, but somehow Jonathan had inveigled Paul into acting for him. Could Victor now refuse?

Paul stared at him, dismayed by his vacillation. He had never pressured Victor before, but he would in order to protect his investment.

'Vittorio, you do this thing for me, please.'

It would be futile to protest.

'When do you want me to go?'

'In a few days. I'm just finishing some business with Jonathan.' Paul rose, extended his hand to Victor. 'See, I knew you wouldn't turn him down. This boy's going to be a friend to us, Vittorio.' His statement had a curiously hypnotic effect on Jonathan as though intended as a warning.

Twenty–three

David's apartment was neat, filled with books, and he had a corner view which overlooked the campus. He waited with proud expectation for his brother's reaction.

Wearily Jonathan sank into the sofa. 'Well, it looks like you've done yourself proud,' he said, relaxing for the first time in days. His contact with Paul had been disturbing.

'You really pulled me out of the shit,' David said. 'Man, I was sinking.'

'Next time you'll stand up for yourself.'

David opened a couple of beers and brought out a package of pretzels. 'I spoke to Mom and Dad on Sunday, Jonathan. They're still very upset,' he said tentatively. He could not take sides in a family conflict and he did not want to lose Jonathan's support. David might be the older brother, but he needed Jonathan behind him. 'Is there anything I can do ... to make peace?'

'I didn't know we were at war,' Jonathan snapped back.

'Don't take it out on me. I just want us to stay together.'

'David, you're in over your head,' he replied. 'I laid it all out on a plate for Pop. It comes down to one thing – growth. He's not capable of it. Give him his lousy little ring, his fighters sparring, and he's happy. I can't spend my life sitting in a gym and bullshitting about which yo-yo has a better left hook. He had a chance to come in with me like a gentleman – an executive – but it's against his nature. He lives in the past.'

'And you?'

'I couldn't let this opportunity go by. I had to act.'

David continued warily: 'But he offered you money and you turned him down. Why?'

Jonathan rose from the sofa and walked to the window. He saw students scurrying with books and briefcases. They had a gaiety, a sense of childhood still clinging to them in their school sweaters, white bucks, and chinos, and he knew that he had missed something, the experience of youth with its fads, innocence, and games.

'He didn't offer the money in good faith.'

'How can you say that?'

'Because it's true. I'd have him on my back till I paid him off. The moment he gave me the money he'd start telling me what I ought to do. I don't like answering to people – parent nor not. I can't go around with my eyes lowered because he lent me a few bucks. I won't be involved with someone who doesn't treat me as an equal. You know this has been going on for years. If I didn't fight to have dances, roller skating, wrestling, the club would've been dead. Shit, David I made him take a lease on it then buy it outright.' He reached for the beer and drank from the bottle. 'I can't be controlled, father or not. We parted friends, shook hands like gentlemen. I took nothing. My conscience is clear.'

And that, he knew, was precisely the trouble. He had made his father pick a side. If Jonathan's venture failed, then Alex would regard him as someone he could never trust again. But by the same token, if Jonathan succeeded, Alex would be beaten by a better man. Their differences were irreconcilable.

'He loves you . . . more than me or even Mom,' David said without grievance.

'It's the self-image he thinks he sees in me that he loves. The difference between us is I love him for what he is and he loves me for what he thinks I am.'

In a disgruntled mood, he refused his brother's invitation to spend the evening together. He had to meet Paul for dinner at eight o'clock. He took a shower while David shaved and the temporary intimacy reminded him of the days in Brooklyn when they shared the same room. He thought of the companionship they'd never had except out of necessity.

'I wish you'd change your mind and come down to Mario's with Linda and me,' David said. 'Nothing fancy but the spaghetti and pizza are as good as you get in New York.'

'Not tonight, thanks.'

There was an eager expression in David's eyes as he rubbed Wildroot on his hair and molded down his pompadour so that it was high and pushed forward. He put on glen plaid slacks and a navy blue cardigan.

'Linda's very pretty and she made it clear she's got a crush on you.'

312

David's face shone with pleasure. 'You approve?'

'Well, let's not make a big deal out of it. She's Victor's daughter. And if you mess around with her, you better be serious.'

David stretched his long legs contentedly on the coffee table, sipped his beer, and smiled.

'Just between the two of us . . .? We're in love.'

'You're always in love. I didn't expect you not to be in love with someone.'

'Honestly, it's the real thing,' David said earnestly.

'David, it's your business. Just don't screw her up. You both want to finish school. Think about it after you graduate. Victor's been very good to both of us, and I wouldn't want to antagonize him. His daughters are holy.'

'Like hell.'

'What's that mean?'

'Georgie's wild. The stories I've heard about her . . . Georgie fucks.'

'Do you know that personally?'

'No,' he admitted.

'Then never repeat it. For Christ's sake, she's Victor's child. He took you into his house. So if someone gossips about Georgie you should defend her. I mean, this makes me sick.'

'Jonathan, she was at UCLA for three years and quit. There was a lot of talk about her then and there still is. Whenever one of the fraternity boys I'm friendly with finds out that Linda is her sister, boy, do I get looks. Like I'm taking out some tramp. How do you think I feel?'

'Look, it doesn't take a whole lot of guts to tell a guy who talks about Georgie to knock it off unless he wants his ass kicked in. David,' he shouted, 'can't you stand up for your own once and for all. My God, when I think of what we've all been through together – Paul, Victor, Pop, and Sam, we're thicker than blood.'

David was furious. Jonathan invariably chastened him, put him in his place, humiliated him. Why couldn't they be equals? Did he have to be told what was right and wrong as though he were a child?

'I accept people for what they are. If Georgie whores around, that's her business.'

'I'm not arguing about that. But you don't have to listen

to what other guys say about her. You're just giving them fuel.'

David looked at him blankly, then turned away. A horn blew downstairs. Jonathan's stomach churned when he saw Carmine leaning out of the driver's side. He called out that he was coming but he remained in the living room, despising himself for having taken David apart. They were together for such a short time and he had wanted it to be light and pleasant.

'You won't say anything to Victor about Linda and me?' David asked.

'No, you will when you're ready.'

*   *   *

The pylons supporting the pier shuddered as they were thrashed by the heavy surf. A strong saline odor clung to Jonathan's clothes. He was sitting in the car with Paul in the parking lot of Jack's at the Beach, a seafood restaurant in Santa Monica. On the pier, the neon light above the restaurant dazzled him. He had been staring at it for more than two hours.

Paul was staying close to his alibi. Juan wove his way through the cars on the lot and got into the back seat.

'Bugsy's asked for his check.'

'Who's he with?' Paul asked.

'Virginia's brother, Chickie, and his girlfriend, Jerri, and Alan Smiley. I don't know if Bugsy and Smiley have any business together. I heard they were friends.'

'Where's Carmine?'

'He was two tables away and Jo-Jo and me were on the other side of him.'

'I hope he enjoyed his dinner.'

'He was too busy talking to eat much. He just never stopped. Pauli, think it over, will you? We could blow him right here in the lot.'

'Forget it,' he said, sour, belligerent.

'But with the boy here?'

'You're okay, aren't you, Jonathan?'

'Fine.' Sweat dripped into Jonathan's eyes, and the dank, stale tobacco air of the car nauseated him. He'd feel better when they drove and he could stick his head out of the window.

Bugsy and his three guests walked down the steps of the pier. Siegel had a toothpick in his mouth. Chickie started the car and headed it north toward Sunset, the long way home. Carmine followed in the Chevy. At the first light he would pass Bugsy, so that they had the car sandwiched.

At the junction of Sunset and the Coastal Highway, they swung right and continued for twenty minutes along the road. Paul was calm, emotionless. He sat beside Jonathan fingering the trigger on the ·30-caliber carbine as though it were a lover he was caressing.

It was ten thirty when Bugsy's car pulled into the driveway of 810 North Linden Drive. The sound of friendly voices echoed from the alleyway. Siegel mentioned a horse which was running at Santa Anita the following day. Then silence. The shadows of palms fronds cloaked the empty street.

Carmine left the car. He carried a sawed-off shotgun crooked firmly in his arm. He went round the back of the house.

'I've never really taken pleasure in icing a man. This time's an exception,' Paul said to Jonathan, who squirmed nervously beside him.

Paul fitted the clip of bullets into the rifle.

'Now I'm as guilty as you ... is that what you wanted?'

'We're partners, aren't we?' he said. 'We look out for each other ... and I need you.'

It was ten forty-two when Paul left the car. Jonathan saw Siegel and another man sitting on a pale yellow sofa in front of the window. Siegel picked up a newspaper and was pointing to an article as Paul crept through the thick clump of azalea under the window. Jonathan stared at the back of Juan's head.

'Don't let him do it.'

'There's no stopping him. He's a real cowboy.'

Paul raised his rifle and took aim.

Bugsy's head tilted to the side. He gestured to someone else in the room.

The rifle fired. Bugsy was lifted from the sofa. Paul fired again ... four, five, seven ... times. He trotted back to the car, followed by Carmine guarding his flank. Both cars edged away from the curb. They headed directly up Coldwater Canyon in convoy.

'You hit him real good,' Juan said.

'First hit popped his eye out of his head. I must've hit him four-five times.'

They stopped at Mulholland Drive and Juan buried the rifle in a deep ravine in the hillside.

Paul was in high good humor. On the drive back to Encino he talked about his future plans. He would appoint Jack Dragna his lieutenant in California and he himself would continue to keep a low profile in Miami and Arizona.

'Besides the personal side of this,' he told Jonathan, 'I just inherited Bugsy's ten percent of the Flamingo in Las Vegas. Now you, me, and Vittorio are going to have a nice quiet drink together in the house to celebrate.'

Hollow-eyed and weak from the shock, Jonathan barely made it into the house. When he attempted to speak his voice croaked. Victor held him under his arm, assisting him to a leather armchair.

'What happened?' he asked.

'I think he ate a bad clam at dinner,' Paul replied. 'Next time, Jonathan, I'll let you pick the place.'

The complicity Paul had forced on him had fouled him, poisoned his being. There was a marked difference between Bauer falling off the fire escape and this premeditated murder. He knew that Paul's influence might destroy him if he didn't keep his distance. The lesson he had learned would not be wasted.

Jonathan did not get up till late in the afternoon, by which time Paul and his crew had left for Miami. Both the *L.A. Times* and the *Herald Examiner* had banner headlines announcing Siegel's murder. A fuzzy photo of Siegel, his plaid suit and tie splattered with blood, a gaping cavern where his left eye had been, was featured in the center. Jonathan looked at it, then tried to block the murder from his mind. He had to if he were to survive.

He spent what remained of the afternoon at the pool, lying under the trees which towered over the pool decking. Then he methodically attended to his business, speaking both to Charlie and Bill Gardner to tell them of the arrangement he had made with VCA. Both men told him they were pleased with his progress and eagerly looked forward to his return to New York. Charlie had given him a furnished apartment

316

on Park Avenue and Sixty-fifth Street in a building he controlled. The prospect of new surroundings and his desire to see Frances again – it had been six weeks since his last weekend at Vassar – made him all the more eager to return home and settle down to the construction of the Arena. He had hoped to book a flight that evening, but Victor was unable to go with him for a few days and this increased Jonathan's frustration. He had come to loathe California with its leisurely life-style, its unhurried attitudes, and its bronze, statuelike people.

Georgie and a lithe, dark-haired girl with fine delicate features were on the tennis court just within view. They stopped after a set to drink lemonade served to them by a Mexican maid who bowed when she carried away the tray. They went back to their game, looking like white lilies on the red clay court, oblivious to the man carrying groceries through the side kitchen entrance, the florist delivering flowers, the two Japanese gardeners hosing the leaves off the terra-cotta tiles. It was as though all these people were created to serve them. They took their aristocracy for granted.

When the game was over they joined him at the pool. They were going to a party that evening, and Annie, Georgie's playing partner, through a mixture of childish cajolery and 'pretty pleases' persuaded him to go with them.

There was an element of conspiracy which made him uncertain, for Georgie warned him not to mention their plans for the evening. Georgie in fact told Victor that they were going to a movie and would then cruise around the Strip to show Jonathan the sights.

It was after nine when they drove through the Bel Air gate and stopped at the hotel for a drink. They took a table by the piano and when Annie went to fix her makeup, Georgie's mouth curled in contempt.

'She thinks she's your date,' she said, her dark eyes roving over the men at the bar. 'At Ronnie's parties, there no such thing. You grab anyone you like.'

'And if I don't?'

She gave a deep, hoarse laugh. 'Then it's hard luck. The prettiest girls in L.A. will be parading around the pool.'

'Georgie, just out of curiosity, why'd you lie to your father?'

'He'd shit a brick if he knew I was seeing Ronnie. The two of them have been fighting for months. Ronnie's got a seven-year contract with VCA and he wants to get out of it. He hasn't reported to Warner's for the movie deal Dad made for him. Jack Warner's suspended him and he's sore as hell at my father. So Dad and Ronnie are suing each other. It's a helluva mess. And Ronnie hasn't seen me for days and he won't even answer my calls ... as if poor little me is to blame. After all, I'm just Victor's daughter, I've got nothing to do with the business. What the hell can I do about Ronnie's situation?'

'How long have you been seeing him?'

'From the time I quit college. On the QT because my father would murder me. I left school because of Ronnie, so that I could see him whenever he was free.' She took out a bottle of pills, swallowing one with her drink, then offered the bottle of Benzedrines to him. He looked at the bottle. There was no doctor's name on the label. 'I get them on Hollywood Boulevard, as many as I need. One thing about L.A., you can get whatever you want, no matter what it is – boys, girls, pills – if you can pay.'

He sympathized with her predicament but realized that Georgie was one of those girls who thrived on pain and if someone did not punish her she would do the job herself. World-weary, indifferent to others, at twenty she looked a hard, reckless thirty.

They had a few more drinks when Annie returned because the girls did not want to arrive early. Flynt himself, it seemed, usually appeared about two or three hours after his own party had begun.

Annie, it turned out, had done a few bit parts at MGM in musicals. She rabbited on interminably about how an agency like VCA could turn her career around.

'Did your father get a chance to screen my reel?' she asked Georgie.

'Annie, I told you a hundred times you have to give it to him yourself. My father is a very suspicious man. If I give him the reel, he'll think you're using me and then you can kiss your invitation to the house good-bye. Call him at the office and make an appointment.' She turned to Jonathan with hands outstretched, gesturing with futility. 'If you make a suggestion to Alex, what's his attitude?'

'He laughs in my face.'

'Exact – ly.' Her eyes were spacy. She'd had four drinks and another Benzedrine. 'See, when you've got a famous father, he'll indulge you personally. He'll try to ruin you so that you can't be a threat to him. I took acting lessons for years, dancing, singing, you name it. When I told my father I was thinking about a career, he sent my mother and me to Europe for three months. Annie, I can't help you.'

The starlet gazed at Jonathan hopefully.

'Who's your father?'

'No one you could turn to, honey, unless you can punch.'

'What's that mean?'

'He's got a boxing club in Brooklyn.'

'Terrific,' she said sardonically.

'See, you're wasting your time on me and Georgie.'

'Not on you, Jonathan,' Georgie said. 'My father said you're going to build an Arena in New York.'

'I sing,' Annie shot out quickly.

'On your back you do,' Georgie said, signing the check.

The bitchiness continued on the drive up Bellagio to Flynt's estate. A Japanese houseboy in a starched white shirt with blue braided epaulettes opened the door, and Georgie asked anxiously:

'Is he around, Aoki?'

In the living room music was detonated from enormous speakers and about fifty people were standing around drinking, nibbling on hors d'oeuvres.

'I haven't seen him since early this evening when he came in with Miss Sanders.'

'Rita's here?' Georgie's face relaxed, suffused with pleasure. 'If anyone can talk him into going back to work, it's Rita. She's his co-star at Warner's.'

A waiter brought Jonathan a glass of champagne and he walked to the glass doors and watched half a dozen couples throwing a volleyball in the pool. The girl in the middle who was 'it' lunged from side to side to try to get the ball. She leaped up under the diving board, and Jonathan saw that she was naked. Beside the pool, two cooks were lighting the brick barbecue and laying out steaks, hot dogs, and hamburgers on platters.

It was his first Hollywood party and although he wanted to enjoy it, meet the movie stars, the showboat behavior of the men and women vying for each other's attention dismayed him. There was no question: California was disagreeing with him. And Georgie's comments on the unattached girls made him think he was in a whorehouse; 'She's supposed to be real good; Blondie over there will make it with anybody, so don't believe you're the one; the brunette by the pool, her claim to fame is that the King gave her one.' A man in a brightly printed Hawaiian sports shirt passed her a stick of marijuana.

Jonathan walked out to the pool, found an unoccupied chaise lounge, sipped his champagne, and got quietly tight. By midnight the crowd had become totally uninhibited. Girls were reeling around, many of them naked, others partially dressed plunged into the pool. Some couples were making love on the grass, while others watched and cheered them on. He spotted Annie sitting beside the fireplace stroking an older man's cock and playing with herself.

Floating past him were a gallery of bodies, bronzed perfumed flesh, a nudist colony. They were willing initiates of the strange habits of their absent host who epitomized glamour while they simulated debauchery. The luxury of Flynt's cruel humor permeated their exhibitionism.

'Every fuck-up and hophead in town comes by,' a man in white ducks and a candy-striped red polo shirt said to him. 'Who're you ... you look like an agent?'

'I'm a friend of Georgie Conte.'

'Is that cunt here?' the man asked, forcing open his mullioned eyes and lumbering forward. 'I'd like to kick her teeth right out of her ass.'

A burst of applause was heard. Some of the guests had spotted Flynt talking to Jonathan. But Flynt ignored the outburst.

'Maybe we ought to leave before you really lose your Southern hospitality,' Jonathan said.

Flynt peered at him, then howled with laughter, raucously forced. Jonathan disliked him at once. The first thing he noticed about Ronnie Flynt were his hands: thick, hairy fingers with long rounded nails coated with a thick colorless polish. He visualized them scratching a woman until she screamed. But nothing could alter the dreamy lassitude in those eyes, fixed, virtually expressionless. In his film roles, Flynt projected always this mask of indifference: people died, women ran off, men blew their brains out while Flynt wandered through their tragedies, a sleepwalker, impervious to them. Jonathan could not conceive of anything touching him or rousing him from the intoxicating oblivion that was his natural state.

'What's your name?'

'Does it matter?' Jonathan stood up. 'I'm not exactly important to your career. And I'm about to haul my ass out of here.'

'Hang on,' Flynt said. 'It's just the way I talk. Means you're welcome here. My country manners.'

Slinking behind Flynt, a bright orange bath towel knotted around her body, was the redheaded Rita Sanders. She had a dazed half smile on her face. She was staggering; it was evident that she was very high on something. She stopped and leaned against Flynt to support herself.

'Friend of Georgie's,' Flynt informed her, 'but he's shy.'

'Funnnnnnnnnnnnnny ...' Rita said.

'My father and Victor are old friends, and Victor and I are doing some business.'

'Well, when you see Victor you tell him that two of his clients hope he falls under a truck,' Ronnie said.

Rushing toward them, her arms outstretched, was Georgie. She embraced Rita flamboyantly, then hid her face coquettishly behind Rita's shoulder to determine Flynt's mood.

'Are we going?' Jonathan asked.

'Hey, don't you like funnnnnnn?' Rita asked.

'Don't hide, cunt,' Flynt said, grabbing hold of Georgie's hair.

'Cunt,' Georgie said, savoring the word. 'That means you're not angry with me any more,' she shouted. 'Ronnie, you haven't been fair ...' She grinned, waiting for him to agree.

'Did you do some smoking?' Flynt asked.

'I'm outa my head,' she admitted. 'Three smokes and four bennies. I'm totally flipped but I was afraid to come near you. I mean, every time I look at my father I could stick a knife in him for what he's doing to you.'

Flynt smiled with cultivated malice, sat down on a chair, and extended his hands. She fell on his lap.

'It's not just me he's hurting, but Rita, too. And that's bad,' Flynt said.

'Real bad, Georgie,' Rita said bitterly. 'You don't know how I'm hurting. Your father turned all the switches off. Not a single connection in Hollywood will deal with me. Fucking Victor,' she said tearfully, 'wants to stick me back on the funny farm. All he cares about is how many drugs I take. What does he expect of me? For years I was his dirty little secret, then he dumped me.'

Jonathan lay back, confused, as though he'd walked into the middle of a film he couldn't get a line on. Georgie's groveling embarrassed him and the animosity she bore Victor was unworthy. He had learned earlier from one of the guests that it was based on a complete misunderstanding of the agency's role in Flynt's career. Victor had signed Flynt to a seven-year agency contract and because Flynt did not like a role Warner's had offered him, he had turned on Victor – ignoring the fact that Victor had taken an obscure sidewalk cowboy and made him into a major star.

Georgie snuggled up against Flynt. The abandoned look in her eyes and his own lurid seductiveness, playing one woman off the other, was chilling. His was the depravity of the incorrigible rake. Around them nude guests stuffed hamburgers into their faces, poured champagne on bare-breasted exhibitionists, and busily switched partners the moment orgasms had been achieved.

Jonathan found himself dragged along with Georgie to the poolhouse. The room was fitted out as a small gym, with barbells, pulleys, a leather horse for handstands, and an exercise bike with a mileage counter. There was a small portable steam cabinet in the corner and a couple of wooden benches against the wall. In the center of the room was a massage table with a clean white sheet and hard pillow.

'Here's where I keep my stash,' Flynt said, rooting through a closet. He held out a small dark blue bottle. Rita licked her lips reflexively, and Georgie giggled inanely. 'S'posed to be the best coke you can get ... pharmaceutical stuff.' He spread half a dozen thin lines of the powder on a mirror and handed a glass straw to Rita who greedily sniffed it, then lay back on the table crooning.

'Ohhh, wow, wow.'

Georgie, somewhat tentatively, took the straw and filled her nostrils.

'I'll pass,' Jonathan said.

Georgie slithered to the bench, and Flynt was beside her, whispering lovingly, cajoling her, unzipping the back of her low-cut dress. In a minute she was naked, her firm, well-shaped breasts in Flynt's hands. Stroking her nipples, he pulled her up from the bench, wrapped his arm around her waist, and urged her to the table where Rita lay giggling. He flipped the towel off Rita and took hold of Georgie's neck. When she resisted, he took another line of coke from the mirror with his index finger and forced her to lick it. Rita lay splayed out on the table, exposed, groaning, and Flynt took more of the coke and rubbed it along her clitoriis.

'That's so good, Ronnie.'

'Come on, Georgie,' Flynt cooed softly.

But she was recalcitrant, frightened. 'Please, Ronnie, don't make me do this.'

Jonathan stood by dizzily, his mind blurred.

'Just think, your old man's fucked that pussy hundreds of times,' Flynt said. 'Just touch her ...' He guided Georgie's hand to Rita's vagina, spread the lips. 'Come on, Georgie, you're doin it for me.'

Georgie's face was twisted. There were tears streaming down her cheeks. 'Oh, Ronnie, Ronnie, why do you want to hurt me like this?'

Rita had her eyes closed and lay numb as a statue, her body white. Flynt's fingers closed like a vise around Georgie's neck and pushed her face against Rita's vagina.

'Open your mouth, cunt, and start eating her.'

'Don't make me!' Georgie pleaded.

Jonathan roused himself from his stupor and pulled Georgie away. 'Georgie, let's get the hell out of here.'

Jonathan had no idea where the two men came from, but one hit him in the eye and the other kicked him in the stomach when he fell to the floor.

Georgie was crying, 'Leave him alone,' but the men kept pummeling him. They sat on him and slammed him repeatedly in the face and the stomach. The bile rushed to his throat and he caved in, falling flat on his back.

'You always have to give me trouble,' Flynt said.

'Don't hit him again,' Georgie implored him. 'I'll do it ...' She lowered her head, moving her tongue between Rita's thighs, and Rita blinked, opening her bleary eyes with satisfaction as Georgie's tongue spun along her clitoris.

Flynt's fingers thrust open the lips of her vagina and he said in a raspy voice:

'Get inside it. You lap it up, cunt.'

He moved away and one of the men at a signal began snapping photographs of the two women, both groaning now in helpless, ecstatic agony.

'Eat it, eat it, shitface,' Flynt stormed violently, holding Georgie so that the man with the camera could get her in the picture. 'I love it. When I get through with that guinea cocksucker of a father of yours, he'll wish he was dead.'

Jonathan was pulled to his feet. His nose was blocked, clogged with hardened blood, and he had a gash above his eye where a ringed finger had gouged out a piece of flesh. He was dragged through a side entrance and dumped into Georgie's car. He fought to keep his eyes open but they continued to close no matter what he did. He had no idea of the time when the door opened and a soft hand touched his face.

'Jonathan, Jonathan, I'm sorry. I didn't want this to happen', Georgie said, her mouth pulled to one side. 'It was the drugs. He didn't know what he was doing ...'

'Why'd you let him? We could've got out before it started.'

She gave a short, bitter chortle.

'Why? Why? Because I'm no fucking good. He could always turn me around. Anything. God, Jonathan, I loved it. I went back for more.'

Twenty–four

Jonathan was with Victor in the bedroom when a messenger delivered the photographs from Flynt. Victor flinched for just a moment, then continued to pack his briefcase. He was relieved that Tina hadn't seen them. He carried his bag down the stairs, kissed his wife and Linda good-bye. Georgie was still asleep. If he had any obvious regret it was for the beating Jonathan had received – a purplish-blue swollen eye and four stitches over his brow.

During the flight they played gin rummy on a bar table in first class and drank Scotch. Jonathan felt compelled to bring up the subject.

'That bastard ought to be dead.'

Victor's eyebrows rose and an ironic smile played across his mouth.

'That's much too simple.' His voice was controlled, dignified. No one could imagine that he was suffering at all. He picked up the small pencil they were scoring with and used the eraser on the pad. 'There's a word for this – attritus – and it means "pulverizing matter by constant friction."' He held up the pencil. On the table, shreds of the eraser scattered when Victor blew on them. 'I have a lawsuit against Ronnie. Maybe he expects that this will cause me to drop it ... who knows what's in his mind?' he said without any show of bitterness. 'I'm a man who lives in the present. I can't undo what happened. I can't restore Georgie's virginity or alter her character. Before I received the photos, I phoned Jack Warner and told him to replace Ronnie. Jack's a sensible man; we're old friends. He'll try to bring Hawks and Bogart in, and I'm sure they'll have a better picture. But Ronnie owes the government two hundred thousand dollars and he continues to spend twice that every year. I no longer cosign loans at the bank for him and so nature will take its course. You see, Jonathan, he can't work again ... not even in summer stock for fifty bucks a week.' He gave a short, bemused laugh. 'Having Ronnie beaten up or killed isn't my style. But, believe me, I'll see to it that everything he has will be taken from him. There'll be a time when he'll come running to me for help and I'll rip his eyes out of his head.' He paused, still serene.

'As for Rita, well, I'll tell you about her. She was my mistress. I loved her dearly. I gave her a career. I never sold her short as an actress or as a human being. But then she fell in love with dope. It replaced me as the center of her life. The battle was over before I could do a thing. The drugs have destroyed her mind. I've sent her to one sanatorium after another. But I'll never forgive her for letting herself be used with Georgie just because Ronnie had some coke for her. Believe me, when she wants to buy drugs now, I'll see to it her connections will only be too happy to supply her. She's one step from an institution and I'm no longer dedicated to saving her.' Sadness flashed like a scimitar in his dark eyes. 'And Georgie ... Georgie's going to have to face herself – and that will be trial by fire.'

Victor's hand trembled when he fitted a cigarette into his ivory holder. Jonathan filled his glass with Scotch.

'I'm glad you told me,' Jonathan said, 'because I didn't know how you were going to react. Fact is, I thought you were going to lay back and swallow it all. My father always said that you never let anything interfere with your business.'

Victor ruminated for a moment. 'Well, I haven't, have I? I've just chopped off the dead wood.'

Jonathan couldn't get Victor out of his mind even when he saw his new apartment. He inspected the rooms, the surroundings, discovering the air conditioning in each room, the all-electric kitchen, the sturdy, hard, horse-hair mattress, the liquor cabinet stocked with the best brands on the market. The refrigerator bulged with fruit, cheeses whose names he couldn't pronounce. He saw a clear path ahead for himself, free of sentiment. But as he girded for his flight into the future, he knew that he could never, like Paul or Victor, build his life on revenge. He had touched death twice: he wanted no part of killing again. He sat down on a leather armchair which faced the fireplace and picked up a bottle of champagne. He opened the small envelope and read:

Missed you like mad. Call me as soon as you get in.
I love you!!!!!!!!!
FRANCES

*   *   *

Lenore enjoyed looking at her reflection in the mirror of the small beauty parlor in Liberty. The metal curlers and clips reminded her of something but she couldn't think what. There were several other women in the shop, sitting under hair driers, reading magazines, and smiling pleasantly at her. The manicurist wheeled her trolley to the side of Lenore's chair.

'Which color polish do you like?' the woman asked.

This was Lenore's first time out of the hospital on her own, and the act of making a decision was problematical. Her eyes traveled over the colors. One was too pink, another too darkly red.

'Don't you have green or blue?' she asked, and the manicurist got the impression that she was being teased.

'I'm expecting a delivery next week,' she replied wryly. 'In New York they've got all the colors. Here we deal with red and all the stepsisters, cousins and *fercockted* in-laws. But green or blue on nails, not at Salon Shirley. Now soak the left hand and think red.' She examined Lenore's cuticles with disapproval. 'When's the last time you had a manicure, when you were sweet sixteen? For you, honey, I don't need nippers but fish-hooks.'

'I never had a manicure before,' Lenore explained as the woman massaged her fingers. The sensation was pleasurable. She'd have to tell Dr. Green when they met later in the day. She delighted in the hairdresser's manipulations, the way she swirled the comb, creating ringlets. The relaxed atmosphere and the natural friendliness of the woman touched her. She wondered if she had a daughter and plaited her hair, shopped for clothes, listened to confidences. How she missed her mother, she thought, but when she tried to visualize her own, the effort exhausted her and she remembered Dr. Green's injunction. 'When something begins to worry you, concentrate on the present, what's actually happening to you. As far as you're concerned, the past is dead. You're in control, so don't let events you don't understand trouble you.'

327

Her hair was done in a French roll with ringlets over her earlobes. She thought she looked beautiful. Her self-image was gaining strength with each passing day, fortified by the compliments she received at the hospital. No, there was nothing wrong with her, she told herself. It was like arising from a long, troubled sleep. She was sure now that some cataclysmic event – the earth falling off its axis or swallowed by other planets – would not occur if she thought about it. She had tested these patterns and she had come to realize that the actual process of thinking could not cause catastrophes.

Walking through the busy town with its women marketing, she felt at ease, but she was still nagged by the need to return to the hospital. Would she ever, she wondered, have a place of her own with friends her own age? Frequently she wanted to wander aimlessly through the strange cities she was reading about in her geography books. But Dr. Green had given her his trust and she must not make the mistake of ignoring him as she had her father when he had told her not to walk near the brewery. It would cause trouble. Better to do what she was told.

But, even though she was a few minutes late, she could not resist the corner drugstore. Displayed in the cluttered windows were cosmetics and perfumes. She went into the shop, paused at the counter. In a glass case she saw little boxes labeled Coty, Chanel, Revlon. Lipsticks, mascaras, brushes for applying pancake makeup, compacts, powders. They all tantalized her. No, there was no green nail polish. She was studying *Vogue*, squinting at the models' makeup and clothes. An elderly man left the sofa fountain opposite her. He wiped chocolate syrup off his hands and asked if he could help her. He waited patiently, while she made her selections, but after a while he left her, for she became increasingly confused. Ultimately she spent, to his surprise, almost ten dollars on cosmetics and fashion magazines.

On the way back, though she knew she was late, she stopped at the high-school sports field and sat in the stands watching the baseball team practice.

Clattering on spikes along the wooden stands, a tall, freckled, muscular boy in uniform waved to her and jauntily leaped two rows to reach her.

'Where've you been all my life, beautiful?' he said, winking at her.

She did not know how to respond to his question or whether to speak German or English. This ambivalence sometimes occurred when she was asked questions. Dr. Green had assured her that there was nothing to worry about and she should always reply in English.

'I'm a visitor.' Her standard line with strangers.

'Where're you staying?' The boy doffed his baseball cap. 'If you want a ticket to the game on Friday, I've got a pass. You can sit right by first base. I'm the first baseman and I bat fourth,' he observed proudly, crinkling his eyes and chewing bubble gum. 'What do you say?'

'I'll come if I can.'

'The game starts at five o'clock.' He extended his hand. 'My name's Larry Mayer. Every big league scout'll be at the game. They're after me. I'm major league material.' He sat down beside her, wiped the sweat trickling from his brow with the back of his cap. 'What's your name, beautiful?' She hesitated and he said, 'Listen, I'll hit a homer just for you. Come on, tell me your name.'

Blushing she said, 'Lenore West.'

'Any relation?'

'What do you mean?'

'West ... West's Hotel.'

'No.'

'Just a coincidence, huh, the name,' he said, scratching his brawny, freckled forearms. 'I work up there every summer on the athletic staff. Are you staying there?'

'No.'

'Mystery, mystery, mystery, huh.' He peeked in her bag and squealed with delight when he picked up a handful of lipsticks. 'Boy, I'll bet you look great in them. Wow. Come to the game, Lenore. We're playing our rivals, Monticello High, and we're going to shellac them. With you in the stands, I'll just go ape when I'm at bat.'

She pointed to the bat.

'Is that yours?'

'Thirty-six-ounce Louisville Slugger which I bone and take to bed with me for good luck. I belted sixteen homers this season with this baby. If you hang around till practice is over, I'll buy you an ice-cream soda at the drug-store.'

She looked at her watch. It was four fifteen.

'I can't ... but I'll come to the game if you give me that.'

'My bat?' Larry asked in astonishment.

'Yes.'

'How about another one?' he pleaded.

'Will it look like this one?'

'You bet your life.' He bolted down the stands, steamed across the field to the bat rack, and pulled out another bat, then breathlessly rushed back to the stands. She was heading toward the exit when he caught up with her.

'Hey, what is it with you?' he demanded in consternation.

'Oh, I'm sorry. I had to leave.'

Awkwardly he handed her the bat. On the field players were calling his name and his attention wandered from her to the pitcher on the mound signalling him.

'Will you come?'

'I'll try.'

'Hey, this is a free country. Can't you go to a ball game if you want to? There'll be a ticket at the box office with your name on it.'

'Thank you.'

He stared after her, ignoring the taunts of his teammates.

Lenore carried the bat and her supply of cosmetics into Dr. Green's office. He welcomed her, looked somewhat curiously at her, then sat on the edge of his desk and waited for her to explain why she had bought a bat.

'They did a wonderful job on your hair. Did you enjoy it?'

'Yes. I spoke to everyone.'

'Is something bothering you?'

'I was invited to a baseball game. Can I go?'

'Of course you can. Do you have a date?'

'I think so.' She seemed distant, distracted, and he reached out to her.

'Why don't you tell me about it?'

She flinched, as though frightened of being struck. He lighted a cigar and offered her one but she declined. She was lost in some mystical plane of consciousness. He had been having some difficulty with her lately. The calmer, more normal her condition, the more she was holding back. It was a natural progression. As she gained control, became more secure within herself, new inhibitions, blocks arose.

330

At the beginning she had spewed forth an endless list of complaints, real and imaginary, but as the course of her treatment progressed, her resistance became more pronounced, her confidences rarer, more generalized, intentionally vague.

He had meant his compliment on her new hairdo. Lenore was strikingly beautiful and her lack of self-consciousness about her looks heightened her physical presence. Her clear gray eyes were large, almond-shaped, and crowned with long delicate lashes. But ultimately, despite the litheness of her long legs, the melody of her body, what stood out was the pristine composure of her face, no longer childlike but still guileless. He had decided he ought to release her conditionally, allow her to make direct contact with the world and see how she adjusted to the exposure.

She had progressed remarkably in the months following the shock treatments. Her delusions involving natural and mystical forces controlling her conduct had been exposed and no longer troubled her. Obsessive topics of thought involving her mother had also been clarified. Gone was the restiveness, the negative attitudes, the repetitive patterns, and the fugues of compelling ideas which had previously dominated her. In fact, she could not be classified as a schizophrenic at this stage, for with his help, the symptoms as well as the condition had been ameliorated. She was a confused seventeen-year-old but this was hardly a justification for continuing to keep her in the hospital.

Lenore's catatonia had been a classic regression, a return to an infantile level of integration after the rape. The mind had its defenses: injured, it withdrew, but this was actually a positive sign, a desire within the unconscious to survive in some form. The death of her mother in childhood had constructed a state of tension which had developed into a case of massive anxiety. This had been coupled with Sam's strictness as a father, his warnings, which had, in a sense, functioned as a magnet to the other profound anxiety. The two halves, prior to the attack, had existed in a psychological matrix, trapping Lenore. Too young to deal with these forces – the one the voice of her dead mother, the other Sam's restraints, his constant reproaches – Lenore had all the qualifications for the perfect victim. But the condition of catatonic schizophrenia with its process of elisions, loss of association, withdrawal had, to a marked degree, saved Lenore.

Silences were still a part of her therapy. When Green made no effort to force the conversation, Lenore eventually gave way.

'Are you angry with me for being late?'

'No, why should I be?' he said affably. 'You're on time mostly.'

'You still trust me?'

'Sure I do. You're a very trustworthy person. You must've been enjoying yourself.'

'I was, I was. There's so much to see and do . . .'

'You're starting to investigate life outside the hospital. That's a good thing.'

For a moment her mouth dropped and she retreated. 'Do you think Jonathan's going to hate me?'

'What makes you ask that?'

'I stopped and watched some boys playing ball at the school.'

'Nothing wrong with that,' he insisted.

'I . . . I *spoke* to another boy.'

'Well, why should anyone disapprove of you talking to a boy?'

'It's so confusing.'

'What is?'

She stood up and moved into the corner, hiding her face, her composure abandoned.

'I can't say this to your face.'

'Okay, if you prefer not to. You don't even have to tell me.'

'You won't think I'm horrible or disgusting?'

'Why should I?'

'Ohhh, I don't know. It just isn't nice.' She shuddered, her body tautened.

'Lenore, you have free choice. If it's something you'd rather not discuss, then don't worry about it. On the other hand, if it's making you miserable, then by telling me we can see what it is and why it's bothering you.'

In a whisper she said:

'I touch myself . . .' The anguish in her voice suggested a reversion to their earlier session after the electroshock treatments when the girl had been paralyzed by guilt. He allowed her time to compose herself. 'I'm so ashamed of it, but I don't know what to do. At night just as I'm trying to fall asleep ... I get hot there and I rub it. I put my finger inside! It's wrong and I have to stop.'

The confession drained her. She stood frozen in the corner, a contrite child pleading for grace.

She waited apprehensively for his reaction, fearing that she had shocked and disgusted him. She had held nothing back, trusting him with her soul, and he regarded this manifestation of integrity as a personal triumph. He offered her a cigarette, lit it for her. She began to relax, her mood swing had run its course and the small gesture of a reward reassured her. She perceived that her offense was not as serious as she had imagined.

'Lenore, there's no need to hide. You haven't done anything wrong and you feel better – I can see – now that you've got it out.'

'You're not angry with me?'

'No, of course not. Let me explain a few things to you.' He stood up, glanced out of the window at the rose gardens, the gorgeous fulfillment of summer. The apple and pear trees in the fruit orchard were bountiful that year and he remembered how, when she was a child, he had taught her how to plant and nurture the trees that were now vibrant with fruit. 'Lenore, what you're doing is called masturbation. It's kind of a natural investigation of the human body – of what belongs to you ... to all of us. We're curious about other people, and intensely curious about ourselves. There's nothing unhealthy, dirty, or shameful about masturbation. If you didn't, then all the energy that's stored up inside you wouldn't find any outlet. People who don't admit their sexuality have time bombs within them that one day explode. So this is a voyage of discovery for you. Enjoy it. It won't harm you. There are times, especially before going to bed, when you're drowsy and you feel an irresistible impulse to explore. The exploration is pleasurable, relaxing, so give in to it.'

She smiled but then her expression changed. She worriedly bit her lip. 'Do you think Jonathan still likes me?'

'I assume so. There's only one way to find out. Write to him and invite him up to visit you.'

'Here?' Scandalized.

'You're going to be discharged at the end of the month.'

Elation and fear mixed in her reaction.

'When will I see you?'

'Oh, we'll keep going two or three times a week. Depending on how you're adjusting.'

'I don't want to leave you.'

'You're well enough to begin your life in different surroundings.'

But Lenore had a skeptical, distrustful look on her face when she left. Dr. Green knew she did not believe for a moment that she could cope on her own in the world, but still his only recourse was to give her the chance.

* * *

The networks treated Jonathan and Victor with great courtesy. But as one meeting led to another, Jonathan came to the conclusion that they were stalling, avoiding an outright refusal just because of the high esteem they held Victor in. After a week of maybes, the executives became even more dilatory, and Jonathan knew that he was getting the runaround. Meanwhile, Victor had clients to see, theaters and clubs to look at, and he left Jonathan to his own resources.

Jonathan had had enough. He made an appointment to visit the owners of Channel 10, a local station in New York controlled by two Texans, the Marchands of Dallas, father and son. They ran their station as a hobby. They didn't care that the station lost money – it provided them with a tax write-off. Besides, what they wanted most was to be accepted by the New Yorkers named in society columns, to pick up tabs for movie stars at '21,' be seated promptly at a ringside table at the Copa, and to be on party lists.

Jonathan arranged for their dreams to come true. After a week of frenzied party-going with Charlie and with clients of Victor's, they virtually handed over the deal to Jonathan. A twenty-year contract was negotiated; the Arena would provide the Marchands with free sporting events of their choice in exchange for twenty minutes of air time per week, and Jonathan would control the prime advertising spots.

Before returning to California, Victor somewhat shamefacedly met with Jonathan in his apartment. He explained that he had worked out a friendly agreement with Sam regarding Georgie's future.

'Georgie knows a helluva lot about entertainers,' he said enthusiastically. 'Apart from booking Sam's acts, she could come down to New York and check out new acts, go to the theater, and operate as a liaison with my office here.'

'Any change would be for the best.' Jonathan agreed.

'She'd have you and your folks to visit,' Victor continued. 'I'd like to feel that I could count on you to help her when she's in town.'

'Victor, do you have to ask?'

He fell into an easy, relaxed posture. Maybe Georgie could, in a different environment, work out her problems, change. In L.A. she had fallen in with the wrong group, was headed for destruction.

Jonathan fixed them another drink. He was wary of Victor's formula, the package he had developed for Georgie. 'What about her studio job?'

'That? It's a joke. I fixed it and now she's off the film. I had Johnny Rosselli put some pressure on the studio ... to get rid of nonunion people, so it didn't look like I had her pink-slipped. When I get back, I'll give her the choice of going to work at West's or walking around L.A. without a penny to her name. Good-bye Saks and Magnin's charges, good-bye car, no lunches at the Polo Lounge. Her options are to sling hash at a counter or to wash floors. Thank sweet Jesus, I've got one daughter who won't tear me apart. When Linda meets the right boy and gets married she's going to have a church wedding like nothing they've ever seen in L.A. I'll bring in the whole chorus from La Scala to sing ...'

The limo driver rang the doorbell and explained that they'd be caught in rush hour traffic if they didn't leave for the airport immediately. Victor downed his drink and embraced Jonathan. His gratitude was real but his reasoning seemed shaky. He had hired Jonathan as a watchdog, demonstrating that he little understood Georgie and the range of her depravity. Georgie would resist pressure.

'Don't think I'm telling you what to do, but on the flight back, think how you're going to put it to Georgie.'

Anger upset the fine symmetry of his handsome face. 'She disgusts me. ... You think it's wrong for me to send her east?'

'Victor, at least get her on your side first. Don't just threaten her. She knows you've seen the pictures. She's been humiliated. If you make her believe Sam knows how to run a hotel but messes up the entertainment, that your agents in

New York aren't aggressive enough in acquiring clients, in other words how much she can help you by coming, you'll give her back some of her confidence. Besides, isn't that what you intend her position to be?'

Victor squared the crease in his gray fedora with the side of his hand.

'No, Jonathan. In a plain, simple word, this is exile. I've got to get rid of her. I have to live for the rest of my life with the image of her with Rita. But don't worry, I'll play it your way. After all, didn't I figure out a job for her? So long as I don't have to have her around me.' His eyes had the blunt chill that he had observed in Paul's when mentioning Bugsy Siegel. 'As far as I'm concerned she's a corpse.'

* * *

From the moment ground was broken on the Arena, Jonathan had been plagued by a series of disasters which seemed to occur without any plausible reason. He did not believe that he was a victim of the implacable forces of fate. He had a simpler, more direct response.

'Sabotage,' he told Charlie as they rode the construction elevator ten stories up to the top of the concrete shell. The formwork had been completed and hardhats were welding the steel girders. More than eight hundred men were in the work force, and they were bare-chested in the humid September morning, sweating and swearing at crane drivers below who were shifting huge slabs of concrete at lower levels. Although they had employed more men than necessary, they were running behind schedule.

Charlie was in a foul temper, for he was involved in a whole series of enterprises that had nothing to do with the Arena.

'What about the lawsuits from the local residents?' he asked, pulling off his seersucker jacket.

'We anticipated those,' Jonathan said. 'They're chicken-shit suits. You owned the property and we're not driving people out of their homes. The noise is a temporary inconvenience. All of that was made clear when we were issued the building permits.'

They reached the roof where men with beet-red faces, sun-bronzed backs and arms were using acetylene torches to burn and join steel tubes. To an untutored eye, the Arena was taking shape. 'Materials aren't being delivered on time,' Jonathan said. 'We've had people out sick, sometimes as many as ten percent. Some of the electricians aren't union, and that's causing bad blood with the union. Every other day, they're threatening to walk off. And when they don't, they're on a go-slow.'

Jonathan had rings under his eyes, his skin was sallow, and he looked like a man who needed a rest cure. He had aged years since returning from California, sleeping four hours a night, arriving at the site at six in the morning, staying up till two or three going over blueprints with the architects and contractors. Maybe he had bitten off more than he could chew and a more experienced man ought to be brought in. At least that was Gardner's and the bank's opinion. But Jonathan would not accept this dismissal.

'What do you expect me to do about it?' Charlie was becoming increasingly defensive.

'Al Lazar asked to meet the two principals, so that's why you're not having lunch at Fraunces Tavern today.'

'Who the hell's he?'

'The business agent of Local four fifty-six, of the construction union. He's God on this job.'

'Couldn't we have met at a bar or a restaurant?'

'Lazar likes the roof.'

There was no place to take shelter and they waited for fifteen minutes under a blazing sun. The noon whistle blew for lunch, and the men put down their tools, opened their tin lunch boxes. Lazar finally showed up, wearing a straw hat, a dark green suit, and hand-painted tie featuring a horse at the starting gate. The horse's mane had been squashed in the double Windsor knot and the tie itself was as abbreviated as the five-foot-two Lazar. His eyes never settled on a face but shifted restlessly.

'Al, this is Charlie Packard.'

'The boss, right?'

'No, we're partners,' Charlie said.

'Well, the kid can't make decisions about money without talking to you, right?'

'We make them together.'

Lazar jiggled some wax in his ear.

'This job's a real disappointment,' he said. 'My men are unhappy about the working conditions.'

337

'Like what?' Jonathan demanded.

'Safety for openers. Too many accidents.'

'Yeah, but they always seem to happen to nonunion people,' Jonathan said.

The fact did not register on Lazer.

'Well, whatever.' He scratched his ass. 'Next thing you know, a bomb could go off.'

'Al, what's that supposed to mean?'

'A bomb's a bomb. Five sticks of dynamite tied around an alarm clock and put at the foundation.' Charlie was horrified, listening with disbelief. 'Or if that don't happen, then something else could hurt you like the union's position on holidays and overtime.'

'We're paying top dollar.'

'That's your opinion, Jonathan. Let's hear from your partner.'

Jonathan had never seen Charlie intimidated before, but this was a new environment for Charlie – the streets with their imminent violence. This wasn't discounting municipal bonds, taking on a new stock underwriting, or collecting rents on Park Avenue.

'You want to make a deal?' Charlie asked.

'See, your mother didn't raise crazy children, Mr. Packard.'

Jonathan caught Charlie's eye, signaling him to withdraw.

'Let's hear your side of it,' Jonathan said.

Lazar's lips puckered in a half smile and he clapped his hands together.

'The figure I had in mind was a hundred now and a hundred on completion. Man, you'll be open by Easter for High Mass.'

Charlie began to nod. He had millions already tied up, what did two hundred thousand mean? It could be added to the construction costs by the accountants as overtime or fiddled on padded bills from the contractors.

'That means no go-slow, no more accidents, no extra holidays?' Charlie asked.

'I'll have their asses out on Thanksgiving and Christmas,' Lazar affirmed. 'Easter Sunday, Dewey and O'Dwyer can cut the ribbon. You got my word on that.'

The prospect of paying extortion money infuriated Jonathan, but at least now he knew why he had been beset with problems which had nothing to do with his own management. The bank and Charlie could not accuse him of fouling up the project or suggest that he had acted irresponsibly. Now he could show Charlie how he could control a difficult situation.

Jonathan lit a cigarette, offered one to Lazar, holding the light for him.

'If I can discuss this with Jonathan –' Charlie began.

'Take all the time you like – two minutes,' Lazar said, blowing smoke out contentedly.

'That's not necessary. You know, Al, what confuses me a little is the way you keep using *I*. "I want this," "I figure," "I'll have the men working." ' Jonathan noticed Lazar pulling back cautiously. 'You asked to see the two of us – principals – but who the fuck are we talking to? You're a piece of schmuck bait. You don't exist. Your Local four fifty-six is a paper job. You've got a shitty little store on Broome Street next to the Grotta Azzurra. You got a desk, a toilet, and a phone in there. You know, Al, when you make demands on people you have to come out smoking. Bombs, well, you should have had one with you ...' Charlie had turned white and he started to remonstrate with Jonathan, but Jonathan went on. 'You're a nothing bagman who walks around this site with a pint of Schenley in his pocket and you chew on stogies. Al, call a strike, right now!'

Lazar retreated a few steps. 'I don't have to take this crap from you.'

'My friend, you eat it up. You can't make a deal but *your* principals can.' Jonathan started to walk away. 'Al, I wouldn't piss on you if you were on fire. The people behind you can make trouble. If they've got names, I'll be happy to talk about anything they want to complete this job. They're interested in a sweetheart contract, I'll listen. But they can't send you as the rabbi to us. If we do this, then, let's have it proper ... an *Argomentazione* with *Fratellanza*. Everybody has his say and we come to terms.'

Lazar's lips moved but no sound came out. He raised his fist, then under Jonathan's unyielding glare dropped it. 'You talk this way to Johnny Dio and to Ducks, you won't have to worry about a union problem.'

'I only talk this way to an *Indian* like you.' Jonathan pointed to a drug-store on the corner. 'You call them now and say I'll meet them at the Grotta at eight. They're my guests. And, Al, I catch you on the site again I'll burn your fucking head off with a torch.'

Lazar backed off, catching a loading elevator, and rode amid piles of cement. He never once raised his eyes to Jonathan standing there above the chute.

Charlie had still not recovered from the force of Jonathan's action. 'You're a crazy kid. Pay him the money and let's not have any more headaches.'

'I'm sorry you had to be disturbed with this sort of thing. But he wanted to see both of us. Charlie, I'm nobody's boy. I'm my own man. I don't get a shakedown for two hundred thousand dollars.'

'What're you going to do?'

'Handle it.'

Twenty–five

He had not been consciously avoiding Frances, but there never seemed enough time for them, and even when they spent an evening together, Jonathan talked endlessly about his plans for the Arena. Somewhere along the line she felt she had been lost, forgotten, and she was assailed by resentment. She had hung around the city all summer waiting to see him, ignoring stacks of invitations from friends at the Cape, Martha's Vineyard, not to mention the season at Antibes. She had spent a few days at the family summer house in East Hampton, but passed up parties and dinner dances.

Her summer had been ruined.

Night after night, eating alone or with her parents when they were in town, going to the movies alone, fragmented her nerves. She floated down to the Village, sat in Rienzi's drinking espresso or drifted into the Champagne Gallery to listen to the soft, romantic piano music. She was saving herself for Jonathan. It was the thought of him which had made her junior year at Vassar endurable.

Yet now again he was late ... hours. They were to meet at the house at five thirty, have cocktails at the Pierre, then go on to dinner at the Colony. She had even made the reservation. At eight fifteen he finally called.

'Honey, will you catch a cab down to Broome Street?'

'What happened to our plans?'

'I got held up. The Grotta Azzurra.'

'Can't you pick me up?'

'We're meeting two people for dinner and I'm down here. Dress casual.'

'Jonathan ...'

'Hustle it. Bye.'

His manners had always been questionable. But now he was actually ordering her around.

And yet here she was taking it. She made her way down the steep stairway of the restaurant, battered by a mob clogging the entryway, physically pushed back by a waiter carry-

341

ing a steaming, oversized tray of lobsters swimming in a hot red tomato sauce. She leaned against the wall and studied the backs of men's heads. She caught his gaze when he turned to shift his wooden chair to let another party through. He rose, hand cutting through the air, beckoning her. She struggled past cramped tables.

'Johnny, Tony, this is my lady, Frances.'

Two sets of suspicious eyes, one face pudgy, jowled, the other starkly handsome, hair matted with pomade, nodded and emitted 'hellos.' A stack of clamshells rested on the paper tablecloth against the plates. Jonathan poured Frances a glass of wine from a pitcher filled with slivers of apple and pear.

'Here's lookin at you,' Ducks Corallo said, banging her glass. He had pale blue cynical eyes. 'Does she forget what she hears?'

'Uh-huh,' Jonathan said, squeezing her hand under the table.

'We were having a conversation,' Johnny Dio informed her, giving her the benefit of his smile. He was white-skinned, greasy, and had the looks of a third-rate matinee idol of the twenties.

'I'm just baggage,' Frances said, glaring at Jonathan.

'Well, then you know your place,' Corallo advised her amiably. 'You relax, Frances, and enjoy your dinner. This place's got the best guinea food in the city.'

Frances decided the two men probably made their livings stealing tires or breaking gum machines in the subway. But she had come for Jonathan's sake and she would not allow herself to be baited. She removed her hand from his under the table, sipped her wine demurely. She would have her say later, if she ever managed to get Jonathan alone.

It was out of consideration for her that Jonathan had asked her to join him. He felt he owed it to her not to cancel again at the last minute. Still, she had to know he was fighting for survival. If Frances could not appreciate his situation, then it would be best to end their relationship.

He had antagonized both of these men by his treatment of Lazar, but the strategy of aggression appealed to him. Paul had schooled him in tactical maneuvers of this kind. Dio and Corallo considered him a loudmouthed, ignorant young man who needed to be taught a lesson, but still, they had agreed to sit down with him and discuss their demands. Jonathan knew he had made an inroad and he proposed to capitalize on it. From the moment they had met at the table, he had acted in a deferential manner to Corallo, the more important of the two.

They ordered dinner, drank several pitchers of Valpolicella, idly chatted about the resurgence of the Cleveland Indians under Lou Boudreau, who was managing the team as well as playing shortstop. Both men were baseball fans and over chicken, country style, the atmosphere became relaxed and at times jovial. As they all stirred their espressos, shared a zabaglione, Jonathan took command of the situation.

'You might think Frances is just my window dressing for the evening, but I wouldn't embarrass either Ducks or you, Johnny, by pulling a stunt like that. She's Charlie Packard's daughter, so obviously she's here to protect his interests.'

'Fair enough,' Ducks Corallo replied, fixing his eyes benignly on Frances.

'I think then it's time we settled this,' Dio began. 'Nobody wants to hurt anyone. Your Arena is important to the city and we all want it to be finished on time.'

Frances sat back attentively, watching each man in turn.

'Then let's cooperate,' Corallo said with the practiced air of the fixer. His lazy eyes scanned the faces of the two young people. 'Jonathan and Miss Packard, you have to trust me. We're bona fide union officials. Johnny is the business agent of Local one oh two here in the city. I'm an officer of Local five sixty in Hoboken and some New York locals.'

'Then why'd you send an errand boy to lay this on me?' Jonathan asked.

'We can't be everywhere at the same time. Al Lazar is one of my assistants,' Dio explained. 'Believe me when I tell you, it's important that our people are employed.'

'He tried to shake me down for two hundred thousand.'

Still amicable, Ducks Corallo smiled expansively.

'That was no shakedown. It was the price of peace. You know every job – and especially one your size – has industrial disputes. I wouldn't like that to happen with the Arena.'

'It's not going to,' Jonathan informed him.

'Well, you've got to see our position. As officials, we got to keep the work force happy and in line. You know on your job we've had a lot of serious complaints,' Dio said.

343

'For two hundred, no more trouble or complaints?'

'I can guarantee that,' Corallo said. 'Our drivers have been giving us heat about the depot's procedures at both ends – the pickups and the deliveries . . .' For the next five minutes, he cited imaginary infractions and safety measures, suggesting that one calamity after another had caused the men distress, and that he as their spokesman had a legitimate claim to reparations.

'Can I have my say now?' Jonathan turned to Frances. 'And I'm also representing my partner's point of view.' Both union men seemed confident that the bargaining would now begin. 'Besides my partner, I've got a few friends, too, and I had to take them into my confidence.'

'Well, if your banker can keep his mouth shut, then there'll be no problem. If he starts calling Feds, then the Arena – what there is of it – is going to wind up a hole in the ground. You'll be able to parachute into that hole, my friend,' Dio observed starkly.

Jonathan touched the empty glass and the waiter brought over more espressos. The restaurant had thinned out and the tables beside them were unoccupied. Jonathan broke a lump of sugar and sucked it. 'Look, I'm young but I wouldn't have been given this kind of responsibility if Morgan Guaranty and Charlie Packard didn't believe that I was the right person to handle a venture of this size. They didn't pick some yo-yo off the street.'

'I'll buy that,' Corallo said.

'You know I haven't given you this spiel to build myself up, but to prove a point. How come other people are putting millions of dollars on the line for me to carry the Arena? Do you think maybe they checked me out?'

Ducks was becoming uncomfortable with Jonathan's line of reasoning. They had thought to terrorize a young boy and a well-known millionaire. Easy pickings, a few threats, followed if necessary by a show of force. No, Ducks did not like to be on the defensive.

'Well, what are you going to do?' Dio, sensing Corallo's uneasiness, asked mildly.

'Explain the facts of life,' Jonathan retorted vehemently. 'If other, more important people can take the trouble to check me out, then how come two businessmen, labor officials no less, can't be bothered to find out who the hell Jonathan Stone is.'

'Are you paying or not?' Corallo asked.

'Well, I discussed it with a few of my friends after I saw Lazar, and they agree with me. Nothing, not a fucking penny, and' – he extended the palms of his hands in Dio's face – 'if you're looking for trouble, then let's have it. Pauli Salica's with me. If I make a call, he'll be up here tomorrow and he already discussed the payment with Frank Costello. So maybe the two of you ought to get your act straight. Frank's really pissed off with you. He's got a lifetime pass to the Arena and he'd like to use it. So, Ducks, let's be sure you're ready and now's as good a night as any.' Dio stammered something, averting his eyes. 'Tonight, just to prove a point, I gave the security guards time off. Between twelve and three. You got a bomb, put it there or stick it up your ass . . .' He nodded apologetically to Frances for his language.

Corallo seemed mesmerized, and when Jonathan rose with Frances and threw a hundred on the table, he implored him to be reasonable.

'There's no need –' he began. 'Pauli's one of us. No one's going against him or Frank.' His voice quavered and he looked to Dio for support.

'Why didn't you tell us you were connected?'

Jonathan put his hands on Dio's cheeks and patted them like an affectionate parent.

'You never asked me, schmuck. You're a tough guy, you worked for Lep. He told you to throw acid, you did it. Johnny, you better make up your mind. You're in control. You want to throw acid, you do it now, and if you don't, man, there better not be one single labor problem or fuck-up on this job again.'

Corallo extended his hand, waiting an eternity for Jonathan to react. Finally, at Frances's nervous urging, he shook.

'No problems, Jonathan. My word on it. Thanks for dinner.'

Frances clung to him under the sheets. Her fingers touched Jonathan's brow, slick with sweat. His eyes were open, but he felt isolated even in the familiarity of his bedroom.

'What's happening to us?' Frances asked without reproach. 'Tonight . . .' she leaned up on a pillow, 'was that a benefit performance for me?'

'Is that what you thought?' He turned his sleepy eyes on

345

her bare breasts. He did not enjoy making love to resolve a quarrel or to prevent one, and she had caught him just as he was aroused.

'I don't know any more with you.'

'There's a simple explanation. I wanted to be with you but I had to see two animals and make sure they didn't shit on my corner.'

Instinctively for comfort she stroked her breast with her nails and a small rose grew before his eyes, and he found himself tantalized by the spirit of reprisal motivating her. She gave off a scent, pungent as an Oriental aphrodisiac. The need to touch her was becoming overwhelming.

'You, you're an opportunist.' She did not look directly at him, but seemed to be confiding in a third party who would make a decision in her favor.

'Since when's that a crime?' he asked. Her other breast firmed, hardening the pale nipple. She was becoming hotter by the minute. Maybe that was the mood he required of Frances.

'Is it money? Christ, you know goddamn well you never have to work a day in your life.'

'Nobody, not you or Charlie, is going to stick me under a Christmas tree, honey.'

'Well, people say you're power crazy and tonight's demonstration showed me you're one real bastard.'

'With you?'

'All the time. You treat me like some whore you run into once in a while and then say – "I've got to give her a call when I remember."' She threw the thin blanket off her side. She opened the balcony door for some air but only the tepid, sultry breeze of the city's sewers entered the room. Her naked form silhouetted against the low lamplight emphasized the arch of her back and the contour lines of her thighs. The Packards had honed a fine product.

'First summer I can recall without a tan. I haven't been in the sun since June. I spend my time hanging around waiting for you.'

Steam was coming out of her, giving her substance, enhancing his desire. He left the bed, stood behind her, and rubbed his hand over the swell of her ass. They turned belly to belly, their legs pressing the edge of the bed.

'You look ready now,' she said as though the thought of

346

intimacy never crossed her mind.

'I'll put the tan on you.' His tone was intentionally glib.

'What a treat!'

'In your condition, a cock's a cock.'

She wouldn't stand for that and fell back on the ethic her parents had carefully excluded from her upbringing. 'Do you want to marry me?'

'Is that important?'

'I didn't think so when I first started going to bed with you.'

'Why now?'

'I was going to say I'm entitled to an answer without giving my reasons. But the fact is, I'm not on the shelf yet. I've had *calls*' – she pronounced the word as though it were filled with foreboding – 'which I haven't answered.'

'I haven't stopped you,' he goaded her. 'Have I?' Blameless. 'What're you after, an open relationship or ending it.'

She turned, belligerent. 'You did some job on Charlie. He thinks the sun –'

– 'shines out of my ass. Still, what's that got to do with us? In case you haven't heard, he's not carrying me. I came up with my end. This isn't a poor boy from the slums who meets a rich girl, bangs her often enough for the father to pay for a wedding and take him into the family business.'

'My God, Jonathan, I wish it was the case. If you only knew how I've prayed for that.'

'Frances,' he continued to stroke her, 'for what it's worth, I wouldn't have taken you home the night I met you if I couldn't back myself up. Nobody was out there behind me, so if I flopped, it wouldn't be into Mommy's arms. Charlie's money was never a consideration. I came after you for you.' He broke off suddenly in a cold sweat.

'Do you still want me?' she asked in a husky voice which fell between hope and skepticism.

'Naturally.'

'As what?' There was no defiance or servility in her question. 'You're not really sure . . . friend, lover – mistress.'

'Not all three?'

'You're not ready to get married?'

'I guess not.'

'Just out of simple human curiosity, is there something about me you don't like?'

347

'I'd be a liar if I said yes, and a fool to say no.'

'That's some straight answer.' She smiled at him, the familiar worldly Frances he adored, a girl filled with natural confidence and intelligence.

'Last question, please.' His hand lightly floated along her inner thigh. 'Is something missing – in me?'

His fingers slid inside her. She was moist.

'Frances, we have to start seeing more of each other. You're flipping out,' he assured her. They fell together on the bed and her legs arched in a triangle, her tight ass leaped into the air, as he thrust into her.

'Hold it back,' she whispered. 'I don't want it yet . . .'

They changed positions, her knees squashing her breasts, legs on his shoulders. He probed deeper, until there was nothing left of him.

'I love your cock . . . dream about it. I want it all the time.' She started to gasp, her moans music that he would never tire of. 'Fu-uck it, fuck it, fuck it, honey . . .'

He came, an explosion of semen, draining him. She held firmly to his balls, squeezing them. When he finally withdrew she was still not satisfied. She smothered his cock with her tongue, licking it dry, then stroked herself.

'Christ, Frances, you're an animal.'

'That's the nicest thing you've said to me in weeks.' She did not neglect him, putting her mouth down on him. 'I love to feel it get bigger in my mouth. Means I can – oh . . . She held it in her fist, squeezed.

He rolled her over on her side near the mirror he used for dressing. The images had a starkly erotic effect on them. She raised her legs, mesmerized by the view of his entering her. Their legs entwined and he reared back and thrust, shoved inside her, the excitement embracing the two of them as though they were observing two strange participants. He gained momentum. He couldn't stop, but he fought not to come, the pain in his testicles excruciating as she yelped, cried, bit her bottom lip. Over and over again she came and each time there was a different note, a variety of enticement that drove him. In her eyes he witnessed a degree of beguilement, a mystery that he had not been aware of previously. Frances's seductiveness had no real peak. He sensed he could never again have enough of her.

Gone were memory, plans, the present. They had reached

time indefinite, molded together, each venture more radical than the last. The sheets had been torn from the bed and they clawed at each other on the raw mattress, their bodies heaving, rolling, one moment Frances on top, the next Jonathan billowing down her thighs, his head between her legs, tasting her, eating her, until she pleaded with him to stop. They swirled into each other's arms, bruised, virtually wrecked.

He clung to her and asked with considerable perplexity:

'Frances, what happened to you since the last time we made it?'

'I guess I knew you better than I thought I did. I assumed if I had to be your mistress, I'd better be damn sure you didn't marry someone else.'

Twenty-six

Time moved in rapid spasms after Frances returned to college for her final year. The raw hunks of days and weeks were for Jonathan unnoticed passages. The seasons went unmarked for him. Sun, snow, the temperature, the light of day, were only relevant as they affected the construction of the Arena, and he neared his objective of opening for Easter. The driving force was his race with the deadline he had to meet.

Jonathan allowed his mail to pile up on the mantelpiece, on his bedside table, in bathrobe pockets, even in his laundry hamper. If anyone important wanted to contact him, he could always be reached by phone. All of his bills were paid by the Arena Corporation and he drew a salary. He paid cash for his daily needs and entertainment expenses. He seldom saw his maid, their communication consisting of scrawled notes on the backs of shirt cardboards. But finally the woman's patience ran out and she stacked the mail she had gathered from various coveys. She left a note on his pillow.

> Mister Jonathan – What do I do with all this?
> Throw it in the cinerator or what?
>
> IRENE

His response was as she hoped. He pulled the garbage bucket out of the kitchen and whipped through the post in a matter of minutes, crumpled letters, ads, offers for charges in department stores, brochures to travel to Miami, valuable coupons for buying magazine subscriptions, until he came to one which was printed in light blue Waterman ink with a thick-nibbed pen. He recognized the buff-colored envelope, the back of which in flourished script announced West's and underneath it, Sam's slogan, West Is Best. Without curiosity, he opened it, took a puff from his cigarette, extended his legs on the leather ottoman, and sank back into the smoky-green-leather men's club chair, a recent present from Frances. It was probably another request for a donation from Sam who constantly held fund-raisings at the hotel for displaced persons or Zionist charities. He opened the letter and in astonishment gazed at a child's simple printing on lines that had been ruled in pencil on the hotel stationery.

Dear Jonathan,

I hope you will be happy to hear from me. I have written to you many times. Letters which I did not send. I also thought of calling you. But a letter is best. I have been out of the hospital for almost a year now and living with Papa and Sylvia in this huge place. Will you come to see me, please? I have asked Papa about going to New York. He says it might be too much for me. I have never stopped thinking about you. I have not told anyone about this letter.

Always yours,

LENORE

He read the letter three times, then got to his feet, dizzy. He was tempted to call Frances, his closest friend and confidante, but how could he?

He had to go it alone.

Yet it was irresponsible for him to leave the city. Easter was only a week away and both the union and the workmen had fought through a virulent winter to keep to the schedule. Frances was due in for the Easter break from Vassar in a day and he had agreed to pick her up and spend the evening with her friends at dinner in Poughkeepsie. Emotionally they were on the crest of a wave which he sensed would lead to marriage when she graduated in June. He had brought her home over the Rosh Hashanah holiday to meet his parents. She had even accompanied him to synagogue on Yom Yippur and told him that if it were important to him or his parents she would convert. When he had asked her, 'Don't you have any religion, Frances?' she had replied, 'You're it.'

His parents approved his choice. Just about everybody adored the couple, considered the match perfect.

351

At a Christmas party held at the Packard home with friends and relatives present, the reins of marriage had grown tighter. His mother, wearing a new gown bedizened with beads and sequins from Loehmann's had excitedly asked:

'Are you going to make an announcement?'

The corners of her mouth drooped when he replied:

'Merry Christmas.'

'Well, your father and I are going to be disappointed.'

'I want to keep you and Pop young and how's that possible if you become a grandmother?' he said with deceiving gaiety.

'Jonathan, we like this girl' – he was standing by the bar with his mother and she was drinking her semiannual cocktail, a pony of Cherry Heering – 'Frances has something very good in her. Don't ruin her,' she barked at him as though he were still a child.

Apparently most of the guests shared his mother's anticipation. Cliques of people hovered around him and Frances most of the evening. Their faces glowed expectantly. Aunts and uncles who had flown from Newport, cousins from Palm Beach, encircled them, tittering, gossiping, sizing him up, offering invitations, suggesting European honeymoons. One of Frances's uncles informed him he could fix it so that they had the director's stateroom on the *Queen Mary* and even went so far as to write out a list of hotels throughout the Continent in which the mere mention of his name would guarantee the treatment accorded royalty. He was a millionaire of some kind. They all were. Both sides of the Packards seemed to have some genetic claim on money. Before the war they had all been quietly wealthy, but now thanks to airplane parts, real estate, astute investments in the stock market, pieces of airlines, pieces of shipping companies, oil leases, they had constructed a dynasty of wealth that was awesome.

'You've been courting her a year,' Alex said, receiving one of those signals from Miriam that the partners in durable marriages respond to without having heard any part of the conversation.

'This is just a Christmas party,' Jonathan said, growing uncomfortable.

'Some Christmas party,' Alex jeered. Relatives from all

352

over are here ...'

'They'll just have to wait till we're good and ready,' he replied with an air of both injury and rebuke. 'I don't see that it's anybody's business but mine and Frances's.

'What've you got, ice water in your veins?' Alex asked, surly. 'I've just been in the library with Charlie discussing it.'

'Well, if you came to an arrangement, I hope *you* can live with it. I won't be bound by anything but my word.'

'Jonathan, I wish I could understand you.' Miriam's face was pinched and her eyes roved from Alex to him in dismay. 'What does Frances have to say?'

'We haven't talked about it since the summer.'

'She's got feelings. Surely she must have hope?'

Across the room Frances smiled ruefully at him and gestured, subtly apologetic, through latticework of arms in dinner suits and an assortment of diamond and gold bracelets. She, too, was at the mercy of other people's designs. She broke through the cordon of bodies as the sixteen-piece band Charlie had engaged took up their instruments. The Persian carpets had been banished to the basement and the paraquet floor highly glossed.

'Come on, let's dance,' she said to Jonathan. The band was one of those society groups permanently wedded to Cole Porter. It started with 'Night and Day.'

'I'll dance with you if he won't,' Alex offered.

'I guess you'd do anything for him,' she said with a disarming wink.

'He doesn't deserve you,' Alex persisted.

'What gave you that idea?'

'We expected – or should I say *hoped* for – something more,' Miriam said, stolidly staring at Jonathan.

'Like what?' Her disingenuousness was obvious, since the subject had followed her like the plague from one relative to another.

'Well, Frances, and don't take this the wrong way,' Alex said, his voice mellowly affectionate to her, 'but when are you two going to get engaged?'

'When we're ready.' Her hand touched Jonathan's, their little fingers entwined, and she exerted a small pressure to prevent open warfare. 'Alex, now don't you take this in the wrong spirit, but Jonathan's not going to be stampeded by

353

you or anyone else.' Her eyes were luminous in his defense. 'I'm in no hurry ... we have a loving relationship. That doesn't mean we have to run into marriage.' She was trembling. The stress was unremitting, and on his parents' faces she saw disbelief give way to consternation.

'Frances, you're a lovely, beautiful fool,' Miriam said, 'and even though he's my own son, if you let him have it both ways, you'll wind up alone. As a woman I find it unjust for you to let him play games with you and your family.'

With the reproach ringing in her ears, she started to the dance floor with Jonathan, but she could not resist a final word.

'I can live with it.'

It was not the last word however.

'For how long?' Miriam retorted.

Jonathan held her tightly while they danced to the approving glances of the guests.

'Is it true?' he asked, mortified by the compassion he felt for her.

'I don't know, honey.' Her lips grazed his cheek. Her pain was so tangible, so tactile, it reached out and embraced him and he gladly would have signalled Charlie and asked him to announce their engagement at that moment, but Charlie was not in the room. She clung to him.

'Am I messing you around?' he asked plaintively.

'Does it matter any more?' she replied, battered.

But it did matter profoundly to him as he drove through the sleeping towns of New Jersey to be reunited with his past if only to be freed from it. He told himself as he went that he could never let Frances go.

He had not visited the Catskills for years and the area struck him as alien though it had not changed much. Women, heads covered in babushkas, strolled along the roadside, trailed by sallow-faced children, the boys with wiry side curls, yarmulkes on their heads. The season had not begun; the towns were sparsely populated with the permanent residents, the landscape curiously European. The village had a kind of burgher complacency, reminding him of Germany with its costermonger stands on the shoulders of the roads, the hand-printed signs bleating cut-rate prices for TOMS, CUKES, POTS, the abbreviations themselves representing the hawkers' own estimates of their worth; knife sharpeners in rotted-wood, horse-drawn carts, metal wheels jangling, the driver squealing in Yiddish offers to exchange everything from table linen to drapes for his gleaming cleavers and cutlery – free sharpening included.

The atmosphere changed radically as he approached West's. Gone were the Burma Shave billboards with their ditties and slogans. In their place giant signs announced the mileage to West's as though the end of a mystical pilgrimage were in sight, a new Taj Mahal.

In a way West's lived up to its assertions. The road miraculously changed to a two-lane macadam on the turnoff. A gate with a barrier was manned by three uniformed security guards, one of whom gave him a map of the grounds and directed him to the main building, a tawny-brown stucco edifice striated with marine-varnished pine over which trained Virginia creepers were woven. A battalion of bell-hops and parking attendants, jangling change, worked like trained commandos, handing him his parking ticket, coding his alligator two-suiter, all in a matter of seconds and still finding time to admire his new dark blue Lincoln Continental.

Guests were coming out of the dining room, some complaining that they had eaten too much, while they examined the broadside listing the daily activities. He followed the bellhop to the registration desk and listened to an elderly couple theorizing about the dangers of archery instruction.

'Name, please,' a handsome woman in her mid-thirties asked. He wondered if this was Sylvia.

'Jonathan Stone.'

She checked the file of ruled index cards.

'There's no record of a reservation, Mr. Stone.'

'I came up on the spur of the moment.'

She examined a master chart on the wall.

'I'm sorry, we've got a full house ... it's Passover. People have made reservations a year in advance,' she noted reprovingly as though he were an interloper. 'If you're a single, I could make a call and try to get you into another hotel nearby. You'd have all the guest privileges here.'

He became flustered, torn between revealing he was a family friend or remaining anonymous.

'I'm a friend of Sam's.'

355

'You and a million others,' she said with the hapless resignation of one who has heard the statement an infinite number of times. 'Frankly, if you were his own son –'

'He's only got a daughter,' Jonathan interjected.

The woman peered at him over the desk. The poised manner gave way to troubled suspicion.

'Are you . . . ?'

'Alex's son.'

'My God, *Jonathan* . . . it's really you.' Snooping clerks gathered around to observe the arrival of a celebrity they hadn't recognized. 'You'll stay with us in the house. Sam'll be thrilled. What a surprise.'

Her gaze had become a positive embrace, framing him.

'Golly, I've been reading about you in *The New York Times* and even in Lee Mortimer's column about this new Arena. Sam always said you were as smart as a whip. How're your parents?' she asked with that buoyant enthusiasm which does not permit reply. 'David, we heard from Georgie – she's up here booking the entertainment – David's going to school in California and doing terrific.' Her ebullience was exhausting him.

'Sylvia . . . about the room. I'd rather be on my own.' He knew that Sam would be ill at ease if he and Lenore were under the same roof. 'Privacy, you know how it is when you're single . . .' She'd be certain to reassure Sam that he was an incorrigible ladies' man.

She took the bait.

'Oh, of course, and are we packed with singles. Some of these girls – for the life of me I can't understand how parents allow them to come up here on their own. Wildness, you can't imagine. Times I think we're running a . . . a . . .'

'I follow you.'

'You've got the FDR suite. Sam named it after Roosevelt before he died. You know how many times we invited FDR here? Maybe a thousand. Sam has a letter signed by him thanking him for the invitation which he had to decline because of the climate. FDR had to go to Hot Springs for his polio.'

The bell captain was dispatched to take him to his suite, after which at Sylvia's insistence they would meet at the pool. But he had no intention of swimming and had not packed trunks. This was not a holiday but a reunion.

He changed into a plaid sports shirt and a pair of light-weight blue slacks, white loafers with no socks. He studied his face in the mirror and saw an image of self-control. But as soon as he turned away, his nerves betrayed him. He put on a pair of dark glasses, and followed the signs to the pool.

A crazy madrigal of sounds enveloped him, hollering men, giddy, clamorous women, while mischievous eyes examined every inch of him, the glaring raw sunshine his enemy. The voices were drowned by the unrestrained noise of a Latin-American band under the spell of a demonic bongo player.

Sam stood by the lifeguard chair. He was stony-faced; when they shook hands, it was with the caution of rivals. But he nodded and smiled in his role of genial host.

'Come on, Jonathan, let's sit on the terrace. I'll order breakfast for us. . . . How long are you going to be staying with us?'

'A couple of days. I haven't had a break in months. It's been hectic . . .'

'So I've heard,' Sam said guardedly. Jonathan was surprised at the development of Sam's physique, his arms tanned and muscular, carriage erect. He now wore a thick mustache and moved among his guests with the easy manner of a paternalistic baron inspecting his lands and his subjects.

'Just coffee,' Jonathan told the waitress who had a menu in her hand.

'The suite comfortable?' Sam asked.

'Couldn't be better.'

They took each other's measure. Sam's timid disposition was clothed in the facade of the prodigal landowner, flattered by his guests and case-hardened by expansion. A man of property was not a clay ball, malleable or shaped by forces outside his demesne – not when he was feeding more than a thousand people a day. Jonathan had no wish to challenge him.

'You heard she was out?' Sam asked.

'Uh-huh.'

Sam digested the admission without apparent concern. 'Is that why you came up?'

Jonathan decided to play it straight. 'Why else?'

Sam blinked in the bright sunshine. He had not expected candor. He tapped the wrought-iron table nervously.

357

'She's made tremendous improvements –'

'She can talk,' Jonathan shot out. 'That's more than an improvement. It's a miracle.'

'You've spoken to her?'

'Not yet.'

Sam saw his absolute mastery was slipping away. 'Lenore still has a long way to go yet. She's an outpatient twice a week.' Sam toyed with his teaspoon and looked to his guests. A complimentary rumba lesson was in progress and a man barked over the microphone: 'Side together forward – pause – side together back – pause ... you're doing your basic box step.' Hundreds of pairs of feet, mainly in wooden clogs, clacked on the decking.

Jonathan gave Sam the initiative. 'What do you suggest?'

'I'm not sure. Obviously she'd like to see you.'

'Then what's the problem?'

'I'm a little apprehensive. She's been on a kind of plateau emotionally. I'd hate to have her get depressed when you leave.'

'Maybe she won't. It's been such a long time. We're very different people now.'

'Exactly, you're not children.'

'Sam, the last thing I want to do is upset Lenore. I think you realize that.' Sam muffled a sigh. He knew he was being manipulated but he couldn't for the life of him figure out how Jonathan was doing it.

'Did Lenore's doctor think it would be best if she avoided certain people or situations?'

'No. He recommended a normal, everyday life.' He paused, his self-containment abandoned for the higher purpose of truth. 'Fact is, he advised me that it would be a good idea for Lenore to see you.'

'Any reason?'

'Because she wanted to, and to deny her would suggest punishment.' Jonathan looked to Sam like a panther ready to spring. 'I suppose I still think of you as a little boy who wouldn't listen to anybody.'

Jonathan pushed his coffee away and decided to crack the nut wide open.

'Sam, suppose I let you make up your mind.' He looked at his watch. 'Let me know by one o'clock. I've got some calls to make. If it's *no*, I'll just shoot back to the city and no harm done.' The energy in Jonathan's eyes frightened him. What the hell was he made of? 'I wouldn't go against you ... there's no reason to.'

'Aren't you engaged? Your mother mentioned something about Charlie Packard's daughter. That's *the* Charlie Packard, isn't it?'

'Yes, but we're not engaged.'

'Well, if you do get married, I'd consider it a privilege to do the wedding myself up here.'

'Thanks for the offer.'

Sam was running out of delaying tactics. 'By the way, I suppose you've heard that Georgie's running the entertainment up here now. She knows so much more about it than I do. We're getting acts that I never dreamed we could pull.'

Jonathan gave Sam a melancholy smile. 'Georgie – I'm happy for her success.'

'Look, how about Georgie joining you and Lenore for lunch at the house? Quiet, intimate – the dining room's a madhouse ... and the thing is Lenore feels very secure with Georgie. They're great friends. What do you say?'

Jonathan got up from the table and Sam was disconcerted by the severity of his gaze.

'What time?' Jonathan asked harshly.

'Twelve thirty – one, whatever suits you....'

* * *

Jonathan made a few calls to his office, then spent the rest of the morning roaming around the grounds. He avoided the pool because it was too noisy and public. He craved solitude, so that he could compose himself. He could not remember when he had ever been this close to panic.

He took the path down to the lake. The water was clear, and by the sandy shore schools of minnows, flecks of silver, swam rapidly in fidgety bursts. He dipped his hand in the water, scattering the fish. It was ice cold. The sign prohibiting swimming seemed superfluous.

He declined a free fishing lesson and took out a rowboat. Coursing along the shoreline, he made out a large two-story house with a cherry-red brick facade camouflaged with pine and fir trees. He saw the figure of a girl. He knew it was Sam's house but he wasn't sure who the girl was. He took off his shirt, closed his eyes, and let the boat float in the breeze which started and stopped. He fixed the cushions and rested his head on them. A legion of memories floated hazily through his consciousness, agitated intrusions which made him shiver.

He rowed back, found a changing room, dank-smelling but with a sink and tarnished mirror. He threw some cold water on his face and wiped himself with coarse brown paper. His face was reddened from the sun. He made his way along the shore like a spy, his pulse throbbing.

On the grass outside the house, he finally caught a glimpse of her. She was leaning back in Georgie's arms, her long hair streaked silver-gold by the sun. Georgie was brushing her hair, and he shrank back, startled by the vision of intimacy he had observed, galled by the sight of Georgie's touching her, a lioness guarding her cub. Tanned mahogany, her black hair pulled back, the whitish cleavage of her breasts exposed, Georgie had a rank voluptuousness like a spoiled peach.

He climbed up a small hill. They still had not seen him. Lenore jumped to her feet as though sensing something. In her floral patterned yellow sun-suit, she looked like a ravishing spring goddess celebrating the discovery of her own birth. He pushed aside the high shoots and she walked toward him.

He held out his hand awkwardly. She threw her arms around his shoulders, pressed her face against his, her enormous gray eyes exultant.

'Oh, Jonathan, I've wanted to see you for such a long time ...'

There was a gorgeous candor in the admission and in the unaffected warmth of her embrace. She was, as he remembered, the most beautiful girl he'd ever seen. He stood holding her, stunned by the realization.

He kissed Lenore on both cheeks and she led him by the hand to the blanket where Georgie squatted. Georgie's face was grim, weighty, like a starved raven. The reckless hostility in her expression startled him.

'See, I told you he'd be good-looking,' Lenore said with unabashed adolescent delight. 'We're going to have a picnic and I'm doing it ... I'm in charge,' she said rushing into the house.

He was on the point of greeting Georgie when she raised her hand.

'You cooked this up with my father,' she said venomously.
'What?'
'Sticking me up here in this fucking hotel – this wilderness.'
'That's not true.'
'This is my exile,' she protested vehemently, 'and you fixed it.'
'You've got it wrong, honestly.'
'You lying, miserable bastard ... I hope you live to suffer.'

There was nothing he could say to disabuse her of the demented fixed idea that he was responsible for her banishment. The odious curses rang in his ears.

'Georgie, as far as I'm concerned, you can screw gorillas if that makes you happy. If you want to blame me because you're fucked up, then be my guest.' Her eyes, set close together, were frightening in their rage. 'You, you're introducing Lenore to the world,' he said contemptuously. 'Just make sure she doesn't wind up with clap.' She lurched to her feet, about to accost him. 'Georgie, why don't you go wash your hair, swallow some pills, smoke a reefer, or whatever it is you do to live with yourself. But, honey, just vanish before I kick your ass in and dump you in the lake.'

Georgie darted off, her haunches bunched up in tight red slacks, a dray horse released from its cart, maddened by its abandonment. Lenore had a tray in her hands, a distracted but genial look on her face.

'I don't understand her,' she said setting the tray down. There were plates of chicken, cold cuts, and chunks of buttered French bread. 'She's nice most of the time but then she gets these moods.' She smiled at Jonathan, effortlessly, with an infectious hint of intrigue. 'I'm glad she's not joining us. I wanted you all to myself. . . . Is that wrong?'

He was entranced by her playful innocence.

'No, it's not wrong. Being honest is all that counts with me.' He reached out and her head swung onto his lap. He fixed her face in his mind, dazzled by the clarity of her eyes in the sunlight. He bent low, holding her tightly, and kissed her. After a moment he withdrew. Her mouth had been like that of a child's, sweet, pristine.

'I can't tell you how often I've thought of you kissing me.' She held nothing back, and her incapacity for guile or the shabby artifices of seduction touched the deepest chord

361

within him. 'Oh,' she said with anguish, her fingers gliding over his cheeks, 'you mustn't cry. I'll make it better ... I want you to be happy.'

But he was at variance with reason, inaccessible, a victim of impulses too strong for him. Clasping his knees with his hands, he rolled on the ground, bawling like an infant, the wrench of pent-up emotion pouring out of him with such frantic, jarring turbulence that he thought he would never stop.

'It's all right,' she said softly. 'We're together.'

He was inebriated by the treachery of his pain, never having conceived that it would be he who could not stand up to the shock. He had been haunted by visions of Lenore collapsing, a beautiful imbecile, ill beyond reckoning. However, she was calm, soothing him with affection, understanding, patient with him. The tears had run their course and he was chagrined by his breakdown. What upset him was the unpredictability of the attack. Could it be that she was the stronger one?

He cleared his voice: 'I didn't know what to expect ...'

'How could you? I've been sick for an awfully long time and it takes people a while to get used to the idea that I'm better now.'

They barely touched the food, talked until late afternoon. Her memories were vague, amorphous bursts, fused with her years of treatment. She trusted him with all her thoughts, but the trouble was that the burning away of her early life experiences brought her to that dangerous state of grace in which she trusted everyone.

'Even in the bad times when I couldn't express myself, I thought of you.' He realized why Sam was so concerned about her welfare. Lenore, in her present condition, needed a keeper.

They walked up to the baseball diamond where members of the staff were playing an exhibition for the guests. She pointed to a rawboned, muscular boy on first base.

'That's my friend, Larry Mayer. He's going to play professional ball next year,' she exclaimed.

Mayer caught sight of her, doffed his cap, winked, and fielded a ground ball with studied elegance.

'That was for me,' she said with exhilaration. 'He's coaching me.'

'In what?'

'Everything. He's taught me how to hit ... play basketball.' She tittered with laughter. 'He says I'm a tomboy.' She was lost to him now, leaning forward intently, the child fan caught up in the thrall of hero worship. Her intoxication with the softball game troubled him. She was arrested by time, a nine-year-old with the body of a woman.

Twenty-seven

Fortified by half a dozen Scotches and sitting with Billy Davis and his publicity man, a hawk-faced, chinless man with a voice like a shoemaker's lathe, Jonathan listened to the breathless pitch while dancers glided across the Taboo Room's marble floor.

'With Israel becoming a nation on May fourteenth, you'll get more publicity for the Arena than if Joe Louis signed to bang Betty Grable on the hump of a camel's back,' Harry Swan bellowed.

In the background, Billy's white teeth flashed with approval. 'It's never been done,' Billy observed with animation. 'A black man working all night for Jewish charity. For Israel! That's your opening, man.'

'Victor and me'll get every star from stage, screen, and radio to work for nothing,' Swan noted, then rattled off names, ranging from Sophie Tucker to Clark Gable.

A star-filled charity event would establish the Arena as an institution overnight in the minds of everyone. Furthermore, it would open up a whole new society to Jonathan. Wealthy philanthropists from all over the country would come and pledge money and he would donate the Arena for a cause which would enlist him in their ranks. The prospect of coming to Israel's aid engaged his sympathy. He would be a benefactor.

'We can hold just over twenty-five thousand, but think of the millions of people all over the country who'd want to give a few bucks. They'd be shut out.'

'But you'd have a packed house,' Swan said without seeing the potential.

'Listen, my friend, in terms of population figures, that's no audience. I've got a contract with Channel Ten in New York to carry a certain number of events. Just suppose this was one of them. We'd go out live in New York. If network affiliates want to carry it, then they pay a fee. Some will bite, others might hedge, so we'll kinescope the whole evening, edit it, and Victor can sell the syndication rights.' He thought for a moment. 'Night of Stars,' he pronounced.

'It's exposure for everyone,' Swan agreed.

Billy clung to his sleeve, his eyes watery, filled with gratitude.

'You know, I could get a number one album out of this as well as a single. Man, I want a gold record.'

'You're all charity, sweetheart,' Jonathan said, motioning to Lenore who sat at the other end of the long table. He guided her like a brother through the swarm of people lined up at the entrance to the dining room. It was the first night of Passover and dinner was to be served a bit late in order to allow the staff more time to arrange the tables with matzos, bitter and sweet herbs, and to distribute prayer books at each place. Choir, cantor, and rabbi had been rehearsing all afternoon for the occasion. A contest to find the youngest boy who could read was held. The boy would ask the four questions from the *Haggadah* as was traditional. This celebration of the Jews' exodus from Egypt and their deliverance was a festival which Jonathan always rejoiced in. This would be the first time he had missed it with his parents, and when he had called his mother earlier in the day to apologize for his absence, there had been a distraught note in her voice. With David in California the family had, she said, broken up.

'There's nothing left but your father and me,' she said tearfully. The offense had been compounded by his failure to tell her that he would be at Sam's hotel.

A small boy stood at the dais reading from the *Haggadah*. 'Why is it on this night we eat unleavened bread . . . ?'

Lenore had no interest in the ceremonies of the Seder. She had on a lime-green chiffon dress with puffed sleeves embroidered at the cuff with lace. The rounded neckline was cut low and the swell of her breasts had a provocative effect on him. In between the prayers, she elicited a promise from him to dance with her afterward, then with a toss of her leonine hair she leaned close to him and asked:

'What do you do, Jonathan? I was trying to follow it in the bar, but I didn't understand.'

'I'm the managing partner in the Arena in New York.'

'Is it like a job?'

'Not really. I'm one of the owners.'

'Oh,' she said blankly. Her attention drifted to the service and when Elijah was mentioned and the reward for finding the matzo, she fluttered with excitement, the exotic thrill of a treasure hunt stimulating her.

'Tell me about Elijah?'

'He was a great man, a prophet,' Jonathan said. 'He was given a mission by God to destroy the cults of Baal which were brought into Israel by Jezebel. They were wicked people without morality ...' Sam listened approvingly. 'And he had a contest with the priests of Baal to see who had greater powers, and the story goes that Elijah was able to raise a widow's son from the dead. When he finally left the earth it was in a chariot of fire.'

'What a beautiful story,' she replied in a childlike voice. 'Is that why we eat matzo?'

'It's a kind of remembrance of the Jews' exodus from Egypt when they had to live on the desert and had no leavening for bread.'

She clapped her hands with fervor, leaned over, and kissed his cheek. There was a scent of lily of the valley cologne on her ears.

Holding her later on the dance floor, his child love, the hopeless mute, irretrievably lost, his mind fed on the despotic flumes of the past ... boat rides on the Isar, the plangent waltz in Yorkville. Her face was serene. In the dark corner he felt the shape of her womanly body under the light chiffon dress. She was unconsciously pressing against him. She raised her head and he kissed her lightly on the mouth. Her eyes remained closed, and the glimmer of a smile played across her lips. Her fingers grazed the back of his neck and he was mortified by the excitement, the way she aroused him. He found himself in an intolerable quandary, wanting her, but inhibited by her past. He couldn't be the one to take her. And maybe that was the trouble with idealizing her. The years away from her had been a rehearsal for this moment, but he was still unprepared for the actuality.

'Are you going to marry me?' she asked artlessly, and when he hesitated she gripped him tighter. 'Jonathan ... ?'

'Baby, you've only been out of the hospital for a year. Give yourself some time.'

There were no grays in her world view. Only acceptance or rejection. She laid her head on his shoulder.

'Don't you love me?'

'Naturally I do – always.'

'Then what's stopping us?'

'I want you to be sure that I'm the right one.'

She dismissed his statement. The inclination to touch and fondle her, seek out each part and fold of her flesh, was overwhelming. The foxlike, inviting expression on her face assured him that she would not resist him, and in a sense she was taking control of him. Her breasts touched against his chest and it almost seemed that her innocence had become a reckless weapon which she was using against him.

'Of course you're the one ... Larry tried to kiss me a couple of times but I wouldn't let him.'

'Lenore, you need some time.'

'For what?' she answered, taking him literally.

'Well, to go out into the world, explore it, find yourself. It wouldn't be fair to take that away from you. Honey, you've lost so much –'

– 'That's why this is so important ... I've waited for you, Jonathan.'

At the table he sulked over his drink. Her eyes never left his face and he felt trapped by the intensity of her puzzlement. It was as though he were with a child who'd been denied a sweet and was attempting to probe the logic behind the prohibition. She clung to him, relentless in her pursuit, boxing him in. The placid grace of her face imperceptibly took on the rough edge of indignation.

'Talk to me ... tell me what's wrong with me?'

'Nothing, absolutely nothing.'

'Do you have a girlfriend?'

Lying to her about Frances was the only solution in his inextricable position.

'No.'

'Swear to God?' she asked suspiciously, appeased only by absolutes.

'Yes.'

'Well, then why can't we tell Papa that we're engaged and we'd like to get married in June? I've got all the fashion magazines in my room,' she continued as though the resolution was in sight, 'which show the new wedding dresses girls are going to be wearing. I want to be a June bride.'

He took hold of her hands, pressed them to his lips, and she sighed, releasing the tension.

'Haven't you been listening to me?' Her eyes were vague

and spacy. 'Lenore, no matter how I feel about you' – he faltered – 'the thing is, you're not ready to get married to me or anyone else.'

The sadness clouding her face suggested that her world had collapsed. She was immune to reason, martyred by adult subtleties beyond her perception, and when he reached out for her, she drew away from him. The action startled him and for a moment Frances's face flashed through his mind, Lenore's twin in the emotional upheaval he created. He wondered if there was some kind of willful pattern in his own behavior which he inflicted on those he loved.

'You don't love me. You've been lying,' she said forlornly. Tears flowed down her face, swamping the makeup she had so carefully applied before dressing. She rose from the table, a woman deceived, without resources, caught in a maelstrom.

'Lenore, calm down.'

'Ohhhhh, Jonathan, I've never been so unhappy,' she wailed, lost and bereft, then she dashed through the tables and up the stairs to the lobby. He ran after her, calling her name, pleading with her.

He caught up with her on the porch. Clouds of ground frost rose up from the grass, and her convulsive sobbing echoed crazily. From the other end of the porch Sam darted between them and she fell into her father's arms.

'Oh, Papa, Papa,' she groaned. 'He . . . he . . .' She gulped in air.

'What?' Sam asked. He was even more distressed than Lenore. 'What have you done, Jonathan?'

Lenore broke away from him, threw off her dancing pumps, and lurched across the wet lawn. Sam stared at Jonathan with repugnance. The recollection of the day Jonathan had taken Lenore out of the hospital flooded back.

'She was being unreasonable . . .'

Sam glowered at him.

'For a year now she's been full of fun, laughing, enjoying herself. She's made tremendous progress, and now you have to come up here and open up all the old wounds. Don't you understand that she's not for you?'

'Sam, she thinks she's in love with me.'

'What does she know about anything, let alone love?' Sam stretched out his hands in supplication. 'Leave her be. Haven't I suffered enough with her? What are you trying to do to us?'

'I love her, Sam, but she's not ready for me.'

'You disgust me.' He scowled. 'You, of all people, because you were there, shouldn't even dare to think things like that about her.' Like a shrike Sam had impaled him on the nightmarish memory which had tormented him and fed his imagination. Again he was losing his perspective. 'You're no good for her ... your father told me how you dumped him and sold yourself to Pauli. Aren't you ashamed of yourself? You stab your father in the back, you stab me by hurting Lenore. Where's your conscience?' he shouted in the still night. 'If she has to go back to the hospital, it'll be because of you –'

'Sam, you're wrong. I don't want to hurt her.' He was traumatized by the virulence of the attack and wondered if indeed he was as unworthy as Sam made him out to be.

Sam raised his fists and flailed them with frustration. 'You're rotten – you always were, even when you were a kid. Now get out of here once and for all. This is my property and I never want you to set foot on it again.'

* * *

Not even the swirl of press parties, brimming with celebrities and film stars sent from the West Coast by Victor and Harry Swan to provide fodder for all the major magazines and local newspapers could relieve Jonathan's depression. Mayor O'Dwyer's smiling face appeared on television when he cut the blue ribbon officially opening the Arena. But in the forefront, 'the mover and brains behind the entire operation was an obscure young man from Brooklyn by the name of Jonathan Stone,' according to a capsule in the business section of *Time* magazine. He was variously described as a financial wizard and a sportsman by the New York daily papers, and he grew accustomed to phone calls from Dan Parker, Winchell, and Jimmy Powers. He had a regular table at Toots Shor's.

It was a funny sensation to hear his name on the lips of strangers, to be claimed as a personal friend by people he'd met over a drink. His connection and partnership with Charlie Packard and the fact that he was a client of Bill Gardner's at Morgan gave him instant respectability on Wall Street. The bank didn't do business with nobodies and Jonathan was judged by the company he kept. By being seen at '21,' the Colony, Le Pavillon, his name appeared in society gossip columns regularly and became familiar to readers grabbing a doughnut and coffee at the Automat as well as to the Transylvanian organizers of debutante balls looking for fresh blood. He had become well known for being well known.

And he didn't think about it much. He was wretchedly unhappy. Lenore had once more been torn out of his life and he suspected that this separation was final. What made his situation unbearable was the fact that he would never have the chance to discover whether he was still in love with her.

Denied his hope, he easily fell victim to a new passion that transcended his personal tragedy. He believed in Israel, felt a need to come to the assistance of the newly born country. He called a press conference and announced that the Arena would have a marathon 'Night of Stars,' all proceeds to benefit Israel. He extended invitations to socialites, civic leaders, United Nations representatives, and political powers in Washington. But he was not satisfied with the results of the press coverage and so he taped a message on Channel 10 which hit people where they lived.

He stood before a map of Texas and Israel to demonstrate the relative size of the two states.

'Texas is more than thirty-three times larger than the new nation, and has many more resources, just as you watching in your homes have more money, free time, gadgets, and conveniences than this country with a population of just under two million. They're starting from scratch. While we were winning the Second World War, many of the people who have arrived in their new homeland were living in unspeakable conditions in concentration camps. They deserve a chance to survive. Can't New Yorkers and all Americans find it in their hearts to contribute something to the cause of freedom? We're supposed to be the most generous people on the face of the earth, so let's prove it by giving on the "Night of Stars." '

The remaining five-thousand-odd tickets were sold an hour after the commercial, but more importantly New York fell in love with Jonathan. The Arena opened as a kind of shrine to good works. Jonathan sat in a box with his parents, the Packards, and the Gardners. On the stage a battery of telephone operators took pledges from callers and a totalizer board registered the amounts contributed. Billy Davis introduced entertainers, pitched for Israel, sang. He was a dynamo,

370

tireless in his exertions. Guest stars came between their shows at nightclubs, and casts of Broadway shows performed until the packed audience reached a point of exhaustion from cheering and applauding

Jonathan had arranged a private midnight dinner in the executive offices high above the Arena. He led the group to the elevator which went directly to his tenth-floor suite. The view was spectacular – a glass wall framing the entire Arena and another floor-to-ceiling window overlooking First Avenue. Architecturally Jonathan had achieved his goal. The building was domed and supported by cantilevers. Not a single post had been used and the view from the cheapest seats was unobstructed. Each row of seats had been raised so that even the taller spectators would not block the row behind.

Champagne bottles rested in tubs, and white-gloved waiters moved around the room with trays of hors d'oeuvres and exquisite crystal tulip glasses filled with Dom Pérignon. Jonathan stood at the window observing his creation. Beside him stood Frances, her eyes filled with adoration. But his sense of achievement was still injured by the way he had been humiliated by Sam. It was galling to find acceptance in New York society and at the same time to be treated like a wayward boy by Sam.

Alex had taken him aside early in the evening.

'You're a real human being.'

'We can still be together.'

Alex laughed wryly. 'You're smart in lots of ways, but you'll never understand me, will you? I'm the last of the one-man operations and if I go down it'll be on my terms. But let me give you some advice, not that I think you'll take it for a minute. Build your life with Frances. Sam called me and told me what happened. He'll never let Lenore go – he thinks he has to protect her the rest of his life – and you can't go back to the past. Jonathan, make do. You've got a beautiful future. Don't let what happened with you and Lenore spoil your life.' Alex's face tightened. 'It's none of my damn business, but I did take your side, plead your case, but he wouldn't listen. He's running a successful hotel and he thinks he can control people's lives. I wish I knew what the hell was wrong with him.'

Jonathan nodded and placed his arm around his father's

shoulder. The closeness of their earlier relationship had returned when he needed it most.

'Pop, I appreciate what you did ... but have a heart. "Make do?" What's that supposed to mean? Honestly, look me in the eye and tell me that's what you would've done in my position.'

Alex laughed self-consciously and with a hint of belligerence.

'Me, I'd have hit the bastard. He was once my dearest friend. Before I said good-bye, I told him that we were finished, I never wanted to speak to him again. What he's doing to you and Lenore is unforgivable. There's no reason for the two of you not to see each other. You're a good, decent man. You're at least entitled to a chance to manage your own life. Sam has no right to interfere.'

He looked coldly through his father.

'I'm going to see to it that he's very sorry.'

'*Alav-ha-sholom.* I'm not saying I don't approve of your attitude, but you've got to ask yourself how much of a price you'll pay and is it worth it. You're going to be unhappy for a long time whether you succeed or fail.'

He had been grateful for his father's support. Now he excused himself from Frances and caught Bill Gardner's eye at the buffet table. They held up their champagne glasses and clinked them.

'How does it feel to have the city's balls in your hand?'

'That's a helluva way for a banker to talk to his client.'

Gardner, somewhat tipsy, roared. He was the complete gentleman and it amused him to lower his social tone. 'The opening is an outrageous success. Do you know you've sold better than fifty percent of the season tickets to the Roller Derby!'

'Seventy-eight percent,' Jonathan replied. 'Bill, I want you to do me a favor.'

'Name it.'

'Well, last month I spent the night up at West's Hotel. Packed house. They've got some operation up there.'

'I've never been up there,' Gardner replied.

'They're expanding tremendously. Workmen everywhere. It's like a goddamn city.'

'What's the favor?' he asked, becoming intrigued.

'Well, they have to be borrowing money from some bank.

372

I'd like to find out which one it is and how much they've got outstanding in debt commitments.'

'No problem. We can run a credit check on them in the morning. If you're interested in buying in, why not approach the owners?'

'It's one man and he'd never sell.'

'Well, we can see how their paper stacks up and then decide if it's worth buying. For all you know, it could be paper that the lender wants to unload and would discount.'

'That's what I had in mind.'

Twenty–eight

It had been more than a year since Jonathan had seen Lenore. The last he'd heard of her she was living in the Village on West Eleventh Street and was enrolled in some kind of college program at Washington Square. Georgie was living with her as a guardian of sorts. He'd learned from Victor that Lenore's psychiatrist had been instrumental in persuading Sam to let Lenore go out into the world. Sam had yielded to the doctor's arguments: a hotel was no place for her.

He was embittered by the fact that she made no effort to contact him. All she had to do was pick up the telephone, yet all through the year during which bike races, rodeos, circuses, the Roller Derby, and basketball came and went in the Arena, he heard nothing but rumors from his brother David, a continent away: gossip he picked up from Linda about Georgie's feeble progress as VCA's sometime representative in New York.

It seemed Georgie got drunk a great deal in small night-clubs while scouting for talent, and so Victor had banished her entirely from his office but still kept her on a small retainer. Jonathan was overwhelmed by Sam's ignorance in entrusting Georgie with his most precious possession. Apparently Georgie had demonstrated that she could control Lenore. In a sense Sam's naiveté had worked in his favor. Who better to protect Lenore than a woman who knew all the tricks and hated Jonathan? Georgie, the willful, corrupt woman who scorned authority; Lenore, the compliant, fragile, vulnerable princess. What would their relationship bring?

But there was a limit to how much Jonathan could worry about it. He was caught up in the endless details of running a huge enterprise, planning a year in advance for concerts, sporting events, negotiating to buy a basketball team which would be in direct competition with the New York Knicks. The business had become a parasite, and he gladly played host as it consumed fourteen to sixteen hours a day, with constant traveling, meetings with crazy promoters in the

South who wanted to bring demolition derbies to the Arena, sponsors of body builders, impresarios in search of the world's most gorgeous women, dance troupes, symphony orchestras who could not get Carnegie Hall. He worked for months on end without a day off, never noticing the passage of time or his exhaustion.

He and Frances had reached a tacit understanding, and they resided on the time-tested plateau of emotional compromise. She sensed his inner turmoil without knowing the cause of it and she prudently kept out of his way except when he wanted her, never chided him for his indecisiveness. She was working part-time in Charlie's office and daily growing more knowledgeable about his operations. Three night's a week she took graduate courses in political science and economics at Columbia. She was determined to keep pace with Jonathan and not let him slip out of her hands by outgrowing her.

But her mother inquired about Jonathan. Frances and her parents were on their way out to dinner with the Gardners. Isobel and she were waiting for Charlie who had been detained at a meeting. The evening was pleasantly balmy and they decided to walk along the river and then over to the Gardners' town house on Fifth Avenue.

'My attitude is to let him have the best of both worlds,' Frances said as they walked beside Carl Schurz Park.

'Is he fooling around with someone?' Isobel asked.

'More than likely ... as long as it isn't one girl.'

Tug horns sounded mournfully on the river.

'Doesn't it bother you?'

'Isobel, woman to woman now. If Charlie has his occasional fling, does it worry you?'

Mother and daughter enjoyed a sophisticated candor given to very few. Isobel laughed complacently.

'So long as he comes home to me.'

'That's the point.'

'I wouldn't like to face the prospect of your father leaving me for another woman.'

'That's why you've given him so much freedom.'

'Is it obvious?' Isobel asked.

'Naturally. Charlie worships you because you understand him. Tail, as Jonathan calls it, is a kind of boys' own game. They get tired of it.'

375

'How predictable is Jonathan?'

Frances sighed uncomfortably.

'Tough question. If by predictable you mean being able to get hold of him day or night, then he's predictable. Even when he's out of town he calls me. I'm his anchor. But there's been something bothering him for a long time. Since we met. I don't know what it is. It hasn't got anything to do with us ... as we are now. But he's strung out. That much I know. I think if he's given enough time to disengage himself, then we'll be married.'

'Then it's something from his past?'

'Probably,' she admitted ruefully.

'What do you think about taking Miriam to lunch next week?'

'That's kind of underhand. And maybe she doesn't know anything.'

'Would it hurt to sound her out? Wouldn't you be happier if you got a fix on where you were with him?'

'Frankly, it scares me to death.'

'Honey, we wouldn't push. Just sort of choreograph around it. You know what I mean – find out what he was like when he was a kid. It'll be tactfully sentimental. A voyage back to the past ... innocent enough.' Frances stopped and leaned against a rail. She felt cornered. 'Frannie, you love him, don't you?'

'Yes.'

'Then why live in doubt? I'll tell you something. It's not knowing that kills people. You're a strong, intelligent woman. If there's an enemy, best to know and go to war. Whether you win or lose, at least you'll have the satisfaction of having fought like hell.'

They continued to walk in silence to the Gardner house. Bill was late as well. He and Charlie would be coming directly to the house. After Frances's second martini, she approached Isobel and said, 'Call Miriam tomorrow.'

'That's my honey. If blood has to flow, let's make sure it's not yours.'

*　*　*

Over the months, Bill Gardner had done more than his homework. He had a complete breakdown of all the assets and liabilities of West's Hotel, as well as a statement of

Sam's personal net worth. Sam, the master builder, had not taken the rudimentary precaution of incorporating. He had charged ahead with his expansion, fully confident of his abilities, secure in his vision of conquest. But his flank lay exposed. He was like an inexperienced chess player who brings his queen out at the opening, then spends the rest of the game retreating in the hope of saving the piece.

Sitting in Charlie's capacious office with its view of Wall Street was Isadore Schwartz, a timid, hollow-eyed man with the frightened manner of a bookkeeper who can't explain discrepancies. He was the president of the Bank of Catskill, Sam's primary lender. He had as an act of goodwill and friendship cosigned loans, extracted second trust deeds and mortgages from neighboring local banks with no more collateral than Sam's good name. On the balance sheet, West's annual net profit was ninety thousand dollars in its best year and that was on a gross in excess of three million dollars.

'Under three percent,' Charlie stated contemptuously. 'West doesn't know what the hell he's doing.'

'The hotel's famous ... every guidebook recommends it,' Schwartz replied. 'Don't forget that the net profit is after taxes and bank charges.'

'We can read,' Bill said sourly. 'But according to these loan papers, the long-term debt is four million dollars. If the hotel has one bad season, West will default and then he'll have to go into receivership. Where's that leave you and all the lenders you suckered?'

'I didn't sucker anybody. Our area depends on the people West's draws. It was in everyone's best interests to let Sam expand.'

Jonathan had persuaded both Charlie and Bill that under new management, West's could form the flagship of a chain of resort hotels throughout the country. He had discussed the possibilities with Salica the previous week and Paul had endorsed the acquisition, seeing in it an eventual tie-up with his interests in Las Vagas. There was always the possibility that legalized gambling would spread through the country and Sam was not the man to take charge of that operation.

'Isn't it obvious that if Sam opened the hotel to conventions, he'd have guaranteed bookings a year to eighteen months in advance?' Jonathan said.

377

Schwartz looked cornered, but he still retained a degree of stubbornness.

'No, Sam would never go for that. West's is built on a tradition of personal service for individual guests. He hates the idea of conventions.'

'Is he being naive?' Jonathan asked.

'In my opinion, yes. But he insists on running a high-quality hotel with no compromises. No one can move him.' A waiter came in with drinks and Isadore Schwartz reached for his straight shot of rye. The waiter left the bottle for him on the table. 'My God, if Sam even knew that I was here discussing his situation with you people, I don't know what he'd do. Our friendship would be out the window.'

Gardner took a hard line. 'Mr. Schwartz, as one banker to another – and let's forget personal relations for the moment – what do you think the state bank examiners and federal auditors would have to say about this kind of loan? Don't you know you'd be in danger of losing your charter? They'd fry you alive.'

Schwartz winced, horrified by the prospect.

'You, Mr. Schwartz, are a candidate for a grand jury indictment. I understand your predicament,' Bill continued. 'Banks do a lot of off-the-cuff transactions to oblige a good customer, especially when the borrower is a friend. But your paper's unsecured. You've let West borrow without proper collateral, and he's also pledged the same assets to four banks ... you, Monticello, Liberty, and South Fallsburg. Sure, you all respect and admire the man. You saw a chance to help him and yourselves, but any way you look at it, this is an illegal transaction. And when the examiners find this sort of thing, they stick their noses in all the bank's transactions. They poke into corners. They question every loan you've got outstanding.'

'How'd you expect to get away with it?' Charlie asked.

'The truth ...?' Schwartz wavered, confused and horrified by his dilemma. 'By cooking the books.'

'But now you've got a way out,' Charlie insisted, pressing his case. He sensed a rout.

'How do I tell Sam that I sold his paper?'

'You don't. What you're doing is legal,' Gardner informed him. 'Charlie Packard and Morgan just buy you out.'

'How long will you let Sam float?'

'We're not going to push him out. But if he gets into trouble, at least he's got major support, and you're off the hook,' Jonathan assured him. 'No one's trying to squeeze you ...' He looked at Charlie and Gardner for confirmation. 'And believe me, no matter what decision you reach, no one in this room is going to blow the whistle on you.' He could see that Schwartz was ready to cave in. 'Just think, at your next audit, some nosy clerk might find out on his own what you've been doing. Why take unnecessary risks when you've got a perfectly legitimate way of getting out of this without having your head chopped off?'

In the warm summer evening the banker sweated, torn by loyalty and his fear of exposure.

'I hope Sam appreciates the kind of friend you've been.'

'He's the best human being I've met in a lifetime,' Schwartz avowed. 'The man is solely responsible for building a new wing on a hospital in Liberty. There's no end to his charity and generosity. He's a humanitarian.'

'I don't doubt it,' Jonathan noted without expression.

Schwartz poured himself a stiff shot from the bottle. His eyes watered. 'Can I have a few days to think this over?'

'It's now or never,' Charlie said. 'Yours isn't the only deal we're considering.'

Charlie's light blue eyes appeared colorless.

'What's the deal?' Schwartz asked.

'Fifteen percent discount.'

'That's robbery. You're stripping it.'

'The interest on the seconds is twenty percent over thirty years. You're walking away with five percent for selling toilet paper. Not to mention that you come out of this clean. No one's going to question the transaction, not with the Arena Corporation and Morgan as buyers. What the hell are we going to do if the hotel goes bad, sell the beds and lobby furniture?'

'You're bastards,' Schwartz bellowed, clutching his chest. 'You don't give a goddamn about the little man.'

'We're guaranteeing the hotel's solvency and we're bastards?' Jonathan said.

'You take away a man's pride –'

– 'Cut the shit,' Jonathan interrupted. 'You're talking about your points, so let's forget about human dignity and pride. Sam's an incompetent businessman and you as his banker

379

should have known better.'

'Out of nothing the man came up to the mountains and built something. His blood's in the place and I'm selling him out.' Fruitlessly he searched the men's faces for some sign of concession. Then he picked up the pen Gardner offered and signed the transfer documents. 'Sam won't be told about this. Will you give me that assurance?' he pleaded.

'Not unless he misses a payment,' Jonathan replied.

'And if he does?'

'Why not take an optimistic view?' Gardner suggested.

'I asked a question ...' His eyes fastened on Jonathan's face.

'We'll give him a testimonial dinner, and a gold watch for his good works, then throw him out,' Jonathan said stoically.

* * *

Georgie's behavior had become more and more erratic through the year and Lenore had no idea how to contend with her. If she complained to Sam, she would lose the small freedom she had gained. If only she could turn to Jonathan for help. However, she was convinced that he wanted nothing to do with her.

Georgie lived on a cycle dictated by pills – roused from her drugged sleep she immediately swallowed two heart-shaped pink tablets, followed by multicolored capsules with her coffee, which inspired her to roll a joint from the stash that she kept in a milk bottle on top of the refrigerator. Eyes rolling, she would then reminisce about her halcyon period as Ronnie Flynt's one true love, work herself up into a demonic rage, curse Victor with such venom that Lenore would leave the table and slink into her room. But Georgie would be at the door a moment later, pleading for an audience – solitude was unbearable – and then Georgie would go to work on Jonathan, accusing him of bewitching her father with his Machiavellian tricks.

'Everything was perfect until that fucker showed up. He twisted my father around his finger and caused all the trouble between Ronnie and me.'

That was her version, and Lenore had no doubt that she was lying but she had no way of having the details confirmed, for Sam had so violently denounced Jonathan that she lived in dread of ever accidentally running into him. She kept to herself, spent whole days in the library, rarely frequented the student hangouts on Waverly Place for fear that Jonathan might wander in, although she had no reason to believe that he was still in the least bit interested in her.

Everywhere she went in the apartment, from the bathroom to the kitchen, the sweet, rancid smell of Georgie's marijuana trailed after her, clung to her blouses and dresses. For months, Georgie had conducted a relentless propaganda campaign on the virtues of marijuana in an effort to convert Lenore.

'But you still drink, even after you've smoked,' Lenore said one evening when Georgie was paralyzed by her daily intake of Scotch and drugs and had almost let the bottle of Black and White slip out of her hands in the kitchen.

'Tastes better.' Georgie put on the record player. It was a recording of 'This Nearly Was Mine' from South Pacific. Through some connections she received records free. 'I've been at the Baby Grand up in Harlem listening to a few new singers. I've made up my mind.'

'To do what?'

'Go back to the Coast. Ronnie needs me. I'm a big girl. I can't let Victor run my ass forever. I'll look for a job and Ronnie and I can at least be together.' She added. 'Your father'll have to pay someone else a hundred a week to room with you.'

'He's been paying you?'

'Well, how do you think I live? What I get from the agency wouldn't support a dog. My half of the rent and forty a week for food. Victor's worth millions and I've barely got walking-around money. It's a joke. In any case, you don't need a baby-sitter. You're doing damn well in school and it's also about time Sam let you go.'

'Do you think he will?' she asked.

'Well, I'll give you straight A's. Just do yourself a favor and listen to him. Jonathan's not for you. He's a rotten, two-timing bastard. I don't suppose he mentioned when you saw him that he's engaged to marry Charlie Packard's daughter.'

'No, he didn't,' she admitted, thunderstruck.

'Well, that's Jonathan for you. The world's finest backstabber.'

Dolchstoss. She remembered the German word and the sinister sound it had when the Nazis used it. She watched

Georgie toy with the phone, first picking it up, then placing it back on the cradle.

'I really ought to call Ronnie to let him know about my decision. He'll want to pick me up at the airport if he isn't shooting.'

Throughout the year, whenever Georgie had spoken of Flynt and Victor, Lenore found herself sympathizing with the woman. But there had been the nights when Georgie didn't come home and others when she brought men and women home to sleep. Once there had been a couple and the man had appeared early in the morning when Lenore was leaving for class and had been embarrassed and flustered. For months the man's cryptic remark floated through her consciousness. 'They told me to shove off ... go figure it, I thought I was the prize,' he had said, accompanying Lenore down the stairs.

In a world made up of books, solitary visits to the Metropolitan Museum, and movies, Lenore had walked an un-wavering path with the vigilance of a parolee. She knew that Georgie reported on her to her father. But in two weeks the term would be over. Sam was still considering her request to remain for the summer semester so that she could pick up six more credits. If Georgie left, he would make Lenore return to the hotel for the summer months. Three meals a day with Sam telling her how evil Jonathan was.

Georgie picked up the receiver and dialed the operator.

'Long distance, person to person. To Mr. Ronnie Flynt.' She sipped her drink, then took a long drag off her joint. She waved her glass at Lenore for a refill.

'Hello,' came a grouchy voice, and almost simultaneously the answering service said, 'Flynt residence ...' Clinking the ice cubes in her glass, Georgie waited. 'Who's this?'

'Ronnie!' Her voice had a high-pitched exuberance. 'It's me, Georgie.'

'Goddamn,' he shouted, 'you still on the line, operator?'

'Yes, sir.'

'Didn't I tell you never to put through this bitch?'

Georgie smiled with bovine complacency.

'Never mind, I'll talk to her,' Flynt snapped.

'Ronnie ... just give me a chance,' Georgie said. 'I'm coming back to L.A. I'll be able to fix everything with my father. Honestly, there's nothing to worry about. I can't

382

stand it without you. Honey, trust me, it'll be like old times.'
She seized her opportunity enthusiastically. 'Ronnie, if we
got married, Victor would have to stop persecuting you.'

'Let me tell you somethin, sister. I haven't worked for
years. Every studio in town shitlisted me, and I've got
fuckin lawyers crawlin out of my ass. I've given depositions
till I'm blue in the face. And I've got you to blame.'

'Ronnie, why'd you send the pictures of me?'

'To shove it down his throat. The contract he had me in
was slavery with loan-out clauses that gave him a commission
and me nothing. And as far as you're concerned, you're a
two-bit piece of twat that I wouldn't piss on, so lose my
number, Georgie, take an overdose, or fall under a fuckin
bus. You're dead out here.'

The receiver fell from Georgie's hand and she slumped
over.

Lenore picked up the receiver and hung it up. Georgie's
face was contorted. The ice cubes from her glass had spilled
on her red dress. She shivered and then pathetically stretched
out her arm.

'Would you get me my bag? I think it's in the kitchen.'

Lenore fetched the bag and fixed her another drink. She
bent down on a knee and began to wipe Georgie's dress.

'Don't bother ...'

'What's the matter with that man?'

'I got what I expected,' Georgie said, rooting through her
bag.

The admission confused Lenore and she sat down on the
arm of the sofa. 'Then why'd you call him?'

'I couldn't help myself ... Oh, Christ, I can't explain it.
There's something inside me that makes me want to crawl ...'

She took out of her bag an orange-colored piece of rubber
tubing, then opened a vial containing a milky white powder.
Lenore followed her to the kitchen and watched her cooking
it on a teaspoon. Georgie filled a syringe, bound her left arm
with the rubber tubing, then plunged the needle into her
vein.

'Georgie, what the hell are you doing?' Lenore cried. The
pain remained on Georgie's face as permanent as a birth-
mark, but her eyes became lazy and she dropped her head
listlessly.

'I scored at the Baby Grand. Good junk,' she muttered.

Then with a trancelike, lurching movement she staggered back to the sofa. She lay down, hypnotized by the impact of the heroin.

'What are you talking about? What junk?' Lenore's alarm increased. She sat beside her, held the head that was nothing more than two glowing eyes.

'I'm so cold ... hold me,' Georgie pleaded, and Lenore took hold of her icy fingers.

'Should I call a doctor?'

Georgie's hands groped at Lenore, the hands and fingers were everywhere, clinging to her breasts and her neck.

'Let me touch you ...'

'No, it's not right.'

Georgie's hand crept under Lenore's skirt. Georgie inserted a finger into her vagina.

'Why, why're you doing this to me?' Lenore pleaded. 'Don't, it's sick, I don't like it.'

But Georgie was relentless, dropping to the floor next to Lenore's legs. Lenore struggled to get away and she struck Georgie with her fist. When Georgie stripped off her panties, her anger was uncontrollable. She clawed at her until Georgie withdrew, gagging on her tears. Georgie bolted into the kitchen and picked up the syringe which lay on the sink, and Lenore was terrified that she was going to come after her with it. She pulled up her panties and rushed to her bedroom, but as she passed Georgie, she saw her once again plunging the syringe into her arm. This time the tube was not on her arm and the veins were bleeding. Repeatedly she stuck the needle into her flesh and forced down the plunger.

In a corkscrew motion Georgie slowly fell to the floor. Lenore stood frozen, waiting for her to move. The needle was still attached to her arm.

'Georgie?' She inched up in terror to the fallen body. The eyes were open, as though dazed by shock. 'Georgie, get up.' Lenore touched her face. It was cold, the sweat on her forehead was chilled. Her panic increased. She rushed out of the apartment, hailed a taxi on Seventh Avenue, and gave Jonathan's address. The doorman, accustomed to laconic calm women who asked to see Jonathan, was affected by Lenore's distress and accompanied her to his apartment. It was after midnight and he touched the doorbell provisionally. The chimes carried into the corridor. Lenore leaned against the wall, crying.

384

Jonathan came to the door, shirt opened, a drink in his hand, and with a look of mild surprise. At first he did not see Lenore, and as the doorman was about to open his mouth, Lenore tearfully moved into his line of vision.

'It's so awful ... she's dead ... Georgie,' she blurted out. Jonathan frowned, nodded to the doorman, and took Lenore into the apartment.

'Jonathan, she killed herself ... I couldn't stop her.' Looking at her, shivering and frightened, he forgot for the moment where he was. A woman's voice from just beyond the threshold of the living room called to him.

'Anything wrong?' She moved into view, both arms raised above her head clasping the hook at the back of her dress. Frances dropped her hands. The two of them looked guilty, she thought, conspirators plotting against her. She had never seen Jonathan so uncomfortable and off balance. She looked at the tall blond girl, eyes filled with tears, but Lenore avoided eye contact, glumly, childishly, bit her bottom lip.

Before she could bring herself to speak, Frances had a presentiment of intimacy that ravaged her. This was definitely not one of Jonathan's occasional whores.

'What happened?' she asked.

'This is Lenore, Frances. We've been friends since we were kids.'

'My roommate killed herself.' Lenore raised her eyes and caught the rancor on Frances's face.

'Victor Conte's daughter,' he explained, pulling a jacket off the doorknob and flinging it over his arm.

'Do you want me to come with you?' Frances asked.

'No, it'd be better if you went home. Do you mind taking a cab?' He didn't wait for a reply, but walked out to the elevator, fidgeting, his head lowered, and the girl wan and shaken.

'How'd it happen?' Frances heard him ask, his voice carrying down the corridor.

'She injected herself ...' The elevator arrived and they were gone, Jonathan and his terrible secret. It had always been there, waiting to spring up, menacing her. Miriam had skirted around the girl all through their lunch. She knew Miriam was on her side but she was aware the woman was holding back, afraid to commit herself, until over coffee, Frances had taken hold of Miriam's hand and in a soft voice said:

'Please tell me about *her*. So that I can understand why he's afraid of marriage.'

Miriam's throat had tightened. Coughing nervously, flustered by Frances's prescience, she knew there was no way, short of barefaced lying, she would deceive her, especially in front of her mother.

'I wouldn't make much of it. But he was very attached when he was a child to our friend's daughter. Lenore's been seriously ill for years and she's been in a mental institution. That's all there is to tell,' she added, refusing to give any more ground than the situation called for. 'If I were you, I'd never mention her to Jonathan. Let the dead be buried. Frances, I want the two of you married more than anything. Just don't ever let him think he's being pushed. It'll be a good marriage. The problem is we're all so used to seeing him take charge of people that we lose sight of the fact that he's still very young in many ways.'

Now she had met the phantom from his past. Lenore! She hated her with an overwhelming passion.

The door to Lenore's apartment was still ajar when they entered. Jonathan could see the tremendous effort of will it took for Lenore to enter it. She covered her face as Jonathan stood over the body.

The needle hung obscenely on Georgie's arm. The blood had coagulated. He bent down, felt her pulse, then let her hand come to rest. Beside the sink was a small bag filled with heroin.

'Was it an overdose?'

'No, I don't think so. She just kept sticking herself in the arm with the needle.'

'Nothing inside it?'

'The first time it was filled.'

'She killed herself,' he said aloud. 'If the police see the needle in her arm, they'll know that she committed suicide. She won't be able to be buried as a Catholic. It'll kill Tina.'

He walked through the room, limp, oblivious of the surroundings. All this year, Lenore had been just within reach, a few minutes away by car.

'What set her off?' he asked.

'She called Flynt and he was insulting . . . then . . .'

He sensed that she was retreating. 'Lenore, tell me for God's sake.'

Her head sunk onto the cushion. She made a gurgling sound. She was becoming intensely nervous.

'I ... well, she – Georgie. After the call she injected herself. I didn't know what she was doing. She went crazy. She – it happened so fast. She came after me, touching me, and I wouldn't let her. I pushed her away. God, maybe if I let her she'd be alive, but it was so disgusting and I couldn't stand it. So I fought her off and she ran into the kitchen and started to stab herself with the needle. There was nothing I could do. I thought she was giving herself more dope – and all at once she keeled over and when I touched her she was cold. I didn't know what to do.'

He resisted the temptation to comfort her.

'It's a horrible story,' he said at last. 'Don't ever mention it again.' She nodded submissively. He took a handkerchief from his pocket and walked back into the kitchen. He pulled out the syringe and let it fall to the floor.

'What'd you do?'

'Lenore, I'm going to call Victor and tell him that she died of a drug overdose. After that, you phone the police and say you just walked in and your roommate's dead. You were at a movie or the library or something. It's a mess and telling them the truth is going to hurt you and the Contes. The papers will play up the story as it is. The less anyone knows the better. By the way, I wouldn't mention that I was here. Your father'll only make life harder if I'm brought in.' She stared at him vacuously. 'Lenore, have you got it straight?'

'Yes,' she muttered, 'just one lie after another.'

'Exactly. Nobody wants to hear the truth.' Including himself, he realized. The thought of Georgie making advances to Lenore curdled his blood. Dialing the operator, he glanced over at the immobile pair of legs.

A servant fetched Victor at the other end of the line.

'Victor, it's me, Jonathan. I'm sorry, but it seems Georgie had some kind of accident.' He heard the knowing sigh. 'She was messing around with some pills and drugs and it looks as though she had a heart attack. Yes ... she's dead. Lenore found her when she came in and she called me. Please give my sympathy to Tina. Yes, of course I'll meet you at the airport.' He held the receiver away from him. He had never heard Victor cry, and the thin wail, filled with the final agony of loss, wrenched at him. 'Good-bye, Victor. She's at peace.'

Jonathan felt awkward alone with Lenore. The poignancy

387

of her situation drew him, but he rebelled against his instincts. He could no longer trust them. They had led him astray and caused him immeasurable pain. Now he had restructured his life to include Frances and other women who made no emotional demands. Lenore deprived him of all the forces that held him together.

'Are you okay?' he asked.

'I think so.'

'You'll be able to handle it ...?'

'I'll have to, won't I?'

He waited in silence until she had phoned the police. He wanted to stay, see her through the ordeal, yet he had no choice but to leave.

She did not have the energy or resources to hold him, but she looked at him oddly when he went to the door. He had not even touched her hand during the taxi ride. The desire to reach out and feel him against her had been so overbearing that she could have cried. Now he was leaving her again and she didn't know how to stop him. She stood by the door then crept out on the landing with him.

'Is she special ... is she your girl?'

He turned slowly to face her. A smile died on his face.

'Sometimes she is ... when I stop thinking about you.'

And he was gone, a blurred shape in the night.

* * *

A cortege of limousines followed the hearse to Our Lady Queen of Martyrs cemetery on Staten Island. Lenore caught a glimpse of Jonathan riding with his family. Frances was sitting beside him. The cars stopped at an open gravesite. Men leaned on their shovels and an elderly priest clutching a Bible walked to the car bearing the Contes. Tina wore a black veil and Victor soothed her as she walked sobbing behind the priest.

It was the middle of June, a cool, sunny day with the promise of summer still unfulfilled. Sam and Sylvia wore dour, serious expressions. Lenore herself could not explain the light mood of expectancy which welled up inside her: the prospect of seeing Jonathan again with her father powerless to prevent it.

On the ride down, Sam had been silent and reflective. Was it possible that he had had a change of heart? she wondered. She knew that her behavior would be examined critically. She must act docilely, follow his orders. Her apartment had been closed and all her belongings had been moved back to the hotel. She was waiting for Sam to make up his mind about returning to college in New York and she did not wish to jeopardize her chances. She had to demonstrate that she was capable of functioning on her own. Sam had been pleased with her progress. She had a B-plus average and the letter informing her that she had made the dean's list had been framed and placed in the Hall of Fame corner. She knew that her encounter today with Jonathan would be the test to determine her future.

Pauli stood solemnly by Victor and beside him, Chou was subdued. A welcoming smile came to her lips when she spotted Lenore. Chou embraced and kissed her.

'My baby!' she exclaimed. 'You're beautiful and a woman.'

Sam walked along the line of men as though running the gauntlet. He nodded severely to Alex, shook hands with David and Paul. When he was forced to pass Jonathan and Frances, he averted his eyes, but paused to kiss Miriam. The priest raised his hands, beckoning them to move closer. The sun sparkled, illuminating his bald spot, and Lenore kept her eyes fixed on his face during the short service.

'Ashes to ashes . . .' he intoned.

Jonathan stood erectly beside Frances. Lenore wished she could reach out to him.

'Dust to dust . . .'

The brass casket was lowered on ropes by the grave diggers.

'In the name of the Father, the Son, and the Holy Ghost, we commit thy child, Georgette Mary Conte, to thy loving care and pray that her immortal soul will reside with thee, Christ our Lord and Savior.'

The priest made the sign of the cross and the others, genuflecting, weeping, lifting their right hands and crossed themselves. In the babble of dolorous sounds, the women encircled Tina whose lowered head seemed permanently fixed on the hole in the ground which was being filled with fresh earth and a claylike loam.

A brief reception was to be held at the Stones' apartment, after which the Contes were to return to California and attend a requiem mass at their local church. It was Victor who had decided that Georgie was to be buried in New York. Victor had banned Georgie in life and now in death her exile was fixed eternally.

Lenore waited by the limousine for her father to break away. He and Alex stood to the side, talking by the grave. She watched in the outside mirror as Jonathan and Frances passed behind her. She and Jonathan had not exchanged a word.

She was surprised when Frances left Jonathan at the car, turned, and walked toward her. The two women were face to face.

'He told me he can't marry me,' Frances said. 'I guessed as much. But one thing you can be damned sure of – I'll never give him up. So where does that leave you?'

'Nowhere,' Lenore said brusquely as Sam approached. 'It's over with us.'

BOOK FOUR

Twenty-nine

There is an unnoticed spatial emptiness that invests the lives of men destined to be bachelors, and at thirty Jonathan looked forward to some idealistic Indian summer which would rescue him.

Until he met Sandy Wells, Jonathan had carefully removed himself from those situations that might pose problems and present a crisis. He kept to fugitive liaisons, lasting an hour or a weekend, devoid of emotional contact; he preferred to float unhindered from party to party, collecting women who would make no demands on him. He was like a man who approached a gambling table with a set sum of money, lost it, and left the casino never to return.

It would have surprised him to learn that he had a reputation as a ladies' man. Never cruel to women who passed through his bed, he made no promises, told no lies, gave no basis for hope, disparaged optimism, lavished no presents. In fact he hardly ever appeared in public with a date unless it was to round out a dinner party. Romance, at least until Sandy, did not exist even as a possibility.

Once a month, when he was reminded by Machado, he and the Kid would drive over to Alex's place and go a few rounds. He still had his wind and his weight was a constant one sixty. Stripped and at five eight, built like a mule, he looked a promising middleweight, but once in the ring, he demonstrated a conspicuous lack of skill, fought like a brawler, hit on breaks, and invariably lost his temper: he loved infighting, clinching, butting heads, and he never responded to the bell or to Machado's injunctions.

'Move laterally, Jonathan; you're in my line of fire, comin straight at me.'

Machado shot snaky combos lightly against his headgear to teach respect, but still Jonathan kept advancing, punching wildly, ultimately arm-weary, at which point Machado would turn on the speed and Jonathan would find the lithe Cuban behind him, smiling and tapping him on the shoulder.

'Man, I'm here.' He would handcuff Jonathan from behind with his gloves to prevent another bull charge.

After the workout he, Alex, and Machado would go over to Lundy's, swallow several dozen Little Necks at the clam bar with pitchers of beer. These were the best times for him these retreats into the carefree man's world. After his third beer, Alex would return to the fundamentals of self-defense.

'It's a good thing God didn't make you a fighter....' He froze into a stance to illustrate his knowledge. 'Your left side is offensive ... you attack with your left and defend with your right. See' – a shadow punch was released – 'when I throw a left my right guards my jaw. Now even first-rate boxers don't realize that the three points of attack are here. Piff-piff-piff,' he breathed deeply through his nose, pulling the punches. 'The liver, the heart, and the temple. It's not the solar plexus or the point of the jaw. Sure, you'll see a guy going down after a shot to the chin. But remember, you're hitting one of the strongest bones in the body. The temple – particularly the left side – is how most fighters get knocked down.'

'Right, boss.' Machado verified the lesson, threw up his wrists to glance at his watch. 'How we doin for time, cause I gotta cook two eighteen-year-olds *guapas* like about seven up on Columbus Avenue.'

'Okay, you can run me home then start banging,' Jonathan said.

'On that very important subject of ladies, what's doing with you?' Alex asked.

'A strong maybe.'

'I'm not prying, but can you give me a little form? With David and Linda coming up for another wedding anniversary, your mother is still waiting to buy a dress for your affair. Fact is, she heard you were seeing Frances again.'

'Just when we're at loose ends.'

'Well, it's your life.' They shook hands. 'Keep in touch little more often,' Alex said, reluctant to let him go.

'Come to work for me at the Arena and you'll see me all the time.'

'Wise guy. You can't fight for shit, so how can I work for a man whose ass I can kick in?' He accompanied Jonathan to his dark brown Rolls Silver Cloud II. 'You could do a lot worse than Frances. Remember us to her....'

'You got it.'

Alex watched the Rolls pull away from the curb. His son lived just across the bridge but they might have been in different countries. It was a strange sensation to read Jonathan's name in the papers and then show Miriam the article; the latest had been about winning a franchise from the newly formed American Basketball Association and forming a team to be called the New York Scimitars. The grainy news-wire photo made him look older and Alex strained to remember if his son had ever been young.

'They still on your ass about Frances, huh?' Machado said as they headed for the Brooklyn Bridge, soon to be relieved of the sight of these decaying neighborhoods. On nearby streets, black kids pissed on fire hydrants whose water they couldn't release and teenage Puerto Ricans with pencil-thin mustaches and tattooed arms vigilantly patrolled street corners and clustered around moon-faced gang-bang girls. Like his father, Jonathan thought, they were staking claims to abandoned territory and perhaps on another level, Frances also fell into that category.

As far as Jonathan was concerned she had, like a prospector, bought into a played-out mine. But she just refused to accept that affairs wither like flowers and have to be thrown out after a time.

A year after Georgie's funeral, she had succumbed to a Wall Street lawyer. But she soon surmised that her attraction stemmed from the connections her husband could make through Charlie. The union lasted four months.

Europe was next. The house in Antibes attracted a variety of suitors and during the Cannes Film Festival, Frances met her second husband. The Comte d'Anviers owned a nightclub behind the Croisette. He had a taste for buying expensive presents for himself and charging them to Frances, and an eye for the young waiters he hired from the provinces. She soon tired of roving the casinos while the comte sipped Pernod with the liquid, doe-eyed boys.

Shorn of the Frenchman, she traveled Europe alone, battering Jonathan with letters of her wretchedness. When these elicited no response, she tried setting out in great detail her erotic adventures among bellboys in Positano, ski instructors in La Rosa, fishermen in Rhodes. Her letters were so long and graphic that he wondered how she found the time to attend to the appetites she described. Her postcards were more concise. 'I found my calling. I'm a whore. How do you like that?' Still others were like coded shop orders. 'Three Arabs in one afternoon. One after the other.' This from Tangiers. He sent her a cable: 'Safety in numbers,' to which she replied fretfully, 'Not funny. Your fault.' His sympathy had expired and he wished she would find another confidant.

She returned to the States and, at Charlie's instigation, took up residence in Reno and legally disposed of d'Anviers who had been using her name to get loans from Lazard Frères and other bankers.

'I can pick them,' she told Jonathan when they finally saw each other again. 'A tax shelter hustler and a French buggerer who came to bed wearing eye cream and who tossed himself off on black satin sheets. Ahh, first love . . .'

Divorces, like mink coats, suit some women, and these harmless dissolutions brought out in Frances a quality of gaiety and self-ridicule and that amused Jonathan. 'Could you imagine becoming my third husband?' Her tactics never gave any indication of the pain she felt. She had become a consummate actress. She was too well attuned to Jonathan's responses to exert any pressures. They became casual friends, lunching together, occasionally going to the theater, and once away for a weekend, but to her consternation they did not sleep together.

Sitting on the bench in the Arena, Jonathan watched in exasperation as the Scimitars practiced. He had been on the road for ten months during the year, recruiting players from college teams. What the team lacked was a star, someone who could make things happen, and he thought angrily of his encounter with the directors of the Arena the previous week.

Sitting at opposite ends of the table in the boardroom next to Charlie's office, he and Charlie had glowered at each other, opponents rather than partners in an enterprise. The four do-nothing directors had made the trek to New York for the meeting because they'd been told of Charlie's plans to take the Arena public. Cash and stock options were involved.

Jonathan had regretted taking Gardner's advice on the selection of the board. 'Let Charlie handle it, for Christ's sake,' he had been told all those months before. 'These guys are major industrialists. With them sitting on the board,

Wall Street's going to take this new issue seriously. The market's been soft.'

They had been at lunch at the Bankers' Club. Jonathan had just flown in. His suitcase, tattooed with labels, was parked in the checkroom.

'Well, who the hell are these guys?'

'James Dale of Dale Asbestos ... Big Board. The company is second to Manville. Look, I've got the Standard and Poore reports.'

'Bill, do me a favor, don't give me reports. I want to know about these men. They're strangers.'

'Charlie's known them for years.'

'That's not good enough.'

'Jonathan, relax. Take a few days off. You're wiped.'

'Well, how the fuck do we get a team together if somebody doesn't pick the players and hire a coach?'

'These people are going to lend prestige.'

'Terrific,' he said sourly. 'I've got the franchise and they're going to tell me what to do.' He scraped the hollandaise off his poached salmon. He'd been living on hamburgers and chili for the last week at East Texas State, drinking beer with the team in college dives, and sleeping in a roach-filled college boardinghouse near the campus.

'Nobody is going to give you orders.'

'Who else did Charlie get?'

'Albert Cope of Allied Insurance. Cope is chairman of the board and he controls a group of pension funds. Evan Lawrence of Lawrence Electronics. American Exchange. They make microcircuits for Sperry Rand.'

'Next?'

'Tom Ruth of General Affiliated Paper. Also Big Board. They have twenty percent of the market in cardboard containers. All these names mean something to mutual fund managers, pension plans, and to sophisticated investors.'

Jonathan reflected for a few minutes on Gardner's endorsement, but he could not overcome his negative reactions. All he knew was that, while he had been on the road, Charlie had put together a team of industrialists without consulting him.

'Don't I have a say-so about board members? After all, look at the logic,' he snapped. 'We've got asbestos, electronics, insurance, and cardboard. What do any of them know about programming the Arena? Are they experts in putting on hardware shows, conventions, the roller derby, a circus, show jumping, dog shows, concerts?'

'No one's claiming that. That's your province and you've done a damned good job of it.'

'Thanks a lot.'

'Jonathan, spare me the sarcasm.' Gardner's relaxed attitude turned militant. He was under orders to man the board with conservative members of the financial community who would restrain Jonathan's spending. 'These people are running successful companies and they'll give us the credibility we need.'

'Six million in profits after taxes isn't going to persuade the public that *I* know what I'm doing?'

'It'll help....' Gardener had not expected an altercation. 'Have I misled you before?'

'No.'

'Then what's the problem?'

'They all have votes.'

'Yes, but they'll go along with your plans.'

But they hadn't. They demanded to control the contracts he had offered players. They insisted on ceilings and cut corners on advertising. They were in it for the buck. Dale, a lanky, stubborn man from Detroit had come to New York to escape from his wife for a week and get laid. Tom Ruth, headquartered in Toronto, brought his wife in with him to catch Broadway shows. Albert Cope spent most of his time attempting to work out a deal with a group of Lloyd's underwriters to buttress his company's foreign investments. And Evan Lawrence, an airplane buff, hoped that he could buy a Beechcraft which would be partly financed by the Arena.

They had managed to show up for the meeting, but all they were concerned with were salaries, free stock, and options to buy at below the market price. They listened attentively to the financial program Charlie laid out. However, when Jonathan presented his plans for the New York Scimitars, they dug their heels in.

He stood up, walked around the table, disconcerting the men. 'I assume everyone in this room has heard of Tim Avery.' They nodded blandly. 'Fine. He's been drafted by Philadelphia in the NBA and the sports pages have been filled with stories about the contract disputes he's having.'

'I think the boy's an idiot,' Dale observed captiously. 'He's twenty years old and to turn down three-quarters of a million dollars –'

'He's a three-time All-American. With a thirty-two-point average at UCLA. He's a superstar.'

'What's all this leading to?' Cope asked. 'You've got your team ... the average salary of your players is close to forty thousand a year, plus expenses.' He thumbed his finger down the list of figures as though it were an actuary table.

'My brother David, who's now running VCA, the agency that supplies us with most of our talent, has been close to Avery since he was a junior. I think that with Avery we will become a viable team. Our attendance will shoot up. We'll sell season tickets with no problem.'

'Jonathan, we've already pumped three million dollars into this franchise,' Charlie informed him. 'The Knicks are the big team in New York.'

'They've had two lousy seasons. Besides, league schedules are set up so there won't be any conflict. We're at home when they're on the road. We don't play a single home game on the same date. Avery can make the difference between a winning team and a bunch of deadasses. I believe because of Avery's relationship with my brother we can get him to jump leagues.'

Cope peered at him through his thick-lensed glasses.

'How much?'

'A million dollars.'

'You're crazy,' Lawrence charged. 'Nobody's worth that kind of money.'

He was stymied.

'Jonathan, what you're suggesting is just irresponsible,' Ruth added. 'It's embarrassing to listen to these figures.'

Not one of his arguments carried weight. They bagged him. Five against Avery, two for. Gardner had supported him, but Jonathan was convinced that it had been a token vote, dictated by Charlie so that Jonathan would not believe there had been a gang-up.

He'd been squeezed and it had been done subtly, all in the name of sound financial practice. Jonathan's power was ebbing away. He suspected that his difficulties with Charlie and his cronies were directly related to his rejection of Frances.

Now, watching the practice session, he made some notes on a pad he kept by his side. The ten men on the floor couldn't shoot a lick and passed sloppily. They resembled a bunch of schoolyard pickups rather than a team of pros. Ludicrous. His disgust increased. The time and effort he had put into acquiring a bona fide professional team was down the drain. He doubted whether the four-month training period would make any difference. The Scimitars would be hooted out of New York.

Making his way across the gleaming wooden floor while the players assembled at the far end of the court was Charlie. Perhaps if he watched the team, he'd see the error of his decision. Jonathan wearily got up to meet him. The coach intercepted them. Grim-faced, sweating through his gray shirt, he, too, was despairing. Jonathan had recruited Bill Mullins from Notre Dame. He was a hard-line defensive coach who believed in ball control. Now he looked ready for a morgue slab. The pressure had been intolerable. After every practice his hairline seemed to recede an inch.

'Run, just keep them running,' Jonathan said sharply. 'I want to see these bums fast-breaking for four quarters. That's all we've got going for us, Bill.'

'Mr. Packard, maybe you can talk some sense into him. Nobody can run for forty-eight minutes.'

'With all due respect, Bill, Charlie Packard isn't running this team. I am. City College won the NIT and the NCAA championship because they ran! They didn't have a shooter on the team! Everybody we signed has speed going for him. Now you make this bunch of dumdums into a unit and they'll win ball games.'

Head slumped, Mullins returned to his players. He had picked a good shooter, a seven-foot giant from New Mexico, but Jonathan had refused to offer the boy a contract because he was plodding and deliberate, needed too much time to get himself set.

Charlie joined him on the bench.

'They're pathetic, Charlie. What brings you into town?'

'Lousy weather and I wanted to take Frances to lunch.'

It had been a freakish summer in New York: unendurable humidity and a sultry rainstorm almost every day. Spending most of his time indoors, Jonathan had little appreciation of the weather. The small consolation was that West's Hotel had fallen off more than sixty percent because of cancellations. Sam was four months behind in his loan repayments. Jonathan had held the bank off.

'How is she?' he asked noncommitally, his attention wandering to the boys racing across the floor in a speed drill.

Charlie's eyes were pronged with the spokes of half a century of fine champagnes and brandies, but his expression had settled into the cast of melancholy old age. 'Can I pull you away from this for a minute?' he asked.

'I'd rather talk here if you don't mind.' Jonathan detected trouble hovering around him.

'You'd be doing me a personal favor if you took Frances to lunch instead of me. Lutèce. The reservation's in my name.'

'Why?'

Solemnity gave way to exasperation. Charlie didn't expect puppets to talk, certainly not to ask questions.

'In all the years, well, with this on-again, off-again thing with Frances ...' He stammered. 'Jonathan, she's hurting.'

'Charlie, Charlie, I'd do just about anything for her – but don't ask me to lead her on.'

'What harm would it do now? You dragged it out for years and I never got the impression you were conscience-stricken.'

'I don't think that's fair.'

'What the hell's fair got to do with it? The girl's falling apart. I'm not coming to you as her father but as a friend.'

'Charlie, I've always cared for her. I've never stopped, even when she was married. But for reasons I can't go into, we missed our shot.'

His words had no effect on the distressed father.

'I've taken an option on a beach house out at Malibu. If she likes it, I'll buy it.' He gave Jonathan a faint smile. 'If you went out there, you could see Tim Avery. Buy him, Jonathan, okay.'

'What?'

'I got the board to reconsider. Please ... a few days. What does it matter to you?'

'What happens when I walk out? Won't she be worse off? Charlie, for God's sake, you're a man of the world. You've broken a few hearts –'

'My daughter's a different case.'

'But it doesn't make sense.'

'It's for me and Isobel ... the girl's sinking.' Charlie's mouth quivered. 'Admit to me that you never loved her and we'll forget this conversation.'

Players gasping for breath, dragging their feet, wobbled across the court, bodies gleaming with sweat.

'Charlie, I did love her, but not enough.'

'Give her this last chance. Maybe something unpredictable will happen. She's the best. We both know that. One of a kind.'

'A bleeder.'

'That's not her fault. Give in. Make the effort.'

Charlie Packard, a man who squeezed blood out of business, dismissed executives wholesale when he took over a company, had driven all the way from East Hampton to beg for his daughter.

'Do you think an unhappy marriage for both of us would have served your purpose?'

'Not mine, but Frances's. The pricks she married were hardly reasonable substitutes for you. What are you made of? I've got one daughter, one wife, a hundred million dollars, and our lives aren't worth a shit.'

'The sadness of the rich is always touching in its way.'

'Jonathan, Jonathan, do it. Back me.'

'You're such a smart old cunt.'

'Malibu isn't exactly a torture chamber, and Frances doesn't look like a door hook.'

'I'm talking to a wall.'

'No, just somebody who behaved like a friend to you from the moment you walked into my house.'

Charlie started across the floor, oblivious of the players rushing past him, twisting out of his path.

Jonathan followed him, protesting at his unreasonableness. 'Charlie, this is going to hurt her again. I'm seeing another girl and it's serious.'

'Really? Since when did any piece of ass get under your skin?' His tone was acidulous. 'I told you I'd deliver Avery, didn't I?'

'Oh, it's a trade.' Animosity embraced them as though in communion. 'This isn't beef on the hoof.'

Charlie discounted his feelings. He might have been

bartering for a piece of property. 'Give my baby this break. I won't ask again.'

*　　*　　*

A whirlwind of people jammed the downstairs bar at Lutèce. Waiters flurried by. André's supercilious eye scanned the reservation list for unfamiliar names. Suntanned women in gossamer summer dresses whispered about wandering husbands, affairs that were growing serious, inheritances that were expected if a stubborn parent would drop dead, balancing checkbooks, and who was drying out again. They moodily sipped champagne eye-openers and worried about the traffic problems back to the Hamptons. Men with alligator attaché cases and Brioni suits left their chauffeured cars under umbrellas. A summer rain slanted against the restaurant windows.

Jonathan spotted Frances in the early-bird's corner. She was smiling at nothing in particular, as though the laughter surrounding her made her eligible for inclusion in a club she might not otherwise join. She was still lovely with a freshness that gave the lie to her reckless claims of sexual freedom. As the unwilling instigator of her grief, he had not got off entirely free. In the flesh, she inspired guilt.

For a moment she stared at him, perplexed, then looked over his shoulder, expecting her father.

'What happened to Charlie?' She sounded concerned and flustered.

'Knee injury rebounding. And I was promoted to the first team. Okay?'

'Sure.' She glowed, made room for him by her side, and he ordered a drink. 'I didn't even know you were in town.'

'Charlie couldn't get hold of you, so I volunteered to fill in for him. I'll even hack the check. What more could you ask?'

'Not much.' She tentatively kissed his cheek.

He detected no conspiracy and was convinced that if she had any inkling of Charlie's tactics, her humiliation would have been crushing. She took pains to avoid touching his hand, a mere inch away from hers beside the ashtray. Cloaked behind a broad, worldly, counterfeit smile, her effort to appear relaxed was disheartening and merely served to crumble the intimacy they once had. They behaved with insufferable consideration toward one another and he thought that mortal

403

enemies have an easier time of it than people who have shared a bed.

Their first martini celebrated remorse, the second lost them their table for half an hour, and over the third he was halfway on the plane to California with her. She was alive again, the future a challenge she would eagerly accept.

'We're both white as ghosts. What a summer,' she added as though merely a season had eluded them. 'I'm going out to Malibu later this week.' A tacit invitation. 'I'm fed up with New York. I'm fed up with every place. Maybe I'll like California. Everything seems so unimportant out there ... and I could use a place that's unreal. I guess you're too busy with the team to get away now.'

There it was. A suggestion. Uninsistent, but still a hook. She was bargaining for a weekend. Charlie had laid a snare, a beauty. He could sign Avery and accommodate Frances at the same time. It was a pernicious trade. Flesh for flesh.

'I might but it would be tricky.' Why couldn't he say no and tell her the truth about Sandy? The imploring eyes prevented disclosure.

'What's a few days?' Rain slashed the window like razors and they both watched for a moment. 'I'll leave it up to you,' she said, her fingers nervously toying with a balloon of Armagnac.

'I'll have some business to do.'

'Well, naturally.' She laughed. 'If you were on a desert island alone you'd find a way of doing business.' Her hand touched his affectionately, then she withdrew it self-consciously.

'Okay,' he said with resignation. 'We could catch a night flight.'

She didn't know why she was forced to ask a question which might upset him, but she wasn't using her head.

'Do you ever see her? The girl I met ...' She turned white under his blank stare.

'No, why should I?' he replied evenly. 'It was kid stuff, filed away.'

She couldn't leave it alone. 'I can't help wondering what she's been doing ... you know.' The sharp ratchet sound of rain might have been a coffin being nailed as it ricocheted off cars and hammered the awning.

'I'm not sure.' He seemed genuinely vague. 'Let's see,

somebody mentioned ... yeah, it was David. He saw her when she came out to the Coast. She's getting into some kind of cosmetics thing. Door to door. Kind of schlock.'

'Schlock?'

'Cheap stuff. Nothing much. David mentioned something about her trying to get one of his clients to endorse the junk she sells. Friendship aside, he told her to forget it.'

It was still drizzling as they waited for his car.

'How were the *carnitas* in there?' Machado asked.

'At fifty a head, they've got to be good,' Jonathan replied. 'Let's drop Frances and then call Irene and ask her to pack me a bag. I'll be on the Coast for a few days.'

She settled back in the car, keeping a respectable distance from him. He must never again feel she was smothering him.

'Is she married?'

'I wouldn't know. Is it important?' He became curt and distant.

She had overstepped the boundary. 'I'm really glad you're coming,' she said, regaining her spirit. 'Separate bedrooms ... if you like.'

'Frances, you still think of everything.'

Thirty

Paul's boat was anchored just outside of Nassau harbor. The four unshaven fishermen, copper-skinned, sat on deck barefoot in shorts and thin cotton polo shirts. They had skirted some blue marlin and barracuda earlier in the day, but had been outsmarted. All they had to show for their adventure was a broken rod and several torn lines. None of the men fretted unduly. They had not come aboard that morning for the fishing but to present reasonable proposals to Paul. He had avoided discussion and attempts to corner him during the day. Wait till evening and they're beat, drunk, sun-dazed, he thought.

The men were his guests in a manner of speaking, since he had categorically refused to appear in New York after the attempted murder of his closest friend and ally. He might be next. Things were dangerously unsettled in the organization. If a slob like Vinny Gigante, a three-hundred-pound barrel of jelly who couldn't even make it as a button man, could dare to try to take out Frank Costello right in the lobby of the Majestic, the apartment house he'd lived in for years, then who was safe? Certainly not him. He'd spoken to Costello after he'd left Roosevelt Hospital. The bullet had grazed his right temple and just missed taking off his ear.

'I made him when he called my name,' Frank Costello had informed him. 'Gigante, the Chin. Used to fight six-rounders. He couldn't hit for shit. He catches me by the mailbox near the elevator and he's got the fuckin nerve to say – "Hey, Frank, this is for you . . ." So I turn around. He's maybe ten feet away. He fires and catches me and then runs . . . Ever see a tub o' shit move? Well, I did.'

'Should I come up, Frank? You need protection.'

'Stay put, Pauli. Believe me, you show your face in the city, they'll give you a banquet at the Boot's place in Fort Lee. They're waiting for you. Everybody in town is scared shitless that you're gonna open fire. Pauli, stay put is what I'm telling you. Let the shitheelers come to you.'

'Frank, forget about me. You need me, I'm there.'

Costello cleared his throat. The cigarette cough he had sounded like the grate of a subway train.

'Listen to me. Let whoever you see make you a proposition, but you be careful. If there is somebody you can trust outside the organization, then take him in. Somebody clean that isn't known. You'll add ten years to your life. But if it's not possible, then for Christ's sake, play ball. It's all changin, Pauli, and I don't want you left out in the cold. They isolate ... everybody's got big eyes on you and the publicity you're gettin is hurtin you. It's the wedge. So let the thing settle down and you'll find out who's with who.'

'Did Vito order this?' Paul asked.

'Who else? Fuck it, the guy sold out his own country to Mussolini to save his ass so what could you expect from him? Pauli, the hit on me is called off, but you watch out.'

Vito Genovese had agreed to allow Costello to retire in peace. Frank was worn out after his time in prison, without ambition, but he had counseled against a further expansion into narcotics. And Vito had never been anything else but a junk dealer. During his years in Italy he had supplied cocaine to Count Ciano, Mussolini's son-in-law. How could he stay away from it or accept Costello's ban?

'Come on, you bums, there's ice and booze. What're you drinkin?' Paul asked his visitors. He had wondered who would be sent down to see him and what offers would be made. He knew that he would be asked to take in an active partner, but in which side of his business? And was it just his action they wanted? Frank was now cut off in his estate in Sands Point, recovering. He refused to see visitors or answer calls.

'What's a bottle of J and B run you, legit?' Carlo Gambino asked, lumbering to the bar which had been set up under the blue awning of the Chris Craft. Bull-necked, nearsighted, with his slow, deliberate way of speaking, he might have been mistaken for a warehouse clerk. But he was a central figure of power in New York. He had planned and orchestrated, in collusion with Vito, the murder of Albert Anastasia in the barbershop at the Park Sheraton Hotel, and in the changing alliances, he had inherited Anastasia's position as boss. It was evident to Paul that he was priming his protégé Joe Columbo for a sudden move up the hierarchy.

'A deuce. Duty free.'

'Shit, we pay that for a shot at the fuckin Waldorf,' Joe Columbo said testily.

'But we're seein the show,' Sonny Franzese, the man-about-town noted. He was clearly in attendance as Columbo's bodyguard.

'Asshole, I know that,' Columbo snapped at him. 'It's the fuckin principles involved. I mean to say, hijacked it costs us more.'

The steward climbed the galley steps and laid out trays of giant gulf shrimp, raw clams, anchovies and peppers, thin sweet slabs of prosciutto.

'Some spread,' Gambino said, grabbing a plate and loading it.

Columbo jiggled the ice cubes in his glass and scratched the mosquito bites on his stubby arms. He was not much of an outdoorsman and he disliked traveling. The fishing trip in rough seas had frightened him. With the port in sight and the boat rocking gentle as a cradle, he had regained his confidence. He pulled a crumpled article from his pocket.

'Pauli, you seen this?' he asked.

'No, what's it about? My glasses are below.'

'From *Confidential*. You don't read?'

'It's nothin special.'

'Well, there's a guy out there, reporter, name of Joey Fields, and he must use the same shower as you. Listen to what it says: "The Phoenix community has ignored organized crime. An investigation carried out by this reporter has revealed that Paul Salica, a syndicate boss with interests in Miami, Los Angeles, and now Phoenix, has been buying property over the years at Lake Horseshoe. Salica's other activities include bookmaking, loansharking, and prostitution. His newest venture is control of the pornography trade from Arizona to California ..."'

Paul remained impassive, staring at the water while Columbo continued to read.

' "... Junkets to the Bahamas set up by a Phoenix travel agency for high rollers," ' Columbo's singsong voice continued. Paul had seen the article. Attempts to track down the reporter's sources had failed. Where was Columbo heading?

'He's got a helluva pipeline,' Franzese observed.

'I don't know where he's gettin it. My people are water-tight.' He leaned against the deck rail facing the men and

Gambino joined him.

'Fuckin problem with these writers is they're untouchable. These people are holier than cops. They can't be fixed,' Gambino advised him.

'I never was gonna bother. He'll run out of gas and it'll be forgotten. . . .' Paul waited for a reaction.

Gambino smiled broadly, revealing stained, crooked teeth.

'Pauli, you're supplyin Joe here with the movies and pictures and maybe it'd be better for you to get that stuff outa Phoenix.'

'To L.A.,' Columbo shot in. 'Other thing is, Paul, the stuff your people send me is garbage. Grainy shit in black and white. Ugly broads with seams on their tits and scars on their bellies. I made a connection out on the coast in L.A. with a guy which makes 'em in color with gorgeous young pussy. I seen some of his stuff and I'm tellin you, it's as good as a real movie. He's a pro. Now there's no conflict with us. I have the East Coast and you're out West. It's the product we're discussin. . . .'

'I'm listening.'

'You hook up with him, throw him a percentage, and you and I bankroll some developin labs. We got production and accordin to my man, the color costs maybe two fifty to make. We run off a few hundred prints and sell them at sixty a hit. Plus the French card decks which runs maybe seventy-five cents and can be taken off the film. Magazines cost say a buck and we unload them at a sawbuck a hit. This move gets Fields off your ass and we're all happy. The product is better and the profit is higher.'

'How much do I throw the guy that makes them?'

'Twenty-five percent. You keep fifty and for my investment I get twenty-five.'

'Doesn't it sound like a good deal?' Gambino asked in a cajoling voice. 'Everybody is happy and all this publicity stops. The pie gets much bigger and you don't lose, Pauli.'

Interesting that they had picked on this relatively obscure part of his operation in an effort to force his hand. Although pornography was growing year by year, the profits were nowhere as large as those gleaned from narcotics.

Paul recognized this as the first step. Ultimately he would be asked to share his junket business, his gambling territory, but perhaps by yielding quickly, he would gain time and be able to marshal support from other out-of-state bosses who resented the New York families' raids as much as he did. Maybe he could split the organization right down the middle, with Chicago as the boundary. Vito could have the East, and he would lead the West. Chicago would remain under Sam Giancana, who in any conflict would side with him, since he also despised Genovese.

'First thing you ought to know,' he replied after a long silence, 'is that I sold out of Horseshoe a year ago to a property boiler-room bunch. So I can't be tied to the property. Now suppose I agree to share with you, Joe. Does it end there? Or are you interested in opening more of my territory with Carlo?'

Gambino and Columbo protested vehemently, swore that they had no further interests in Paul's activities.

Despite their assurances, this was an opening for Vito's junk. Pornography was one thing. It was something that people wanted and it didn't hurt anyone. Junk was too big a risk. Filth. Ultimately they would squeeze him out because he would not support Genovese.

'You're growin with the times, brother,' Columbo said expansively, smiling. 'Workin with you is somethin I always wanted.'

'You got it.'

Gambino's inscrutable moon face, however, was still vaguely troubled.

'The other thing Pauli. That thing with Frank was bad business. Foolish ... the man wanted to retire in peace and he should have been given the right.' Paul allowed him to continue the charade. 'Nobody feels worse than Vito. It was a misunderstanding. Vito thought maybe Frank is playin possum and he wasn't sincere. Well, he should've taken Frank's word is all. Pauli, let there be peace. Vito wants it. We all do. Don't you be the one to take up Frank's side. What's done is done.'

They had come to ensure that he remained neutral, but because of Vito's paranoia, Paul knew that no matter what his intentions, his motives would remain suspect. A wall was being built to contain him.

'I want peace. But leave Frank alone.'

Gambino embraced him and over his shoulder he saw Columbo nodding to Franzese.

* * *

After Vito's messengers had left, Paul visited the Englishman who had been his trusted confidant since he first moved into the Bahamas. Arthur Glendon was a shy man, middleaged, with excellent family connections, but he had been forced out of his legal practice in London by small-minded partners who objected to his personal life. Glendon had the misfortune, from their point of view, to have fallen in love with and married a young black Nassau schoolteacher. He had quit London with his new wife and set up a practice in Nassau. His special field of interest and expertise was international finance and, as he nicely put it, 'Tax avoidance.' In the five years since Paul had been his client, millions of dollars had been secreted by Glendon in offshore corporations and Swiss discretionary accounts, and he had doubled Paul's money.

The two men met for drinks on the terrace of the Royal Brittania for the signing of a will Glendon had drawn at his client's insistence.

Warm sea breezes flapped the papers that Paul was examining.

'Initial at the bottom of each page,' Glendon said.

'Now if anything happened to me – and I'm not counting on it –'

'I will see that the money goes to your heir if Chou is also deceased. The will is not subject to probate and the money will flow into the discretionary trust we set up on Grand Cayman.' Glendon lowered his eyes. 'How is she? ... I'd hoped to see her.'

'She's a fighter,' Paul replied with conviction. 'I hate to be away from her, but she finds it too tough to travel.'

'Give her my love.'

Paul decided to fly directly back to Miami and have the crew sail the following day. Each moment away from Chou affected him. When he was with her he could share her pain, console her. When she was alone, Carmine reported that it took four Seconals for her to sleep. Her cancer had reached an advanced stage. God, he thought brokenly, he was losing her and he could not conceive of a life without her.

Thirty-one

On the plane to Los Angeles, Jonathan was subdued. He had not been truthful with Frances. His insatiable curiosity about Lenore had not ceased. With a miser's obsession he had gathered and hoarded every scrap of information about her that he could.

She had begun work after college as a cosmetics demonstrator at Saks Fifth Avenue. Surreptitiously he took to buying his ties there on the ground floor while several counters away he watched her apply new shades of pancake and eye shadow on fortyish women fighting losing battles with their husbands' reasons for staying in town once a week. She traveled Fifth Avenue. Bonwit's for six months, then to Lord and Taylor, where she was promoted to assistant manager of the department. She seemed to have an innate desire to shield the human face.

She still lived in the Village in a brownstone ground-floor apartment on Fifth Avenue and Eighth Street. At odd hours of the night he would cruise past, sometimes on weekends, to see if the lights were on and whether or not she was entertaining a man. But he never saw one there. It became evident that she had settled into the sheltered life of a reclusive spinster. He could not resolve the paradox of the two persons he observed.

During the day she was glamorous, well dressed, a beauty who turned heads on Fifth Avenue. As time passed, her physical appearance grew more startling. Once away from work, she retreated, wore baggy jeans, ill-fitting jackets, thick, shapeless turtleneck sweaters, and used no makeup. He doubted whether anyone from her business would recognize her. It was as though she spoke to the world with lowered eyes in a whisper: Ignore me, pretend I'm not here ... don't notice me. On her home grounds she had achieved perfect anonymity.

Her habits were as regular as a clerk's. She liked to drink and go to the movies. The Waverly on Monday night when they changed the program, browsing for books in the Paperback Gallery, coffee at Rienzi's or the Peacock, a concert once a month, museums every weekend.

But only when she was at work did she reveal any animation. On her own a solid caste of regret was imprinted on her face. Year after year he grew increasingly bewildered by her tolerance of loneliness. There were times when he actually wished she would meet a man who would rescue her from the gray shadows of solitude. Through all these covert intrusions which ultimately left him humiliated, he had never heard the sound of her laughter.

It was impossible to discover whether Lenore had found a method of conserving herself, or if the life had gone out of her for good. Estranged from involvement, she was a sad young woman living only a short distance from him, but light-years away.

He let her be. He was afraid to intrude on the cloistered existence she had created. He knew that he had failed her, that neither she nor Sam would ever understand that he had loved her too much to take advantage of her when she had been his for the asking.

Ultimately he had given up on Lenore, relegated her to the past. It had been ten years since Georgie's funeral. He had been convinced that he was incapable of loving another woman again until he met Sandy Wells.

Now for the first time since his childhood obsession had bled him, he allowed an adult passion to carry him along, freeing him from Lenore.

* * *

At the Malibu Colony the dog walkers were out. The beach was community property, so the poodles shat where they pleased but never in the ocean. Women of all ages and sizes, young mistresses trailed by their old men, bellies skiracked from weight losses, skins baked to fine parchment, and sour ex-wives who'd won their beach houses in costly divorce settlements sauntered past the house. Jonathan and Frances lay on the deck, their bodies slick with oil, vodka tonics within reach. She had played her hand skillfully. They'd had hamburgers with David and Linda at Jay's in Santa Monica the previous night, then crashed into bed ... separately. Breakfast on the terrace, fresh orange juice, coffee from an espresso machine, croissants.

Weekends with her at Vassar flooded through his mind, dinner at college dives, signing in late at roadside motels, and the wild hunger they both felt in the middle of the night, the sadness as Sunday evening approached.

But what a different weekend this was. No motel this time but a cedar beach shack treated to look old and weather-beaten, containing a stone fireplace with a surround that could seat eight people, tiled floors with Aztec symbols, four bedrooms, three bathrooms, a sauna, a group Jacuzzi, a Mexican couple in attendance, a kitchen out of *Home Beautiful*, hidden speakers operated by bedside switches – all the gentle trappings of a quarter of a million dollars.

Her very happiness was an accusation, an indictment of his behavior. He knew that all it would take was a piece of paper at city hall to rescue Frances from squandering her life on men who didn't deserve her.

'I'm curious,' she began, topping up his drink, 'do you mind my asking?'

'Frances, since when do we have to be so formal? Friends don't need permission to ask embarrassing questions. They just do it.'

'I gave up trying to outsmart you a long time ago.' She climbed onto the steps leading to the beach and they shared the same board plank. 'Would it have been different if I'd been pregnant?'

'Come on . . .' Act out of guilt and loyalty, he thought, and you need a knockout to win the bout.

'Seriously. Would you have just walked out or made me have an abortion?'

'Oh, shit, can't we just get our bodies brown and relax?'

'You wouldn't have come with me this weekend if there wasn't some vestige of feeling.'

'Honey, I'll never stop caring about you, but we would've had a bum marriage.'

'You never gave us a chance.'

'Let's go for a swim.'

'You'd rather not discuss it?'

'What's to be gained?'

An elderly couple, the woman with rings, gold bracelets gathered from heaven knew how many trips around the world, the man holding two Yorkies in his arms, stopped to stare at them, then walked on.

414

'I always say the wrong thing,' she admitted. 'Jonathan, honestly, I don't know what the hell's going to happen to me. Frankly, it hurts to see you, but after the two stiffs I married, I thought, what the hell, roll the dice again, throw yourself on his mercy. I'm thirty-three. I don't care if we live together without being married. I just have to be with you.'

He walked down the steps and pushed his way into the water, ignoring the fierce shock of cold waves slamming against his chest. He swam some distance from the shore then turned. She was still sitting on the steps, a mere speck. He floated serenely on his back, drifting with the tide. He'd allowed Charlie to use him, but he was no longer Charlie's boy. He swam into shore, carried by the crashing breakers, and for a few moments he lay in the sand and let the water churn over his back. He took a shower and cleaned the tar off his feet.

When he went into the house she was sitting on the sofa in a thin yellow diaphanous wrapper. The bottle of vodka was beside her and it was clear that she had made a substantial dent in it.

'I sent Miguel and Rosa to Jurgensen's to pick up some steaks and goodies for dinner.' Her eyes were pinkish and she was intent on not slurring her words. She extended her arms to him.

The moment of maximum danger had arrived.

'Please ...' Her voice was sibilant, coaxing. 'We've been together hundreds of times. Once more won't matter, will it?'

He padded barefoot across the tiles, ignoring her invitation. The idea of sleeping with her again after all this time had a certain unholy taint, like screwing the wife of a close friend. Their future was behind them. He stalked into his room and was about to close the door when she stopped him.

'Why're you making such a big deal out of this?' The drink in her hand sloshed accidentally on the wall. Self-basement was her province, and she whimpered patheticlly.

'Frances, let me come clean with you for once.'

She shrank back, daunted by the menace of a revelation. Jonathan, I don't know, maybe the excitement of being together ... you know I don't drink much ... never in the morning ...'

He held her firmly by the shoulders.

'Listen to me for a minute, goddamnit.'

'Don't, please. I'll get by with illusions.'

'Frances, once and for all you've got to get me out of your system.'

She was shivering. 'No,' she cried.

'I never led you on. You were the one making the plans until I made you stop. I wanted Lenore but I can't have her. . . . She lives in her own world and I can't be included. You want me to tell you about her?' he shouted. 'She goes through the motions of living. She worked in department stores for years and now she's trying to sell some line of cosmetics. She doesn't let a man near her. Well, I can't go on mourning. Lenore and I are dead. Now you know, does that make you happy? But that doesn't mean that I'm any more in love with you now than I was then. I tried, Frances – I really thought we might get together. But it was never there. I just don't want you as a wife. Isn't that clear by now? Do you think you'd feel any better if we had a screw? What would that be but another promise?'

She sat on the floor, numb, immobile.

'You've got to stop hoping, Frances. I know what hope does. It eats you up, ruins all the good things, prevents you from really feeling alive. You'll find somebody real for you. I know what I'm talking about. It happened for me last May. You know me. I was about as interested in classical music as I was in Impressionist paintings. But one afternoon while the Boston Symphony orchestra was practicing at the Arena I happened to walk through and I stopped and sat down. I've never heard anything so beautiful in my life. Brahms's Third Symphony. I listened for about an hour and when the orchestra broke for lunch a girl walked down the aisle past me. She plays the viola, as if I knew the difference between a viola or violin. But she stopped to talk to me.' He laughed at himself. 'She thought *I*, I, of all people, was a music critic! I faked it for about thirty seconds and then took her out to lunch. Nowhere grand because she just had an hour. We went to a deli. I've been seeing her for the last three months whenever I can. The orchestra's on tour – Cleveland, Detroit, Seattle – and about once a week I manage to jump on a plane and fly to wherever she happens to be playing.

'Frances, I think I'm in love with her. When I'm with her, I'm a different person . . . I stop feeling guilty about you and

416

omehow I can accept that Lenore and I weren't meant to be
ogether.'

She was battered and her eyes were unable to focus.

'Frances, isn't it better that you know the truth?'

'Maybe for you it is. I would've been happier without it.
'ake your things with you and don't come back. Your mis-
on of mercy is over,' she said coldly. 'Just one thing, what
nade you agree to come out here with me?'

'I thought we'd be on a different footing. Just friends
pending a few days together.'

On her tightened face he saw the ruined channels of time.

'I went to a dance and you gave me a ride home that lasted
or more than ten years.'

'They don't have settlements for that sort of thing.'

'You're damn right they don't. I was managing, getting by.
Vhen we saw each other, I always bought it. Graciously, too.
Vo demands, no pressures. You go your way, I go mine.
Vhat was my sin? Loving you? But this is punishment. If
ou'd told me all this at lunch, I wouldn't have gotten on
ne plane with you.' She ripped the sleeve of her wrapper,
rumpled the chiffon, and threw it on the floor. 'I'm such an
liot. Doesn't this look familiar?' He hesitated, confused by
er action. '*You* bought it for me the first weekend we spent
ogether up at school and I've been saving it for years. My
loset at home is stuffed with all the clothes I used to wear
those days ... the saddle shoes you teased me about, my
prority blazer.'

'Frances, stop torturing yourself.'

'The sensation agrees with me. I'm used to it. I married
man who counted my father's money when he was in bed
vith me, but that didn't matter to me. He just bored me
lly. My second liked everybody, but when it came to me or
beachboy, well I got tired of finishing in second place.
till, it was no heartbreak. I wasn't wounded, so I didn't
ave to worry about healing myself. I realized that he was
relevant.

'Everyone was irrelevant, because I loved you. Saintliness
as never a state either of us set much store by. So when we
esumed our *friendship*, I didn't make any pitch for you.
Veeds were growing over me, but Christ, I had the courage
o respect your privacy and the fact that you rejected me ...
ut when you agreed to come away with me ... well it had

417

to mean you still felt something. I've been living on nervous energy,' she shouted pitiably. 'No pills, just adrenaline. Could this be some elaborate joke on your part? But I don't see you laughing –'

'Frances.'

'Don't offend me by offering any explanations. I've had enough of those. You and your girl have a very happy life, lots of kids, and fuck Frances. Go, Jonathan, just go ...'

*   *   *

He arrived at the Polo Lounge before David and he sat at a corner of the dark bar gripping his drink. The whipping he had received seemed to him unjust, but he could hardly have disclaimed responsibility for the weekend by explaining that Charlie had set them both up for such a confrontation. He tried to put her out of his mind and decided that once his business was completed, he would fly to Boston to see if his relationship with Sandy could stand up. He was tired of running after dreams while he was pursued by the dreams of others.

David located Jonathan at the bar. Suntanned, wearing the obligatory dark glasses, a beige Dick Carroll suit, and a dark brown voile shirt open at the collar, he carried a brown crocodile attaché case which matched his shoes. He comported himself like a man fighting recognition, but the greetings he received from waiters, producers, and directors suggested that he had fallen victim to that counterfeit image that Hollywood spawned so naturally. If you weren't important, just pretend. He had a new assurance about him, but how deep it went was impossible to determine. He was an *agent*, and as he had confided to Jonathan some time ago when he joined VCA: 'There isn't a single man in the business who ran to his parents when he was fifteen and said, "I know what I want to do with my life. I want to be an agent more than anything else in the world." But since I'm in this business under the handicap of being Victor's son-in-law, I'm going to prove that I'm better than anyone else. In the trades, I'm referred to as the Cobra. Hard to believe that the student of literature, the would-be painter, could become such a creature, isn't it? But I'm good at what I do. I've learned how to hustle, lie, make promises that I'm not aware f, sell people, and spend money like it's inherited.'

Now David was reveling in his independence. Victor had taken the job of head of production at General International Films. It was an oater factory and Victor had a program of musicals lined up. One of the restrictions laid down by the New York financiers of the studio was that he had to leave the agency so there would be no conflict of interest. David had been the logical candidate to succeed him, but the old son of a bitch had tortured him for weeks before he finally approached him.

'You passed the test,' he told David on his last day at the office. 'You played a cool hand. No complaining. You carried on with your work as though nothing was happening. See, David, I had to find out if there'd be a difficult transition and you'd fold up.'

David would have liked to cut his throat, but he merely smiled humbly.

'Victor, I appreciate the confidence you've shown in me.'

'Well, VCA is your baby now.'

'Are you sure you're right in going to GIF?'

Victor's eyes glinted malevolently.

'I can't turn the job down. Every agent in this town dreams of running a studio and turning it around, especially a dump like General who've made nothing but shit and associates for years. Quality will sell. The other thing that's irresistible is sitting behind a desk and being in a position to say "fuck you!" to all the people who've given me a hard time. Actors and directors who came to interview *me* to see if I'd be right to represent them and then walked out to other agents. They're going to come to me for work with their tongues hanging out and, David, am I going to shove it to them.'

The industry would soon have an opportunity to judge how successful he had been in gauging the public's taste. A sneak preview of his first film would be held in a few weeks at Grauman's Chinese Theater.

'We've got a garden table,' David said to his brother. 'Tim likes exposure.' He looked at his gold Piaget. 'He's due in ten minutes but stars are always late, so we can talk for a while. Now do me a favor and explain what the hell you're doing here with Frances?'

'Charlie suckered me into it. But Frances and I had it out this morning. Shit, what a mess. This time it's really over.'

419

'Dummy, you should have married her years ago. You don't know what's good for you.' He picked up a white phone and told the hotel operator to put through any calls from his office.

'Have you got the deal with Avery?'

'Not yet. But I brought agency papers with me. He signs or he leaves legless. Jonathan, what are you prepared to pay for him?'

'A million for five seasons. Charlie got the other directors to go for it.'

'Okay, I can get lots of mileage out of this.'

Avery made his entrance and all heads turned in his direction. He had the blond California good looks that had put him on the covers of sports magazines, and Jonathan knew that he could be the cornerstone of the franchise and give the new league instant credibility. Waiters and strangers surrounded him. Everyone was accustomed to film stars, but the man considered the finest basketball player in the nation awed even the jaded regulars at the Polo Lounge. He headed to the table, a permanent smile on his lips, his long straight hair over his left eye. He might have been polished by a jeweler's rouge. But like all perfect human specimens, there was a singular lack of charm about him. It was as though the gods had finally run out of ideas during his composition.

He sat down between them and not at the place setting. 'I like to face the room.' He shook hands with them in turn and peered distantly across the garden at a girl miming an invitation which she sent over a moment later on a cocktail napkin. 'Another blow job,' he advised them. He ordered a large orange juice and for a moment the awkward provincial boy emerged from the hard shell. 'I'm very flattered that you want to represent me, David.'

'Tim, this is an unusual situation, me dealing with my brother, but since the papers have reported your problems with Philadelphia, we all know that you've turned down their offer of seven hundred and fifty thousand dollars. I can do better,' David said.

'With them?' Tim asked.

'No, with Jonathan.'

'Jonathan, did you bring your checkbook?' Tim asked.

'Naturally. You're the new girl in town and everybody wants a screw. Give David a big smile and he'll have you

420

selling toothpaste on TV next week at five thousand a pop plus residuals.'

'Are you serious?'

'The tip of the iceberg,' David replied. He propped his case on the table and pulled out a memo pad with a list of names. 'Tim, let me establish my position. I'm going to make you the best deal ever made in basketball. But before I can legally represent you, you'll have to sign agency papers. Now why should you do that and pay me ten percent? Because with me you'll make more money in the off-season than you do playing basketball. I'll merchandise you. You shave, well Gillette wants you to sell their blades. Colgate wants you to brush your teeth with their toothpaste. Ford would rather have you driving their cars than anyone else's. Wheaties needs you to eat their cereal. Voit will make your signature basketball, and Keds will design sneakers made to your specifications. The key to this is New York. The Knicks can't draft you because Philadelphia has the rights to you. So you can forget about the NBA if you don't play for Philly. In ten years you'll be thirty, a veteran. You may have slowed down. Your future's uncertain. Who knows, maybe you'll have a freak injury – a knee goes.'

'My blood's curdling,' Tim said.

'What David's saying is that even if you're in a wheelchair there'll be thousands of dollars coming in for the rest of your life.'

'I want you to have acting lessons,' David picked up, 'so that when you're through playing ball you'll have another career waiting for you with an audience primed for you instead of selling insurance in San Bernardino.'

When the phone rang, David handed the agency papers to Tim to study while he settled a dispute with a writer and producer who were threatening to leave a film.

'Suppose I put myself on the open market?' Tim asked.

'You won't get the press coverage in San Francisco or, God forbid, Detroit or Cincinnati. You'll make the same money but New York is where the big bucks are.'

'David, suppose I sign?'

'Then we open negotiations and see if we can hammer out a deal with Jonathan now.'

Tim asked for a pen and was handed David's gold Parker. 'Okay, you got yourself a client.' Tim listened with growing excitement as the two men went at each other like tigers. He couldn't believe they were brothers.

'If Tim has any legal problems with Philadelphia, we would expect you to pay all attorney's fees.'

'Since he's jumping leagues, how can they sue him? No one can prevent him from playing ball, earning a living outside the NBA.'

'Jonathan, neither of us is a lawyer.'

'Look, Warren Berliner, my attorney, gave me his legal opinion. It would be a nuisance suit and would be dismissed.'

'A hundred thousand then, in the event of litigation.'

'You've got it. And we're prepared to offer Tim one million for five seasons.'

David fell silent and Tim waited apprehensively for him to accept. Philadelphia had held firm to their offer of seven hundred and fifty thousand.

'Tim, frankly, it's awkward to conduct a negotiation with a client present, but since I never want you to think that I sold you down the river because Jonathan's my brother, I'm going to insist that you be the one to make up your mind. You call the shots.'

'I just don't know.'

Jonathan realized he had to put the squeeze on.

'Look, I'm not crazy, David. You can't shop my offer and then come back to me. If you want Tim playing in Kansas City or Portland, then take him there. Let him collect his clippings from the *Star* instead of *The New York Times*. Not to mention the sports show I'd fix for him. You want him to sell products, he's got to be in L.A. or New York, not the boondocks.'

'How long will your offer hold?' David asked.

'Till I leave the table.'

'Tim?'

'Well, it looks like I'm playing for the Scimitars.'

'You'll report on Monday. We're training a month early because we've got a bunch of guys who never played together and I hope you're in shape. You'll do us all a favor by saving up your blow jobs till the season's over.'

David made notes while he nibbled at his salad.

'Now let's get down to the crunch. If Tim's injured during the period of his contract, we have to have a clause that he still gets paid.'

'If we're talking about him missing a few games, well, that's realistic. But if he breaks a bone or needs knee surgery and sits out a season, then we can hardly be expected to pay full salary. We'll pay fifty percent and all medical expenses. Furthermore, he gets two thousand a month living expenses and I'll even throw in an apartment.'

'I want a no-trade clause,' David insisted.

'The man's paying me a million bucks, why would he trade me?' Tim asked.

'Let's say you have four great seasons and another team is prepared to pay two or three million dollars for your services. Why should Jonathan pocket the money? It's like the old studio deals on loaning out stars. You pay someone what seems to be big money. A hundred thousand a year guaranteed, and then you loan him out to other studios for a couple of films at three or four hundred thousand a hit and you wind up making money without ever going to your pocket.'

'David, you're being unreasonable.'

'Just trying to protect my client. Jonathan, let's split the difference. If Tim gets traded for anything in excess of one million dollars, after recouping your investment, he should share fifty-fifty with you.'

'We've got a deal.'

'Just like that?' Tim asked in astonishment. 'What if Jonathan backs down or withdraws?'

David smiled. 'Well, I pretend he's not my brother and sue the ass off him. My dear Tim, nine hundred thousand dollars may be a lot of money to you, but believe me, my hundred thousand commission is simply a fortune to me, so we'll collect. Right, brother?'

While they waited for their cars at the entrance. Tim's battered Chevy was set apart from the flood of Cadillacs and Rolls-Royces in the driveway as though it might cause a plague.

'Why don't you get your client a decent set of wheels, big shot?'

'How about a new Thunderbird every year if we take Ford's offer?' David asked Tim, grabbing his parking ticket and tipping the carhop for him.

'White?'

'Any color you like and a mink coat to go with it,' David

said ebulliently as Tim got into his wreck.

'You were very convincing,' Jonathan informed hi⟨s⟩
brother.

'Convincing? I tore your eyes out. You wouldn't have
gone any higher' – David stared quizzically at Jonathan –
'would you?' Jonathan raised two fingers and Davi⟨d⟩
blanched. 'Two million. I don't believe you. You're a goddamn liar.'

'You didn't ask, so how would you know? Tim's marquee
value. Without him I've got just five guys in a track meet.
David, I'm going straight out to the airport. Will you cal⟨l⟩
Charlie with the terms and ask him to hold off any pres⟨s⟩
releases until I get back to New York?'

Elusive, unpredictable, David felt robbed of his brother'⟨s⟩
company. They saw each other so infrequently now. Family
reunions once a year in New York and the occasional flying
visit never lasting more than a few hours. Jonathan worrie⟨d⟩
him. Always in motion, a bird that never came to rest. Th⟨e⟩
years were passing rapidly and still Jonathan was so deepl⟨y⟩
submerged in his business that he appeared to be living in ⟨a⟩
vacuum he had constructed for himself.

'Can't you stay for a day or two?' he asked.

'Not now.'

'Where are you running?'

'To see a girl.'

'Is it serious.'

'Christ, I hope so ... this time.'

The doorman honked the horn of his car which was blocking the driveway and he dashed to it.

'I've missed you,' David called out, but his brother wa⟨s⟩
already out of earshot. 'I've missed you,' he repeated t⟨o⟩
himself.

Thirty-two

Jonathan checked into the Ritz-Carlton and was given a room which overlooked Boston Common. He tried Sandy's number repeatedly but there was no answer. He stretched out on the sofa, forgot to eat the sandwich he had ordered, and dozed off. He awoke at midnight, disoriented by the time change and his strange surroundings. He again called her number. He had sent a telegram from the L.A. airport, but obviously she hadn't got it. Then he recalled her mentioning that the orchestra was playing a series of concerts throughout New England. She might have been in Tanglewood, or at the music festival in New Hampshire, and it was too late to get any information from the booking office.

At two in the morning his phone rang.

'I'm in the lobby. I told the switchboard it was an emergency and they put me through.'

'Can you come up?'

'I'll ask.'

'If there's any problem, I'll get dressed and we'll go to your place.'

He switched on the lights, caught a glimpse of his haggard, pink, sun-blotched face, and went to the door when the bell sounded. Sandy was a pale, slight, lean girl with dark chestnut hair. Her eyes were a mixture of sorrel and brown, set wide apart, and her face had the imperturbable self-possession that one sometimes came across in religious paintings. She was still wearing the cream satin blouse and long black skirt that was orchestra dress.

Her fingers touched his face tentatively and she pressed her lips against his.

'I didn't expect you,' she said withdrawing from him. 'We got in from Pittsfield just a while ago, and I found your telegram.'

She was one of the few women who never appeared to be in a hurry. Perhaps it was because she reserved her passions for music rather than people.

He caressed her hair. 'I couldn't stay away.'

She blushed and the veins in her neck throbbed. 'I've been thinking about you all week long,' Sandy said. 'I thought of calling you, but I didn't want to disturb you. Would it be a problem for me to stay here with you?'

'I don't think so.'

'Hotels like this can sometimes be funny about women. I'd love to have a bath,' she said as though the request required special permission.

She took nothing for granted. He wondered if she had developed this attitude during the years she was the mistress of the married teacher she had studied composition with at Juilliard. He had been her only lover, and when they parted there was no question in her mind that he would return to his wife and children. She had remained unattached until meeting Jonathan. She was twenty-seven, entirely self-contained, and in the months they had been seeing each other, she had never attempted to establish any claim on him.

It seemed she had never remotely considered the odd chemistry of their coming together or the possibility of falling in love. As she stooped to turn on the bath taps, he stroked the long arch of her spine.

'Are you coming in with me?'

'I thought it was just Europeans like my parents who still took baths.' He thought with amusement of the large sack of Epsom salts, the eccentric-shaped bottles of oils and gels that surrounded his parents' tub. Sandy wrapped a hand towel around her hair and he leaned over, kissing her on the neck and mouth. She always waited docilely for him to make the first move, never presuming to take the initiative, even though she was more responsive and sensitive than any woman he'd ever been with. Her tact neutralized his naturally aggressive instincts, raising him to a new level of consciousness. Her skin responded to his touch with a reflexive shiver. Slender, with small breasts, her delicacy was almost a wound in her character, and when they climbed into the tub, he kissed her forehead and her exquisitely shaped lips. He had no doubt that for once in his life he was acting out of free will.

'Are you going to stay in Boston for a while?' he asked.

He couldn't keep his hands off her and held her against him.

'We've got a few weeks off. Then we go up to New Hampshire for the music festival.'

'Did you make any plans?'

'Nothing definite. I thought I might go home to Maine and spend some time with my parents ... and, well, think about my future plans.'

He observed her retreat and it disturbed him to think she could be evasive with him. But she hardly owed him any explanations.

'Have you been offered something with another orchestra?'

'No ... I wouldn't think of leaving Koussevitzky ... it's something personal.' Her head was bowed, her fingers toying with soap bubbles.

'Sandy, what is it? Have I upset you in some way?'

'Of course not ... it's just that ... I don't want you to feel as though you've been boxed in.'

'How? I'm here – we both are – because we choose to be.'

'Jonathan' – she raised her face and gazed resolutely at him – 'I'm pregnant. I think it must've happened the first time we made love. We both had a bit too much to drink and, well, I'm not blaming you or myself for that matter. These things happen. But I'm afraid. I've got my career to think of, and I'm not really sure whether I ought to have the baby and try to manage or go for an abortion. I could get a leave of absence.'

His hand touched her stomach. The thought of her carrying his child galvanized him.

'Did marriage ever cross your mind?'

She sighed deeply, twined her long graceful fingers in his.

'You're too good to be saddled with something like this. No, marriage isn't the alternative. And please understand, I'm not sorry for myself. I'm not some abandoned woman with no one to turn to. My parents are good people. I know that my mother would agree to look after the baby if I had it, and I could go back to the orchestra.'

'Sandy, Sandy, don't you think I'm entitled to *my* rights?'

His vehemence startled her.

'Naturally, but under the circumstances marriage strikes me as improper. It's not as though we were kids and you've got to do the right thing by me. It's been wonderful knowing you, the happiest collision of my life outside of music. We're

427

such an unlikely pair.' She smiled, holding his hands to her breast. 'Music to you is Frank Sinatra. And sports to me are equally meaningless.'

'I'm not asking you to study batting averages or become an expert in basketball.'

'I know that ... and I'm not suggesting that you run out and buy Beethoven's symphonies.'

'But you love me – just a little?'

She flicked some water at him with her index finger, playfully, like a child. 'Where I come from, a declaration of love isn't usually a question.'

'I love you and I'd like you to marry me,' he said unwaveringly, looking at her to gauge her reaction.

'I thought you might ... that it would come to this. But don't you think you're being unfair to yourself? You see, I don't think I'd be happy living on the scale you do. Chauffeurs, maids, expensive restaurants. I don't want to talk to caterers about menus for parties or to traipse around guests as the charming, well-organized hostess seeing that everyone's glass is full and insisting on their trying the quiche Lorraine. Yet, that's the kind of woman you ought to marry. Really, Jonathan, I'm a very private person. I have no great ambition or special causes to convert other people to. I enjoy my solitude.'

'Does that mean you don't love me?'

'No. The fact is that I adore you. I don't understand half the things you do. Your energy level intimidates me. You're one of those elemental forces of nature that I used to read about. A man of destiny, a builder, and all I really want for myself is quiet, no great peaks of happiness or depressions. ... The idea of having a child and being married to you or anyone somehow overwhelms me.'

All during the night, watching the placid, beautiful face, the dark hair blanketing the pillow, he could not accept that the life she was carrying inside her could be denied him. He ran his fingers across her belly, imagining he could detect the swell of the forming child. She was afraid of change, but she didn't need to be afraid he would change her.

At breakfast later that morning, he was unnaturally quiet. He drank black coffee and chain-smoked.

'I didn't mean to upset you, Jonathan.' She fondled his hand. 'I just hate to play games or lead people on. I'm no

428

good at it anyway.'

'Would you marry me if you weren't pregnant?'

'Well, there wouldn't be any coercion.'

'Sandy, suppose I was in favor of your having an abortion on the understanding that we got married afterward?'

'Are you serious?'

'I'm in your hands. But please don't sell me short. You can throw all the obstacles you like at me if you don't feel the same way I do, but at least give me credit for being honest about us. We could both do with some time out of town. You want to see your folks. Would they object if I came with you?'

'You don't have to sell yourself to them.'

'I'm not selling myself to anyone. I'd like to meet them. They sound open-minded, and maybe it is a good idea to talk it over with them. Not that you need any advice, but before you kill *our* baby, it wouldn't do any harm to think over the consequences.'

'Jonathan, don't put it like that.' Her eyes were perplexed by the severity of his remark.

'Then why are you tearing your life apart? Couldn't you go back to playing after you had the baby? You started out playing chamber music in a quartet. Don't they have quartets in New York? Doesn't New York have symphony orchestras, music schools? Don't musicians get married, have children, and still play?'

Tears filled her eyes, and she wiped them with the back of her hand.

'This is awful,' she protested. 'I'm not used to crying. Since I've been pregnant the least thing sets me off. I hate not having any control.'

'Sandy, if you can honestly look at me and say that you don't care, then I'll leave and never bother you again.'

'I'll tell my folks we're coming.'

* * *

Jonathan rented a convertible Oldsmobile and they stopped off at Sandy's apartment so that she could pick up some clothes. He listened while she telephoned her mother, explaining that she was bringing a man home. 'Someone special . . .'

It was the first time he had been in her apartment. She had

always met him at hotels or flown down to New York and stayed at his place. He felt like an intruder. It was a one-bedroom apartment with a small terrace, immaculately clean and orderly. Music scores layered the top of the piano and alongside it were two metal music stands. She collected old pieces of pottery and had framed posters and concert programs along most of the wall space. Her records stretched across the room on eye-level shelves. There were herbs growing in old tea tins.

He heard the peal of her laughter as she responded to some remark her mother made. He stood at the threshold of her bedroom. She slept in a queen-sized four-poster with a canopy and matching yellow challis bedspread. The walls were lined with family photographs. In the background he saw a harbor, a sign of Falmouth, and fishing boats. Near the bedroom door was a photograph of Serge Koussevitzky inscribed: 'To Sandy Wells, my lovely fiddle, Affectionately, S.K."

Her face was suffused with elfin gaiety when she hung up the phone.

'You've given my mother a reason to bake. Maine lobsters and corn for dinner. We should get there by seven if we leave now.'

'Are you happy?'

'Very.'

'You didn't tell her, did you?'

'I thought I'd wait till I got home. But I've never brought anyone to meet them before. My mother just went on and on.'

'Did you put everything together,' he asked with wonderment, 'in the apartment?'

'Uh-huh.'

'Incredible. At least I'll know who to call if the sink leaks or I need some carpentry.'

'I grew up in a fishing village. My father had one boat when I was a kid and we all had to learn how to do things with our hands – clean the catch, repair the nets, and set the lobster pots. We all worked together. It's still a family business. My brothers work with Dad. I guess they aren't terribly adventurous. They come down to Boston once a year, but they've never been to New York or anywhere else. My grandmother was the piano teacher in town and she taught me how to play, then I went on to violin and viola....'

She seemed to drift back through the years as they drove
along the coast road, the thick clouds burning off in the late
morning, the squall of gulls alighting on the beaches jammed
at Marblehead. Every now and then he glanced away from
the road to gaze at the fine-boned, delicate face, as she transported him back to her magical childhood, dances at the
school, musical evenings on Sundays.

As though Sandy weren't enough, he had also fallen in
love with her memories, her past, and the rhythms that
governed and shaped her. It was nothing less than a miracle
that this sweet, warm woman was harboring his child. He
felt reborn himself, in touch with the harmonies of life.

He thought about Frances for a moment, but with no
qualms. He had not misled her, not lied to her. She had
forced herself on him, refusing to accept the truth. He was
confident that she would overcome her disappointment. In
any event, Charlie was responsible for the fiasco in California,
and when he returned to New York he would set matters
right with him.

The towns rolled by – Kittery Point, York Harbor – all
with a touch of English seaside, the air permeated by sea
spray as off the coast yawls and ketches whipped in the wind
at crazy angles. He drove without a shirt, and they ate giant
hoagies and drank beer which they bought at a roadside stand
outside of Portland.

They reached Falmouth at dusk. Boats were coming into
port, horns tooting, sliding past each other in the narrow
channel. They parked on a bluff, got out of the car, and
leaned over the concrete embankment, arms around each
other's waists. She pointed out the slips used for the four
Wells boats. Below them were boatyards with men scraping
hulls and at the end of the pier a weather-beaten shack used
by the harbor master. Running beyond the road was a double
railroad track, and he noticed a group of boys ensconced
above them on a hill and he was thrust back to his childhood.

'Do they still have books to record engine numbers? When
we were living in Munich my brother used to collect them
after school.'

'They throw stones nowadays,' Sandy said, pushing her
windblown hair out of her eyes. 'Just a local milk train on

431

this route now. . . .' She paused and regarded him quizzically. 'Did you say Munich?'

'München,' he said in German.

'Really?'

'Yeah, we got out in 1938.'

'You're a European; I never would have guessed. Have you been back since the war was over?' she asked excitedly, as though his place of birth had given him a cultural pedigree which invited new respect.

'No. I don't think I'll ever want to see it again.'

'You don't like talking about it.'

His flight across Germany intruded on him unexpectedly. Lenore in the back of the car . . . bleeding.

'Let's go meet your folks.'

The family house was a large, sprawling Cape Cod in a cul-de-sac at the end of a small street. A rusted Chevy pickup was parked outside the garage. From the garden Falmouth Bay could be seen. As he carried the two suitcases down the uneven flagstone path, he felt a flutter of nerves. The Wells family would be appraising him. He was a boy again about to be tested.

Her father insisted on relieving him of the suitcases after they had shaken hands. Bob Wells's hands were as coarse as sandpaper and torn from hook cuts. He was tall, with a thick clump of white hair, his skin the color of saddleskin, his shoulders broad, and he wore denim overalls.

Jonathan was given a room with dormer windows, low-eaved, which had obviously been occupied by one of Sandy's brothers, for school pictures and a photograph of a boy holding a large fish on the deck of a boat hung over the iron bedstead. A tarnished brass telescope set on a tripod was angled out at the bay.

'I guess Sandy must be serious about you,' Bob Wells said in a friendly voice.

'I hope so.'

After showering and changing his clothes, he joined Sandy's parents in the living room which was paneled with old barnwood and filled with mementos of the sea. In a way he felt as though he were entering America for the first time.

The temperature had dropped, and Alma Wells was on her knees fixing kindling for a fire. She wiped her hands on a striped blue apron and her mouth puckered into a smile. She was a plump, handsome woman in her sixties, with a sun-lined face and alert sparrow eyes. She took both of his hands in hers and invited him to sit at the window seat so that he could watch the sunset reflect on the bay. Bob brought him a glass with about four fingers of neat Scotch. Jonathan was entranced by the warmth exuded by the two of them.

A few moments later Sandy came downstairs, dressed in faded Levi's and a fisherman's knit turtleneck sweater. When she saw Jonathan in his cream Palm Beach linen slacks and his white-on-white patterned shirt, she laughed.

'At long last a Sulka shirt appears in our living room. The first ever.'

'I'll have to remember the next time I travel that it's not to the Beverly Hills Hotel.'

'Are Frank and Dennis coming over?'

'They'll be here for coffee. We didn't want Jonathan to think we were ganging up on him,' Bob replied.

'See,' Jonathan said banteringly, making room for Sandy at the window, 'everyone thought you were on the shelf.'

'Well, we did wonder,' her mother said. 'Sandy's always been a loner.'

After declining a second drink, Jonathan made a call to his office. He wrote down a long list of messages, but the only one that concerned him was an urgent one from Paul. Still, Paul could wait and so could his business. It was his time now.

He was persuaded by Bob to have another drink, and he went into the kitchen, brushing past the two bustling women secure in their domesticity. He chipped some ice off a block, and when he ran the water over it in the sink, four greenish-black, seaweed-covered lobsters gyrated listlessly under the cold spray, claws moving in a helpless pavanne. The women surged past him, carrying in hot biscuits, a mound of butter, and occasionally Alma inserted a large wooden spoon to stir the chowder bubbling in a cast-iron pot on the range.

Bob made no effort to ferret information out of him, but sat silently in a deep worn chair facing the fire, drink in hand as the tongues of flame snared the dry wood. Jonathan relaxed. Her parents had taken him at face value. He was *with* Sandy, credentials enough. He divined no undercurrents, no fears of a misalliance.

433

Bob lent him a large oversize sweater when Jonathan accompanied him outside to stir the coals on the barbecue. Bob carried a thick fork and a tray of buttered corn cobs which he wrapped in foil, setting them on the edges of the grate to let them smoke. Below them thundering crescendos of waves reverberated as they bit into the rocky shoals. A beam revolved intermittently from the lighthouse beyond the channel.

'You may as well know ... Sandy hasn't agreed to marry me,' Jonathan said as the two stood at the edge of the garden. Gristles of sand thrashed against the stone windbreak.

'Is it worrying you?' Bob asked gently.

'Well, I've got to admit that I feel kind of off balance.'

'From what I know of Sandy, she isn't the sort who leads people on. She made a commitment to become a professional musician and it just might be that she's now discovered there's more to life than a career, no matter how fulfilling her music is.'

'Does she want to see just what you think of me or how I fit in?'

'I doubt it. Maybe she's trying to bring together her childhood with what she is now. Fuse it. But, Jonathan, the less time you spend figuring out women's motives the saner you'll be,' he added.

They dined leisurely on raw clams with hot biscuits, thick chowder, drinking beer between courses. From time to time when Bob was outside basting the lobsters and Alma was in the kitchen, Jonathan gazed across at Sandy, enchanted by this woman he wanted for his own. Although she looked back at him with affection, something else played on her mind, some heightened anticipation of things to come.

'My mother's fallen for you.'

'How about you?'

'Me? Oh, I'm easy,' she said, her eyes on the front door. 'You're very different since you've come.'

'Your parents've made me feel comfortable. I don't have to prove anything. New York's a long way from here.'

'I think you're starting to understand what I was talking about.'

He reached across the square table, barely touching the

434

tips of her fingers. It was hard for him to conceive how he could sleep the night under the same roof without her beside him. But it did not occur to him to formulate any plan. The Wells house was not the place for hatching plots, no matter how romantic the inclination.

At about nine, when they were sated with lobster but still anticipating Alma's deep-dish pie, Sandy's brothers and their wives arrived. In the excitement of the reunion, the chatter, the promises of visits not kept, the tinkle of brandy glasses, the family gathered closely together, swapping names of old friends who had moved, died, changed wives, he felt like an outsider cut off from her. Their music, the constellation binding them was for him a denial of his rights. He had expected boisterous, half-drunk fishermen who arm-wrestled for amusement, sports fanatics who would fall on him for inside information on athletes they only read about in the sports pages. Frank, the eldest, bearded, a squat man with the stark gray eyes of an anchorite, spoke in a sonorous low voice. He fished for a living and played the cello for the good of his soul. Dennis, a few years Sandy's senior, was the friendlier of the two, but after a moment of polite conversation, he turned back to his sister and with her approval went to the hall cupboard and quickly assembled music stands rusted from the salt air, then wiped off bridge chairs whose seats were dank with mildew.

The brothers had brought along their instruments, and with Alma's pie growing cold on the uncleared dining table, Dennis arranged the chairs and stands in an arc while Alma lifted up the storage seat of the piano and handed out scores.

After apologizing for being out of practice, they took their seats: Alma and Dennis on violin, Frank tuning his cello, and Sandy on viola, the princess at court.

Jonathan stood back, intimidated by the prodigal display of talent. The brothers' wives sat like widows on the sofa, knitting. At the beginning of Debussy's String Quartet there was some disharmony and a confusion of timing, but as they progressed, the color of the thematic lines, clear, mellifluous in its profusion of melody, fused the instruments.

With his brandy glass tightly clamped, Jonathan retreated unnoticed into a corner of the room. It was not so much a case of being out of his element, but a strong feeling of rejection. He had heard the piece before. Casting his mind back, he recalled a day on the river with Lenore when they had beached their canoe and listened to the same music. The epiphany of a time warp enclosed him, upsetting his equilibrium.

Sandy's eyes were closed, and as her fingers ran nimbly over the strings, the bow crossing mournfully, he knew that in her was a depth of feeling which she could never hope to share with him. When she opened her eyes, glancing for an instant at him in the shadows, she revealed a spirit of intimacy which had been denied to him even when they had been making love.

They continued to play after he had gone upstairs. He lay on the narrow bed, imprisoned by loneliness, the smell of salt air clinging to the blankets. Gradually the music became lower and the dreams took over. He saw David sitting on the railroad siding, book in hand, the student of locomotives, while he rushed off to meet Lenore at the boathouse, clutching his sweat-stained, crumpled marks.

He woke with a shudder when Alma entered his room at seven in the morning. She carried a tray with a pot of coffee and a plate of toast. She sat down on the edge of the bed.

'I didn't mean to startle you. Sandy looked in on you before she went out and she didn't want to disturb you.'

'Where'd she go?' He propped himself up on his elbow and lit his first bitter cigarette of the day. 'She didn't leave?' he asked, somewhat shrilly.

'No.' She poured two cups of coffee and offered him sugar and cream. 'She's gone out on the boat with Bob and her brothers. It's been years since she's had the chance. They were up most of the night ... and when Frank suggested it, she jumped at the chance. It seems she needs some time on her own.'

He rubbed his bleary eyes and regarded Alma's stolid face with anxiety.

'Would she like me to leave?'

'No ...' A note of doubt he thought. 'And Bob and I wouldn't think of it,' she replied.

'Then what's the problem?'

'I suppose by coming home and seeing all of us she thought some solution to her predicament would present itself.'

'Am I the predicament?'

'Partly, and the other is having the baby.'

'I appreciate your honesty,' he said severely. 'Do you have any influence over her?'

'About as much as you do. . . . Sandy can't be stampeded.'

'So I've discovered. If you were in my position, what would you do?'

'I'd stay.'

He spent part of the morning wandering around town in frustration. He bought a couple of pairs of jeans, some work shirts, and a pair of tennis sneakers at a local Levi, Sweet-Orr general store and then drove down to the harbor. Falmouth Bay was like a strand of frayed rope cowled in a gray veil, but beyond the breakwater the open sea foamed a diffuse blue-green. He drank his lunch at a bar near the jetty. What, he wondered, could Sandy be thinking out there on the boat with her brothers? Had she devised some test by which to judge his steadfastness?

He made his way out to the pier, passing trawlers unloading herring and cod. At a slip he stopped by a sign which read WELLS AND SONS. Boats hacking black spumes of smoke, engines bellowing and roiling, chugged into port. He sat on the edge of the pier and drank the bottle of beer he had bought and stared down at the oil-slick water. In the distance three boats steamed around the breakwater, then cut their speed and idled gradually toward the dock. Squinting, he made out the name Wells on one of them. He was encouraged by the waves of two men on deck – her brothers.

At the wheel above deck in a sheltered control house, he saw his viola player easing the boat into the slip. Her concentration could not be diverted and he waited patiently for recognition. Bob shouted, 'Cut it now, honey . . .' The engine died and Frank and Dennis, with grapples, speared the pier, leaped off, and made fast the ropes to large metal rings. Behind the boat the water exploded when the anchor was winched down. Most of the deck was filled with spiny lobsters trailing moss and seaweed.

'We had a really good day,' Sandy said to him when she jumped ashore. 'I brought them luck . . .' She averted her eyes. Her skin was windblown dry and her lips were caked. 'Jonathan, you were so peaceful this morning I didn't want to wake you. You smell of booze.' She thrust her arms around

437

his neck. 'I love you so; how're you going to put up with me?'

He clasped his arms around her and kissed her in full view of the men.

'I know it's Falmouth, but is there some place we can find to go to bed?'

On Sunday they were married by a justice of the peace in the Wells garden. It was a clear day, and the sun glinted in his eyes as he joined hands with her. He had bought a navy blue suit and two plain gold wedding bands in Portland. Sandy wore a simple white linen dress and a wide Panama hat with a white veil, and when he lifted it to kiss her, it was with such tender reverence that he thought he'd break down. Eyes closed, he drifted for an instant in time to that high place he had always dreamed of but never seemed able to discover in the quest for himself.

When they settled in at his apartment late that night she felt uncomfortable. Disquieting echoes seemed to cling to the place. And when he started explaining how the finances would work – she would have her own checking account, charges at any stores she selected, a complete new wardrobe – she fell into a morose silence. Yes, she could keep the apartment in Boston and he would pay the rent, but he insisted on her visiting a gynaecologist before she rejoined the orchestra and they would have to be told that she was having a baby.

It all came at her so fast that when she finally climbed into bed she felt exhausted and battered. She found herself retreating from him. Yet when he touched her, his loving gentleness returned. He rubbed her belly with coconut oil, and as she began to doze she heard him say:

'You won't have any stretch marks. I'm going to do this every night.... It's two in the morning. Should I call my folks and David? We've got to arrange some kind of reception for my people.' But she was asleep, and when he closed his eyes finally, he realized that he needed to be more gentle with her. It was natural for him to treat people in an authoritative fashion. He had to guard against this with Sandy.

438

Thirty-three

Machado dropped him off at Charlie's office, but as he breezed past Charlie's secretary and the woman became flustered, muttering that Charlie was in conference, Jonathan bluntly asked, 'Since when do I have to wait?'

When Jonathan entered the office, Charlie leaped from his desk and shouted, 'Didn't I say never to let *him* in.' The secretary burst into tears and Jonathan was so startled that he gesticulated futilely, then froze. He detected the presence of another man in the room, sitting with his back to him in a deep wing chair, but his attention was riveted on Charlie.

'What's wrong with you?'

'Ey, since when don't you return calls, big shot,' Paul said, moving between the two of them. Jonathan was stunned.

'Pau – li?' he asked, as though to confirm that he was not in the throes of some nightmare.

'Yeah. Now, Charlie, he's got a right to be here an I couldn't care less about how you feel personally. I've sat down at the table with people who've tried to kill my wife. So let's cut this shit out and wrap everything up.'

Charlie brandished his fist, then slowly let it fall to his side. 'You fucking shit,' he snarled, 'what the hell did you do to Frances?' Before he could respond, Charlie's head dropped and he moaned so bereftly that again Jonathan was paralyzed. 'She stuck her head in the oven.'

'Jesus,' he muttered, 'I didn't –'

'You didn't what? If not for the Mexican couple coming back, she'd be dead. She was barely breathing. She was in a coma for two days.'

'Charlie, I'm sorry.'

'You're sorry. What made you hurt her so badly that she'd do such a thing?' he asked.

'Is she going to be all right?'

'She'll live. Why, why, why, Jonathan?' Charlie pleaded.

'I told her I was in love with another girl. I just married her.'

'I hope you'll make her as happy as you did Frances.'

439

'Charlie, please, you know I went away with Frances for your sake...'

'You went to get Avery, so don't lie!'

Charlie moved uncertainly back to his desk and sagged into his high leather chair. Then, utterly crushed, his voice shaking, he presented his case to Paul.

'There was no difference in how I felt about Jonathan and Frances. I loved this boy as though he were my own. Anything he wanted I gave him. Bank credit, contacts, property. He wanted to take over that hotel in the Catskills, well, I fixed it so he could. I gave him his head, never interfered. Yes, I tested him. Deliver a million dollars on your own and you're my partner, I said. Split down the middle. But if he didn't put up a nickel I would've backed him because my daughter loved him.' Tears streamed down Charlie's cheeks.

'A million dollars arrives out of the blue. For Christ's sake, he must think he's playing Little League ball with me. I insisted that my man at Morgan take down every serial number. We traced all of it to Nassau. Paul, I found out it was your money and I knew that the choice tickets to all the Arena's events were going to your ticket agency.' His eyes glinted angrily at Jonathan. 'It suited me to do nothing. I just wanted you happy. You beat the odds. When we had union trouble you were the one to straighten it out. You had a strong connection and they weren't going up against Paul.'

Jonathan was a model of civility. 'Charlie, I didn't marry Frances because I don't love her enough to be the husband she deserves.'

'Someone better than you,' he said, flaring again.

'Why did you drag Pauli in when this is between us?'

'Jonathan, what I gave I'm taking back! If I could bury you I would without a second thought. You burned your options with Frances.'

Paul stirred himself as though out of a deep sleep.

'Jonathan, we're in a boxcar. Charlie's got a report which he can turn over to the commission office at the ABA on our involvement. You'll be declared unfit to be associated with the Scimitars. I been sittin in a fuckin hotel for days waitin for you to show up.'

'I'm out – just like that?' Jonathan asked with disbelief. 'Charlie, you can't do this to me.'

'It's been done,' Charlie replied vehemently.

440

'If you try to fight it, then everyone'll come after me,' Paul informed him. 'FBI, Justice Department ... and my *own* people. And that puts my head on the block. My associates are nervous as it is with the publicity I've had. Jonathan, if I fall, I'll never make prison. Gambino and Vito would have me hammered because I'm against them now. They'd think I'd expose them.' He spoke with such candor that it hardly seemed possible to Jonathan that Charlie Packard was present. 'If I go, then you're next,' he noted firmly. 'It's business, see? We come unstuck. No way Charlie can be taken out. *Your* friend Gardner knows. Charlie's prepared to deal. Our end stinks. We cop a walk and Gardner turns over the report on the money you invested.'

It was inconceivable to Jonathan that everything he had striven for should collapse this way. What did the years he had put in add up to?

'After all we've been through, Charlie, does it come down to personalities?'

'It comes down to my daughter sticking her head in an oven. You're married now. Maybe if you ever have a child and watch it suffer and bleed before your eyes, you'll understand.'

What could Jonathan say to this man – and what could he salvage of their partnership? Was Charlie going to throw him out after all he had done for the Arena? Who else would travel the hundreds of thousands of miles he had, visiting the chairmen of companies, persuading them to hold their annual conventions at the Arena? More than a third of their income came from this source, but that wouldn't matter to Charlie. He'd write off the loss – as he was writing off Jonathan. And all because Frances had been told the truth.

And Jonathan was right. Charlie conducted the meeting directly with Paul, as if he didn't even exist.

'Four million for his share of the Arena?' Paul asked incredulously.

'I turn the paper of West's Hotel over to him. They've missed their payments for four months. Unless someone comes up with the money, the bank will move in and take over. Another of Jonathan's adventures that didn't pay off, but I backed him.'

'Pauli, this is robbery,' Jonathan interrupted. 'The Arena is worthy twenty-two million, and we're averaging fifteen thousand a minute on television time. With the Scimitars it'll go up to thirty thousand.'

'What do we do, sue him?'

'So I've lost even my television time which I split with you as an act of goodwill,' Jonathan charged Charlie.

'Isn't it clear to you yet that you're out? You have no bargaining position. The only reason I'm paying you four million is so that it looks like a legitimate transaction for the IRS. Otherwise, I'd give you nothing. Another one of his follies,' he continued: 'On Jonathan's recommendation we bought five hundred acres of unfilled land outside of Monmouth at a thousand dollars an acre.'

'To do what with?' Paul asked.

'It was one of his harebrained schemes for a sports complex. The tender just for landfill came in at ten million dollars. But I indulged Jonathan like a father would a crank son. Since it came out of money we diverted from TV advertising time, I'm making it a present to him. It's unsalable. He can choke on the taxes. They're running fifty thousand a year.'

'All this cause he wouldn't marry your daughter?'

'Yes. This is strictly personal,' Charlie averred.

But was it? Jonathan wondered.

'And now you'll take the Arena public, issue five million shares at ten dollars a pop, and unload my piece with it,' Jonathan said. He turned to Paul. 'He'll place the underwriting with one of his friends' companies, pay them a commission which they kick back, give them options to buy stock at five dollars a share, so while the public is shelling out ten, Charlie and the assholes on the board make a quick profit on shares he's placed at their disposal. The suckers who buy the stock won't ever know what happened, and what makes the scam so beautiful is that it'll be perfectly legal with the SEC and read like poetry in the prospectus.'

'How do you know this?' Paul asked, staring coldly at Charlie, who did not react to the indictment.

'Well, Pauli, I thought it up. That's why I went after our own basketball franchise, just to make owning a share of the Arena irresistible to the public. I wanted to offer something they understood – not some complicated business deal but a team out there on the floor that they can watch, criticize, cheer for, read about in the papers, that's got the feel

442

of reality. I busted my ass and used my brother to deliver Avery so that when we went public, the man on the street would know about it and want to get in. You don't read about new issues on the front page of the *Daily News* or the *Post*, but this time you will.'

'I was the weak link, wasn't I?' Paul said, unnerved.

Jonathan went to Paul with outstretched hands and embraced him.

'Pauli, you're nobody's weak link. We've got an outraged father who decides to blame me for his daughter's problem and at the same time sees a way of making millions as a result of my work.' He nodded at Charlie in a congratulatory spirit. 'A master stroke, Charlie. I wind up with peanuts, a hotel going bankrupt, and a five-hundred-acre marshland in New Jersey.'

Through all of this Charlie remained taciturn and withdrawn. 'Your trouble is that you have no feelings,' Charlie said finally in a low, hoarse voice. 'Frankly, all I wanted to do was get rid of you.'

'Get rid of me? I wish you had a legitimate grievance. I never wanted to hurt Frances. You're the one who insisted that I take her away and give it another chance. I've always been true with her and with you. Maybe that was the trouble ... that I didn't have the guts to cut her out years ago and maybe I was too trusting with you. You let me run the Arena because I turned in profits year after year. Sure, you provided the capital, but mine was the know-how and the fucking sixteen-hour days. Why didn't you threaten to throw me out when we first started together unless I married Frances? Why didn't you make it a condition? Charlie, what hurts more than the money you're stealing from me is your fucking hypocrisy.' His voice trailed off mournfully and he locked arms with Paul and walked with him to the door. He looked over his shoulder at his ashen-faced former benefactor. 'Charlie, you've made a mistake. You left me with my balls. ...'

The full shock of his situation did not register until later when he phoned Bill Gardner at Morgan and was told by his assistant that he could come into the bank after hours to sign a quit claim so that Packard's funds could be transferred to his account. But even then the only emotion that betrayed

443

him was a tremor around his mouth as he instructed his baffled secretary to pack his personal possessions – including photographs of the Arena from the time it was a mere excavation hole up until opening night. The office staff was bewildered when he walked through and, without explanation, said good-bye, thanking them for their loyal service.

He took the elevator down from his office and walked through the empty Arena. From a seat in a back row he watched the Scimitars toweling themselves off and heading for the showers. Equipment handlers gathered the basketballs in large hampers, cleared the benches of warm-up suits, then disappeared down the long passageway which led to the dressing rooms.

The stillness was disconcerting, unnatural. It was as though he had entered some giant mausoleum and not the place where thousands of people had laughed and cheered. When he got up and walked the long way out through the lobby, he had to pass the giant blowup of himself and Charlie with the Arena in the background. He turned away and left.

Standing beside a taxi with the meter running was Warren Berliner, his attorney.

'Jonathan, what the hell's going on?' he asked petulantly.

Berliner's consternation provided an incongruity on his boyish face. The puckish, trusting expression, wide-set brown eyes, the regular front teeth with a space between them, and the high forehead beaded with perspiration gave intimations of a quixotic child being sent off to school for an indefinite term. His brown-striped seersucker suit had patches of wet under the arms as in the taxi he wrestled with papers billowing out of his briefcase. It was he who had persuaded Jonathan to acquire the swampland in Jersey as a site for a stadium, since it provided a central point among four states. 'I don't care what kind of spot you're in' – he brandished legal documents – 'you can sue the ass off Packard.'

'There can't be any litigation,' Jonathan said matter-of-factly. 'A third party is involved.'

'Who?'

'I can't discuss it.'

'Jonathan, I don't care if there are fifty parties involved, I can't represent you without knowing the facts. Shit, you

444

know we have a confidential relationship I'd never betray. I'm only concerned with protecting your interests. Okay, so there's blackmail, obviously, but there are ways of combating it. I'm not going to let you lie down and die. You're being robbed of everything. Now in your own interests, tell me.'

Berliner continued nonstop through midtown – suggesting suits, injunctions, freezing company funds and assets, claims of fraud, appeals to licensing authorities – hammering Jonathan with all of the weapons available to him in his legal arsenal.

'No! Now get off my ass. I have to do this.'

'But look what you're sacrificing. Charlie's just a fucking moneylender. You made the Arena. Why would you let him do this to you? Give me one logical reason and I won't open my mouth again ...'

'Friendship.'

'The party you're protecting is your friend, well, fair enough, but what could happen to him if you fight it out in the courts? Jonathan, you own fifty percent of the equity of the Arena. Surely your friend understands what's at stake for you?'

'Warren, he'll be killed if this comes out in the open. And I'll be next. So let up. You're coming with me purely as a witness and to make sure that four million dollars is transferred to my account after I sign an agreement relinquishing all rights and claims to the Arena. Have you got it!'

Gardner came out of his office to greet them.

'Hello, Warren ... Jonathan. No one's sorrier than I am about what's happened,' he said ruefully, guiding them into his office. He sat down on the edge of his desk and there was a solemn dignity in his careworn face, but behind his glasses the eyes were caverns. 'Charlie wouldn't listen to reason. I think he's going to kill off the Arena without you.'

'Bill, nobody's irreplaceable. I did my job at the beginning. A general manager can handle it.'

'You're taking it very well.'

'Do I have any choice?'

'It's a squeeze,' Berliner said waspishly.

'Bill, answer me honestly. When I delivered my end of the investment, whose idea was it to trace it?'

'Charlie's. I had no alternative. I wasn't curious. I'm a

445

banker. You gave me assurances that you'd produce a million and you lived up to your word.' His contrition appeared genuine.

'Do you have any idea when Charlie will take the Arena public?'

'It was put into the works the minute you signed Avery.'

So much for Charlie's grief, Jonathan thought. He knew now that he had been deftly outmaneuvered. Frances's attempted suicide was just an excuse Charlie employed to unseat him. If Charlie wasn't able to use his daughter, he would have thought of another way of mousetrapping Jonathan. Even the board's opposition to signing Avery must have been a smoke screen. The master had taught him a lesson. The same dutiful parent, he recalled, had years ago at their first meeting defended the male position, said that knocking up a girl was no reason for marriage.

Berliner was turning pages and pages of legal documents which Charlie's lawyers had prepared, assigning his share of the Arena to Charlie. 'They're in order,' Warren said.

Gardner handed Jonathan a pen and as he signed the blood drained from his face. Gardner handed him a manila envelope.

'The report's in there.'

'Any copies?'

'No.'

'Bill, there better not be.'

'It's never left my safe. . . . Jonathan, what do you expect to do about West's mortgage? They're in the hole for a quarter of a million. I think you're pouring money down a sewer.'

'I'll make the payments. And since I've got the assignments to that jungle in Jersey, I'll swing for the taxes.'

'You're coming out of this with some capital,' Gardner advised, 'so why let these two losers swallow it up?'

'I don't think they're bummers. Risky for sure,' he said exhaustedly. His stamina was rapidly going and he thought he might collapse if he didn't get some air.

'Jonathan, just remember that this door is always open to you.'

'Just have the funds transferred to my account and I'll let you know in a few days which bank I'm going to use.'

'Why?' Gardner asked, offended by Jonathan's attitude.

'You'll always be Charlie's boy. I need a guy who's hungry and has cast-iron balls, because with me as a client, he'll need them.'

*   *   *

'The doctor told me I was a bit anaemic and gave me some iron pills – but you look as though you need a transfusion. What's wrong?' Sandy asked. He lit a cigarette from a dying butt. 'Can't you tell me?'

'It's too complicated to explain. I'm no longer connected with the Arena or the Scimitars. I was bought out.'

'I don't understand. I thought it was yours.' She was shaken by his turmoil.

'Stop worrying. We'll come out of this okay.'

'I've brought you bad luck.'

'Oh, Sandy, don't talk nonsense.'

'Did it have anything to do with us getting married?'

'No, honey ...'

'Are you sure you're up to going out with your parents? Couldn't we leave it for a while till you're in better spirits? If you're depressed, they'll think there's already trouble between us. First impressions are so hard to overcome. I want them to like me.'

He refused to draw her any further into his shattered world. He poured himself a tumbler full of Scotch and sank into his club chair. The apartment itself, belonging to Charlie now, had an aura of malevolence about it. He told her he wanted to move as soon as they could find another place. He suggested buying a town house on the East Side. They'd need more room for the baby and a live-in housekeeper. Besides, he added, 'I'd like you to have a music room so that you can practice and blow yourself out listening to records.'

'Can we afford to buy something that costs a hundred thousand dollars? It's such a lot of money, Jonathan, and I don't want you to have to sweat a mortgage. I'd rather live conservatively ... within our means. We don't have to impress anyone.'

'Sandy, I love you for being so concerned, but you just find a house in the Sixties between Madison and Park and let me worry about the finances. I'm not flat on my back. And we need the room. This is a bachelor pad and it's served its

447

purpose. If your family comes to visit, I don't want to have to shove them into a hotel. So think of it as a place for them as well.'

'Everything's so complicated here.' Her confidence was being drained.

'This is New York, not a fishing village in Maine, but don't let that scare you. I've had a setback, but believe me I'm built for endurance.'

For reasons he couldn't begin to comprehend, his spirit had not been defeated, merely injured. Maybe it was because he had Sandy on his side.

She suggested a number of sensible economies, like selling his Rolls, firing Machado, giving his maid notice, eating in, and living on a fixed budget. She insisted on paying the rent for her apartment in Boston and would, until she took a leave of absence from the orchestra, contribute to the household.

Gazing lovingly at her as they walked down the stairs to the Pierre Grill to meet Paul and Jonathan's parents, he took hold of her arm and said:

'Sandy, please keep off the subject with my folks. I can't go through an interrogation with them.'

Ever punctual, the Stones were waiting with Paul at a table in the bar. Miriam immediately put on her glasses when she spotted them. Alex had beseeched her not to antagonize the newlyweds by bringing up what she considered the insulting exclusion from the wedding. She and Alex had rights, and Jonathan had shown profound callousness by keeping his plans secret and presenting them with a fait accompli.

'It's not as though he's a kid and we would've forced a big affair on him,' she had complained to Paul. 'Couldn't we have had a small informal dinner with you and Chou ... Victor and Tina, not to mention his brother?'

'Miriam, he's happy finally. He found the right girl, so celebrate,' Paul had replied.

Alex was sitting with his back to the doorway. He said sternly: 'Don't describe her to me. I want to be surprised.'

'Thin as a rake, like a model,' Miriam advised him, assuming the post of commentator. 'Pretty. If she weighs a hundred pounds it's a lot. A size six and that's giving her the benefit of the doubt.'

'She's a honey,' Paul observed, tempting Alex to look

448

while the couple made their way around the archway. 'She's got somethin.'

'I'll bet it isn't a Star of David around her neck.'

'Since when's that so important? Is that stopping David from being happy? Do you hate your grandchildren because they favor Linda?'

'That's different. Linda's like our child. Please, God, don't let her speak with an English accent and be related to the queen. That's all I need.'

'She moving up fast on the outside post, Alex,' Pauli announced. 'Chestnut filly, good legs, not breaking stride, terrific pace, finishing fast ...'

'Thin! Bones sticking out of her face,' Miriam countered. 'Small nose. It's a wonder she can breathe.'

When they arrived, Alex turned sharply and jumped to his feet.

'My God, you're beautiful.' He embraced her, kissing her on both cheeks.

Paul was next, smothering her affectionately in his arms.

Miriam regally offered her cheek, then emerged from her sulkiness. 'Up close you're so much prettier,' she said exuberantly. 'Why'd it take forever to get from the stairs?'

'I was walking slowly, Mrs. Stone,' Sandy replied breathlessly. 'Afraid you'd notice me.'

'Him' – Alex pointed to his son – 'we don't want to know. I guess he was ashamed of us ...'

'No. It just happened so fast,' Sandy attempted to explain when a glass of champagne was thrust into her hand and Pauli was on his feet, proposing toasts of joy, health, fertility and:

'*Fortuna a mi bambini ...*'

'Got a few snaps of the two of you and the priest in front of the altar?' Miriam needled Jonathan.

'A justice of the peace performed the ceremony, Mother.'

'Her people don't believe in priests?'

'They're Methodists.'

'That warms my heart. At least if you have daughters we won't have the problem of another Italian *bris*. Believe me, I can live without another morning of prosciutto and sponge cake with a rabbi and a priest fighting each other over the Bible. It's a good thing Victor is our own or I would have committed murder.'

449

'Miriam, what do you want? He's happy and off the streets.' Pauli poured more champagne into her glass.

'Oh, you're getting me drunk. I need hangovers on top of everything ...?'

The questions were flying as though they were in a court-room.

'No phones or telegraph office up there?' Alex asked.

'Of course they have them.'

'Well, couldn't you use them? Airplane routes up there in Maine?' he rattled on. 'It may be a shock to you to learn that your mother and I fly in planes. In case you don't know, she's never more relaxed than when she's airborne. It's the only time she don't worry about dying. That's the pilot's headache.'

'One thing Sandy ... you won't need the milk farm,' Miriam advised her daughter-in-law.

Sandy caught Jonathan's attention, leaned over, and whispered, 'They're a scream. Are they always like this?'

'Every time I get married.'

Alex held her hand in his and examined her fingers.

'Are you an athlete? Miriam, you wouldn't believe it, but she's got calluses on her fingers.'

'You golf?' Pauli asked.

'Let's see.' Miriam commandeered the fingers in question.

'She plays the viola for the Boston Symphony Orchestra,' Jonathan explained.

'Well, would you believe that?' Alex said. 'Is that a violin without an *n*, Sandy?'

'No, Mr. Stone. It's sort of a cross between a violin and a cello. Larger than a violin.'

'Leave it to Jonathan to bring home somebody different, eh, Pauli?'

Sandy had entered the spirit of the evening. The warmth of the Stones and Pauli gave her a sense of security, belonging, having ties. New York was no longer quite so imper-sonal.

'How'd it happen?' Miriam asked.

'We met in May when the orchestra played at the Arena and Jonathan just happened to walk through during re-hearsal.'

'It's only the end of July ... Talk about working fast.' Miriam sipped her bubbly, beamed, overjoyed, confused and heady with drink. 'Lightning, like his father.'

Sandy looked directly at Miriam. 'I hope it's not going to upset you,' she said softly, 'but I like to begin every relationship honestly.' She faltered and Miriam waited. 'I have to tell you that I'm pregnant.'

'When did he get the chance?' She was dazzled but not surprised. 'Are you both happy about it? Forgive me, it's not my business and you won't find me an interfering mother-in-law – that I promise you – but was that the reason ... ?'

'No. He wanted to marry me before he knew I was having a baby.'

'Sandy, can I tell Alex?'

'Sure, it's not a secret.'

'Alex, guess what?' she called across the table.

'Sandy's pregnant.'

'News travels fast around here. You could see from her walk?'

'Jonathan just told us,' Paul said ebulliently. He left the table, conferred with the maître d' of the dining room who treated him like visiting royalty, for Paul always stayed at the Pierre and tipped lavishly. Two more bottles of Dom Pérignon were put on ice to go with the caviar already waiting for them on the dinner table. Paul moved around the table, examining the centerpiece of flowers he had ordered and the orchids wrapped in cellophane for the ladies. Jonathan looked wonderfully relaxed after that disastrous morning, Paul thought. Paul waited at the table while the party was escorted into the dining room. There was no more loyal man than this boy he considered his son. Jonathan had given in to Charlie without any struggle, sacrificing his fortune to save him. He had to secure their positions so that neither of them would be vulnerable again. He was determined to pressure Jonathan to join him. The two of them in league would form an invincible combination. Besides, Jonathan was ripe for an offer to run his operation.

The Stones were careful all through dinner to avoid references to Frances and Lenore. Jonathan had made a good choice. This girl was certainly different from any they could have imagined him marrying. She had a tame, malleable personality. She would provide the companionship he needed. Besides, the child would give him stability. Over coffee, Miriam leaned over to Alex.

'He seems to have come into his own.' But is he really in love? she asked herself. Or is he settling for fatherhood as a substitute?

Alex gave her a long look in which she read all the doubts of the past. 'He's got Lenore out of his system. Sam made him walk on hot coals. I hope he has peace of mind now. I suppose Frances will be hurt . . . it can't be helped.'

Miriam took hold of Alex's hand and he raised it to his lips and kissed it.

'We were lucky,' she said, 'to have found each other young.'

'It's a pity we couldn't pass that luck onto Jonathan. I can't ever find it in my heart to forgive Sam. Just think how different his life would have been with Lenore.'

'She was sick for so long. God knows what her mind is like even now.'

Miriam shuddered, whether from the air conditioning or the memory, she couldn't be certain.

The three men had ordered Sambuca with their coffee and watched the waiter light the bow-shaped ponies. The liquor and coffee beans bubbled and they waited for a moment for the lip of their glasses to cool before raising them. Alex seldom worked out nowadays and Jonathan observed the flaccid pouches of flesh below his chin and the tight creases of skin on his neck. The former brawler had developed the unheroic sags of middle age, along with thinning steel-gray hair, slower reflexes, and an uncharacteristic temperateness. It was as though his bent for rage had been replaced by the indigence of apathy, the specious currency that men past fifty are forced to spend when it has become clear that they are not infallible. The gnarled hands had become arthritic, gone passive in the captivity of time. He talked about *his* club only when pressed. It was open two days a week.

'All that draws is roller skating on Sunday, and women wrestlers! And what do I get? Hoodlums. Black and Puerto Rican kids with steel pipes and chains.'

'Why don't you retire?' Paul asked. 'Come down to Miami and we'll do something together.'

'One bank robbery a lifetime is enough for me.'

The three broke into a loud, guttural, uninhibited bout of laughter.

'I should've packed it in when you asked me to, Jonathan.'

'Well, I'd invite you in with me, but I'm not connected with Charlie any more.'

'What? You've given up the Arena?' he asked, startled.

'For greener pastures,' Paul advised him.

Seeing Jonathan's flustered expression, Alex was not at all sure about Paul's assessment.

'Pauli, let him answer ... why?'

'I agreed to let Charlie buy me out.'

'Then what're you going to do?'

'I'm thinking about a few ventures.'

'Jonathan, be honest with me. Are you in trouble?'

'No. Just the opposite, Pop. People have to grow. I gave it ten years. I made it into something and there's no challenge left for me.'

'That's not the impression you gave me last time we talked,' he said heatedly, trying to read the truth in his son's face. 'You got the Scimitars and Avery, so why leave now? I'm not exactly a genius when it comes to business, but please explain me your reasons, if I'm not prying.' Losing his bearings, Alex lapsed into refugee English.

'I have an opportunity I couldn't pass up and the Arena was ... when you come down to it, my proving ground. I know my capabilities and I outgrew it.'

'Charlie must be sick about you leaving,' Alex insisted.

'He'll get by,' Jonathan replied sardonically.

'I just don't understand this change.'

'Leave it alone already,' Pauli said disgruntledly. 'Jonathan's out of it. He knows what he's doing.'

'Pauli, you don't build something out of nothing, then walk away from it,' Alex persisted.

'If the money's right, you do.'

Alex became captious. Paul's logic offended him. 'Forgive me, Pauli, but from bookmaking, shylocking, and broads, you're one of the country's leading experts. If you had a column in *The Times*, everybody would read you on these subjects, but as far as running an Arena, filling it with events the public will pay to see, and organizing a professional sports team against established competition, you know *gornisht*. On this Jonathan's an authority. He came into New York a *pisher*, after running my joint in Brooklyn. Yet he not only stands up to the Garden but he builds something

453

bigger and more successful.' He regarded both men with incisive contempt. 'It stinks. If you want me to believe you left out of choice, then you insult me. Charlie found a way of cutting you out – that I can buy.' He loosened his tie. He was flushed, and his breathing, Jonathan noticed, was becoming labored. 'God, how could he do it to you?'

Jonathan gripped his father's hand and regarded him with affection. He was moved by Alex's outrage.

'It's done, Pop. You guessed right. But believe me, I'll wind up on my feet.'

'You'll have your day, Jonathan. And make him eat shit. If not for you, then for my sake.'

'I'm starting again and I can't worry about settling scores. Charlie has to live with himself, I don't. I wasn't careful, so I got kicked in the ass. I left myself exposed. Next time, it'll be different.'

The farewells were filled with promises of staying in close contact. Miriam appointed herself supervisor of Sandy's pregnancy and Jonathan was delighted by the lack of pretense between his wife and mother.

Before parting Alex took Jonathan aside and stood with him outside.

'No matter what, I believe in you, and this time if you need me, I'll be there.'

Thirty-four

The windshield of Jonathan's car was a bloody smear where bugs and insects had splattered. He drove back to the main road to gain a better perspective. The heat outside was intolerable and the humidity above the swamps swirled in dusky cloud formations. The two men were just above the Manasquan River in the county of Monmouth, New Jersey. Jonathan had taken the detour so that Paul could inspect the parcel of land, but he was reluctant to leave the car. The miasmic, fetid odors were nauseating.

'No wonder Charlie wanted out,' Paul said irritably. The area looked like an organization burial ground. 'Do you have any idea of what kinda money'd be involved in this?'

'Nothing you could raise.' Jonathan unfolded a map and spread it out on the dashboard. 'Pauli, there are various factors favoring a stadium in Jersey. Cheap land which I already own. The best highway system in the East. We're between the turnpike and the Garden State Parkway. We're at a confluence of Pennsylvania, New York, Delaware, Connecticut, and, of course, Jersey.' Paul listened quietly. 'This is the highest population density in the country. The unemployment in the construction business is at an all-time high – even worse than during the Depression.'

'What the hell do you see here?'

'A stadium, with a dome, temperature-controlled so that we're not at the mercy of the weather. A combination flats and trotter track. Dog racing. Fairgrounds. An amusement park the size of Disneyland. Just listen to me. ... Football's growing. There're going to be new teams, more pro leagues. We're at the beginning of a new era in sports. The public is hungry for action.'

Paul was overwhelmed by the scope of Jonathan's plans.

'Who pays? You still haven't told me that.'.

'The state of New Jersey through a bond issue. How do you think states raise money for roads? We've just been on the turnpike and paid a toll. Well, that money goes to Jersey and a part of it to pay off the bonds.'

'It's going to take years.'

'I've been building up relationships with local politicians.'

'The DeCavalcante and DeCarlo families own this state. Without a push from them, you're dead.'

'I don't need them,' he replied furiously.

'They got the *rabbis*. For a change, hear me out. The only thing worth having in a stadium is the food and liquor concessions. Through my Servo Enterprises I control concessions at twelve dog tracks and six racetracks in the Southwest. The rest, of course, is off-track gambling. I've got maybe two hundred bookies who work through a central clearing office in Phoenix. I don't want bricks and concrete to worry about, but a guy with a phone and a pad calling his customers. Between California and Arizona we're handling fifty million dollars a year on all sports. The vig alone comes to five million. If you want to hear some figures about juice,' he added, turning hard, 'let me lay it on you. You paid me back my original investment and we split the other three million. But what if you was just somebody who needed it and I had to carry you for ten years? Well, the rate I get is four for five. On a yearly basis, my friend, that comes to one thousand and forty percent interest. Jonathan, the future is in loan offices for people who aren't credit worthy. The deadbeats in hock who can't get their foot into the bank, who got nada, no collateral, who can't get mortgages and choke on rent, who can't handle their debts to the department stores and then try to get lucky with a bookie and wind up pissing blood. You bet regular, I gotta wear you down. Believe me, I began in fuckin Miami at the dog track when it was nothin and that's where I built my stronghold. For once, let me guide you. Come in with me.'

Paul described how he had made inroads in the pornography trade, using girls who worked in the brothels in Nevada, how the films were developed in underground labs, then distributed nationwide under the counter in dirty bookstores. His hand was everywhere.

'When I whacked Bugsy a few years ago, well, that was the only time I felt anything personal. But the real reason was business. I expanded my territory, tripled the profits in a year. It was a consolidation for me. I already had Florida. With Siegel dead, I inherited his piece of Vegas. Arizona nobody wanted but me, so I got it on a plate, but California was my baby.

456

'In New York you got five families always on each other's backs. And Vito Genovese is counting everybody's money. He watched everyone else. Dio winds up with garbage contracts and throwing acid in Victor Riesel's face. Albert the animal tries to move in on Lansky in Havana so they get crazy Joe Gallo to blow him. They're ignorant, *bestiale*. What's to fight for in New York? I see them a couple of times a year which is more than enough. I'm makin more money than any of them,' he continued expansively. 'Vito sees junk as the future, not me. Smokin a little grass is innocent, shooting smack is another ball game. I want no part of it. My side is different. A man wants to bet his team, a horse, back a fighter, he wants to fuck or look at some pictures, or he needs money, well, all that's normal. There's nothing disgusting or degrading about that. Nobody forces a girl to spread her legs for a few bucks. It's her decision. Maybe she likes it better than an assembly line in Detroit or getting her ass pinched in a diner by every greaseball swillin soup. That's slavery for a woman. Hooking ain't. So in every state except Nevada fucking for money is a criminal offense. I don't see it that way....'

What this was all leading up to, this recitation, was some form of partnership. He was wary of Paul's confidences. The price was too high. They were on divergent paths. He was a builder and Paul the wrecker of people's dreams.

'Maybe the best thing that happened to you was to have Charlie blow you out of the Arena. You learned a lesson – never to trust anyone but your own.'

'And you're my own, right?'

'You got it. Charlie Packard was your blue chip. Holy. Well, what's the difference between him and me? Or for that matter, my people? In our world Charlie would've had to back his move with guns. Against you, he didn't need them. He had a hostage. Me. You took the beating for me. You paid the ransom. It was a high price. Now what I'm saying to you is don't fight destiny. We were meant to be together. Whatever I have is half yours. No contracts, lawyers, not even a handshake. Just nod and it's yours.' When Jonathan hesitated, Paul relented. 'Think it over. We'll straighten this thing out with Sam and then you can make your decision. But this stadium idea ... well, you're beatin your brains out.'

Deflated by Jonathan's vacillation – who in his right mind

would dare turn him down? – Paul lapsed into a morose silence. His face, Jonathan thought, mapped a thousand cabals. He had for so long been the host of vice that it never occurred to him that ordinary people did not share his devious view of human nature. Perversity was certainly a fact of life, but it hardly attracted the religious devotions that animated Paul. Jonathan, no matter what the inducement, refused to be used as Paul's underling. But he needed Paul's support. If Paul withdrew his money, Jonathan's plans of transforming West's Hotel would come to nothing.

'I locked horns with Charlie because your life was on the line,' he said finally. 'Now, I get the feeling that you're holding a gun to my head, Pauli. If I say no, how are you going to take it? I'm not condemning what you do, but somehow, in spite of having had my ass kicked through my teeth, I don't think I could hack running a bookmaking operation or using my imagination to figure out new ways to juice little guys who're hocked over their heads. It's not my way. It could be the chance of a lifetime, but I have to walk away from it.'

'Can you explain why?' Paul asked.

Jonathan pulled off the road onto a verge. The scenery had not changed since his last visit to West's except that the bungalow colonies en route appeared more dilapidated, the people older. Sam's billboard was still the same, filled with grandiose offers of an escape to Paradise.

'Pauli, working with you puts me in an organization. I'm my own man.' He got out of the car to stretch his legs. Paul joined him. 'I've always had this desire to build since I was a kid. I was almost there. The Arena was a stepping-stone to the Dome in Jersey. I came unstuck' – he prodded Paul's chest – 'because I picked two partners, you and Charlie. You were the wrong people for me. Now you can hang me with Sam's paper and get out, but Pauli, I think I'm entitled to a ride – this time without you. If I fall, let it be because I overreached myself and not because of you again. What are you looking at me like that for? So hurt. Have I said I'm against guys betting on horses, or fucking? I screwed hookers for years. I paid. It doesn't embarrass me to admit it. The backer I dealt with wasn't exactly an angel. You've got your money back. If you insist on splitting the rest, then I'm going to have to scramble for my life.'

Paul stood dumbfounded and humiliated. The boy had

458

grown to manhood and had rejected him.

'What do you want?'

'Your million and a half on a long-term note.'

'That'll leave you open for the same thing Charlie did to you.'

'Not if you put it in a bank ... the First National of Miami.'

'And comake the loan?'

'No. You just persuade the president that I'm creditworthy, and if you make the deposit conditional on him giving the loan, he isn't going to pass up the business. You get interest and I pay it. I need a friend, goddamnit, not a boss. Let me know what you decide.'

*　　*　　*

West's Hotel had the ragged, patchy, dessicated quality of an old-age home. Framed on the lawns were a handful of elderly guests in slant-backed wooden chairs which needed repainting. The security hut was boarded up and two middle-aged bellhops stood frowning at the entrance. The wooden facade had been warped by rains and loose bits of stucco hung as precariously as stalactites. The porch creaked; rusted nails from the boards jutted up. The neglect and state of disrepair extended into the lobby where the carpet was worn down to the underpadding near the desk. Jonathan noticed a curious stale odor.

Lunch was in progress and a clerk at the desk made a feeble attempt to welcome them. Standing at the entrance to the dining room which could seat up to twelve hundred, they stared at the rows of empty tables, deserted waiters' stations, all of which gave the gigantic room with its billowing, threadbare drapes the ambience of a ruined mansion.

The glory days were well behind Sam. No new photos had been added to West's Hall of Fame since Jonathan's last visit.

When they asked the headwaiter for Sam, they were told he was at his house. Walking down the flagstone path, Jonathan was reminded of his last visit, the sunlight glistening off Lenore's hair as Georgie brushed it. He resolved to put out of his mind these imprints of the past.

Wearing white gardening gloves, clippers in hand, Sylvia was cutting fat-bellied roses which should have been pruned

459

weeks before. Her gray hair had a bluish tint, and the years of summer sunshine had withered her skin. A victimized expression curled her mouth when she saw the two of them. For a moment she was speechless, locked in indecision.

Behind her, rowboats rotted at the pier.

'Hello, Paul.' She nodded curtly at Jonathan. 'He's in the house with Izzy. We didn't expect to see you this soon, Jonathan. You haven't given us much of a period of grace, have you?' She paused as though having expended the last of her energy. 'You'll forgive me if I don't join you?'

'What do you think's going to happen?' Paul asked when she averted her eyes and resumed cutting.

'The inevitable. Him' – she inclined her head toward Jonathan – 'he'll close us down.'

'You go in, Jonathan,' Paul said. 'Let me talk to her.'

The front door was open. Sitting on a floral-patterned sofa, papers spread out on the coffee table, Izzy Schwartz's drawn face and frightened eyes moved to the small foyer when Jonathan came in alone. In a short-sleeve shirt, baggy khaki work pants, Sam stood at the brick fireplace. In the funereal silence, Sam's shoulders slumped forward involuntarily and his skin hue altered to a nutty yellow.

'What a stroke,' Sam said trembling, his tone a shattered vibrato. 'Who could've believe this?' he asked rhetorically.

Jonathan approached him dispassionately. 'We can't continue being enemies,' he said. 'It's a luxury neither of us can afford.' He offered Sam his hand, and for an instant the mere proximity of Jonathan made Sam shudder, but at last he took it. 'You're up to date on your repayments. I made good the quarter of a million you were behind.'

'I told you not to panic!' Izzy exclaimed, jumping up from the sofa. 'See! See! If I still had the paper I would've had to call it in. *I* couldn't carry you.'

'What torture have you got in store for me?' Sam asked quietly. 'Do we get a chance to pack up our things?'

Paul strode briskly into the living room. His looming, broad figure did little to reassure Sam.

'Eh, Sam, you look more scared than when we was in Munich.'

'Pauli? I should've guessed that you'd be in with him.'

'What? I'm your enemy all of a sudden? I ain't here to dance on your grave. Your trouble was always you couldn't

460

tell which is your friends and your enemies.' He peered at Schwartz. 'Maybe Mr. –'

'Izzy Schwartz.'

– 'You'll excuse us so we can have a private talk.'

Relieved of a burden of elaborating how Jonathan had forced him to deceive Sam, Schwartz wiggled his fingers and trotted outside.

'What do you want from me?' Sam asked.

'Some explanations,' Jonathan replied briskly.

'Pauli, is there nothing you can do so that I can salvage something?'

'Sam, listen to the man. And for once, don't try to box clever. When you first got started, I asked you if you needed me and you told me you could do things clean. I never forgot. I'm here as a friend to the two of you and nobody's going to push your face in the shit. No funny money's going into the hotel. Jonathan'll have enough legitimate funds to see if he can turn the business around.'

'Thanks, Pauli,' Jonathan said. His eyes roved Sam's pinched, harried face. 'I'm not interested in settling old scores. Either you accept that at face value or we have no basis for discussion.'

Sam nodded apologetically. 'You're a bigger man than I gave you credit for.'

'Okay. We've cleared the air so we don't have to bullshit each other.'

Sam took a bottle of Chivas out of the fussy, old-fashioned, barrel-glassed breakfront and set three glasses and a bucket of ice on the table. His hang-dog expression vanished after his first drink.

Jonathan removed his jacket and draped it over a dining room chair. He was, Sam observed, as firmly muscled as Alex had been at his age.

'Sam, this isn't going to be an ass-whipping session. I'm not here to blame you because your business fell off. If it comes to that, so did mine. I've been bought out of the Arena against my will, but I'm living with it and neither one of us is going to fall apart. I'm expecting my lawyer and accountants to come up later this week to audit your books so that we know exactly what everything's worth. They'll arrange for appraisers and then a survey team, architects and engineers I worked with in New York, will be able

461

to give us an idea of how much we'll need to put the hotel back on its feet. Sam, are we in for any nasty surprises? Bills that you haven't paid or other loan paper?'

Sam's face was torn by that manic discordance with which a thief proclaims his innocence. He would be, Jonathan decided, a lousy poker player. In a quivering voice Sam began: 'There's another hundred thousand dollars short. I siphoned it off over the past two years.'

'Why?' Jonathan asked.

'Yeah, where'd it go?' Paul inquired with surprise.

He started feebly with an air of wounded self-commiseration. Suffering, Jonathan observed, had always been his trademark.

'I ... Lenore ... I couldn't turn her down. She came to me with an idea to start her own cosmetics business. Sylvia and I sweated it. Lenore'd been turned down by the banks.'

'Great,' Jonathan muttered.

'Give me a chance, please,' Sam implored him. 'She spent seven years working in cosmetics at department stores. Then she worked for Revlon ... Charles Revson himself hired her in product development. Then she sold his line to stores all over the country. She put on demonstrations for thousands of women, ran shows. She came to me and begged me to help her start on her own.'

'Well, how come nobody ever heard of her?' Paul asked.

'It's like a new concept. She's up with a hundred women. She's holding like a seminar, a convention, whatever.'

'What did she do with the money?' Jonathan asked.

'It's gone into setting up a lab in Sunnyside, Queens. She's hired graduate students in chemistry, men working on their Ph.Ds at Columbia who want to pick up extra money in their free time, to develop formulas for her. Believe me, she can account for every penny. Honestly, she's very capable.'

'What are those women doing up here?' Jonathan asked.

'She's giving them a sales course. Ask her. Look, we're empty and she got seventy-five bucks a head from each of them for the weekend, which is better than I've been able to do this season. Sure, it's a lot of money, but I didn't have the heart to refuse her. Give her a break. Her capital is peanuts and she's working hard to make a go of it.'

462

Jonathan let the plea pass him by.

'How'd you skim the money?'

'I fiddled my tax returns ... how else? My own credit's death.'

Jonathan foresaw a series of personal complications from which he had to extricate himself.

'Well, one thing I've learned is to pay taxes. All we need now is an IRS audit. She doesn't get another penny out of the hotel.'

'There's nothing to give. Her capital is invested in equipment. She knows my financial position. Don't take this little business from her. She's broken her back to get this far.'

'Can we forget about Lenore for the moment?' Jonathan said wearily. 'I'm only concerned with my plans for the hotel and to find out if you're the right man to see them through. The question right now,' he continued, 'is can you do it?'

Sam blanched but could not bring himself to argue.

'Years ago when hotel owners were practically family members and knew the names and quirks of their guests, you were the perfect mine host,' Jonathan observed disdainfully. 'Hotels need good staff, managers who wear blazers with emblems, so if one leaves, nobody gives a rap. We've got two different philosophies: your personal touches or my plastic packages. This hotel needs a new image.'

An expression of fright clouded Sam's face.

'The public is entitled to what they want out of a resort, not what suits you. You've got two dozen suites. They can be chopped up into another sixty rooms.'

'He's got nothing but space already,' Paul interjected.

'Because he's selling the wrong thing at the wrong time.'

'This is a summer resort, a place for families,' Sam said. 'Don't you see that?'

'Listen, my friend, you've got old men in baseball caps and Bermuda shorts screaming at each other over pinochle bids. And women in house dresses drinking borscht, *kvetching* about varicose veins and walking around with curlers in their hair. There are oxygen cylinders outside the dining room. This isn't a place for a vacation but a stop along the way to the grave. If you want to run a convalescent home, then go to Miami and open a joint on Washington Avenue.'

The vehemence of Jonathan's argument numbed Sam. All of his principles of service were being exploded.

463

'For the hotel to work again you need a different concept. We've got to spend money on advertising. I want to build an indoor pool, a gym, saunas. There are half a dozen runs up here that could be groomed for skiing.'

'How do we stay open all winter?' Sam asked in astonishment. 'We've always closed after New Year's.'

'We use the weather. There are twelve months in the year and we have to run at seventy-five percent capacity. The thruway cuts an hour off the drive, and that makes West's accessible in two hours from midtown. The key to the business is attractive rates for conventions. We need a convention hall. We'll hold business conferences and I'll put the packages together with the contacts I developed at the Arena. Every fucking room is going to look the same – like a Holiday Inn. Immaculately clean, plastic, with king-sized beds. We can't reeducate the public and give them European standards when all they want to do is sleep and screw in a room. Turnover, Sam.

'Look at the way you run your dining room. The public is weight conscious. They don't want to shovel food into their faces every two hours. The dining room should be buffet style. People want to move around and check out the action. We put in a health salad bar. Everybody walks around skinny and horny. January, which is traditionally a dead month after New Year's, we do a singles package at reduced rates. Not everyone can afford to fly to the sun and it's high season in Florida and the Caribbean. Sam, we're going to create a playground for adults in which anything goes. Romance, easy sex, the possibility of meeting the right person ... that's what I'm talking about. A place where every secretary and salesman believes he's got a chance to make out. We'll change the name to West's Country Club and this time incorporate.'

Jonathan's dynamism enthralled Sam, but such grandiose plans would require a substantial investment. 'Where's the money going to come from?'

'We'll have everything revalued and mortgage the place to death. It's called leverage. Let the banks pay. The interest and repayments are tax write-offs.'

'Sounds pretty good,' Paul agreed. He watched Sam struggle with the ideas Jonathan had proposed. The prospect of dumping Sam if he opposed Jonathan was unpalatable. Paul's loyalty still ran deep. He would not forget the time in Munich when Sam had taken him and Chou into his pension and risked everything for strangers.

Sam stared vacantly at the two of them, lost and confounded. Finally, he asked, 'What do you need me for?'

Jonathan sat on the arm of the sofa, stoically. He had overcome his conflicting emotions. Sam's hollow, abased eyes gave him no triumph; he could not devise a punishment greater than that which Sam had inflicted on himself. Sam had failed and been rescued by his enemy.

'I can't run a hotel and I need someone I can trust.'

'Do I get a salary?' Sam was quick to ask.

'Fifty percent of the profits. But you can't write checks. My lawyer will do that.'

'You don't have to give me anything.'

'Sam, we're partners. You don't draw anything but basic living expenses. Until we're in profits, I won't take a nickel out of the hotel.'

'You're very generous.' Sam was filled with self-reproach. 'I messed up two lives.'

Jonathan struggled to find an appropriate response, but it was beyond him.

'Why don't I let two old friends get reacquainted and drink a little booze? I'll look around the place on my own.'

Thirty-five

The lawn was muddy and bright green from the heavy rains. He trooped from one end of the property to the other, visualizing ski runs, areas for barbecuing, new stables, a plexiglass cover over an indoor pool which could be opened. But there was a part to this homecoming which he could not have prepared himself for. He had not expected to see Lenore ever again, certainly not in surroundings so redolent of broken dreams.

Around the pool women were assembled, listening to Lenore expound her ideas of beauty care. For a moment, standing on the deserted patio, out of her line of vision, he did not recognize her. She had cut her hair and wore it angled back on the sides. There was a tenacious assurance in her face and her eyes were startlingly direct. It had been years since he had last caught sight of her around her Village haunts. She had gained presence.

He inched closer to hear her delivering her pitch.

'What we're selling in Natura is a line of hair and skin-care products made of natural elements. None of the ingredients can damage the hair or skin. It isn't a new concept. Women for centuries have been using the ingredients from fruits and vegetables to soften and moisturize their skin. Now we've found a way to blend these natural ingredients to work even better. So you'll be dealing with familiar fragrances. Lime astringent, orange moisturizer, strawberry and lemon shampoos, cucumber cleansers. Everything we're producing is nonallergenic and our base materials are organically grown. Now, you're all aware that we haven't got millions of dollars to spend on advertising or launch campaigns on TV and in the magazines. Natura is going to succeed by word of mouth, and your friends and neighbors will have to buy from you because they can't purchase our products in stores. So again we've got something unique because it's personalized. Your customers will be able to try our products in their homes. Some of them will want to work for us because it isn't a full-time job, and, naturally, you'll receive

466

a bonus for anybody you recruit.

'How much money you make depends entirely on you. You're your own boss. No one punches a clock. I'm guaranteeing that any product you can't sell you can exchange for another or get your money back. The most important thing for you to do is to familiarize yourself with our line, which is what this conference is all about. If you have any questions during these few days, bring them to me. I want you to start using Natura and please be sure to fill out the questionnaires before you leave. You have to believe in Natura, or you can't sell it. You're not peddling brushes, cure-alls, or miracle vacuums. You're introducing people to the beauty of Natura. Ladies, we're going to succeed!'

She had concluded her presentation and the women applauded. They filed past a table where sample kits were available for their own use.

When she was finally alone and had gathered up her papers and remaining samples, she threaded her way through the rows of chairs, collecting stationery, handouts, pencils, and placing them in a box.

He left the patio and walked toward her.

She paused, looked at him incredulously, then slowly smiled. She was so prodigiously beautiful that he felt betrayed by his recollection of her.

'Jonathan ...' She extended her hands to him. 'What a lovely surprise.' She embraced him and there was an unfeigned look of fondness in her eyes.

'How are you, baby?'

'Great. Did you catch my act? How was I?'

'You'll put Revlon out of business.'

'Come on, seriously?'

'You've got an interesting angle.'

'Well, tell me what you're doing here.'

'I had some business with your father.'

'You and him?'

Her hands were still in his, and when she touched the gold wedding band on his finger, he was aware of her discovery. For a minute they regarded each other with confusion.

'I'm married,' he said finally, relieved by the admission.

The moment reached out, entrapping them.

'I'm happy for you.' Again there was no undercurrent he

467

could discern. 'Frances and you were right for each other.' When he shook her off she had a moment's indecision. 'Did I say something wrong?' It was impossible to tell if she harbored any disappointment. He was intrigued by the composure she emanated.

'I didn't marry Frances.'

Her mouth opened slightly, eyes wide as though she had been indiscreet.

'You're still unpredictable.'

'What made you go into this – cosmetic stuff?'

'I got tired of working for other people who didn't know what the hell they were doing. And I sort of felt that I had to do something with myself before I lost my nerve.'

The shadowy outlines of yesterdays rose like spectral towers. They walked along the deserted baseball diamond overgrown with saw grass, the base paths loamy ruts, without exchanging another word.

Then they strolled down to the lake, and as though by conditioned reflex, he untied a rowboat, took hold of the warped oars, and rowed out with her. She removed her shoes and stretched out her bare legs on the vacant seat.

'I hope we're going to be friends from now on,' she said.

'We're too old not to be.'

She held out her hand to him and her fingers glided over his face. Her body had a fragrance which he couldn't identify.

'Don't look so serious about it.' The years of isolation had forged a personality entirely self-possessed. 'The fact is, I'd be grateful for any advice you could give me. I've started Natura on peanuts.'

He explained with great clarity his interest in the hotel, but he did not elaborate his reasons for leaving the Arena.

She gave a low, hoarse laugh which he endeavored to interpret without success.

'This is wild. . . . I spend years working up the nerve to ask my father for a start and now you're my boss. It's true, isn't it, that I literally can't sign a check without your approval.'

'That's it.'

'Am I your employee?' she asked, still faintly amused by the swing of events.

'No, you're not my employee, but you run a division of my business and you're accountable to me.'

'I can live with that. But . . .' She became flustered. 'How, if I may ask, do I begin to negotiate for myself against you?'

'You don't, Lenore. All you have to do is demonstrate that Natural –'

'– Natura.'

'That you can make a go of Natura without my sinking a fortune into it.' He gave her no room to maneuver. Sentiment might prove disastrous. 'Right now I've spread myself thin, and I can't afford to have anything that'll bleed me.'

'Will you give me a chance?'

'A year.'

The time pressure made her wince but she nodded with resignation.

'Lenore, I've got all my eggs in this basket.' He gesticulated disdainfully. 'West's. I never wanted it. It's not my kind of business, but I'm going to put it back on its feet. I have to. I'm stuck with it. Once I get it revalued, I'm going to work my tail off raising money to pay for the improvements. It's going to be tight as hell. If you came to me a few months ago and asked me for a loan, I'd have given it to you with no questions. And if you hadn't started up with Sam's money, I couldn't let you go into it at this point. I don't know a damn thing about hotels or cosmetics. I'm completely out of my depth. Once I get a feel of how much I can borrow, I'll make a fair evaluation of Natura and if it's worth continuing and plowing money into then I'll do it. I'll never mislead you or make false promises. If you don't turn the corner, then you'll have to give it up.'

'What if it takes off and I can't meet the demand? Will you let me expand?'

'Let's face that happy problem when it arises. I'll say one thing for you, you haven't got any lack of confidence.'

'Oh, it's going to work, believe me.'

'Okay, tell me why. Sell me. Why should I buy your stuff if I can get Revlon or Coty or whoever manufactures cosmetics. People buy brands, or am I crazy?'

She flushed slightly. It had never occurred to her that Jonathan, of all people, would have the power of life and death over her small enterprise. She must carefully avoid the trap of her feelings. Still, she was relieved that the thrust of his attack was so nakedly impersonal.

'I'd always imagined it would be easier to do business with someone you knew than a stranger.'

'I'm afraid it's tougher. You get tangled up in personalities.' A smile passed momentarily over his mouth, then was erased suddenly, like the unexpected snap of the wind which had come up, furrowing the lake.

'Since your money is invested in my business, you ought to know that this isn't some whim of a half-crazed imbecile. Let's get that out of the way,' she observed harshly. 'I walk, I talk, and I'm not some doll to be stroked. And getting into cosmetics wasn't a line of work I was forced into because I couldn't do anything else. I've always been interested in it. I spent a long time working in major department stores on Fifth Avenue. I served an apprenticeship with Charles Revson learning the business from the ground up.

'Jonathan, for years I've been looking at women with lousy complexions, rotten, ugly hair that splits and falls out. Half the population is allergic to what's on the market. I used to go home after work and experiment with different formulas. Fruits, vegetables, bases, you name it. I've boiled it, steamed it, crushed it with a pestle and mortar and slapped it on my face. So while most girls were out on the town with manufacturers' salesmen, eating and drinking on expense accounts, I was home trying to figure out how there could be room for me in a business dominated by huge cosmetic firms and pharmaceutical companies. I've added vitamins, proteins, acids, and alkalines to my hair care products. I've tested them on myself. I used to wash my hair all the time with the formulas I was making. And I learned, I learned, until I thought, now's the time ... before someone else beats me to it. I'm an expert now. I know more chemistry than half the graduate students working for me.

'So I developed a plan – selling cosmetics on commission. Natural products. Word of mouth. Give each saleswoman a territory, make her her own boss, let her work the hours she can squeeze in between her kids and husband.'

This was no longer a fragile beauty whose childhood had robbed her of the spring and summer of life. Lenore was a mature woman, a case-hardened pro.

They left the boat and headed up to the main house. The dynamic transformation within her excited him. She had emerged from a deep sleep and found herself in touch with the world.

They sat in a small cocktail lounge off the Taboo Room.

470

'Jonathan, I'm no dreamer. I've got a market and I want to hit it.'

'But what's the bottom line? You need volume to make it work.'

'I'm going to spend a week in ten cities throughout the country, holding meetings in Holiday Inns. I expect to recruit a thousand women nationally ... that's my target figure on the first run. What I do is put an ad in the fashion pages of a paper like the *Cleveland Press*. Then I hold a meeting and try to sign up women who're right for sales.'

'What's your markup?'

'Seventy-five percent retail. The sales force makes twenty-five percent.'

He looked at her askance.

'You can get away with that?'

'Of course. If it were too cheap, no one would buy it. I learned that at Revlon.'

'What's a sample case cost?'

'A hundred and twenty-five dollars.'

'I assume some women you'd want to hire can't afford it.'

'You said it.'

'Well, suppose you get them to put a down payment. Maybe fifty bucks and you have them pay off at a reasonable percentage. Whatever the going bank rate is. Do you follow me?' She had a blank look on her face. 'If you're financing five hundred women for a hundred a head at eight percent a month, that's eight dollars a shot. Multiply that by five hundred and you come up with four thousand a month and as your sales force increases and you continue to grow, your profit on financing can run into big money. Fifty thousand a year, depending on the number of people working for you. The other aspect of in-house credit is that you're showing faith in them and the products. It's not a rip-off, if you're backing them up.'

It amused him to watch her reaction. The exuberant girl emerged and she leaned over and kissed him with blithe enthusiasm.

'That's a hell of an idea.'

He had regained Lenore, not the child, not the speechless teenager, but a woman who had learned to function independently. The discovery took some getting used to, for in his imagination she had always been the helpless, abused girl, foundering between sanity and madness. It wasn't merely that her recovery had been complete, but that she was so full of ideas and energy.

Watching her at dinner, sparkling, at ease, keeping the flow of talk going between Sam and Paul, both as high as kites from their afternoon drinking bout, he was becoming distinctly uncomfortable. He found an excuse to leave.

She followed him outside and he realized that now he was the pursued and she the hunter.

'What's your rush?' she asked.

He was bewildered and thoughts within him clamored for expression but dissipated.

'I've got a pregnant wife and I ought to get back to the city.'

'What's she like?' When he demurred, she pressed him. 'Just simple curiosity, Jonathan.'

'She gives me a feeling of peace,' he replied starkly. 'I was lonely for a long time ...'

'I'm glad we both got what we wanted,' she said persuasively. 'I used to read about you in the papers, and I was very proud to have known you.'

He detected no disappointment in her attitude, but rather the solicitude of a good friend who had a scrupulous interest in his welfare. The reversal of roles did not sit well with him. Memories buffeted him.

'I wanted you all my life,' he said.

She gave a smile which negotiated the no-man's-land they were entrenched in.

'Jonathan, we'll always care for what was. But we can't build on it. I'm a different person and so are you,' she said gently.

Thirty-six

The lot at General International Films was crowded with extras wilting in the noonday sun. They were stationed at the set of a Ring of Kerry fishing village. Bulkheads loomed on the backcloth and a tenor who looked like Howard Keel, sounded like Mario Lanza, and was of Mexican descent pummeled out a ballad whose lyrics embraced such diverse subjects as fishing, Irish mists, colleens who waited, and hungry children. Standing imperiously behind the director, Victor gloated, confident that he had backed a winner. He had paid two million dollars for the stage musical *Irish Kisses*.

'Pure fantasy ... audiences will eat it up,' Victor pronounced to the four minions who accompanied him everywhere. 'Let's catch the rushes of *Barbary*,' he said, leaving the set. This, too, was a musical. In fact, he had four musicals being shot on the lot. He was out to give the public movies that would leave them with a good taste in their mouths.

The power was intoxicating. Now when he picked up the phone, no agent, producer, or star told him to hold on because they were on another line. He had no nuisance clients to squabble with. Even Gary Cooper got his name right and stood up to greet him at Chasen's. His every edict was splashed across the *Hollywood Reporter* and *Variety* in twenty point bold type. Returning the musical to its former glory was the challenge that he had set for himself. He whipped his staff producers and directors to finish on schedule and on budget. He had already written three Oscar acceptance speeches.

Meanwhile, to fortify his image as the emperor of Hollywood, he was spending a good deal of his time entertaining the freshest talent who had trekked to Hollywood. This week it was Lydia Terrell, twenty, a blond ex-cheerleader from Jelloway, Ohio.

He frequently did not return home at night. Tina tolerated his excuses. Divorce for her was out of the question. Besides, since Georgie's death she was even more religious;

473

the house seemed to have become a haven for elderly priests. She went on retreats, refused to wear makeup or any color other than black. High-necked, plain black dresses and an enormous crucifix. Mass every day and on Sunday endless devotions. It almost appeared as though she was attempting to expiate the sins of her dead daughter. Between husband and wife a wall of indifference had emerged.

Driving through Beverly Hills in his black Fleetwood Cadillac with its smoked tinted windows, a pile of scripts on the front seat beside his chauffeur, Victor sensed that his imperial visions lay within his grasp. Harry Cohn, Darryl Zanuck, Jack Warner were about to be dethroned by the smartest operator in the business. The car drove up the hotel driveway and he ignored the glances of guests staring at him. *Life* had done a four-page picture spread on him early that month, and his face was becoming familiar to the public.

He strolled through the lobby, and Johnny, the page boy, said, 'Miss Terrell's waiting for you in the Polo Lounge.' Victor gave him a buck. PR people and agents called out his name and Victor stopped for a moment to grant audiences that lasted a few seconds. 'I can't wait to read those preview cards tonight at Grauman's,' he said. '*Bubbles* is going to be the first hit General's had in years. It'll go through the roof when it opens in New York,' he informed Louella Parsons's legman. 'You can quote me.'

In a booth adjacent to the maître d's stand Lydia sat waiting for him. Victor had spotted her in a screen test for a musical. She had a voice like a crow and more curves than a strep bacteria. Although Victor was God at General International, he could not use her even in the chorus. This girl with her swanlike neck, a cleavage which could accommodate two tennis balls, square white teeth, and wavy, shoulder-length blond hair which hung like drapes over a round, ever-smiling face suited Victor's current mood. He leaned over and kissed her. She made him feel young and desirable, and mistresses, heaven knew, had achieved status for lesser reasons.

A waiter brought over a pair of vodka martinis and Victor announced the evening's program.

'Just one drink ... then a quickie, dressed by eight, and a late supper after the preview.'

In his bungalow at the hotel, he had the phones switched